TEMPUS
FURY

TEMPUS FURY

A TIME SHARDS NOVEL

DANA FREDSTI

DAVID FITZGERALD

TITAN BOOKS

TEMPUS FURY
Print edition ISBN: 9781785654565
Electronic edition ISBN: 9781785654572

Published by Titan Books
A division of Titan Publishing Group Ltd
144 Southwark St, London SE1 0UP

First edition: June 2021
2 4 6 8 10 9 7 5 3 1

Visit our website: www.titanbooks.com

A CIP catalogue record for this title is available from the British Library.

Printed and bound by CPI Group (UK) Ltd, Croydon CR0 4YY.

Did you enjoy this book?
We love to hear from our readers. Please email us at readerfeedback@
titanemail.com or write to us at Reader Feedback at the above address.
To receive advance information, news, competitions, and exclusive offers
online, please sign up for the Titan newsletter on our website:
TITAN BOOKS.COM

DEDICATION
Heartfelt special thanks to everyone
who helped us with our move from SF to Eureka.
We could not have finished this book—and kept our sanity—
without your support.
We love you all.

Imagine time seen as a continuum—an infinite line containing everything that was and everything that will be...

Time perhaps as a tangible object. One that can be touched, like a mural on a wall that stretches infinitely in both directions. Portraying everything that has happened, is happening, and will happen. In one direction is the future unfolding. In the other direction the past, much of it forgotten, back to the beginning of time itself.

Finally, imagine time as a stained-glass window. The story of everything laid out in a glittering mosaic of trillions upon trillions of moments, from the big bang to the fiery death of the universe.

Until it shatters, and these shards of time come back together—but no longer in the same configuration...

This is the world after the Event.

1

Exultationist—Gestaltist Disputed Territory
Outside the village of Horváth, Borsod–Abaúj–Zemplén Republic
(Formerly Northeastern Hungary)
July 18, 2216
Three years before the Event

There had been twelve soldiers in the squad three days ago. Now there were seven.

In good formation, they cautiously made their way up the footpath between meadows and vineyards, toward the village. Here and there locals tended the vineyards, showing little interest in the newcomers. A cursory scan revealed no hostility. The mountainous landscape was green and lush, as if unchanged for centuries—aside from a trio of boxy robot shepherds tending a flock of sheep.

Sergeant Myfanwy Cochrane breathed in the crisp fresh air, admiring the view, trying hard not to think of all the burnt-out cityscapes she had marched through over the years. In places like this, however, the forgotten nooks and crannies of the world, she could almost believe they had found an oasis from the decades of endless world war.

A deserter's dream, she thought, careful to mask it from her subordinates.

"Sarge, we have contact."

An incoming thought from Peters, their point man, interrupted her reverie. At the top of the rise, where an ancient tavern stood and the cobblestone streets of the hamlet began, a quartet of village elders awaited their arrival. Cochrane halted the squad and signaled Peters to hold up. She turned to her comm specialist, Silva, who was also her best diplomat.

"Silva, go talk to them," she sent. *"Bradley, go with him."*

The two soldiers cradled their carbines, attempting a less confrontational manner, and approached the elders. Bradley, one of the squad's two sweepers, was a talented esper. He'd already be telepathically scanning the four villagers.

"Jó reggelt kívánok!" Silva greeted them with a friendly wave. He spoke very little of the local dialect, but had made a point of learning a few basic pleasantries. It was polite to speak aloud before initiating a telepathic conversation with a stranger.

After a few minutes, Silva and Bradley shook hands with the locals, and the comm specialist stepped away, waving down to the squad.

"What's the story, Silva?" Cochrane asked.

"Outstanding," Silva replied. *"We have good, better, and best news, Sarge. This place is called Horváth, and they say they're unaffiliated with any factions. We and any other Gestaltist troops are welcome to stay here as their guests. They also told us the*

Exultationist main force left here two days ago, headed over the border, to which they say good riddance."

She nodded in approval. In this case "the border" meant the border with the Mátra-Slanec Federation, formerly a chunk of southern Slovakia.

For the last one hundred and fifty years Europe, like the rest of the world, had dissolved from nation-states into a patchwork of petty fiefdoms. No, Cochrane corrected herself. Patchwork was the wrong word—that would imply there were still large centralized territories left. The world was now a mosaic of tiny local authorities. Various psionic factions had taken up the mantle of governing—or at least raising armies.

Not surprising that the locals didn't take to the Exultationists. That faction was one of the most notorious of the PsiPremicists—to them, the non-psychic minority weren't just second-class citizens, they were outright chattel. Evolutionary has-beens no better than animals.

The only factions that treated the non-psionic worse were the Vorax, psychic vampires that happily fed on them, and the Ouroboros, the psionic hive mind spreading across Asia like a pandemic. Their Gestaltist PreCogs had warned that the Ouroboros sought to absorb the mind and personality of every person on Earth. These people in Horváth didn't know how lucky they were.

"Sarge..."

She glanced at her second sweeper specialist. He was staring intently down at the villagers tending to the vineyards on the hillside below.

"What is it, Dee?"

He turned to her, fear in his eyes.

"Sarge, I scanned again for hostility, deeper, just in case, and—I'm not reading anything. They've been hollowed!"

The field hands had been brainwiped.

Cochrane whirled and sent to the entire squad.

"Ambush! Shields up!"

Not a millisecond too soon. Automatic weapon fire erupted from the upper windows of the tavern and the closest buildings. The spray of bullets ricocheted off their telekinetic shields, illuminating them with a ghostly glare.

Silva and Bradley turned to take cover, but the four villagers—or whatever they were—dropped their psychic masks and went on the attack. Both soldiers stiffened, faces locked in a rictus, and then crumpled.

Hitting the ground, the squad opened up with their spindle-fed TK assault carbines, but the ambushers had raised their telekinetic shields. Peters, still on point, low-crawled closer to the outlying buildings, but didn't bother trying to blast through their shields. A highly rated pyrokinetic, he just focused his attention on first one roof, then the other, igniting a blaze on both.

The rest of the squad focused their fire on the quartet, but their shields held, disk shapes glowing bright with every impact. The four turned to face them. Suddenly Peters grabbed his head and writhed in pain, dropping and curling into a fetal position.

Then Cochrane was hit.

///the sun exploded
ripping the skin of the shrieking
sky apart in a violent, pulsating
nightmare///monstrous
disembodied human eyeballs bubbled up
through the leprous ground
and began devouring
Kwame their heavy gunner///his screams
echoed and reverberated infinitely
in her ears///while his body went twisting
and stretching into impossible
shapes until his torso
burst open///torn inside out like a pulpy
fruit mangled by a raging lunatic god///

Cochrane fought to regain control of her hijacked senses,
but the sensory onslaught was overpowering—

///the sky plunged
into a crushing hopeless black
night///abandoned by stars///the
haunted moon
a howling death's head
staring down on the ring
of grinning corpses
surrounding her///their faces
melting into grave rot///they
reach for her

stretching forth horrid
grasping hungry cadaverous
clawed hands///covetous
of her naked warmth///

Her resistance slipped as the telepaths reached down into the amygdala region of her brain, triggering the emotional center. Forcing herself to remain calm, she tried to concentrate on the location of her four opponents, even as she felt them twisting the knife in her mind—

///a cyclone of a million
fractaling razor blades flailing
through banshee winds///
ripping through her flesh
///face///stomach///fingers///
everywhere merciless
and unstoppable///
slicing her body
in a universe of pure pain///ten
thousand bloody
wounds made of her///

Cochrane screamed in agony. She struggled to stay alive long enough to pour all her mindfulness into one last telekinetic burst—if only she could—

///she was falling///

///she was on fire///
///she was a newborn baby
being eaten alive
by her own mother///

A sudden violent wrenching. The ground gave a single, quick, booming jolt, and then the pain vanished.

So did the flashing hellscapes.

The sergeant found herself on her knees, fingers dug deep into the turf, limbs shaking, body covered in sweat. She looked at the enemy. Her telekinetic attack had succeeded. She had reached around their line of protective shields and pulled apart the wall of the burning tavern—it had smashed them like a giant flyswatter.

Behind the smoldering slab the two closest buildings were engulfed in flames. Inside them, shooters screamed as the fire took them. Then the sounds stopped. No other hostiles in sight. It was a quiet day in the beautiful countryside again, save for the crackling of burning wood and the heavy breathing of her soldiers.

Meyers, their squad medic, ran up. Cochrane waved her away.

"I'm fine," she said in her crisp British accent. "Check Peters and Kwame." She turned to Dee. He was kneeling on the grass, his face slick with tears. The barrel of his pistol was in his mouth.

"Dee?" she called to him. After a few heartbeats, he slowly pulled the gun away.

"How long?" he croaked.

"Dee? Are you okay?"

He stared blankly. "How many years was I gone?"

"Fight's all over. Only lasted a few seconds."

He shook his head. "No, it was decades... I grew old and feeble in there..."

Meyers went over to the esper and crouched beside him, touching her fingers to his temple, talking to him gently while she mentally ran diagnostics. After a minute or two, she returned to Cochrane.

"He'll be alright. It'll just take a little time to shake off the effects."

"How are the others?"

"Silva and Bradley are dead—hostiles crushed their hearts before they could get their blocks up. Peters is shaken, but I think he'll be okay." She looked over at Kwame, their heavy gunner. He was standing stock still, his spindle-fed cannon dangling from its straps and his blank eyes rolled back. Turning back to the sergeant, she shook her head.

"Kwame's left the building. I can put some suggestions into his lizard brain to keep him marching with us, but he's hollowed." Meyers handed over three dog tags.

Sergeant Cochrane nodded. *Walking killed in action.*

"All right," she sent out to what remained of her squad. *"We still have three klicks to go to get to the bunker. Quick sweep up top to secure the area, and then we're on the move again. Dee, you back with us?"*

He wiped his face with the back of his hand, nodded.

"Good. You're on double duty now—comms and sweeper. Stay sharp, everyone."

The squad's survivors moved out. Below, the villagers continued tending to the vines, industrious as bees, oblivious to the world.

When they finally reached the hatch of the spindle bunker, Cochrane breathed a silent prayer of thanks to the Corps of Engineers. It was right where the map indicated it would be, freshly planted and camouflaged. Bending down, she uncovered the square slab of nanowoven ferroconcrete, and mentally asked Dee for the combination.

"Cerulean Lemniscate Anticlockwise," he responded.

Cochrane pictured a deep blue infinity symbol and set it gently in motion, spinning right over left as it hovered above the hatch.

"Zinnober Triangle Inverted."

She set the image of an upside-down chrome green triangle next to the little spinning blue propeller.

"Topaz Pentagon Clockwise."

Last, she added a yellowish-brown gem-toned pentagon, spinning opposite to the infinity sign. She held all three shapes in her mind's eye.

The hatch made a sharp *clack*, unlocked, and began to sink. It descended fifteen centimeters before halting with a second *clack*, and slid away into a recess, revealing a narrow stone ramp. A line of tiny pale blue fluorescent lights, like helpful fireflies, showed the way. The remnants of the squad trudged down, exhausted and grateful.

At the bottom of the ramp lay the recharge chamber, dominated by the bunker's spindle—its psionic power generator—hovering silently in the air between floor and ceiling. It was a black, elongated diamond structure with a hexagonal cross-section about sixty centimeters wide in the middle, tapering to a tiny flat hexagon at either end.

As the spindle sensed their approach, it activated with an almost imperceptible hum, slowly beginning to spin and flickering to life. Pale traces of lightning began to dance in its smoky crystalline interior, growing to an incandescence that suffused the entire generator with light.

The squad's assault carbines and powered equipment operated on psionic batteries as well. Each soldier unclipped their weapon's smaller spindles and spares, placing them close to the mother spindle. They hung in the air like crystal ornaments, orbiting the generator as they recharged.

Activating the spindle's communications array, Cochrane spoke aloud. "Sergeant Myfanwy Cochrane, 138th Kinetic Infantry, Lima one-one-oh-niner." While she reported in, the rest inflated their cots and dug into their rations. At Meyers' instruction Kwame sat, back to the wall, remaining motionless.

"Dee, you've got mail," Cochrane said. After a moment, she added quietly, "… it's from a PreCog."

The whole team looked up at that, forkfuls of food halted midway to their mouths. Mail was rare enough. Private channel messages, sent from HQ to a grunt, were unheard of.

A private message from Military Intelligence?

Unimaginable.

"Probably just foreseeing a dear John letter," Peters cracked. "Or maybe they forecasted you buying the farm." Meyers kicked him and shot him a reproachful glare.

"Sorry, Dee," he mumbled. The sweeper swallowed, then got up and cautiously approached the spindle array, wiping his hands on his fatigues.

"Specialist John DeMetta, 138th Kinetic Infantry, Delta one-two-two-six."

The rest of the squad waited in hushed silence while he telepathically received his message. When he finally turned around and walked back to his cot, he said nothing. Peters and Meyers exchanged worried glances.

"Well, what is it already?" Peters burst out.

"Cut the chatter, Peters," the sergeant snapped. "The message is for him, nobody else. Got it?"

"It's okay, Sarge," DeMetta said. "It's not classified. Honestly, I don't know what the hell to make of it." He frowned and shook his head. "It didn't make any sense... just something about a... a girl. Amber."

No one said anything.

"Dear John," Peters sent to Meyers.

She nodded.

2

Richardson Home
San Diego, California

Amber woke up.

She lay with her eyes closed for a few minutes, trying to capture her dreams, but finding the images frustratingly vague, like a mental itch she couldn't scratch. Broken snippets tickled her brain—swirls of pyramids, Roundhead and French Napoleonic soldiers, dinosaurs, and talking, flying bowling balls... and a man with violet eyes, stars streaming through their depths.

At first it all seemed so real.

Then, in the way of dreams, it made no damn sense.

The image of a man suddenly crystalized—early twenties with strong features, and a scar on his cheek. Dark shaggy hair falling to broad shoulders, a silver torc around his throat.

Cam, she thought. Yes, that seemed right.

Once his name and face solidified in her mind, so did others who had populated her dream. Nellie—a young

Victorian woman with auburn hair and clever green eyes. Harcourt—another Victorian, but older and somehow irritating. Blake—a World War II British soldier who'd saved her life more than once…

As quickly as the images came, they blurred again, and faded. Try as she might, she couldn't hold on to them.

Darn it! She tried one more time to grasp the memory, then shrugged and realized what she *really* needed.

Coffee.

With a yawn she stretched out on her bed, reveling in the crisp clean linen sheets, then looked around her bedroom. A menagerie of well-loved stuffed animals on the shelf. The picture window looking out on Mission Bay. The cast of *Firefly* looking back at her from the poster on her wall, promising her that they aimed to misbehave.

From downstairs the muffled sound of canned laughter came from the TV. She could smell waffles and bacon, and her stomach growled. Slipping an oversized Padres jersey on over her underwear, she wandered barefoot down the shag-carpeted stairs to grab some breakfast. At the bottom she paused for a moment to stare at a tall, stately grandfather clock standing against the far wall in the entryway.

Huh. That's new.

"Mom? Dad?" she called out as she wandered into the dining room. "Hey, when did we get a grandfather cl—"

Amber stopped in her tracks. Neither her parents nor sister and brother were there, but two more grandfather clocks stood upright at either end of the table.

"Okay... that's weird." Her voice echoed in the empty room.

Fighting a rising sense of unease, she backed away and went into the family room, following the comforting sound of the TV. Another grandfather clock stood there like a monolith, parked in front of the television set, the dancing black and white static reflecting off its glassy face. It made no sense.

Amber's heart started racing.

She went back to the entryway and approached the front door.

Nothing scary there, she thought even as her heart galloped in her chest. *Just a door.*

As she reached for the door handle, it seemed to recede, the air thickening around her hand like warm gelatin. Clenching her jaw, she pushed through, grabbed the handle, and shoved the door open, stepping out onto the porch.

There was no one in sight.

Across the street, a grandfather clock stood on the porch, facing her. Two more were on the sidewalk in front of the house, side by side, as if caught in mid-stroll. Another was down at the corner, and yet another in the middle of the front yard next door. Three more stood sentry at random spots along the street and sidewalks.

A low rumbling noise came from down the block, like the sound of garbage bins being rolled out. The street a few houses down rippled like an oasis in the desert heat. Amber watched as the ripple turned into a long sinuous shape rising out of the asphalt—a huge crocodile swimming through the street as though it were water. It drew abreast to her house, then submerged, vanishing from sight.

Heart hammering in her chest, she retreated back into the house, bolting upstairs. At the top she threw open a door before registering that there wasn't supposed to be one there. On the other side, instead of the hallway, there was a small room, featureless and unfurnished...

Another door on the opposite wall.

Running to the door, she flung it open. Another equally sterile room, another unwelcoming door. In full panic mode, she turned back to the first door, but instead of leading to the stairs it opened to yet *another* small room with yet another door on the far wall.

Fear mixing with anger, she screamed, and ran for *that* door. It opened to a small room with a door. She opened it, to find another door.

And another door.

And another.

And another...

Time and again she burst through, great shuddering breaths pumping through her lungs, turning to sobs as she twisted knob after knob. And then, when her terror seemed too much to bear, she opened yet another door and rushed inside—

Into pitch darkness.

3

Evacuation Zone, somewhere in the ruins of the Khan el-Khalili souk El Qahira Governorate (formerly Cairo, Egypt)
February 2, 2219
Twenty-five minutes before the Event

Even when the ancient city had been alive and full of people, its alleys and souks had formed a confusing warren. In the moonlight, the ruins of the lost Cairo megalopolis were a surreal and disturbing labyrinth—yawning holes in twisted chunks of concrete or metal or stone that stood like abstract statues of lost souls. For the pair of soldiers nursing the wheezing, cantankerous hovercraft through the maze, over broken streets littered with dust, ash, and tangles of bones and skulls, it was a waking nightmare.

The vehicle kicked up great plumes of dust, the twin headlight beams barely piercing the haze in front of them. Both soldiers kept their eyes peeled for trouble, alert for whatever might be lurking in the twists and turns of the haunted streets. Sergeant Cochrane gritted her teeth, her grip so tight on the jumpy, uncooperative stick of their commandeered vehicle that her fingers cramped.

"How much further to the extraction, DeMetta?"

"We're close—less than a klick," he answered.

"And how close are the Ouroboros?"

"Still advancing through central city. Everything west of Gezira Island is overrun, and they've reached Tahrir Square. To the north, the main body has just crossed Ramses Street, and there's a division coming down Salah Salem to do a pincer action from the east."

"Just great," Cochrane thought darkly. *"Can we still get out through the south?"*

"If they don't encircle the whole city first."

"How soon before we're in range of their Medusae?"

"At the rate they're closing in, I'm guessing twenty minutes, if we're lucky."

If they failed to elude the dragnet closing in on them, the approaching Ouroboros vanguard would crack their psyches like eggs and absorb them into the hive mind, just as it had done to more than two-thirds of the human population of Earth. It had taken less than sixteen months.

Cochrane increased the hovercraft's speed as much as she dared.

They turned a corner, and the maze around them exploded into light. They caught a fleeting glimpse of a dazzlingly bright, vaguely human shape as a deafening psychic banshee scream tore through them, overloading their senses with raw bursts of pure insanity.

"Berserker!" That was all Cochrane managed to get out before the lightning storm raged through her neural pathways into

the core of her brain. Her body's muscles locked up, causing her to simultaneously slam on the braking thrusters and rev the accelerators. With a queasy lurch, the hovercraft flew into a spin, careening out of control. They hurtled forward, slamming directly toward the shrieking inferno of glaring light.

Something struck them with a sickening crunch and another explosive burst of intense brightness. An instant later they clipped a section of wall and rebounded before finally coming to a juddering halt.

"We're not dead," DeMetta said aloud, sounding surprised.

"As if we'd be that lucky," Cochrane replied, rubbing her neck. "What happened to the scream job?"

DeMetta looked behind them. A pair of blood trails led to where the former human had been torn in two. For a change their shit luck had a silver lining—the hovercraft had crashed into and killed the thing that sent them out of control in the first place.

Bad things happened when psychics overloaded and blew out their psionic power. In most cases they died horribly, brains turned into gray mush. In the case of berserkers, though, the manifestation of self-destruction was more spectacular.

Berserkers were what remained of a flameout case whose brainstem remained just intact enough to become id-driven, walking psionic Chernobyls. Some psychically annihilated any mind they encountered, others demolished everything in their path with frenzied telekinetic blasts. It no longer mattered what faction they'd served—they were, to all extents and purposes, the psychic undead.

"Berserker contact resolved," DeMetta deadpanned.

Cochrane nodded. "I'll take it." She turned her attention back to the controls. "Let's move."

Their hovercraft's turbines caterwauled more than before as Cochrane urged it back to life. Its battered skirt panels rattled as they sped through the maze of rubble. Crossing the wide thoroughfare of Nafak Al-Azhar into a sector of lesser devastation, they pulled up at their contact point—the domed remains of a grand Ottoman mosque.

The ancient wooden front doors were scorched but still finely engraved with tessellated geometric designs. Cochrane stood by, covering DeMetta with her assault carbine while he beat on the door three times, then twice, then three times again, and finally sent the password to anyone within ten meters.

"*Khanda.*"

"*Kirpan,*" came the countersign a moment later.

They pushed open the great doors and entered the sacred space. Chains of unlit brass lanterns hung suspended from the domed ceiling overhead. It was richly tiled with arabesques and ringed with calligraphic verses from the Quran. Below that were rows of broken stained-glass windows, some tall and long, others forming clusters of little portholes. Stray pale beams of moonlight lanced down through them, illuminating a smooth stone floor littered with fresh corpses.

A tremendous firefight had occurred here. There were a few dead Transcendentist troopers in urban camo fatigues and spiked turbans, but the majority of the casualties were wearing civilian clothes—working smocks, facemasks, aprons. Judging from the stacks of crates, overturned tables, and a scattering of spindles, tools, and material, the mosque had been converted into a guerrilla weapons factory.

"Over here," a Japanese-accented voice called out. A pair of Transcendentist soldiers—one Asian, the other Slavic, their impressive beards and mustaches fastidiously groomed—had taken position behind the ablutions fountain. They rose from their cover and saluted the new arrivals with great formality. "Prefect Lance Corporal Anzai and Initiate Svoboda, Unified True Transcendent Forces, at your service."

DeMetta thought of how Peters would refer to them as "Trancin' Dentists." He carefully concealed that memory—the Transcendentists were notoriously humorless. It was strange to be allied after generations of warring with them, but even quasi-religious, deeply controlling cultists were better than a voracious hive mind.

"Sergeant Cochrane and Esper Specialist DeMetta," Cochrane said brusquely, all business. "What happened here? Rogue faction?"

Anzai shook his head. "Unaffiliated. Criminals, in fact. Our intel tipped us off to an underground bombmaking operation here in the ruins."

"So close to the hive advance? That's suicidal." She shook her head. "Never mind, we don't have time for this. We were told there were three of you. Where's your prisoner?"

Anzai turned and pointed behind him.

Nearby lay a sealed metal capsule roughly the size of a sofa. A small bank of system monitors and controls was on one side, instructions and notations all in Cyrillic. It took Cochrane a moment to recognize what it was—a hibernation pod, just like long-range astronauts used in the old days, back when nation-states had space programs. She shot a glance at DeMetta.

"Do you buy any of this shit?"

"Hell no, and we sure as hell don't have time to figure out what their game is, either."

She turned back to the Transcendentists, eyebrow raised. "Your prisoner is in there?"

"Yes, ma'am. In suspended animation."

"Well? Open it up and get him out! Let's go!"

"Ma'am! We can't open the capsule!" Anzai's previously unruffled composure cracked.

"Then he's a no-go," she replied. "We're out of here. Now." Her gaze was steely.

"Surely we can lift it together between the four of us—"

"Look, Corporal, I don't know your TK ratings, but even if we can lift it to the street, there's no way in hell we'll be able to fit it on the hovercraft. Either crack it open now, or he's staying here."

"We cannot leave this in the hands of the Ouroboros," the corporal responded flatly. Cochrane cocked her head slightly and stared at the man through narrowed eyes.

"Okay... just what the hell do you people have here?"

"We have to get it out of the city!" Svoboda insisted.

"What the *fuck* do you people have here?" Cochrane shouted.

Taking a deep breath, Anzai replied, "We—we strongly suspect... it is a PreCog."

The two Gestaltist troopers stared at him.

"A *rogue* PreCog?"

"Precisely, ma'am."

Cochrane and DeMetta looked at each other. Precognitive operatives were among the rarest and potentially most powerful psionic talents. Letting one fall under Ouroboros control would be an irreparable strategic disaster. The ability to forecast the future was the only advantage the Alliance had left over the hive mind.

She put a hand on DeMetta's shoulder. "DeMetta, I need you to see what's really inside there—and do it fast."

DeMetta nodded. Unslinging his carbine, he carefully set it on the stone floor and knelt by the capsule, stretching a hand over its sleek surface. Closing his eyes and probing its interior, he could just sense a glimmer of the mind inside, but any cerebral activity was buried in hibernation. He had to dig deeper.

There.

All at once he had a clear picture of the unconscious figure. It wasn't what he was expecting.

"There's a girl inside," he said over his shoulder. "She's only fourteen."

"Can you hear me?" he asked her.

"Yes…"

A thought occurred to him—something he had been mulling over for three years.

"Are you… Is your name Amber?"

"No… My name is Sensemayá."

"I'm John," he replied. *"We need to get you out of here, Sensemayá."*

"Wait... It is time..."

"What? What do you mean?"

"They are coming..."

The girl shocked DeMetta by projecting an image into his mind—a huge army pouring off the Salah Salem freeway and coming down the Nafak Al-Azhar. Not an army of soldiers. These were—or, had been—ordinary people. Their anonymous numbers filled the wide boulevard like a river, moving inexorably, their advance eerily silent, their blank eyes staring into the distance.

Leading the somber procession were three sallow-skinned bald men dressed in tattered shrouds, their oversized violet eyes glowing brightly. They stood like statues with their arms at their sides, palms facing out as they glided down the road, feet levitating over the asphalt. The Alliance called them *Medusae*—the Ouroboros shock troopers—and they drew their power from the vast entourage that followed them.

DeMetta came out of his trance, eyes snapping open as he leapt to his feet.

"They're here! Coming down Al-Azhar!"

"Get her out of the capsule," Cochrane barked. *"Now!"*

But the capsule was already opening. With a smooth mechanical whirring, a crack of light appeared along the side of the sleek metal tube as the lid automatically lifted open. A slender young girl with long black hair was nestled within the soft foam, dressed in simple white cotton pajamas. Her features seemed South American, or perhaps Slavic-Eurasian.

She opened her eyes.

"It is time," she sent.

"Sensemayá," DeMetta said urgently, "listen to me. I know you're still groggy, but you have to come with us, right now. Here, let us help you up." The girl sat up. Though her face was unreadable, she was neither groggy nor, it appeared, prepared to go anywhere.

"No," she responded, *"this is the moment."*

She closed her eyes. DeMetta frowned in confusion, and reached out with his psyche once more to try to make sense of her intentions. She allowed it.

"Sensemayá? What are you doing?"

The girl wasn't trying to escape at all. Quite the opposite— her mind was racing out in a psychic wave, coursing through the ruins of the city directly toward all the Medusae triads.

"No! Don't get close to them—they'll absorb you!" he warned her.

"No... I will absorb them."

She wasn't a PreCog, he realized with a shock. No, she was something else entirely, engaged in some psionic discipline unfamiliar to him. As the Ouroboros sensed her approach, he felt the Hive's voracious hunger for their surge. Terrified, he could only watch helplessly as they lashed out to seize and assimilate her consciousness.

They failed.

Instead she *phased*—DeMetta didn't know what else to call it—somehow translating herself extra-dimensionally out of synch with them, her psychic presence effortlessly slipping through the Medusae's psionic nets.

"My god," DeMetta said aloud. "They can't stop her!"

Immune to their mental snares, the girl bypassed the Medusae completely, tapping into the lines of connection between the triads and their attendant hive-slaves. DeMetta felt her flex her strength and seize control of their mental reins. Their power supply became hers, and she drank it all in.

"She's some kind of Vorax," DeMetta said. "Some new form of psychic vampire. She's not just co-opting their power supply, she's doing something I've never seen before—drawing on another kind of energy…"

The esper watched her psychokinetically warping space again, extending her reach not just through the million-strong Hive forces descending upon Cairo, but to all of the hive mind's teeming billions—every one on the planet.

DeMetta opened his eyes again and faced the two Transcendentist soldiers.

"This wasn't some faction of criminal bombmakers, you stupid jackholes. They brought her here to take out the Ouroboros! They found a way to warp space so that the Medusae can't get their hooks in her!" He pointed to Sensemayá.

"She's not a bombmaker—she's the bomb…"

The fourteen-year-old held the entire Ouroboros serpent, with all its billions of once-human hive mind components, in her psionic grasp. She was going to kill the snake.

A smell of ozone filled the air, along with a deep hum that seemed to come from everywhere. Tiny strings of white-hot ball lightning suddenly sparked into life, crackling along the sides of the metal capsule. All around them, the chains holding the mosque's lanterns began to sway. Cochrane and the Transcendentists looked around nervously.

"She's doing it," DeMetta said in amazement. He strained his own clairvoyant ability to keep up with the sheer scope of her global reach as the power she channeled built to near-unimaginable levels. And then it reached a crescendo.

Sensemayá threw her head back and screamed, the piercing sound echoing off the stone floors and walls, shattering the mosque's remaining stained glass into flying pieces. The soldiers crouched and covered their heads.

"DeMetta!" Cochrane yelled. "What's happening? She's tearing the place apart!"

DeMetta could see it happening all around the world, as stolen husks of Ouroboros minds flared out and died, their eye sockets smoking.

"She's done it," he answered, voice filled with awe. "She's really done it—she's killed them all! Every last one of them!" He crouched down next to her. *"Sensemayá, you've done it."*

The girl didn't answer. Her eyes remained closed, body trembling.

"Sensemayá? It's okay, you did it, girl. You saved us all."

"It's not okay, John. Something's wrong... the power's still building. I can't control it, it's not coming down." Her fear was palpable. She grabbed his hand. *"There's too much. Something else is here..."*

He stared at her, trying to concentrate.

"Let me help you. Show me—"

She did, letting him further into her mind. He could see it now. The nexus of extra-dimensional energy upon which she was drawing was transforming into something bigger. She had opened Pandora's box, and couldn't close the lid. Now the girl really *was* a human bomb. Energy particles streamed off her.

"*I'm sorry… I'm so sorry…*"

"*Sensemayá!*"

The psychic wave hit him first, followed by a blinding torrent of charged particles that ripped through him. He screamed. Her hand gripped his with a desperate strength. There was a rush, a supernova's brilliance, and then…

Silence.

When sight and sound returned—a moment later? Hours later?—he found himself draped over the metal coffin, arm outstretched. Sensemayá was gone. Sergeant Cochrane and the soldiers were gone. Cairo was gone.

He couldn't make out anything but the roughest details. It was far brighter and hotter now, daytime. There were voices close by, and he could discern blurry figures approaching. Then he felt hands trying to help him to his feet. He was too unsteady to resist as they brought him—no, not to his feet. They were gently placing him in the capsule. His head spun.

"No, please—don't do that," he murmured. They crossed his arms on his chest.

"*Sui-Netherit, wep em wawet. Hru ent kshese neseni, t'a pa ma-ehti,*" someone said in a reverent voice. The lid closed. The capsule's theta-wave generator put him to sleep instantly, and the hibernation sequence began.

4

Place: Unknown
Time: Unknown

She landed on hands and knees, against a hard surface. Wood. Terror-sweat poured in rivulets off her face as the sound of her sobs echoed off the walls. A faint light shimmered off to one side.

Amber sat up slowly, wiping the tears away from her eyes, watching as violet stars began to cascade down one wall, a waterfall of light suddenly illuminating the room... which expanded until there were no walls, just an endless room stretching out for infinity.

Two men in black monk robes, hoods pulled up over their heads and hiding their faces, sat at a small table. She looked closer. They were playing chess. The white chess pieces were on fire, but neither player seemed perturbed by the flames. Further away a funeral was underway. A simple pinewood coffin lay next to an open grave, dug out from the wooden floor.

As Amber approached the casket, the lid slowly opened. Dr. Jonathan Meta lay there in his own black robe, just as when she first met him, looking peaceful with long silver hair, his eyes closed.

"Oh, Merlin…" she said softly. It broke her heart to see him.

"Amber," he answered.

His voice didn't come from the coffin. It came from one of the chess players. Both turned to her, drawing back the cowls from their faces. Both were János Mehta.

They frowned at her.

"Who's Merlin?" the player with the black pieces asked. He sat there, glaring at her while the Mehta with the flaming chess pieces stood up. He looked around the infinite space in dazed wonderment, then turned to Amber.

"You… *are* Amber, aren't you?"

She looked from one to the other. With his hood pulled back, she could now see that under his black robe, the seated János Mehta wore a military-style uniform of some kind—a crisp black formfitting outfit that looked as if it came from the Imperial wardrobe rack in *Star Wars*.

The standing János Mehta pulled his robe off, revealing military wear as well, but drab and worn baggy camo fatigues—more like the twenty-first-century American soldier gear she was used to seeing, even if she didn't recognize the flag patch on his shoulder.

"Who are you?" she asked.

"I'm Esper Specialist John DeMetta, with the 138th Kinetic Infantry unit of the Gestaltist Faction Army." He rattled off his name and rank with a well-practiced flow before giving an almost embarrassed smile. "My friends, however, just call me John, or Dee."

She looked at the two men. Their faces and buzz cuts were identical, dark skin, high cheekbones, silver hair, and those unmistakable violet space-alien eyes with the freaky cascade of tiny stars. Yet there *was* a subtle difference between them, a natural gentleness inherent to Specialist DeMetta—and to her Merlin—that was lacking in János Mehta. He could only mimic compassion—when it suited him.

She turned to DeMetta. "So... *you're* the one who's been haunting me in my dreams, and making me sleepwalk all over the place?"

"Yes," he replied. "I think it must have been me. Sorry about that."

She flashed on the memory of him at the base of the Sphinx. Cam and Kha-Hotep charging him, weapons raised to protect her. Both men crumpling to the ground without warning.

"Hey!" she exclaimed. "What did you do to Cam and Kha-Hotep?"

"Your friends?" he responded. "They're fine. I just stunned them so they wouldn't cut my head off."

Amber felt relieved to hear that, though her mind was still reeling and she wasn't sure she could trust what *anyone* told her anymore. She rubbed her head with both hands.

"Is this really happening, or is this just another dream?" She glanced down at her jersey. "Never mind, this *has* to be a dream. I haven't worn this shirt in months."

"Well, this *is* a dream," DeMetta said, straddling the chair he'd been sitting in, "but you and I are having a real conversation. You and I have been communicating in our sleep all along, so this seemed the fastest way to catch up. But this is the first time we've been awake in our dreams, if that makes sense."

"Um… sort of," she replied. "Not so much."

DeMetta grinned. "It's okay. We're lucid dreaming now. When we're done, you can just wake up. And in the meantime, if you want to change clothes, just think of something, anything you like. I mean, *you're* the boss here."

On a whim, she imagined herself wearing a black leather combat catsuit. The Padres jersey vanished, replaced by something Kate Beckinsale would wear to fight Lycans.

"We really *are* in *The Matrix*," she murmured, pleased with herself.

DeMetta gave a confused smile. "Sorry, I don't know what that is."

"It's a twentieth-century thing," Amber explained. "So where is your shard from?"

"My shard?" He stared at her blankly.

"What year are you from?"

"What *year* am I from?"

"Yeah, you know, the Event? Where have you been, under a rock or someth—" She stopped as she remembered the Sphinx, and realized her *faux pas*. "I'm sorry. You've been stuck in a big metal box for who knows how long."

He nodded. "You know what suspended animation is, right? Basically, I've missed everything since the Ouroboros marched on Cairo. I don't know how long I've been out, but you must've already heard the news through the spindle networks or the Allied PreCogs, about Sensemayá and how she took out all their Medusae.

"Well, I was there with her when it was defeated—at ground zero, in fact," he continued. "It's funny, feels like it only just happened a few moments ago..." He paused, looking back up at Amber. Her blank expression said it all.

"I don't want to come off like a PsiPremicist," he said carefully, "but are you and this Egyptian group from some rogue a-psyche faction?"

"What?"

"The Contras? NeoLudds? Gypsies?" He suddenly looked at her as if just seeing her for the first time. "Hang on. You're not any kind of a-psyche radical, are you? You're a..." His voice trailed off, as though not wanting to say it out loud. "You're a full-on Ungifted."

"Look," she said, "I have to tell you—I really, *really* don't have a clue about anything you're talking about."

He leaned back and scratched his head.

"I guess that makes two of us." He sat silent for a moment, then said, "Tell you what. You debrief me, and then I'll return the favor."

"Sure, but..." Amber frowned. "Wait, so how did you even *find* me, if you don't—" She stopped, nodded to herself. "Right. Suspended animation. Never mind. Okay, first things first. The Event. So... do you know what 'schizochronolinear' is?"

DeMetta raised a hand. "Let me make this really easy for

you. Don't *tell* me, just *show* me."

"What do you mean? Draw you a picture? Do an interpretive dance?"

"Smart ass," he said with a grin. "No, just *think* about what you're trying to explain to me." He sat straight and closed his eyes.

"Oh. Okay."

She closed her eyes, too, and pictured…

Merlin, back at the Neolithic cave in Britain, lecturing them by firelight, as she imagines a stained-glass window of time, six hundred million years long, shattering in a mindboggling cosmic cataclysm, then coalescing again into a patchwork new world… a towering curtain of raw energy roaring just inches away from her face…

Pleistocene wilderness, Gavin dead beside her, sliced in half… making her way cross-country past ruins, hiding from dire wolves… Blake rescuing her…

Cam, charging her with his sword, then falling at her feet… The young Celt laughing with her, cooking them both breakfast… Getting captured by Cromwellian Roundheads and locked up in the bell tower at Lexden… The others. Stearne. Nell. Their escape. Pursuit. Simon. Blake. Fighting soldiers. Cam, dying on the ground…

The Vanuatu… *Flying the ship to North Africa… Stranded… Crossing the desert… The temple… Giant crocodiles… The* Star of the Dawn… *New Memphis.*

The Sphinx.

* * *

She opened her eyes again. The return to the dreamscape was disconcerting, but she shook her head and recovered. After a moment, DeMetta opened his eyes, as well. When he finally spoke, he sounded shaken.

"So time has shattered into pieces, and you... you aren't an Ungifted, you're just from *the past*. A completely *different* past."

"What do you mean?"

He was silent for a moment, then looked at her with a solemn gaze.

"Let me show you."

He closed his eyes, and images began to stream into Amber's head...

A stark building—a Soviet hospital facility in Czechoslovakia, in 1969. A researcher pulling one card after another from a deck, the young patient unfailingly reciting the symbols off of cards she cannot see.

A shag-carpeted therapist's office in Berkeley, California, 1972. A teenage boy gazes intently at a fountain pen on the parapsychologist's oak desk. Slowly the pen begins to rotate, then rises, hovering a few inches in the air.

Checkpoint Charlie, West Berlin, 1974. From the trunk of the car, an American boy and Czech girl stare at the barrel of a Kalashnikov rifle. The two lock eyes with an East German border guard. He stares back, unable to move.

"Alles klar," he calls out, and waves the car on.

The Czech girl and the American boy stare up at the Iguazú Falls, cascading down from three hundred and fifty feet above them, creating a one-hundred-foot cloud of spray and the most gorgeous prismatic rainbow display either has ever seen.

They remain in Argentina, hiding from both the CIA and KGB. They and their children begin to search out others like them from all around the world.

The Psionic Underground is born.

The twenty-first century unfolds: global superpowers and nation-states splinter into smaller and smaller political units, as psionic adepts seize the reins of government… Within a generation, the Ungifted, those without psychic abilities, dwindle away to a tiny minority.

Spindle technology yields psionic batteries, amplifiers, weapons… and a global utopia.

Then frightening pathologies arise, producing psionic berserkers and vampires, along with ugly brands of psionic supremacism and totalitarian thought. Competing ideologies give rise to psionic factions.

The Psychic Wars begin, endless cycles of combat that rage for more than a century and a half. Factions employing precognitives gain the upper hand. Whole cities are burned to ash, and large swaths of civilization revert almost to medieval conditions, little better than petty kingdoms beset by wandering military units.

Esper Specialist John DeMetta in a bunker in the Eastern European war zone, 2216... driving in the ruins of Cairo, 2219... the Ouroboros invading... Sensemayá... a psychic explosion.

Cairo gone. Hands lifting him up. The capsule lid closing. Too late, he senses their intentions—he is a god, they believe, sent to them by lordly Osiris—and like Osiris, he must be reverently placed in the sacred sarcophagus, so that Thoth and Anubis may restore him to life again...

Sleeping beneath the Great Sphinx... His dreaming mind reaching out for psionic activity of any kind... A spindle, thousands of miles away in a bunker in Great Britain... a girl named Amber.

"Help me Amber..."

* * *

The visions faded away, and the two of them opened their eyes, still in the dreamscape. Both remained quiet for a moment. Amber blinked a few times, and then shook her head. DeMetta took a deep breath and rubbed his temples.

"That helped," he said at last. "I'm starting to remember some things, and understand others, but I still have questions."

Amber snorted, then caught herself and covered her mouth, embarrassed.

"*You* have questions?"

He laughed. "Alright. Ladies first."

"How can you not know what's going on? I mean, that was *you* at the weird bunker back in England, wasn't it?

You sent me the combination. And then that freaky floating dark crystal thing had me dangling in midair while it kept zapping me—what the hell was *that* all about?"

"The spindle. It's a psionic resonator, among other things."

"Well, it scared the shit out of me. I didn't know if I had just dreamt the whole thing. In fact, you've had me walking in my sleep all over the place ever since—you got me to change the course of the *Vanuatu*, without even waking me up!"

"I can explain—"

"Hypnotically controlling me, getting into my dreams…" She looked at him and shivered. "That's creepy. I mean, you could have just *talked* to me about all this!"

DeMetta looked embarrassed. "Listen, you have to understand—I *couldn't* talk to you. I've been asleep. All this time, my subconscious has been talking to your subconscious. We haven't been dreaming about each other. We've been dreaming *to* each other."

"But… how?"

"When you're a telepath in suspended animation, you're never really asleep. There's a part of you, even in a deep REM state, that can communicate. I'm not particularly good at it— it's slippery, like trying to eat with greased chopsticks."

"Oh!" Amber said, suddenly making the connection. "*That's* what your subconscious kept trying to tell me in my sleep. It wanted me to come find you."

"I guess so." He shrugged. "I can't remember any of it very well, just flashes, really, all very surreal. I vaguely remember an artificial intelligence—I can remember scanning through it to get what I needed. That was your ship, the *Vanuatu*, right? And all those Egyptians, especially their priestess, Nefer-Tamit. She was hard to forget."

"Okay, that sort of makes sense, I guess," she said, then she stared as realization struck. "Then it all started when I first got close to the—that… the spindle, right? That's how you found out about me?"

"Not exactly… I've known for years to be on the lookout for you. That's the one thing that my subconscious seems to have locked in on during all this. Getting you to me."

"But *how*?" Amber asked. "How could you possibly know anything about *me*? Are we even from the same dimension?"

"I don't know. I really don't know anything about you at all."

"Then *how*?" Amber gave an inarticulate cry of frustration. "And *why*?"

The soldier looked thoughtful, but didn't reply. They sat there in awkward silence a little longer, until she spoke up again.

"What are you thinking?"

He looked up.

"Sorry," DeMetta said. "It's this 'Event' of yours—I'm still trying to wrap my head around it all. I don't know where I am anymore, and then there's *them*." He gestured to Merlin lying in the coffin, and János Mehta, still glowering at the chessboard. "That one looks like my evil twin."

"Pretty much," Amber replied, her voice bitter. "The other one, the one in the coffin? He murdered him."

Walking over to his doppelganger, DeMetta leaned over

46

the table for a closer look. Mehta didn't respond—didn't seem to notice him. DeMetta frowned.

"What *is* that?" he asked. "Why are his eyes so strange?"

"Are you kidding me?"

"What do you mean?" He seemed genuinely puzzled. Amber concentrated, and handed him a mirror.

"See for yourself."

He stared at his reflection in shock.

"What the hell happened to me?"

"I was hoping *you* would tell *me*."

"So you don't know why these two look like me, or what happened to our eyes?"

"Not a clue."

Nonplussed, DeMetta came back and took his seat again, folding his arms and resting his chin on them as he stared off at nothing.

"So," Amber said. "What next?"

DeMetta looked up.

"You remember the scare you got from the spindle? When it was, you know, 'zapping' you?"

"Yeah."

"It makes sense to me now. That was just an activation sequence. Conditioning you, getting you ready so I can teach you."

"Oh okay, *that's* not totally creepy…" she muttered. "Teach me what?"

He raised an eyebrow.

"How to be a telepath."

5

**Somewhere in the Western Desert
Northeast of Alam el Halfa ridge
Nine days after the Event**

Wachtmeister Schäfer sang as he drove the half-track.

> *Es rasseln die Ketten, es dröhnt der Motor,*
> *Panzer rollen in Afrika vor!*
> *Panzer rollen in Afrika vor!*

The treads are rattling, the motor is droning, Tanks are rolling forward in Africa! It sounded like a sea shanty, and that was fine with him. In a strange way, he felt like a sailor. War here was more like being at sea than any land campaign he'd ever experienced. There was no real territory to seize—most parts of the *Gott verdammt* desert were indistinguishable from any other, and provided little cover. Few of the "ridges" on the map were much higher than the rest of the flat landscape.

In this empty expanse between the Qattara depression and the Mediterranean coast, their tanks and armored cars might as well have been old ironclad ships sailing the high seas, lobbing cannon balls at each other. Sure, the wet salt spray was replaced by dry clouds of dust, and oceanic tempests by desert sandstorms. The pounding of rough seas became the rugged grind of the treads over rocks, and instead of being becalmed they got beached by the lack of petrol.

The thought of being stranded wasn't entirely academic. His half-track was bringing up the rear, lagging behind the main column. The front of the vehicle had taken damage from an Australian mortar, and the engine was struggling along at half speed.

Still, there was no chance of getting strafed by a Brit fighter plane, or of having an enemy tank sneak up behind them. They were moving slowly but steadily, and while the battle at El Alamein had come to a bizarre and inexplicable end, at least the war against the Tommies, the Second World War, was finally over.

Alexandria lay dead ahead and, according to the scouts, miraculously restored to its ancient glory by the same inexplicable wonder that had brought back the pterodactyls and made the Allied forces disappear. The jeweled city would be their reward for months of bloody fighting. Rommel would only need a tank or two and a handful of infantry to get the job done—and the Germans had much, much more than that. With no trace of any modern defenses, the Korps need only roll up and take what they wanted.

A pleasant thought—as long as their half-track didn't get left behind. Ahead of them, a few miles off, the dust kicked up by the rest of the column made a helpful beacon, even if it did look ominously like a sandstorm.

Schäfer squinted.

Something else, closer to their position.

He frowned. The Allied tanks and planes might have vanished, but there were still enemy commandos lurking about the Western Desert, harassing the main column. They had escaped from the base camp back near El Alamein, but not before throwing the camp into chaos—with a herd of wild elephants, rumor had it—stealing lorries and torching a good portion of the German petrol reserves before escaping into the night. It would be very bad luck to run into them out here. Most likely, however, they had fled ahead of the main column.

Whatever lay ahead now, it demanded a closer look.

He pulled to a halt.

"Hey! Driver! Why are we stopping?" one of the troopers called from the back. Schäfer lifted his gloved hand and pointed.

"Somebody's left a Stumpy behind."

It was one of theirs, a Panzer IV, and not a wreck, either. The big tank appeared to have taken its share of enemy fire, but it was intact and looked to be in better shape than their half-track. Its bulk listed slightly to one side. All the hatches were open.

Must have broken a tread, Schäfer thought. He called out to anyone who might be inside.

"Jemand da?"

No answer. Frowning, he pulled his goggles off his sunburned face. Stepping down from the driver's seat, he approached the tank carefully. Behind him one of the soldiers, *Soldat* Brenz, called out.

"What kind of *vrwurschdeld Feuerzauber* is *that*?" he asked in his thick *Schwäbisch* accent, pointing off to the right. A great patch of ground, more than a hundred meters long, and nearly as wide, was scorched black.

"It must be the crash site of the plane we saw come down," Schäfer called back. He rapped his knuckles on the hull of the Panzer, then climbed up onto the hulk.

"*Ja,*" the Swabian agreed, "but where's the debris?"

Schäfer poked his head cautiously into one of the side hatches. No one home. He hopped back down again, saw the soldiers clustered together, and went over to see what had caught their attention. The terrain certainly showed signs of the fire, but Brenz was right to wonder—where had all the wreckage gone?

The others headed back to the truck to take a cigarette break. He continued to study the crash site. His high desert boots crunched on the blackened, vitrified sand. Something strange caught his eye. He crouched down for a closer look.

At his feet, there was a slender rivulet, about as wide as his little finger. It snaked out to the edge of the scorched earth. It wasn't flowing with water, however, but with a gentle steady stream of fine sand. He turned his head to trace the flow—it snaked all the way back toward the center of the blackened zone.

There were more of them, he saw, all appearing to branch out from the center. He rose and followed the root-like little canal. It wound its way inside to a manhole-sized opening, where all of the rivulets came together. The pit reminded Schäfer of the underside of a sand dollar, with its spidery network of lines tracing out in all directions.

His curiosity growing, Schäfer began walking toward the pit, but a bright spot in the black crust caught his eye. He crouched down and picked up a pearl, the largest he had ever seen. At least the size of a quail's egg.

"*Heilige Scheiße…*"

"Hey, what did you find there?" one of the others shouted.

He stood and held it up for them to see.

"Look! It's a pearl!"

"What? *Quatsch!*" Brenz sneered.

"No, honest! Come see!"

Each of the three took a last puff and stomped over to see for themselves.

"I'll be damned and stitched…" Brenz muttered. One of his comrades grabbed him by the elbow.

"Jesus Maria!" He gestured around. "Look! They're all over the place!"

He was right—the blackened ground was riddled with the tiny spheres. He'd been so intent on the rivulet that he hadn't noticed them. Muttering with enthusiasm, the four men scrambled to scoop them up.

"Hey! What's this?" Brenz held out his findings. In the hollow of his hand, the clutch of tiny pearls was *moving*. First vibrating, then jitterbugging about like agitated little drops of oil in a frying pan. Then all at once, the dancing pips came together, coalescing into a single, bigger object.

"Menschenskind!" the wide-eyed Swabian gasped in disbelief, but didn't drop it. He showed it to Schäfer. "Look at this—the pearls all came together, and it's acting crazy. Like a *mexikanische* jumping bean!" The pearl was quivering again—and then it jumped from Brenz's palm to Schäfer's, merging with the pearl that lay there.

"Hey! You ate my pearl!" Brenz yelled. Before either man could react, however, the billiard-ball-sized object jumped to the ground and began moving across the scorched ground. It didn't roll, but flowed away like a glob of mercury, heading directly toward the open pit.

It dropped into the hole without a sound.

The men stared in wonder. Abruptly a metallic wrenching sound came from behind them, and they spun. The Panzer began to wobble, then heave to one side before sinking into the blackened sand. They ran toward it, but there was nothing they could do. Though the ground had looked as solid as any other part of the inhospitable plain they occupied, it swallowed the tank as if it was quicksand.

Brenz whistled appreciatively at the spectacle of the big armored vehicle slipping below the surface. It did so at an angle, its tread rising up then vanishing, followed by the turret and, lastly, the long barrel of the 75mm gun—disappearing inch by inch until the entire tank was gone.

Schäfer broke the silence.

"We need to get the hell out of this place," he said, his voice tinged with dread.

"What about all these pearls?" Brenz asked.

"Did your brain fall through your ass? Forget those things! We're up to our necks in shit here!"

The others agreed, and the four sprinted back to the half-track. It started up without a hitch, and Schäfer punched the accelerator. The engine roared—but they went nowhere.

"*Ach du Scheiße!*" he swore, and he jumped out to make sure they hadn't slipped the tread somehow.

They hadn't.

The tractor tread was still connected with the wheels, but its frayed ends hung over the front and rear sprockets, dangling just above the ground. Below that, there was no tread to be seen.

The bottoms of all the wheels were sunk into the ground. No, that wasn't it... They had been etched away, as if the entire vehicle had been dipped in acid. Shaking off numb disbelief, he poked his head down to look at the undercarriage. The crankshaft was swarming with a shimmering silver glaze, boiling away like ants.

"Get out!" he bellowed. "Get out of the truck."

"But we have—"

"Get out *now!*"

The three didn't argue the point. Jumping out, they moved away from the vehicle as if it was going to burst into flames at any moment. Schäfer wiped the back of his hand against his chin.

"Grab the water cans," he said. "We have a long walk ahead of us."

As the men rushed to obey his order, a stray gleam from below caught his eye. The edges of his boots appeared rimmed with a glistening, silver hoarfrost.

It spread rapidly.

6

Palace of the Prefect in Alexandria
Nine days after the Event

Seven and a half centuries earlier, a twenty-five-year-old Macedonian general had strode the beach, gazing out at the glittering Mediterranean Sea and the rocks of Pharos island.

The place had been called Rhakotis then, no more than a string of five sleepy Egyptian villages harboring fishermen and pirates. They stretched along a slender needle of land between the briny sea and the marshes of a freshwater lake. But the Greek general saw much more—a fine harbor, access to the Nile, ample freshwater, a pleasing climate, and an eminently defensible location.

Drawing in the sand with his finger, the Great Alexander had begun sketching out the plan for a massive seaport. A palace, a gridwork of streets arranged to capture the cooling sea breezes, a canal to the Nile, and stout walls at either end to protect the only two ways to approach from land. And a great lighthouse—the tallest in the world.

Thus the city of Alexandria had sprung into being.

* * *

Distant screams and sounds of violence came up through the open windows, faintly echoing off the marble floors of the council chambers. The sounds did nothing to sooth Hypatia's apprehension as she stared down at the city map.

Small wooden *latrunculi* tokens marked areas of rioting throughout the five districts of the city. A cluster of tokens marked the gates and walls of Delta, the Jewish quarter and the northernmost district, a city unto itself. The Jews were used to the fragile and uncertain nature of their rights outside those walls.

In response to the reports of his soldiers, the prefect Orestes added tokens to the Rhakotis district—the native Egyptian quarter in the city's southwestern corner, as well as major thoroughfares and the *agoras*—even along the harborside outskirts of the Broucheion, the Greco-Macedonian noble quarter enclosing the palace and its grounds.

Hypatia started to comment to her colleague Calix, the prefect's special agent and her friend, but he was dead—killed only yesterday by the same kind of fell device that had later rescued her from certain death. The fresh memories still cut deep.

Stifling a sigh, Hypatia looked to Nellie, the pale-skinned woman who stood silently by the far window, staring out to the southwest with sharp gray-green eyes. The morning sun lit her cream-colored skin and soft brown hair. She was still a mystery, this Nellie. A slave who had escaped the marvelous aerial craft commandeered by János Mehta, and had saved Hypatia's life.

At first Hypatia surmised that Nellie was Galatian, or possibly from one of the Visigoth tribes—her unfamiliar garb seemed ill-suited to the heat, and her pale complexion and slave status hinted at origins in the barbarian north, even if her command of Greek was flawless.

Yet the truth—if the woman could be trusted—was stranger still. Nellie had told them she was from a land on the other side of the world, centuries *ahead* of their own time. It sounded insane, yet Hypatia had seen the evidence with her own two eyes.

Nellie had shared what had happened to her and her companions before and after Mehta had taken over the airship *Vanuatu*, spoken of Mehta's mind-controlling drugs, and how she had returned to Alexandria after the ship had been destroyed. The young woman did her best to explain the events that had shattered their world, but by her own admission, she didn't really understand it herself.

"It was some kind of machine," she'd said, but what kind of machine, she couldn't—or wouldn't—say.

Hypatia chose to believe the former.

Nellie Bly kept a close eye on everyone while ostensibly staring out the window, a strategy that served her well as a reporter. She only wished she had a view over the city walls so she could watch for Blake's return, as well. How he expected to slow the German army, she couldn't fathom. Still, if anyone could do the impossible, it was the British soldier.

This would have been the story of a lifetime, she thought with a pang. Funny, but she hadn't thought about her lost career since the Event. Between the pirate attack, the giant shark, nearly being burned at the stake, and the incredible technology of the *Vanuatu*—so far beyond her imagining it still boggled her mind—she'd hardly had time to consider what she'd lost.

Nelly had built a career by putting herself forward, taking chances few women—and not many men—could or would. When she'd faked insanity to gain entrance to Blackwell's Island, she'd spent ten days in hell. What if her editor at the *New York World* hadn't followed through on his word and secured her release? But he had, and the story had helped secure her career.

One that now meant nothing. How many people in the shard world even knew who she was?

Still, she thought, *I should write everything down. Just in case we manage to set things right.* Although without the *Vanuatu*, that was highly unlikely. And even if they *did* succeed, would the world return to the way it had been? Would any of them remember anything that had happened when the timeline shattered?

Her thoughts scattered when someone placed a gentle hand on her shoulder. Nellie looked up to see the Greek mathematician smiling down at her.

"You look as though you await the return of Mehta's flying vessel," Hypatia said.

"The *Vanuatu*? It was never his." Nellie shook her head. "I don't know what we will do, now that it's been destroyed."

Hypatia's face dropped. "The destruction of such an amazing vessel is a crime."

"Yes," Nellie replied. "Mehta, though… being rid of him almost makes it worth it. Almost." Another thought occurred. "If we truly *are* rid of him."

"If not the airship, then what do you look for?"

"Blake."

"The soldier."

Nellie nodded. Hypatia looked at her thoughtfully.

"Do you truly think he will return?"

"If he doesn't, he won't go out of this world without taking plenty of them with him." Nellie shook her head again, chasing away the thought.

"The guard are on watch," Hypatia assured her. "We will know as soon as they see him."

"What about Alexandria?" Nellie asked. "What will you do?"

"We cannot hide in the palace and let the city devour itself this way," Hypatia replied passionately. At her words, Orestes looked up from the map.

"What choice do we have?" he said. "We are on the ragged edge of anarchy—the guard are stretched thin, and there are already more rioting *parabolani* than there are soldiers left in the Macedonian barracks. We must allow their fire to burn out naturally—let them expend their energies killing themselves, and not our remaining soldiers."

Nellie stood. "Prefect, you must convince the people of the city that fighting one another is suicide, when a greater enemy will be knocking at the gates soon enough. Won't we need every one of them then?"

"She has the right of it," Hypatia said quietly.

"Of course she does!" Orestes raged, slamming his hand on the table. Tokens scattered across the map. He took a deep breath before continuing. "And if they had ears to listen, perhaps I could find the words to extort them—but you know as well as I what the mobs will do if we try to keep them from shedding one another's blood. Or have you forgotten how close you came to being dragged from your chariot and torn to pieces?"

"Yet you are still the law!" Hypatia said. "Who else but you can rally a defense, when the true enemy comes?"

"And what will happen if you do nothing?" Nellie asked.

The prefect turned away from them, and laid a hand on the lion head carved into his seat of rule, as if stroking its mane.

"So..." he said at last. "A woman's eye finds a choice where a man sees none." He faced them again. "Very well. We choose to ride out."

Accompanied by all that could be spared of the Prefectural Guard—a handful of armored cavalry and a dozen foot soldiers—they took Oreste's chariot, the largest *quadriga* in the city, pulled by four handsome Etrurian bays. Hypatia thought sadly of her own charioteer, Onesimus, and her slave Aspasius, lost in the attack on her the previous night. Their fate remained a complete mystery.

Considering how easily the mob had overcome her guard, she was not reassured by the presence of this smaller force. Even so, through the normally-crowded theater district of Aspendia and the Soma—the sacred precinct containing the Temple of

Pan and the mausoleums of Alexander and the Ptolemies—
they made their way without challenge or incident. Along the
great Canopic Way, the city's major thoroughfare, windows
were shuttered and the street eerily deserted.

Finally they approached the *agora*, where the agitated
sound of angry shouts grew steadily louder.

"Listen to the roar," Orestes said. "There must be over three
hundred of them."

Hypatia leaned in to Nellie. "Do you have your weapon at
hand?"

Nellie shook her head. "The pistol? No, it was out of bullets.
Useless, except for show."

Not the answer Hypatia had hoped for.

They came close enough to see the two clashing factions,
their quarrel having passed the boiling point. The patriarch
Bishop Cyril led his black-hooded *parabolani*, the wild,
unkempt monks who had become fanatic enforcers and
foot soldiers. Yet Cyril's forces were clashing, not with Jews
or pagans, but with their fellow believers, the gray-robed
followers of the Christian presbyter Novatian.

"What on earth are they fighting about?" Orestes said in
an undertone.

Hypatia could only shake her head. She couldn't remember
how the two factions differed. Nonetheless, several men
were staggering away, bruised and bloodied, while others
lay crumpled on the street in spreading crimson puddles.
The prefect's guess had been correct. The mob *was* over three
hundred strong. Closer to a thousand, in fact.

"Sound the trumpets," Orestes commanded, his voice quiet but firm. The fracas nearly drowned out the blare of the instruments, but Cyril noted it.

"Prefect!" the bishop called out. "These heretics have committed crimes against the Holy Church and offense against God. Respectfully, the duty to rebuke and castigate them is ours, not yours, *Dominus Praefectus.*"

"Lord Prefect!" the Novatianist leader cried out. "Help us! We are innocent citizens defending ourselves! It is *they* who offend God with their heresy, and they seek to murder us!"

"Lies!" one of the *parabolani* shouted in the forefront. "God will smite you!"

"Patience, Ammonius," the bishop called, reining in his follower. "All of you, make way and allow the prefect to pass undisturbed!" The *parabolani* ceased their assault, and a relative silence fell over the crowd.

"I am not in transit," Orestes said curtly. "I would speak with you, Your Excellency. You and your flock." He raised his voice. "Hear this, all! The defense of the city is at hand. An enemy army approaches. Every man is required to do his duty—every last one of you. There shall be no further unrest. Return to your homes and await my word."

A sullen grumble rose from the sea of black hoods, making the cataphracts' horses nervous. Hypatia shared their unease.

"Prefect, please, I implore you." Bishop Cyril spread his hands wide. "These heretics have provoked the faithful— so grievously, I fear, that I cannot hold back their righteous wrath. Return to the palace at once, I pray you. I will come join you there in due course, to offer my counsel and support." His followers muttered their agreement.

Orestes narrowed his eyes. "I say again to all of you. Return to your homes and await my edict. This is my command. Obey it as Alexandrians, and as my fellow Christians."

"You? You are no Christian!" Ammonius yelled back. He stabbed a finger toward Hypatia and Nellie. "Look at him! See how he parades through the streets with his whores!" The bishop said nothing to restrain him, watching through lizard-lidded eyes as the drama played out.

"*Not a Christian?*" Orestes shouted. "I was baptized by the Bishop of Constantinople! Who consecrated you a monk, you prating priest?"

"Stop this!" Hypatia's clear voice rang out. "Listen to your prefect. Our city is in grave danger from an enemy who approaches even now, and still you all bicker like hateful, quarreling schoolboys!"

"Keep silent, whore!" Ammonius bellowed, spittle flying from his mouth. He raised his fists in the air, stirring up his brothers. "Are godly men to listen to the authority of a *woman*? See how Orestes is in thrall to these vile witches—their slave! He has given his flesh over to Satan!"

"Arrest that man!" the prefect ordered.

Ammonius answered by grabbing a jagged, fist-sized stone from the ground and hurling it toward them. It struck Orestes in the temple, and he collapsed to the floor of the chariot like a rag doll, clutching his head, trying to staunch the stream of blood. It quickly covered his face.

A new roar went up from the mob, and more stones came flying through the air toward them. With a howl of bloodlust, the black-robed tide of *parabolani* rose up again against the Novatianist heretics—and against the prefectural chariot.

The sight of the furious mob made the horses rear up in fright, and the charioteer strained to rein them in. Then a thrown chunk of pavestone caught him in the teeth. Howling, he grabbed his bleeding face and a second stone hit his head, knocking him to the floor of the chariot alongside Nellie and Hypatia and the stricken Orestes. The panicked horses dragged the chariot for a few feet before breaking free and galloping away.

The foot soldiers of the Prefectural Guard rushed to form a shield wall against the rain of stones. Nellie shrieked as rocks bounded off the shields and clattered around them, dangerously close.

We'll be stoned to death, she thought, terrified. Out of nowhere, her panicked mind suddenly envisioned Amber, screaming her name, but the figment was quickly dashed away, eclipsed by the charging mob.

"Oh god, this is it!" she sobbed, grabbing Hypatia.

7

**Aboard the Egyptian barge *Siu-Tuait* – the *Star of the Dawn*
Heading downstream on the Nile
Nine days after the Event**

The *Star of the Dawn* made excellent progress down the Nile, thanks to the crew of twelve Egyptian rowers they had taken on at Giza—all worshippers of the divine and newly resurrected god Siu-Netherit.

They had extended their services gladly. DeMetta had only to make his wishes known to the high priestess Nefer-Tamit, and the worshippers fought one another for the honor to serve. Now they made best speed for Alexandria, the dozen men propelling the barge in strong, synchronized pulls of the paddles.

Amber and DeMetta sat silently in the bow, oblivious to the rest of the passengers. To anyone watching, the pair seemed to be engaged in no more than a friendly staring contest. Inside her mind, a new universe was being born. She had to control her breathing as she grappled with what Dee had awakened. It was as if this terrifying and awesome ability had been lying dormant in her brain, just waiting for the right signal to bring it to the surface. Could this be what they needed? What *she* needed?

"Am I doing it right?" she asked.

"Yes, loud and clear," he responded. *"Okay, come on, keep talking."*

Amber glanced at the Egyptians manning the oars.

"How do they do that? It seems so... effortless."

"I gave them a psionic push to boost their endurance. They'll need breaks for food and water, though, or they'll continue to row day and night as if their lives depend on it, up until their bodies give out."

It was a little creepy, she thought, the robotic way the men went through their paces. It felt like slavery, too, even though Amber told herself they were all volunteers. Their lives really *did* depend on it, too.

All our lives depend on it, she thought.

DeMetta nodded. *"They really do."*

A sudden wave of despair overwhelmed her—their mission seemed impossible. First, they had to find the *Vanuatu*—wherever it was—then, somehow rescue the others from János Mehta and take control of the ship. After that, they had to reach the South Pole to find Merlin's lab. Unless they could reverse the shredding of space-time, the planet would continue to break into tiny fragments...What had he said? *All the way down to the subatomic level...*

At most they had days.

Perhaps hours...

With a jolt, Amber realized DeMetta was aware of her running mental chatter. He was listening to her train of thought, could sense the anxiety radiating off her, bright as a neon sign.

"I'm sorry! I didn't mean to—"

"Forget it," he insisted. After a moment, he continued, *"Focus now. It's going to get trickier. Are you ready?"*

She nodded, and hoped it was true. There was a tingling in her head as DeMetta focused, his features perfectly still. Then it happened. A new part of her mind awakened.

Amber gasped.

She had seen videos of deaf people hearing for the first time, or of the moment when the bandages came off the eyes of a person who had been blind from birth. The instant when someone suddenly gained an entirely new sense that they could never have imagined before. Now she knew what that meant.

A keen new awareness unfolded, the presence of everything around her making itself known. The darkness of the river and the empty desert to either side lit up like Times Square. It was like seeing a galaxy of stars, or maybe hearing an orchestra break into a concerto. The sensations were overwhelming— the invisible light, the silent cacophony.

"Amber…?"

She could feel his concern. *"It's… it's—I can't even describe it all."* She did her best to regain her mental balance, and pushed a collage of scattered sounds and images at him.

///stampeding crowds of screaming fans
at a concert///every face and every animal
she could call to mind///An astronaut
murmuring, "My god, it's full of stars"////

"It can be overwhelming at first, I know," he responded. *"Here, let me show you how to turn down the background noise."* She felt his presence again in her mind, and just like that, she instinctively knew how to turn the roar down to a manageable level.

Better.

With a new, keen sense of awareness Amber glanced around at the other people on the boat. DeMetta, the twelve rowers, Cam and Kha-Hotep, Leila and Ibn Fadlan.

"Wow, I can see—I mean, I can feel—all of us. Do you know what I mean?"

"I do. Congratulations, Amber. You're a telepath now."

Deciding to press further along, she mentally studied her friends. Their Egyptian riverboat captain Kha-Hotep was telling Cam something about the Nile. Ibn Fadlan, a medieval Muslim noble, chatted in Arabic with Leila, a student from twentieth-century Cairo, on some esoteric topic the girl didn't seem to understand. With a start, Amber realized that she could tell that Cam was interested, while Leila was bored.

Their emotions seemed palpable to her in a way she couldn't quite define. No shimmering auras, no cheap special effects. It was as if she'd suddenly gained the ability to read and translate the subtlest of body language.

Focusing on Ibn Fadlan, she saw that he was at ease, buttressed by an almost fatalistic sense of calm. Beneath that, however, she could sense ripples of doubt crashing up against his stony reserves of theological certainty. Leila's psyche showed many of the same fears and more—shock, mourning, and uncertainty—but she didn't enjoy Ibn Fadlan's bolstering assurance. Her doubts were closer to the surface.

Kha-Hotep surprised her with the depths of his feelings. The captain always seemed to be such a cool customer, but he carried an enormous burden of grief at the loss of his crew, especially his younger brother. His hidden sorrow touched her.

Then there was Cam. He seemed even more at ease than Ibn Fadlan, but it wasn't that he didn't understand the gravity of their situation, or that he was in denial. He was just coping in a very different way. Cam had grown up in a less civilized time than the Arab, and his tribal values embraced a world filled with fickle magic and dark, dangerous mysteries.

As she watched the young Celt listening to Kha-Hotep, he always seemed eager to take in more knowledge—he was like a sponge. In the midst of their conversation he glanced over at her and smiled—and with a jolt like an electric shock, Amber felt the power of his feelings for her.

She turned away quickly, unable to keep eye contact.

"Easy now," DeMetta sent. *"Are you okay?"*

She nodded, cheeks flushed and heart thumping. In the abstract, she had known Cam had strong feelings for her. It was one thing to know, however—and another thing entirely to encounter it firsthand, so vibrantly.

He loved her.

He would follow her into battle if need be.

He would die for her.

He *expected* to die for her.

DeMetta leaned in to catch her gaze.

"You sure you're alright?"

"I'm… I'm okay.

"It's just that…"

She struggled to send clearly, but her thoughts were agitated, flying off before she could stop them.

///oh crap///Cam///ohmygod///
///he loves me///oh god oh god///Cam///
///kissing him///Cam naked in the
moonlight///oh god don't die!////
///I think I love him too///

DeMetta took her hands in his and did something with his mind that slowed the unwanted psychic torrent, until it was a trickle.

"I'm sorry," he sent. *"I didn't expect that to happen. I guess I take for granted the training we receive. It's okay. You just sensed a little more than you expected, and got a surprise."* He let that sink in, then added, *"You're a natural empath, Amber. It took me a long time to learn how to properly read surface emotions, and here you are, picking them up without even trying."*

"God, I'm so embarrassed!" she responded. *"I mean, I knew, but…"*

"Yeah, it's different when you get it straight from the horse's mouth, so to speak, isn't it? But don't be embarrassed. It's all part of the process."

She took a few deep breaths, shook her head a bit to clear it, and smiled at him.

"I'm okay. Thanks. Yes, it's just so…" She realized something.

"Wait—you aren't still reading all my thoughts, too, are you?"

"Don't worry, I promise I'm not. Just what you're sending to me."

It suddenly occurred to Amber that she wasn't getting any emotional readings off of DeMetta at all.

"Why can't I sense anything from you—or any of the rowers?"

"There's nothing in their surface thoughts at present. I have them in a sort of fugue state. As for me, my passive defenses are up. Anybody can do it, even our friends back there. I'll teach you all how to shield your thoughts."

Amber sighed with relief.

"So can I learn to hypnotize people, too?" she asked. "'Push them,' you said?"

"Well… yes."

"And animals, too? What about creating illusions?" The implications began to wash over her. "Can I go inside people's dreams? Or hide my mind from other psychics who are looking for me? Can I stun people the way you did Cam and Kha-Hotep, back at the pyramid?"

"Whoa, slow down," he replied. "Yeah, in theory I can teach you all that, but we'll need to start with the basics and—"

"Can I see into the future?"

"I wish," he responded. "No, that's high-level precog stuff, and the thing about PreCogs—sometimes knowing the future isn't such a good thing." A strange look came over him, as if she had reminded him of something. Then the moment passed, and he was in instructor mode again.

"Look, I can't really teach you much about precognition, psychometry, or medical or forensic psi. So we'll stick with the basics.

You need to walk before you can run, including some basic psychic etiquette. There's serious responsibility that comes with ability like you're showing."

"Okay—but there's something I have to do now."

"And what's that?"

"I need to reach the others aboard the Vanuatu. I'm worried sick about them."

"Well, without getting a lock on someone, like I did with you, that could be tricky. Still, we can try. Do you have any idea where they are?"

"Let me see… the ship said they were headed about three hundred kilometers northeast of where we landed, but we've been traveling east and north since then, so… I guess I don't know."

"Well, it's a start. Here, let's try it together." He closed his eyes and focused, and she did the same. Together, each stretched their consciousness across the psychic landscape. With his help, she turned down the background hum from all the non-human forms of life, from the multitude of bacteria to the overwhelming number of viruses, insects, and even the plant life that lived in the vast empty desert.

"See if you can concentrate on just the animals."

Even as she winnowed out vast numbers of living creatures, it still left her with tens of billions of points of contact. Every one of them radiated a struggle for survival—she picked up a panoply of instincts at work, bursts of adrenaline fueled by predators and rivals, the drives for food and sex.

"Good. Keep going."

As she refined her search, she began to detect large groups of humans, each revealing a rich symphony of thought and desire.

"Now, try aiming for just one *of your friends. Concentrate on that specific person as best you can."*

That was an easy choice. She honed in on Nellie, striving to locate her unique psychic signature amid a few hundred thousand others. She sent her consciousness streaming toward the nearest cluster—a large concentration, upriver and to the northwest.

She sensed a city on the coast. Rising above its harbors, a shining beacon, and within its walls, diverse peoples from every corner of the Mediterranean world. *Alexandria*, they called it, and she knew that name from school. Nellie was somewhere in there. Amber could feel it. But where?

Amber called to mind Nellie's face, those mischievous gray-green eyes and delicate upturned nose, her voice, anything.

There was nothing.

"It's no use, I don't know what I'm doing."

"Don't give up. It's not easy, but you can do it."

She chewed on her frustration for a moment, then tried another approach.

… the first time she saw Nellie, disguised as a seventeenth-century peasant.

Confusion—why is this strange young woman slipping her a loaf of bread?

Nellie rescuing her from Cromwell's witchfinder. The ride to break the rest of their group out of the bell tower…

Needling the pompous Harcourt.

The quirky mix of Victorian manners and take-no-prisoners confidence.

And then, just like that, Amber caught the barest psychic flutter of her friend's mind.

"Nellie? Can you hear me?"

A faint thought came quavering back.

"We'll be stoned to death!"

"Nellie! I can hear you! We're coming, Nellie! Cam and I."

Interference of some kind obscured Nellie's signal. She wasn't alone—in fact she was surrounded by other minds, an eye of fear in a storm of fierce, hate-driven emotions.

"Oh god, this is it!"

"Nellie!" Amber shouted aloud.

The connection was dead.

Stones and screams filled the air.

Orestes' blood covered his face like a mask, and his eyes were closed tight—Hypatia could not tell if he still lived. Their charioteer was dead. Staring skyward, his mouth and skull ruined by fresh red wounds, he lay sprawled at their feet. He had been dragged half out of the chariot when the horses fled. Rocks continued to pelt down on his exposed body.

Nellie held her tight, shielding Hypatia from the rain of stones with her own body. The two women clung together, their faces so close that Hypatia could feel Nellie's tears, hot and wet, pressing on her cheek. They flinched at every rock hammering off the chariot or whizzing down, narrowly missing them. They listened in horror to the howling of the mob closing in on them.

Then came the sharp clatter of horse hooves ringing off the cobblestones, shouts, and a commanding flourish of trumpets. The women lifted their heads, and Orestes opened his eyes at the sound. He groaned, stirring a wave of relief in Hypatia. Nellie knelt and cautiously peered over the edge of the chariot.

The cataphract cavalrymen charged to the fore, braving the stones to position themselves between the sea of black hoods and the chariot. Then they advanced, and turned their wall into a wedge—aimed at the bishop himself. As rocks pinged off their armor and their horses' barding, they drew their swords and began to plow through the mob.

The bishop paled to see the cavalry attack centered upon him, but the sheer number of *parabolani* slowed their progress, no matter how many of the rioters they cut down or tried to flee. If this kept up, the horsemen would become mired and brought down.

Then through the din of battle, Nellie thought she could hear more trumpets sounding in the distance. A new commotion rose above the screams and shouting, deep rumbling roars that grew louder and louder. Soon another sound, a high-pitched droning whine, echoed down the Canopic Way, cutting through all the chaos.

Hypatia gripped Nellie's wrist, and she ducked back down. "What is that noise?"

"I think…" Nellie answered slowly, "I think it's 'Scotland the Brave.'"

The fierce yells of fighting gave way to shouts of fear, and the tide turned into a rout as the combatants sought cover.

Nellie risked another look over the rim of the chariot, as a caravan of horseless vehicles rolled in from the west. Two big boxy transports, barreling toward them at impressive speed, their unseen engines making an unbelievable amount of noise. The drivers laid on their horns, adding to the ferocious racket.

Novatianists and *parabolani* alike scattered out of the way of the convoy, bunching up along the sides of the boulevard. The cataphracts took advantage of the confusion to pull back alongside the shield wall. As everyone moved aside, Nellie could see the cause of all the alarm.

Out in front, a familiar motorbike led the way.

"Blake!" she cried out.

In the sidecar, a Scotsman was playing the bagpipes, spreading terror among the Alexandrians. From the side window of one of the big vehicles, a man waved his hat at them.

"Good lord," Nellie exclaimed. "It's Harcourt!"

Blake roared to a stop between the stalled chariot and the mob. MacIntyre ended his playing with a final flourish, and the crowd stared at them in silence. Blake didn't bother dismounting from the motorcycle, standing up astride it instead. He saluted the cataphracts, then jerked his head toward Cyril, who stood petrified with fear.

"You there! This your bunch attacking my friends?"

The man stared, and nodded mutely.

"Who the hell are you supposed to be?"

"I... I am Bishop Cyrillus the Blessed, patriarch of Alexandria, confessor, doctor of the true and Catholic Church, Pillar of Faith and seal of all the Fathers..."

As the bishop spoke, the Scot handed Blake something from the sidecar. He pointed it just over the heads of the crowd, and let loose a spray of bullets, blowing apart a row of amphorae on a portico behind the bishop's head. Shocked, the patriarch ducked for cover while chips of pottery flew into the air like scattershot. The terrified mob ducked, as well.

Blake looked over to Nellie in the chariot. "Alright there, Nellie?"

Smiling broadly, she gave him a thumb's up. Climbing out of the chariot, she hurried over to him. She pointed out one of the monks, who still gripped a stone in one hand. "That one tried to murder the prefect with a rock."

The hooded man dropped the stone and raised his arms in surrender. Blake gestured at him with his Sten gun.

"Right. You're going with the city guard. Chop off his head, or feed him to the lions, whatever you people do here." A pair of the foot soldiers hauled him away, sobbing. A low disgruntled murmur rumbled up from the *parabolani*. Blake stared them down until they fell silent.

"Where's the prefect now?" he asked.

Hypatia stood up from the chariot. "He's here," she said. "He's bleeding, but he lives."

"Alright, *Cyril*." Blake drew the name out slowly. "First, you better remind your flock here of the cast-the-first-stone story. As for the rest of you"—his upper lip curled in disgust—

"if you're going to fight each other, you can do it in hell." He leaned forward for effect.

"You don't have time for this nonsense, you bloody bastards. These people, your fellow citizens you're so eager to murder, may be the ones who save your miserable lives when the real fighting starts." An undercurrent of muttering rippled through the crowd.

"You're afraid of this?" He held up the Sten. "This is nothing. The real enemy is coming, an army with bigger weapons than this—and a lot more of them. That cold-blooded bastard leading them means to take everything you have here—and make no mistake, he'll happily pave the streets with your bloody corpses, and those of your wives and children, to do it. But all the while he draws nearer, you idiots keep merrily doing his murdering for him, so there'll be absolutely nothing standing in his way when he comes for you."

They all remained silent, as his words sank in.

"God forgive us," the bishop moaned. "We are doomed."

"Shut your mouth, you bloody coward," Blake snapped. "The rest of you—do you want to murder each other, or do you want to fight to save your city?"

Another brief silence. Then— "We fight!" someone shouted.

Another person yelled, then another, and slowly the crowd took up the chant. Blake let it ride before he raised his hand for silence, dismounting from the motorcycle.

"Right then," he said crisply. "Here's what we're going to do…"

8

The Lighthouse of Alexandria
Just before dawn
Ten days after the Event

High above the streets, a wayward gull riding the morning sea breeze glided past the soldier on lookout duty. From his vantage point atop the Pharos lighthouse, the lone sentinel could see the entire city, still bustling with commotion like an agitated anthill. Beside him the beacon glowed, its fires kept constant.

All through the night soldiers and workmen, women and children, slaves and free alike had been frantically busy, a hundred thousand lantern lights tracing their movements in the dark. Continuing work in the dim gray light before dawn, the exhausted city still prepared for the coming attack.

Casting his gaze toward the horizon to the southwest, the sentry frowned, then abruptly swore. He leaned against the cold stone wall and shuddered, not from the chill morning air, but from a sudden shock of desperate realization.

Time had run out.

An ashen rippling in the sky marked an emerging dust cloud. Not the familiar signature of a wind-borne desert sandstorm, but the unmistakable mark of an advancing force snaking up the narrowing isthmus toward them, bigger than any he had seen before. It was just as the barbarian warrior Blake had warned—the army from Magna Germania would attack at dawn.

Snatching a camel-leather bucket off its hook, the sentry began flinging handfuls of mineral salts into the beacon's great blazing fire pit. With each throw, the roaring flames flared an angry red.

Outside the city walls, the gardens of the necropolis teemed with scores of diggers and stonecutters plying spades and mattocks while long, twisting lines of porters and slaves hoisted heavy loads past them. A team of men and horses wrestled with the wreckage of a large wooden harbor boat, threading their ungainly cargo between the monuments and mausoleums, their foreman dishing out threats and encouragement in equal measure. Glancing up, he broke off in mid-threat.

"The signal!" he shouted, pointing up to the crimson flames reflected in the lighthouse beacon. "They're coming!"

Blake stopped directing his own team, and came running up to see for himself. The foreman was right. Time for preparation was over.

"That's it then. Battle stations, everyone!"

"Sir, the boat—" the foreman began.

"Leave it!" Blake cut him off. "There's no time. Get to your battle stations now—those tanks will be here faster than you think." When the foreman still hesitated, he barked, "Move it! On the double!"

In the desert a few kilometers to the south of the city, the Afrika Korps moved with the determination of a steel glacier—imposing and unstoppable.

Oberleutnant Dietrich, the lead tank commander, rode upright in the turret, inspecting the vista ahead with his binoculars. For days the remaining army had steadily advanced northward in stages, moving slowly to conserve fuel. The unexpected commando strike on the rear base had done serious damage to their reserves, forcing hard choices on them. In addition to destroying irreplaceable petrol tankers, the assault team had stolen three supply lorries and slipped ahead of the column, where they continued to wreak more havoc.

Yesterday, the Germans lost two more tanks, both crippled by the commandos' newly laid mines, but their biggest casualty was time—the covert offensive costing them another day and a night as they slowed to a crawl, probed for more mines, and kept wary for ambushes.

At last, all that was behind them, and the vanguard was close enough to see the high walls of Alexandria.

Wiping the fine yellow grit from the lenses, Dietrich focused his sights on the city's wide wooden gates. There were two of them, one on the far left-hand, close to the sea, the other in the center of the great wall. Each gateway stood ten meters tall and seven wide—doubtless the iron-bound doors were as thick as tree trunks. No problem there. A single Panzer would reduce both gates to splinters in a moment.

There were eighteen Panzer tanks in Dietrich's vanguard.

Dietrich smiled. Alexandria would be the first fruits of the new Reich, all its splendors there for the taking. And if any of the stray Allied commandos were holed up there, they would soon learn there was no escape from the punishment of the Afrika Korps. Their revenge was close at hand.

Less than two kilometers from the city, the squadron pulled to a halt, waiting in flying wedge formation, two chevrons of nine tanks each. The rear wedge held back in reserve, two hundred meters from the lead wedge centered on Dietrich's Panzer. His earphones crackled.

"Mobile HQ to Wedge Leader, report."

"Wedge Leader here," Dietrich responded. "We are on southwest approach. Objective is in visual range. The Alexandrian *Nekropole* lies immediately in front of our position."

He regarded the extensive cemetery grounds stretching between the Panzers and the high city walls. No way to go around it. The Alexandrian city of the dead was an impressive metropolis in its own right, sprawling with gardens, avenues, and ornate tombs. The Egyptians, Greeks, and Romans had all left their stylistic marks on it over the centuries.

"Defenses are light and scattered," he continued. "There

are improvised obstacles, made from cemetery headstones and other blocks of stone. Defenders have also raised a series of wooden barricades throughout."

He peered closer. The barricades had been thrown together mostly out of ship hulls. They must have dragged them all the way from the harbor. A flutter of movement caught his eye—was that a fringe of spikes jutting up from one of the barricades? He pursed his lips.

"Some appear to have spearmen hiding behind them."

Observing further, well past the irregular lines of crude timber barricades, he saw more definite signs of the enemy.

"The main body of defenders are in two groups. Archers manning the walls, all along the battlements. There is also a line of cavalry arrayed just in front of the main gates. Estimate between one and two hundred horsemen, perhaps double that number of bowmen."

"Shame to kill all those beautiful horses," the wireless operator said.

"Well, horseflesh is delicious," the gunner quipped back.

"How many angles of attack are available?" a new voice crackled. It was *Generalfeldmarschall* Rommel.

"Only one, sir, the wall cannot be flanked by armor units." On the left-hand, the city wall ran all the way to the sea. He turned his gaze to the great freshwater marshland and lake on the right-hand. A herd of long-necked brontosauruses leisurely grazed there.

He stared, dumbfounded, then swallowed and cleared his throat.

"Deep water hazards on both sides."

"Any other opposing cover?"

"Yes, sir, plentiful. Statuary, many mausoleums and temples, and several other smaller buildings—shrines, charnel houses, perhaps."

"That's where the snipers will be positioned—blast every structure you see to the ground."

"Jawohl, understood."

"Your armor will advance, Commander, keeping out of arrow range to protect the troopers on foot. Use the firedrakes to cover the infantry's advance. When you have come to one-thousand-meters range, sweep the ramparts and cavalry with machine-gun fire, and proceed through city gates for stage two."

"Understood. Disposition of prisoners, sir?"

"Standard. March them away from the city under guard and set up a stockade area."

Another voice abruptly cut in.

"Disregard that order! No prisoners." It was the field marshal's new advisor, *Herr Doktor* Mehta. The foreign *Schwarzer.*

"Sir?" Dietrich asked. *Who the hell is commanding this operation?* he thought. There was an uncomfortable pause before Rommel's voice returned.

"You heard the order, Commander," the *Generalfeldmarschall* confirmed. *"No prisoners."* Dietrich stiffened, then collected himself.

"Jawohl, Generalfeldmarschall, understood," he responded, his voice flat. So, it was to be a massacre. Rommel had never

authorized such a thing before. It had always been a point of pride that his units did not operate like an SS division.

"HQ out." The wireless went silent again.

Dietrich noticed the rest of the tank's crew exchanging uncertain looks. The commander didn't have the luxury of doubt. Showing anything less than absolute certainty would be a dereliction of duty. Time to slip on the mask of command and go to battle.

"Driver, advance!"

The vanguard moved into action.

Atop the ramparts, not a single figure stirred, while below them, just outside the gates, the Alexandrian cataphract cavalrymen struggled to hold their line, calming their increasingly nervous mounts. All were armed with peculiar new lances, hurriedly crafted the night before, though no one was certain any of them would work as promised.

Further beyond the safety of the city walls, concealed in freshly excavated trenches, other defenders of Alexandria listened to the unending rumbling of the approaching monstrosities. A fearsome and unearthly sound, like stretched-out thunder, growing louder with every passing moment. Worse than the ominous tramp of marching feet or the din of charging chariots, and louder than either, building continually.

The Magna Germanian war engines were unbelievable. They almost looked like war-elephants, with their long trunk-like pipes. But they were bigger than elephants, and entirely shod in gigantic plates of iron. Strangest of all, they traveled not on wheels, but on great banded belts of metal.

Scores of the Germanian soldiers marched alongside the hulking vessels or rode atop them like fleas. None bore shields or armor, except for funny little half-helmets. All were armed with the deadly hand weapons that killed instantly with a thunderclap.

As the rumbling grew, each soldier felt the squeeze of panic building in his chest. With a low moan, one let his bow fall from his trembling hand and turned to clamber out of the trench. A cooler head snatched him by the collar and tugged him back down.

"Urion, stay down," the older man hissed. "Remember what the barbarian Blake said. Keep out of sight. If we run, they see us, and if they see us, we die." The younger man nodded silently, ashamed. Beads of sweat trailed down his forehead.

"Forgive me, Obelius. I—" His words were cut off by a loud, cracking roar no more than a few paces away. A tall granite statue of Zeus-Ammon fragmented into a thunderous spray of gravel, debris, and smoke.

"Feuer!" Dietrich shouted again. A high Greek-style mausoleum standing on a low hill to their right fell under the crosshairs of the Panzer's 50mm main gun, only to vanish in a roaring cloud of fire. The other tanks joined in the barrage, targeting any stone structure bigger than a gravestone and blasting them all to pieces of rocky shrapnel.

The attack was methodical, thorough, and merciless, the march of destruction slowly steamrolling across the grounds from building to building. By the time they were finished, the City of the Dead would be completely razed, down to the blackened and smoldering earth.

9

Within the city walls, on the high rocky hill that overlooked the southwestern Rhakotis quarter, Nellie Bly watched from the upper reaches of the former Serapeum. According to Hypatia, once it had been the largest and most magnificent of all temples in the Greek quarter, for centuries unrivaled by any building in the world but the Capitol in Rome. Now it was a ghost of itself, long abandoned and fallen into disrepair.

Still, it made a perfect watchtower for keeping tabs on the German advance. She had felt a certain fatalistic thrill in watching the slow sandstorm drawing closer. Now they were close enough to the city's sprawling necropolis that she could make out their hulking war machines, great, lumbering land-dreadnoughts.

Then the bombardment commenced.

She and Hypatia rushed down the staircase and outside, heading for the *agora*. Time to finalize the defenses for the battle to come, the one that would be fought on the city streets.

Dietrich gave the cease-fire order and emerged from the turret to check their handiwork. The necropolis was littered with smoking debris. Apart from the pathetic wooden barricades, no structures were left standing. He scanned the grounds with his binoculars, thorough as a hawk searching out a scuttling mouse, but could find no traces of dead bodies. During the attack, there had been no signs of fleeing defenders, either.

Strange, that.

Had he only imagined the concealed spearmen? Surely the defenders weren't all cowering behind the city walls, leaving only their doomed horsemen outside, shivering at the gates. Perhaps there were survivors still huddled behind their sad little wooden fortifications. Poor bastards.

Time to end this ugly business as quickly as possible.

Blowing his whistle, he gave the hand signal for the infantry. *Panzergrenadiers* dismounted from the tanks and joined the other troopers already on foot, moving quickly to hunt down their prey. Three specialists took point, fanning out to cover more ground as they boldly advanced on the nearest wooden barricades. "Firedrakes," the other soldiers called them.

Horrifying gusts of destruction roared as the trio brought their flamethrowers to bear, scouring what remained of the tattered wooden barricades with coldly efficient surgical bursts.

Stretched painfully thin along the city wall, the armored cataphracts on their increasingly panicky horses stared in growing terror, watching the distant plumes of unnatural fire incinerating the barricades. Each pile of wreckage went up like torchwood, spewing thick, black clouds of billowing smoke. It was all the horsemen could do to keep their lines in good order and their mounts pacified.

The entire body of the enemy—every soldier armed with a long-range killing-lance—advanced directly toward their line, the three scythes of flame in the forefront, clearing the way. Blake had warned them how the Germanian weapons could kill from a great distance. With the pale northern barbarians closing in on them, the cataphracts reached their limit.

It began with a single rider, then another, then another. Then, as if on cue, the entire cavalry force split and bolted away in wild disorder like a flock of startled ravens, half fleeing for the seashore, and the other half for the banks of the lake. If any of the implacable soldiers standing fast on the ramparts tried to call them back, none of the fleeing cavalrymen took heed.

A harsh chemical stench of burning tar and gasoline poisoned the air as the firedrakes left blazing timbers in their wake. The other *Panzergrenadiers* escorted them at a safe distance, wary as cats, fingers on their triggers as they stalked through the cemetery grounds. Spears and bronze swords didn't scare them—but the enemy commandos could be in hiding anywhere. They needed to root them out.

The centermost firedrake made another exploratory sweep of the burial grounds, probing for hidden targets. Ahead lay more lines of wooden barricades, extending back all the way to the city gates. Though the stone structures in the necropolis were nothing but strewn rubble, there was still plenty of cover for an ambush.

"Stay sharp!" the corporal closest to him called out. Heeding his own advice, the man spied a toppled obelisk, big enough to hide a man. He halted, crouched down and stepped quietly toward the fallen pillar, eyes peeled for any sign of movement or a trap. Something snapped beneath his boot, and the trooper froze.

Scheiße!

The firedrake turned at the sound, and both men knew the score. If the corporal had just triggered a mine, a lethal burst of explosive shrapnel was coming in three seconds. It would kill him, the firedrake, and every other man within sixty feet. He had seen a whole British platoon wiped out by just one.

The corporal fought to concentrate on his training. He knew it took precisely twenty-one pounds of pressure to activate the spring-loaded plunger that would fire the ejector charge, launching the primary explosive seven feet in the air…

Standing still as a statue, he gently… oh so gently… leaned back, shifting his weight to relieve the pressure from his boot. There was another, almost imperceptible *click* as he raised his foot. He froze again. Now two of the other nearby soldiers had noticed the situation.

They froze, too.

He lifted his boot completely off the ground, exhaling sharply. Just a scrap of splintered shale. The corporal shook his head and gave a thumbs up to the relieved men around him before taking another step closer to the fallen obelisk.

A strange droning tone came from some point deeper in the cemetery grounds, like the rising whine of an engine powering up. Tensing, the corporal looked about to find the source. With a start, he recognized the skirl of a bagpipe—playing the call to charge.

Flashes erupted from somewhere along their flanks— bursts of submachine-gun fire. The firedrake's dual fuel tanks ruptured, transforming him into a pillar of flame, before blossoming into a fireball that engulfed the corporal and the nearest pair of soldiers. Within a split-second of withering gunfire, twin explosions took the other two firedrakes.

The fragile stillness of the burial grounds shattered again into the howling bedlam of war. In the heart of the necropolis, four hundred paces away, eight hundred Alexandrian bowmen knelt, concealed in trenches. Their captain cautiously peered over the lip of the trench, using a simple but ingenious device introduced the night before.

Blake called it a periscope.

"*Toxótes! Etoimos!*" he cried out. The archers raised their bows to the sky.

"*Véli!*"

* * *

Dietrich only just caught himself from falling back into the turret as the stricken flamethrower teams blazed into a triple-inferno within the advancing infantry. Across the front, a dozen soldiers or more went down, either caught in the exploding flames, or the submachine-gun crossfire that had triggered them. The rest dove for cover and returned fire.

The Panzers opened up with their own machine guns, but no targets were in sight—where were their ambushers?

"Feuer einstellen!" Dietrich ordered into the microphone. *"Feuer einstellen!" Cease fire!* His order was lost amid the cacophony of automatic weapons fire.

As he blew his whistle to make himself heard, a flash of movement from inside the burial grounds caught his eye. Like a ghost, an Alexandrian youth wielding a torch had miraculously appeared out of thin air. With a defiant sneer, he touched his firebrand to one of the barricades. The timbers went up at once, as if saturated with oils, sending heavy black smoke roiling up into the air, and the phantom torchbearer disappeared once again.

All around the ruins, the commander spotted other hints of furtive movement as the other barricades ignited, one after the other. In a matter of moments, dense curtains of smoke obscured the necropolis.

Even as Dietrich tried to take in this new development, a whistling rush filled the air—all but drowned out by the thundering guns—as a sudden cloudburst of arrows dropped out of the sky straight down upon the Germans. His neighboring tank commander suddenly stiffened, a gout of blood jetting from an impaled eye socket. Dietrich jerked his head inside for cover as the arrows clattered off the tank's armor plating like a hailstorm.

Caught outside, the vulnerable foot soldiers had no such luck. Those who dove to the ground for cover further exposed their bodies to the rain of missiles. A forest of arrow shafts sprang to life all around them—and plunged into the meat of thighs and torsos, puncturing arms and necks and lungs. The sound of gunfire gave way to shrill screams.

Moments later a second volley arrived, drawing more screams. The few troopers who could still move scrambled to seek whatever cover they could find, but none was left—the Germans had demolished it.

As Dietrich and his crew looked on in horror through the narrow vision-slits, the troopers who survived the first two volleys ran up in an effort to find shelter by the tanks, only to be struck down by a third volley. Some crouched dangerously close to the moving treads, while others tried to squeeze through rocky debris to get beneath the undercarriage. Others climbed for the unlikely cover of a turret or main gun. None succeeded.

The tankers inside could only watch as their comrades died, pleading for their help. There was nothing to be done for them, nor for the wounded casualties littering the bloodied earth.

"This is Wedge One," Dietrich shouted into the wireless. "All advance full!"

Ignoring the dead and dying infantry, the V-shaped front column pushed ahead into the crumbled smoking ruins of the City of the Dead.

* * *

Secure for the moment in their trench, just an arcing bowshot from the enemy's advancing war engines, the captain of the Alexandrian archers crouched and growled with frustration. Their fog of war had done its job too well. He could no longer see the enemy for the smoke, but he could hear their inhuman tread, could feel the rumbling of the earth beneath them.

Would there be enough concealing cover from the flames and smoke to protect his men if they retreated now? Only the gods knew. Taking a deep breath, he continued to call for one blind volley after another to be loosed.

He dared not stop.

10

Just south of the fringe of the necropolis and two hundred meters behind Dietrich's Panzers in the front wedge, the reserve line fired up their engines and moved forward, following in their own V-formation. The mustard-colored dust kicked up by the tanks blended together with the black smoke spilling upward from the conflagration, gradually encircling the armored unit.

The hard, arid ground behind them trembled, but in their loud, lumbering Panzers the crews could neither hear nor feel the thundering of hooves. Nor could they see the charging Alexandrian cataphracts circling back around, flanking their blind spots from both sides.

On the western half of the cavalry's pincer maneuver, Lucius—the scout rider Blake had rescued from the pit with

Harcourt—rode at the head. Unarmored, he sped in front of the mounted cavalry, directing them around and inside the "V" of the rear tank column. Across the formation he could see the eastern half of the cavalry making the same approach on their end, led by the Zouaves—the three fearless French-Algerian troopers.

"*Epitíthesthe!*" Lucius shouted as his half of the cavalry rounded the hindmost tank. The lead cataphract charged up to it and flung his lance at the back of the turret as he thundered past, followed by two more horsemen doing the same in quick succession.

"What the hell was that?" the forward gunner asked, craning his neck to catch a glimpse as an armored horseman flashed past his viewport, followed by another, then another. "Are they throwing *spears* at us?"

The crew broke into hearty laughter.

"Quit your *verdammt* braying and open fire on them!" their commander growled as another rider rode past and hurled a flaming torch. Smoke began pouring in through the ventilation grills, and the cabin suddenly burst into flame.

The line of riders continued their attack down both wings of the wedge, each warrior throwing his odd lance and peeling off again to attack another war engine further down. Instead of steel spearheads, their fragile new weapons were tipped with narrow glass amphora bottles, lashed in place and filled with a new mixture of sulfur, oil, and naphtha.

Once two or three lances struck their targets, shattering and spewing their contents, additional riders cast lit torches onto the mess. Half the tanks had been hit before the crew of the lead Panzer even realized the formation was under attack.

By then it was too late.

One by one, each tank erupted into flame as the liquid dripping down through gaps in the engine cover and air intakes quickly spread to spots of engine grease, machine oil, gasoline fumes, and any other flammables. The men in the stricken tanks tried to bail out, but it only took seconds for each interior to transform into an inescapable inferno.

The crews closest to the point of the formation rushed to turn their tanks and turrets around, even as the Alexandrian cavalry charged past them. Only the lead Panzer managed to swing their main gun around fast enough to face their mounted attackers. Undaunted, the lead cataphract hurled his lance straight ahead to shatter upon the turret face, just as the tank's forward machine guns blazed to life and cut the man and his horse down.

"Opisthochórisi!" Lucius yelled. He wheeled his horse around, but no one could hear his call for retreat. The guns continued their deadly arc across the charging cavalry, but the tank's own gunfire ignited the spill, engulfing the war engine in a fiery shroud. Still the machine guns roared their defiance, cutting down charging and retreating horsemen alike.

The lead Panzer's victory proved as short-lived as it was pyrrhic. All the tanks in the wedge were ablaze. The few tankers who managed to extricate themselves opened fire with their side arms. One commander, hungry for vengeance, stood high upon the flaming ruin of his vehicle and opened up on the confusion of galloping horses. His submachine gun's ferocious chatter merged with the sounds of screaming horses and men.

An instant later his head snapped back, and with a strangely relaxed grace his body toppled to the ground. On horseback a few hundred meters away, a Gallic sniper in his pill cap leisurely turned his aim toward a new target. His squad of French Foreign Legionnaires had accompanied the cavalry and the Zouaves. They picked off the last of the tanker crews with their stolen German rifles.

In less than three minutes, the defenders had destroyed nine Panzer tanks.

The cramped interior of Dietrich's Panzer rocked as the front wedge trundled over the necropolis's broken ground, navigating near-blind through the smoke and dust. He frowned at the confused radio chatter coming from the tanks in the rear wedge, hidden from sight behind their own formation.

"What the hell is going on back there?" he muttered.

His driver looked up. "Do you want us to turn around to investigate, *Herr Oberleutnant*?"

The commander shook his head. "No, I'm sure they can handle themselves against bows and arrows," he said, instantly regretting his unfortunate choice of words.

No matter. All the infantry had been up front with him. The

tanks in the rear wedge had no such Achilles' heel. Besides, the source of the damnable arrows wasn't far off. Time to press on, cut through this labyrinth of smoke, put a swift end to every last one of these miserable bow-plucking savages, then break down the front doors and ransack their anthill of a city.

One of the Panzers to their right suddenly disappeared into the earth, sending up a billowing of dust and a booming crash— magnified by the unmistakable explosion of an anti-tank mine.

"Was zur Hölle?" Dietrich shouted in shock. He raised the hatch and climbed up to see for himself. Flames rose up from the camouflaged hole where the tank disappeared. Pit trap. Even as he watched, there came another crashing thump and fiery explosion as the treacherous ground swallowed up a second tank, the furthest on the other side of the V-formation. Flames and black smoke belched up from both holes, stinging his nasal passages with the acrid reek of burning oil and hot metal.

The commander shook his head in frustrated disgust.

"All drivers, halt!" he ordered into the microphone. "Ahead quarter speed. Keep a sharp eye out for more pit hazards." He paused before adding, "And when we catch these vermin, we will crush them beneath our treads and bury them."

In the dark of the subterranean catacombs, only the unsteady light of a few small clay oil lamps broke the gloom. Blake cradled his submachine pistol, a stolen German Schmeisser MP-40, listening intently to the noises seeping down from above and idly wishing for electric lanterns.

He leaned against the clammy wall, surrounded on all four sides by carefully stacked stone shelves of skulls and grim mosaics depicting funerary rites. Alongside him stood a marble statue of Anubis, the Egyptian Lord of Death.

Irritated by a sudden prick of anxiety, he shot a look up at the face of his silent companion. The sputtering light of the lamps lent the jackal-headed deity an eerie semblance of life—he seemed to be sporting a sinister grin.

"Go on and laugh, you old bastard," Blake growled under his breath. "Enjoy your bloody field day."

Blake had known what Rommel would surely realize—the mausoleums made perfect strongpoints for armed soldiers. Which was why Blake had kept his forces out of them. Instead, he'd hidden his makeshift army below the surface—in the newly dug trenches, carefully concealed spider holes, and throughout the necropolis's extensive network of underground corridors, catacombs, and galleries.

He and the dozen commandos with him waited in the dark like a tomb full of ghosts, faces dimly lit in masks of lamplight as they sat in silence, listening to the approaching Panzers above. The soldiers he'd freed from the German camp—all veterans of the battle of El Alamein—formed strike teams in place throughout the underground complex. The mix included British and East Indians, New Zealanders and Maoris, and the South Africans, along with the French and Zouave contingent deployed with the cavalry—hopefully attacking the rear of the German column.

Hopefully.

Not for the first time Blake wished they had radios. Coordination was difficult in the best of battlefield circumstances, and this day's horribly mismatched guerrilla skirmish was far from ideal. No telling if the cavalry attack had yet occurred, or if it had been a success or a suicidal massacre.

A sharp jolt interrupted his glum thoughts. The walls shook with a muffled double-burst of thunder, followed a few moments later by a second round, this one nearer to their position. Two of their pit traps had snagged their prey. Some of the men allowed themselves a smile.

Blake stared up at the ceiling of the catacombs as the rumbling of the tanks reverberated off the walls and ceiling, sending a faint rain of powdered limestone down on the men concealed there. His Indian and Kiwi sappers had done the numbers and were confident the layer of stone above them would hold—a Panzer's formidable weight was so well-distributed along the treads, it should simply roll right over them.

Nursing a grim fatalism, Blake was less sanguine about the odds.

Somewhere above, the rumbling stopped for a half-minute before resuming again, closer than before. Blake lifted his eyes to the ceiling. A few moments more, and they'd all know whether or not the roof would hold.

The sound of the approaching tanks grew louder, steel treads and bogey wheels creaking like the chains on a medieval drawbridge above the rising diesel growl of the engine. Another soft trickle of dust dropped from overhead. The men in the stone tomb held their breath as they felt the ground trembling all around them—and then the nearest Panzer passed directly over them.

The roof held.

They exhaled again. Blake thumped the shoulder of Navan Singh, the sapper from the 4th Indian division and Blake's senior demolitions man. The Sikh grinned, then climbed atop the chamber's sarcophagus, pushing aside the small marble headstone concealing one of their spyholes. He peered through his handmade periscope.

"The Jerries are headed straight for the city gates. They'll be on top of our first trench shortly unless we draw them away now."

"Hoots, mon! Let's gang!" The Scots bagpiper, Duncan MacIntyre, stood up, ready to sound the charge again. "We can come up behin' them an' put a right wallop up their crease afair they e'en ken we're there!"

"That's a negative, MacIntyre," Blake ordered.

"Wha'r' we waitin' fur, then? Noo's our chance, mon!"

"We're going to stay right here—and keep your goddamned voice down."

The Scotsman lowered his voice to a harsh whisper.

"Are ye off yer haid, Blake? They'll overrun our line, an' then the whole city's tits up! We're just gonnae let them?"

"If it comes to that, yes."

"For the sweet love ay Christ, why, mon?" The Scot's ginger brows furrowed in disbelief. Blake leaned in closer, eyes locked on MacIntyre's.

"Because we can't win this battle."

11

Aboard the *Siu-Tuait*
Ten days after the Event

Amber cast a baleful look at Dee, lying next to her with his back against the bow. The sound of blissful snores rose up from the hood shading his face from the sun. She envied him. She hadn't managed more than an hour or so of broken slumber since they'd set out for Alexandria.

They had traveled the Nile all day and night and all the next morning. Though the rowers continued with superhuman endurance and speed, to Amber it felt as though the *Star of the Dawn* was crawling up the river on a leisurely pleasure cruise—one she was incapable of enjoying. She was exhausted by Dee's psychic exercises, and sick with worry for Nellie and the men, not knowing if any of them were still alive. She was worried about the *Vanuatu*, and couldn't shake the mental image of a clock ticking inexorably down to zero.

"We'll never get there," she groaned, resting her arms on the bow. A half-submerged log floated in the river below, but a closer look revealed half-lidded reptilian eyes. *Crocodiles*, Amber thought with a shudder. Or possibly something even more dangerous. Luckily it seemed content just to watch them.

"We Arabs say that to travel along the Nile, one must use sails of patience," Ibn Fadlan commented, ever the teacher.

"We have *many* sayings about the vanity of haste," Leila added, winking at Amber from behind Ibn's back, "but don't worry. Really, we're making phenomenal time. We're already on the tributary to Alexandria. We'll be there soon and will find out where your ship and your friends are."

"Really?" Amber perked up. "We're nearly there?" The landscape had remained unchanged for nearly the entire trip, mostly just sand and palm trees, with occasional shore birds or pterodactyls. Now that Leila mentioned it, though, here it seemed more like hill country—and was it just her imagination, or could she smell sea air?

"What's that? Is there a ship ahead of us?" Cam, standing on deck with Kha-Hotep, pointed downriver. What looked like a lone beam of incandescent light came from out of the river, stark white against the relentless blue of the Egyptian sky.

"Too bright for a signal light," Kha-Hotep said, shielding his eyes with his hand.

Dee got to his feet, wiping sleep from his eyes. "Trouble?"

"I'm not sure. I..." Amber trailed off as a second shimmering spotlight joined the first, quickly followed by another half-dozen or so more—all different colors and widths, accompanied by a high-pitched keening sound that carried across the water. The volume increased as the

Siu-Tuait drew closer, the pillars lighting up the skies like a firework show working up to the big finale.

Oh god. Amber's breath caught in her throat as her hair whipped around her face from static electricity. She knew what this meant. Reaching out, she grabbed Leila's hand and squeezed tightly.

A massive wall of brilliant iridescence rose up in the middle of the river, less than a hundred yards ahead of the boat. With a furnace blast of searing heat and steam, the keening spiraled up into a wailing shriek, water bubbling furiously where the pillar bore through the Nile. Dead fish rose to the surface, along with a crocodile unlucky enough to be too close. Amber heard Kha-Hotep's deep voice, shouting to the oarsmen.

"Row for shore! Hard to port!"

A moment later, all the aftershocks vanished together, their ear-splitting wails cutting off as if a switch had been thrown—coring out a deep chunk of the Nile with them.

"Hang on!" the captain yelled.

For a split-second, the boat seemed to stand perfectly still. Then the river surged forward, rushing to fill in the gap even as the oarsmen looked around in confusion. The placid, meandering river became a deluge, the torrent hurling them forward straight into the mouth of a newly formed maelstrom. The hapless rowers could do nothing to stop it. The barge crested the edge of the huge funnel, and then, as its horrified passengers watched, dipped over the top.

Like a leaf carried down a swirling gutter, the vessel plunged down the curve of the waters on a steep spiral heading, threatening to capsize at any moment. But the same forces that had pulled it down the sloping downdraft, listing precariously to the port side, now kept it from overturning as it careened in ever-decreasing circles. Then, with a final roar of white water, the gyre thundered back in on itself, closing off the vortex—and slamming into the stricken craft.

Smashed by the collision of waves, the deck lurched crazily as if the barge were attempting a somersault. Men went flying overhead into the river, while others were thrown against the protruding oars. Amber and Dee clung to the bow, barely keeping their grip as another pounding wall of water swept over them, sweeping up more victims and pitching them off the barge.

Something slammed into Amber, threatening to knock her overboard as well.

Leila.

The girl shrieked and grabbed for them as the angry river rushed in to swallow her up. Amber caught her wrist and held on, even as Leila's weight nearly wrenched her arm from the socket. Strong arms wrapped around her as Dee helped haul Leila back to safety.

"Are you okay?"

Nodding, Leila coughed up a mouthful of water. The turbulence was subsiding, though the barge still bobbed up and down. Amber turned to see if anyone else needed help, lending a hand to a rower climbing back on deck. All around her, those still aboard were helping rescue those thrown overboard. Further back, she spotted Kha and Ibn Fadlan pulling Cam out of the water, bleeding from his head and arm.

"Cam!" Running to his side, she pulled his hair back from the gash on his skull, relieved to see tiny hair-thin silver hexagons beginning to appear as his medical nanites stitched up the wound there and along his arm.

Kha-Hotep and Ibn Fadlan looked on in fascination.

Two crewmen were still missing when the last man was pulled from the water. They called out for them, but there was no sign, dead or alive.

"There!" Cam, back on his feet, pointed at one of the nearby crocodiles, one of the unfortunate rowers dangling lifeless from its jaws. As they watched, a trio of slender tendrils, each tipped with a ridge of curved teeth-like horns, slipped up from the depths and in a moment, snared the big reptile and its meal, dragging them both under the surface.

Shaken, they manned their stations again, and continued on toward Alexandria.

A short time later Amber heard a new noise coming from up ahead.

It sounded like the fourth of July.

When they finally caught sight of the ancient city walls, there was no mistaking the sound of bombardment. The wild river turned into a wide aqueduct and they followed it, threading between the city's southern wall and vineyards, and the marshy banks of Lake Mareotis where long-necked dinosaurs grazed, until finally it turned abruptly northward, through an opening in the wall.

It proved to be a dark vaulted tunnel that opened up into a canal that cut through the city. They could see roofs and obelisks, and a majestic building atop a high hill, but no place to tie up until they had crossed nearly the entire width of Alexandria. There, near the edge of the sea, the canal dumped into a square inner harbor ringed by a neighborhood of markets and warehouses. The docks seemed oddly deserted, perhaps because of the growing sound of cannon fire from the southwest.

Kha-Hotep steered the barge to a landing, and Cam swiftly tied it to the mooring. Once the rowers banked their oars, they immediately slumped forward, unconscious.

"When they wake up, we're going to need to feed them—a lot," DeMetta said. "They deserve medals. For now, just let them sleep."

The six of them ascended the stone steps to the street level. DeMetta stopped just before the final step, a concerned look on his face.

"Wait," he said. "There's something—"

Thick fishing nets, weighted with heavy stone sinkers, came flying overhead, entangling them on the steps.

"*Seize them!*"

"*Quick, kill him!*"

Those shouts and more were followed by a crowd, armed and angry. The closest assailant ran up brandishing a boat hook like a spear. DeMetta couldn't even raise an arm to defend himself as the attacker lunged at him, but the fatal blow never landed. Instead, the would-be spearman stiffened and fell backward, the barbed pole clattering to the flagstones.

Two more attackers were right behind, clubs raised, but they abruptly stopped in their tracks and crumpled as well. At that the leader of the mob, a grizzled old fisherman, suddenly froze with a blank look on his face, then raised his hands.

"Stop!" he shouted in a commanding voice. The other attackers halted, confused and frightened. "This man is *not* János Mehta," he pronounced. "This is his twin brother, come to destroy him. We must offer him and his companions all our help!"

The crowd's attitude flipped at once, and they rushed forward to help pull the heavy netting off of the prisoners. The trio of stunned attackers began to move, sitting up and rubbing their heads. That was when Amber realized that all three were teenaged girls. The small gang was composed entirely of young boys, adolescent girls, and old men—all slaves and street urchins.

She looked at DeMetta, impressed. He raised an eyebrow.

"Keep practicing, and you'll be able to do that."

"No sense in triggering further attacks." DeMetta borrowed a short cloak from one of their erstwhile attackers to use as a concealing hood. Then the gang of defenders led them out of the square inner harbor they called *Kibotos*, "the Box," and past the rows of warehouses, the old arsenal fort and the *Heptastadion* causeway, down to the open-air *agora* marketplace.

The wide city square was bustling with women and girls, the elderly, and young boys. It looked to be everyone who couldn't fight with the army outside the gates, but was still able-bodied enough to pitch in, making preparations for the defense of the city.

Amber was surprised to see three big army transport trucks parked in a row.

"Amber! Cam!" Nellie's voice rang out from near the trucks, and she ran across the wide-open space to grab them both up in a hug. She didn't bother trying to hide tears of joy and neither did Amber.

"My daring girl, my Celtic prince. Look at you both!"

"We made quite a journey to find you," Cam said proudly. "Worthy of a song."

Another woman in some kind of toga stepped forward. She was striking, with Mediterranean features and aristocratic bearing. Nellie broke away from the embrace to draw the woman into their group.

"These are more of our companions," she said in Greek. "Amber, Cam, this is the famous Hypatia of Alexandria! Isn't it amazing?"

Hypatia gave an elegant little nod in greeting. "You and all your company are most welcome here."

Amber felt a bit tongue-tied, but responded with a simple, heartfelt "Thank you," and then quickly translated the lady's salutation for Kha-Hotep, Leila, Ibn Fadlan, and DeMetta, introducing the newcomers before turning back to Nellie.

"I was so afraid we'd never see you again," Amber said, squeezing her tight. "The ship told us where you were, more or less, but then our rover broke, and… anyway, we can tell you all that later. What's going on here?"

"The city is under attack from the Germans," Nellie explained. "From Blake's war."

"Holy shit, *Nazis*? Where did you park the *Vanuatu*? We need to get out here!"

Nellie's face darkened. "Amber…" she started.

"What's wrong? Is it Blake?" *Oh god, is Blake…*

"No, Blake's fine," Nellie reassured her. "At least for now. He's outside the walls with the soldiers. Harcourt's somewhere around here." She shook her head. "He's fine, too, the crafty old good-for-nothing. It's… it's the ship."

"Where is it?"

Nellie stared silently for a long moment. "It's difficult even to say it. I'm afraid it's just… gone."

"*Gone!* Did Mehta steal it?"

"No, Mehta's thrown in with the Germans. The *Vanuatu*… It's been destroyed."

Amber grabbed Cam's arm. Her worst fear—the one she had been keeping at bay—came rushing back. Suddenly the earth was spinning too fast, and her heart felt like a stone thumping around in a washing machine.

We're screwed, she thought frantically. *The world is screwed.*

She slumped to the ground, gutted, and Cam held her arm. She could sense the distress in his mind, even as he tried to stay brave for her sake. DeMetta had been trying to remain inconspicuous, but then he came forward and crouched down beside the pair.

"Listen to me, both of you. Don't give up. We're not finished here, even if we can't see how we'll get through it just yet." He focused on Amber. "Do you remember what I said about the PreCogs? Somehow they knew it was crucial to bring us together."

Amber nodded, trying to breathe through the panic.

"Alright then," he said. "So no giving up yet." He peered at her, and added, "Agreed?"

"Yeah... okay." One of the hard knots of despair in her chest unkinked itself. Maybe he was right. Maybe there was still a chance. The two helped her to her feet as Professor Harcourt emerged from in between the trucks, carrying an armful of different guns, weapons, and ammunition belts, toting them all like some kind of lanky Victorian Rambo.

"What the devil?" he said, spotting them. "The colonial girl and her barbarian. Capital!" He came over at once. "Look at all the dashing new recruits." His gaze fell upon DeMetta, whose makeshift cowl was slipping. The Victorian's mouth opened in horror. "You!"

Nellie gasped.

Amber started to intervene, but DeMetta held up a hand and sighed. She telepathically eavesdropped as he calmed their fears, explaining matters as simply as he could. When he was finished, both Nellie and Harcourt seemed reassured, though Harcourt still looked confused.

Hypatia and Nellie wasted no time getting back to the coordination of the defense efforts—directing porters with timbers to the Serapeum, wagons filled with amphorae of oil to the Jewish quarter, and the Broucheion and Aspendia districts.

A shifty-looking desert monk leading a laden donkey approached Hypatia. They spoke quietly for a moment before he presented her with a tightly lidded basket and some small round pottery jars. Nodding in approval, Hypatia handed basket and jars to Kha-Hotep and Cam.

"What are these?" Cam asked.

"Secret weapons," Nellie answered. "They are coming with us to the royal quarter. Careful with them, now."

DeMetta jerked his head toward the parked trucks.

"Who's motorcycle is that?" he asked Harcourt.

"Blake stole it from the Germans, so I suppose it's his now."

DeMetta walked over and mounted up, starting the engine. He nodded to Amber, patting the sidecar.

"Hop in."

"You and me?" Amber said, surprised. "Where are we going in *that*?"

"We're slipping out the city gates. It's a long shot, but I think I can end all this if I can just get close enough to Mehta. Only I'll need your help."

"Get close?" Amber stared. "Are you out of your *mind*?"

"We're going to save the world, remember?" he replied. "First we need to win this battle."

12

Singh stared down in alarm. MacIntyre looked as though he was about to take a swipe at Blake's head.

"Wha' did ye jist say, ye bampot Sassenach?"

"I said, we can't win this battle." The commando kept his voice cool. His intention all along had been to draw the enemy in—and that part had worked brilliantly, but the most crucial component hadn't gone according to plan. He got to his feet. "Listen to me, all of you. I'm going to tell you what I've already told the snipers. Don't any of you fool yourself that we're going to win this. That's no longer our objective."

"Well, wha's th' feckin' point then?" MacIntyre growled.

"There are two lines of tanks up there, nine Panzers in each. We just killed two of them. If we're lucky, maybe, *maybe*, we *could* knock out all seven of the rest from behind. I'd say our chances aren't half bad. And maybe the Alexandrian cavalry and the French *can* take out the other nine behind us, with one good surprise attack. Christ knows a single charge is all they're going to get.

"Our archers sure as hell made pincushions of their bloody infantry, and thanks to the snipers, those Jerry flamethrowers went up like fireworks." He allowed himself a wry grin, and a few of the men chuckled in response.

"But there's been a change of plan," he continued. "We need to find Rommel's mobile HQ, and it's not up there. That means this is just the advance wave, and he's calling the shots from behind, so more tanks are coming. What do you think that says about our chances?" Blake let the sobering thought sink in for a moment before continuing. "Right. The likelihood is that we can't win this battle, or keep the city."

"A wee late to be telling us noo," MacIntyre said glumly.

"Stow it, soldier," Blake snapped. "Now listen carefully. When the Jerries' real force arrives, we *can* take out János Mehta—and *that* is our prime objective. We *have* to kill János. Everything else is secondary."

"Kill tha' bastard who crossed ye? So *tha's* wha' this's all aboot? How is tha' supposed to save any of us?"

"Damn it, man," Blake snapped, "we're not here to save Alexandria, or even ourselves—*we're here to save the whole goddamned world*. Mehta makes Hitler look like a bloody piker. He's insane, and he's able to sink his claws into your brain… sink them in and squeeze until you're his bloody slave." As he spoke, Blake drilled his finger against the Scot's forehead.

"Worst of all, he can't or won't believe that the planet is literally falling to pieces. So our only chance is to kill Mehta, and try to reason with Rommel. Nellie and Hypatia need to surrender to Rommel as soon as his mobile HQ enters Alex. That'll get them in close. If they can't find a way to all work together to stop what's happening, it's over—for you, for me, the Alexandrians and the Germans, every last person on Earth."

"So we're aw doomed, then? A bloody suicide mission, is it?" MacIntyre's voice cracked. The other soldiers muttered among themselves. Blake said nothing for a moment, meeting the eyes of every man in the tomb.

"I expect we'll probably die here," he said. "But you all could have died in that German pit back there, or at El Alamein—and you most *certainly* will be dead if the whole world goes to pieces, which could be very soon."

That got the men's full attention.

"Mehta's our target, and my money says he's riding alongside Rommel, pulling the strings. Rommel's not one to stay behind in some HQ tent miles behind the front. He's a maestro, and he wants to conduct the whole symphony up close and on the go. He won't be running around blind, buttoned up in a Panzer. The Afrika Korps mobile command is a captured Brit Dorchester AEC. It carries his full communications center, along with the radio crew and equipment. A great lumbering toaster of a lorry, so we won't miss it. Our job is to stay under wraps until it appears—and then fight like hell to take out that bastard Mehta.

"Understand this. The birth and the death of this world began in a physics laboratory in the Antarctic, and to fix it we have to give the others a fighting chance. They have to get to that lab. Nothing else matters. Every last one of us is expendable if we can only give them that."

The other men were very quiet now. A new commotion arose, and Singh took another look topside. He watched for a long time before finally turning back to the men with a sunken look on his face.

"The trenches have been overrun," he said quietly. "It's a slaughter out there."

In the first trench, the archers knelt safely out of sight below ground level. Urion, the youngest of them, had three arrows left. He turned to the veteran by his side for a sign of what to do.

This wasn't supposed to be happening. The roar of their enemy's war engines was only growing louder, and their captain was searching back and forth across the smoke-strewn remains of the shattered necropolis, desperate to get a new sense of their range. All around them the ground started shaking beneath the tread of the machines—still unseen, still coming. Grains of chalky yellow soil began to trickle down from the lips of the trenches.

With the sound of a cracking whip, the top of the captain's periscope suddenly shattered, sending it flying out of his hands. He let out a startled cry and fell backward. Straightening up again, he peered cautiously over the lip of the trench. Urion and Obelius, along with the rest of their company, watched their commander's cheeks turn pale.

When he faced them again, his ashen, expressionless face looked like the shade of a dead man.

"Toxótes! Sikónomai!" he called out, ordering them to stand, his voice more haunted than commanding. After only the briefest of hesitations, Urion and the others dutifully rose to their feet and notched arrows, their heads just above ground level. They could see nothing but scattered scraps of broken stone and thick curtains of smoke rising off the bonfires.

"Etoimos!" the commander cried out. As one, the archers aimed their bows, this time level with the ground. Urion drew back his bowstring, anchoring his hand against his cheek. The clamor was deafening now, but still he could make out nothing. The youth stood as still as he could, but his anxious gaze tracked back and forth, searching for a target. Obelius's earlier words ate at him.

"If they see us, we die."

A solid metal juggernaut burst out of the smoke, smashing through the closest barricade and scattering its flaming timbers to the wind like a handful of kindling. Two more behemoths flanked it on either side, and two more, and two more—a giant spearhead, hurling toward the heart of the city. But first it was coming for them.

"Véli!" the commander howled.

Urion loosed his arrow with the others. The volley raced toward their quarry, but the deadly shafts only shattered against the thick metal plating. In return, the war machines opened fire with their own blazing weapons. All along the line, men screamed and died.

Obelius was struck at once, the impact tearing through his torso and dashing his lifeless body to the ground. Urion raised a hand to his own face—it was wet with the seasoned fighting man's blood. Dazed, the bow slipped from his grasp and he raised up his hand as if he could stop their charge.

Then the closest war machine roared up and crashed down upon him.

13

Lucius stared at the corpses of armored men and horses, strewn over the triangle of bloodstained earth between the V-shaped line of burning tanks. While he rallied the remaining cataphracts, the squad of Legionnaires and the three Zouaves rode up. They spoke no Greek, nor he French, but no words were needed to express what they all were feeling—the flush of victory, tempered by the dreadful cost of the battle.

Sous-lieutenant D'Alsace, the French Legionnaire's commanding officer, silently took a quick headcount of the surviving cavalry. One hundred and twenty rode out that morning. In just the few seconds of the German counter-attack, the machine guns had killed a full third of their riders.

He turned to Lucius, who stared intently into the smoky haze covering the necropolis. After a few moments the two commanders silently came to the same conclusion. Lucius gave a curt nod to D'Alsace, and reined his horse around to address the rest of his men.

"Back in your lines," he shouted in Greek. "Same assault as before—we're going in for twice the glory." The surviving cataphracts cheered. So did the French, who understood the intent, if not his words. The horsemen quickly wheeled about, urging their steeds into formation. In the midst of their maneuvers, a drawn-out whistling sound rose on the air until all the riders could hear it—then came an explosion.

It was as if the sun had dropped upon them. Something impacted with a deafening roar, its inescapable heat blasting apart men and horses alike.

Further from the center of the blast, both D'Alsace and his steed were slammed to the ground. The pressure felt like an elephant rolling over him.

Thrown from his saddle, the stunned Legionnaire lay on the hard earth, watching in a daze as fire rained down around him along with clods of earth, flesh, and blood. With a curious detachment, he watched a gore-splattered Lucius, moving in dreamlike slowness, shouting and struggling to control his terrified, rearing horse. He was yelling something—

"Aposýromai! Aposýromai!"

—calling for his men to take cover behind the wedge of burning tanks they had just killed. But even as the riders galloped for safety, the chatter of machine-gun fire joined the chorus of the wounded and the dying. More riders and steeds screamed and fell to the earth.

With Herculean effort, D'Alsace turned his head to the southwest. Out in the desert, great dark shapes, wavy and uncertain in the scorching desert heat, came into view. He forced his eyes to focus, trying to count the number of new tanks, but there were too many to see clearly through the haze and the scores of enemy infantrymen running to the fore.

A new wave of German forces was coming.

With hatches down and the tanks buttoned up, Dietrich and his seven remaining crews were nearly blind as they lumbered through the smoky ruins of the *Nekropole*, but they were virtually invincible to the small arms fire of the guerrillas. His lead Panzer plowed through another flaming barricade with ease. The interior of the tank suddenly rang with the musical patter of scores of arrows pinging off the armor.

In retaliation, the tankers opened up with their machine guns. At nine hundred rounds per minute, the guns tore apart the entrenched archers in a single burst. The wedge plowed straight ahead without pausing, the tank treads crushing any man caught beneath them. Up ahead, the remaining trenches boiled with droves of fleeing targets. Inside the tanks, the gunners gritted their teeth and made stones of their hearts as they decimated the terrified running men. The tank treads left behind a ghastly killing floor—pulped, red and white shapes mashed into the hard ground, barely recognizable as human beings.

Dietrich kept his jaw clenched and his face a mask as they

rolled out of the cemetery grounds and approached the high city walls. On his order, the wedge pulled to a halt once they came within the thousand-meter mark. To their left lay the sea, scattered groves of olive trees and vineyards along the canal banks to their right. Between them and the gates stood only fields and road.

Peering through the narrow view-slit was an exercise in frustration, but he wouldn't risk opening the hatch for a better view, even if they appeared to be well out of range of the defenders on the ramparts. The bowmen there could not have failed to see the slaughter of their comrades, nor how ineffectual arrows were against the Panzers. Still, the Alexandrians held their line, seemingly oblivious to their impending doom. The gates remained closed.

So be it.

Dietrich lifted the microphone. "All machine guns. Clear the wall." The guns snapped to life, sweeping across the line of defenders. At once he saw something was wrong. Over half the Alexandrians still stood in their place. None had ducked for cover.

"Cease fire!" The machine guns fell silent, and after a moment, the tank commander rose to open the hatch. He raised his binoculars. "*Ach du Scheiße...*" he muttered to himself.

There were no defenders on the wall.

Up and down the city walls, the Alexandrians had lined up stacks of baskets, clay pots, amphorae, or stuffed cloth sacks, each with a staff or pole or stalk of papyrus—anything they could throw together to give the semblance of an archer's head, shoulders, and bow. There were hundreds of the dummy soldiers.

Despite himself, Dietrich began to laugh. The tankers looked at him as though he had lost his mind. He collected himself and pulled the hatch down again.

"Give me an HE round and knock on that door," he said, gazing through the view-slit at the city gates.

The Moon Gate exploded spectacularly in smoke and heat, as if a giant had kicked apart a bonfire. The booming thunder of it sent a wave of panic through the *agora*.

"We're breached!" Nellie shouted. "Everyone, go, go! Off the street!" As people dropped their burdens and ran, she shepherded Cam and the others into the closest truck.

"Come on, into the truck! Go!" As soon as they were all in, she pounded on the cabin, signaling to the English driver. "We're in!"

Loaded up, the three trucks roared across the open marketplace, peeling away from the main road and down the twisting harbor lane. In a matter of seconds, as the column of tanks rolled in out of the smoke, the *agora* was completely deserted.

In the lead tank, *Oberleutnant* Dietrich halted the column and opened the hatch, taking a moment to scan the city with his own eyes. The boulevard before them was impressively wide and open, a hundred meters across. Good: that meant no getting boxed in and fewer places from which guerrillas could strike. No one was in sight, and the houses and buildings were buttoned up tight. That suited him fine as well. Lifting his binoculars, he scanned the rooftops for snipers.

So far, so good.

Retreating back inside, he secured the top hatch again before giving the order to advance. Empty streets or no, he wasn't ready to take any chances. With any luck, their next stop would be the palace itself.

In the underground warren of tombs, the men were still and silent, as though trying on the idea of the grave. Singh had turned his periscope away from the massacre, watching for the second wave of the German attack Blake had predicted. He stood motionless except for an occasional thoughtful tug on his beard, until finally he broke the silence.

"Tell me something, Blake."

"What's that?"

"Have you ever heard of Saragarhi?"

"Should I?"

"No reason you would, I suppose. Saragarhi's no more than a speck on the map—a tiny outpost near the Afghan border, out in the North-West Frontier Province. Back in 1897, when the Empire and the Russians were wrapping up the Great Game, there were twenty-one Sikh soldiers of the 36th Bengal Infantry stationed there. And then one morning, ten thousand Pashtun tribesmen attacked.

"Saragarhi signaled to the closest British fort that they were under attack. No help was forthcoming. So, to prevent the enemy from reaching the other forts, the garrison decided to fight to the last. The Pashtuns in their thousands broke through their pickets, and twice tried to rush the gates, but were beaten back. The Afghani chieftains made sweet promises to entice them to surrender, but the Sikhs would have none of it, and the attack resumed."

MacIntyre and the other men gathered around, listening closely to Singh as he continued his story.

"The Pashtuns tunneled until they breached the wall, and then the battle raged the fiercest. The Sikhs fought hand-to-hand until their sergeant ordered his men to fall back to the inner guardroom, while he remained behind to fight. The onslaught continued all day, until only one man remained. The last survivor, *Sepoy* Gurmukh Singh, personally killed twenty Afghans before the Pashtuns set fire to the post to kill him. The official report said as he was dying, he was yelling the Sikh battle cry to the very end."

"That was a brave man," Blake said.

"Yes," Singh nodded. "That was my father. I just wanted you to know the kind of fighting men you have with you."

Blake nodded. "Good to know."

"And by the way," Singh added, "you were right. The second German wave is coming."

14

First came the screaming of a panicked horse, echoing somewhere in the clouds of gun smoke to their south. The terrified creature emerged from the surreal scene like a waking dream, rider gone and flanks bloodied as it raced away from the German guns. More hoofbeats followed. The cataphracts—those few who still lived—were in full retreat, bolting back toward the city.

Sporadic gunfire sounded from the dusty haze behind them. Spectral figures of Afrika Korps soldiers materialized out of it, stalking the fleeing horsemen and any other targets of opportunity. Then, with a grumbling roar of mechanical treads, the lead tank of the second wave appeared out of the smoke, flanked by two more. And more.

Hunkered down in their spider holes at the edges of the necropolis, Blake's anxious snipers kept hidden as they waited for their real target to appear. The German troopers were everywhere, some marching past close enough that the snipers could reach out and grab them by their boots. But they refrained, remaining frozen, trying to hold their breaths in the hope that their hiding places were camouflaged well enough.

"What do you see, Singh?" Blake hissed.

The Sikh panned across the field with his concealed periscope. "Looks like the rest of the *Panzergrenadier* battalion approaching on foot. More Panzers, too, P-IIIs mostly, I'd say. Three... no, six. No, wait. Twice that—a full dozen of them."

"Forget them," Blake said. "Just tell me where that fat Dorchester is."

Singh made another sweep. "No sign of their HQ. Though they're kicking up a great deal of dust back there. Even a bloody great bus like that could be anywhere south of us and we'd never know." He gave a sharp intake of breath. "Ah, blast them, here they come."

"Climb down," Blake ordered. "If the ground troops spot us, we're done for."

The men huddled together silently in the near dark, the acrid smell of fear-sweat sharp and strong. They could hear the Germans stomping above them, calling out to one another. A spate of excited yelling broke out, followed by the sound of machine-gun bursts. The sound echoed through the tunnel leading to their hiding place.

No, not echoing, Blake realized.

"Move it! They've found us!" he shouted.

Blake bolted from the room. Up top, a pair of German soldiers began to pry away the gravestones and rubble which concealed the entrance into their subterranean passage. Before either could drop a grenade, Blake fired a burst from his Schmeisser, catching them both.

Two of the New Zealanders, a white Kiwi and a Maori, rushed to the fresh breach and popped their heads up, laying down heavy bursts of suppressing fire at the closest enemy troops, a trio of Germans who scrambled to find cover. The entrance had originally been the floor of a great mausoleum—what little remained of its blasted walls barely sufficed as cover for one, let alone three. The trio ducked under the low strip of ragged limestone, lying flat. One trooper pulled out a potato masher, while the others signaled to their comrades.

Releasing the pin, the Nazi pulled back his arm, counting down for the throw. At this range he couldn't miss, but at the perfect moment he froze, struck by a sniper's bullet to the forehead. The grenade exploded, killing all three soldiers.

The sniper's victory was short-lived. He had taken an indefensible risk by exposing himself for the shot, paying for it a second later when a hail of German bullets cut him down. Worse still, giving in to the perverse urge of something unspoken and unplanned, the other snipers opened fire, as well.

The pair of New Zealanders continued to lay down heavy fire before a shrill whistle needled through the air.

"Incoming!" one yelled, but the mortar landed before they could even duck.

* * *

The explosion up top, thunderous in the subterranean tunnels, sent a cloud of acrid smoke and a hailstorm of rocky shrapnel skittering their way. Blake lifted out of a crouch, choking on the fumes as he and Singh moved further into the tunnel.

Slices of light angled in from the enlarged opening, its ragged edges still smoking. There was nothing identifiable left of the two New Zealanders, and the four soldiers who moments ago had been standing closest to the stone steps now lay twisted and unmoving. Singh moved to take up the dead men's position, but Blake grabbed his arm, pulling him back.

"Wait."

They stood in silence, listening intently for the whistle of a second mortar attack. When the sound of shouts and heavy footfalls came instead, both men rushed the entrance, emerging to open fire point-blank on ten charging *Panzergrenadiers*. The hail of bullets slashed the German squad to pieces.

Troopers further back dove for cover and returned fire. Blake and Singh hunkered down for the firefight, taking cover behind the remains of a stone wall.

Moments later a grenade came sailing through the air at them. It dropped a few inches away from Blake's ear. He snagged it on the bounce and slapped it away, an instant before it exploded on the other side of the wall behind them— just as a second one came hurling their way, bouncing off the stony floor and skidding to a stop just out of arm's reach.

Singh was already pulling Blake down when the explosion rocked the mausoleum ruins, so close that even in the relative safety of their cover, the deafening roar jarred their teeth and bones, rocky fragments raining down on their backs. The din of battle, so ear-splitting a moment ago, became muted. Though dazed and shaking, the two men wasted no time coming back up into firing position, ears still ringing.

Blake thumbed his MP-40 from full to semi-automatic. His ammo was already running low—he had to make every shot count now. In the tunnel below them, MacIntyre and the last two remaining soldiers looked up with pale faces, ready to take his and Singh's place if they fell. Smoke and the smell of cordite surrounded their embattled island.

The buzzing in their ears suddenly gave way to the creak of tank treads, and a Mark IV Panzer came rolling out of the yellow-gray mist at their flank, no more than a few meters away. The steel behemoth rumbled to a halt, coming around to better bring its guns to bear on them. For a split-second, Blake's heart froze up even as he switched his Schmeisser back to full auto.

"Aim for the viewports!" he yelled as he opened fire. Singh followed his lead and blasted away at the narrow slits, both men hoping to hit the chink in the armor.

"*Bole So Nihal, Sat Sri Akal!*" Singh roared. The closest of the guns stayed quiet—maybe they'd scored a lucky hit on a gunner. Then the Panzer opened up with its remaining 50-caliber machine gun, sweeping the floor of the ruins with a blaze of heavy fire that chewed up the ground. The tank rotated its turret, lowering the main cannon at its targets.

* * *

Inside the Mark IV, the smell of the forward machine gunner's blood filled the claustrophobic space. The tank's commander, a seasoned Prussian veteran with a seamed face, peered through the thick glass viewport, ignoring the overwhelming copper tang and what it meant.

"Give me suppression fire, and bring main gun to bear," he ordered coolly as the turret rotated with a soft electric thrum. Their loader shoved the heavy shell into the breech and slammed it closed again, while the main gunner targeted the two Allied soldiers who were firing at them.

On the other side of the cramped space, unable to see through his bullet-cracked view-slit, their radioman began blindly sweeping for them, raking the ground with his own 50-cal. The main gunner watched the pair of opponents drop back down into their burrow and finished lining up his crosshairs on the opening.

"I have the target," he confirmed.

"Fire!"

An odd trembling rocked the cabin. The gunner frowned as he lost his mark and hurried to re-align his aim.

"*Gottverdammt*, fire!"

"Trying, sir!"

But the shaking would not subside. The tremor continued, growing worse with each passing second. A sudden sharp jolt caught the commander by surprise, and he steadied himself against the turret walls, his anger souring into fear that he fought to keep under control.

Was it a bombing run? From whom? Had the British returned to the war? An earthquake? Whatever it was, it was growing stronger. He braced himself against the viewport and looked outside. His eyes widened in astonishment.

"Sir! What is it?" the main gunner asked, his voice cracking. The commander did not respond or move a muscle, transfixed at the view-slit.

"*Sir!*"

"Turn the main gun around."

"Sir?"

"*Do it now!*"

The horrendous booming had greatly alarmed the brontosauruses—they'd retreated to the center of the lake, circling their young for protection. Then, without warning, the largest male broke ranks and stormed off toward the marshes at the edge of the water. Another followed, then another, and another, until the entire herd charged forward.

Hugging close to the city walls, a man and a young woman on a German motorcycle watched the gigantic reptiles stampede. Each elephantine body was bigger than a London double-decker bus, with long whip-like tails and serpentine, tree-trunk-thick necks twice as high as a telephone pole. Amber wasn't sure exactly which species these were, but "brontosaurus" felt close enough.

"Good work," DeMetta said. "Now go back to the big guy, but this time replace the fear with anger."

A sense of awe rose at what she had just accomplished under DeMetta's direction, but she shook off the distraction.

She focused her mind on what looked like the herd's alpha male. His reptilian mind felt alien, raw, and crude, vibrating with overwhelming terror. Reaching out, she stimulated a neighboring portion of the brain, setting off a different but equally primal cascade of chemicals. Terror transformed into rage. Gently, she directed the beast's attention toward the tanks to the south.

"Defend the herd," she suggested, pointing out all the tiny, scurrying, hairy little bipeds. *"Egg-stealers,"* she whispered. Then she did the same to the next biggest male, and the next. It went easier and faster each time.

Having penetrated well into the flattened remains of the necropolis, the Afrika Korps troopers in the frontmost *Panzergrenadier* squads halted their advance. They had found a grisly surprise.

All around lay a forest of fletched shafts. Patches of rust-stained earth lay alongside the contorted bodies of their ambushed predecessors in the first-wave infantry. Hardened as they were, the troopers were horrified to see so many of their fellows brought down by such a primitive method. A few glanced about warily, sussing out where any surviving archers might be hiding.

"Wie cowboys und Indianer..." muttered one. He spat on the ground in disgust, and gasped when the earth seemed to bristle at the insult.

Then came another jolt, and another.

"*Erdbeben!*" a trooper shouted.

An earthquake would have been less terrifying. The tremors continued nonstop, accompanied by a new rising sound—the bellowing calls of animals on the rampage. Then the Afrika Korps troopers saw it—a stampede, bursting out of the dust clouds, coming right for them. Most of the men turned and ran. Some froze where they stood, while a few raised their rifles and fired. If any of the enormous saurians felt even a sting, they gave no sign, and the shooters quickly joined the others in trying to flee.

It was useless.

The lead brontosaurus dipped his neck down to snap up one of its targets, flinging the pieces away through the air behind it. Without slowing, it brought its pulverizing feet down on more of the fleeing soldiers. The herd stormed past them all, flattening stone and flesh alike.

The Prussian commander screamed near-incoherent orders to bring the Panzer's main gun to bear. The turret had never moved so damnably slow. As the tidal wave of moving targets swung into his field of vision, the main gunner stared in shock for a millisecond, then fired off a hurried shot that went wild.

The other tanks fired as well, sending hot streaks blazing past the straining necks of the giant reptiles. A nearby Panzer scored a lucky shot, hitting a charging dinosaur square. Its torso exploded like a dynamited whale carcass.

"Reload! Now, damn it!" the commander howled. The loader was already scrambling to get the shell in place.

Watching in horror as the bull dinosaur in his view-slit grew larger by the second, the gunner fired the instant he sensed the slam of the breech—the point-blank shot blew the enormous neck clean off. Its massive decapitated body smashed into the Panzer with the force of a runaway locomotive, crushing vehicle and crew.

The fastest of the oncoming reptiles, one of the smaller adults, fell into the last of the pit traps meant for the tanks. It gave a terrible cry of agony as the anti-tank mines exploded beneath it, but the rest of them overwhelmed the closest Panzers.

One enraged brontosaurus body-checked its mechanical enemy, first knocking the tank on its side, and then muscling it over onto its back. Bellowing its victory, it reared up on its hind legs to stomp the Panzer's underbelly into a crumpled heap of metal before storming off to do the same to a new victim, pounding the earth with each thundering step as the second tank struggled to bring its gun about in time. It failed.

Another tank managed one last fatal shot at the dinosaur coming straight for it before being side-slammed by another, the impact nearly ripping off the turret. A fifth Panzer careened wildly away to escape, but broke a tread, grinding to a halt. The crew struggled to bail out, only to be trampled along with their crippled tank.

With all guns blazing, the last Panzer fought to bring its cannon to bear on the dinosaur attacking it. Slipping its neck under the barrel of the main gun as though it were a rival male, the brontosaurus levered up and sent the tank crashing backward. Within seconds, nothing was left of the entire front formation but a mess of torn metal scrap, and the infantry battalion had been reduced to a tiny handful of badly shaken survivors.

The six remaining Panzers rallied, quickly maneuvering to re-form a single flying wedge and launch a new barrage. Blasting away at the dinosaurs from a safer distance, they set to work turning the battle into a one-sided slaughter once more.

15

"Get those tanks!" DeMetta yelled over the roar of the motorbike as they tried to keep up with the herd.

Sitting up high in the sidecar, Amber closed her eyes concentrating on the bright spots of human minds inside the Panzers. Training was all well and good, but this was the real thing. She had to succeed—lives depended on it.

Going to the tank furthest back on the right arm of the V-formation, she identified the strong-willed commander, and took the path of least resistance instead, honing in on the main gunner. Since she had neither the skill nor experience to overwhelm his mind by force, she used the psionic equivalent of judo. The man was already on the raggedy edge of panic—all she had to do was redirect it. She kept the thought simple and primal, just as DeMetta had taught her.

"These tanks want to kill us."

The gunner swore and jerked his crosshairs onto the Panzer

ahead of him, slamming down on the firing pedal without hesitation. His shell exploded in a direct hit.

"Yes!" he shouted. "Got those bastards!" The rest of the crew stared at him in shock. The wireless erupted in a new burst of frenzied radio chatter.

"*Verdammt* fool!" the commander yelled, grabbing him by the collar. "Are you insane? That was one of ours!"

"These tanks want to kill us!" the gunner wailed.

Another fiery explosion sounded off from their left. The tank commander released the raving gunner and stared in furious disbelief through the view-slit. At the other end of the formation, the hindmost Panzer had just blasted its neighbor apart, as well. He turned away from the sight of the burning vehicle. The loader looked up at him, shell in hand, uncertain what to do. The gunner already had returned to locking in on the next Panzer.

"What are you waiting for? Load it!" the gunner barked, turning to the man, his eyes both blazing and pleading. "*These tanks want to kill us!*"

For a moment, the commander could only stare.

Then he drew his Luger.

"Been good to know you, Singh," Blake said without irony.

"You as well," the Sikh replied.

They stared down the barrel of the cannon, both fully expecting to be blown to pieces. Then the ground started to shake and the big gun swiveled away on its turret.

"What the bloody hell…?"

The two men exchanged astonished looks before cautiously emerging from cover. The German troopers surrounding their position were abandoning their cover and rifles alike, running for their lives. Blake whistled down to MacIntyre and the others, and the three came up to see the spectacle as well.

Then Blake understood the reason for the German's rout, and froze in disbelief. A few of the enemy tried to lob grenades or launch mortars at the gargantuan beasts, but the explosions were lost amid the wave of thundering saurians—as were the screams of the *Panzergrenadiers*.

Riveted, Blake and Singh watched the roaring brontosaurus charge the big Panzer. Its main gun wheeled around at the last second in time to fire on the creature. The blast blew through its massive neck, dropping it like falling timber, just before the rest of the dead beast's bulk plowed into the tank, crushing it with a sickening crunch. Both slammed into the ruins of the mausoleum. Another meter of skidding and their combined bulk would have entombed Blake and his men where they stood. Instead, it gave them new cover.

They took a chance scrambling atop the smoldering wreckage to avoid the stampede raging all around them. From there the soldiers had a decent vantage point of the ensuing carnage. In a matter of seconds, the rest of the German infantry was wiped out, and the remaining tanks in the formation destroyed.

A familiar keening drone rose above the sound of the carnage and burst into skirling music. MacIntyre had emerged with his pipes, as if calling the dinosaurs to war.

Blake thought the man must be insane, but the music was a welcome distraction.

The day was not won yet, however. Off to the south, the remaining half-dozen Panzers repositioned in a new wedge. They opened fire on the charging herd, their barrage taking good effect until one tank suddenly burst into a blossoming flame—followed seconds later by another. Both appeared to have been blasted, point-blank, by their fellow Nazis.

"How the hell...?"

Blake stared in disbelief as the German formation twisted and turned on itself, ignoring the wave of dinosaurs that thundered toward them.

"*What* the hell...?"

He wondered if he was as insane as MacIntyre.

Behind the herd came his stolen German motorcycle. And that wasn't all.

"Amber...?"

Then he saw the driver.

"Christ!" he swore, and raised his gun. "There he is! He's got Amber!" It wouldn't be an easy shot, and his stolen submachine gun was no sniper weapon. He might hit Amber, and taking out Mehta could result in a fatal crash, but it was a gamble he had to take. Silencing his doubts, he focused on taking his shot and brought Mehta's head in his sights.

He held his breath and flexed his trigger finger.

"Blake," Singh said.

The commando didn't respond, concentrating as his weapon tracked the motorcycle. He had a bead on his target.

"*Blake,*" Singh repeated urgently.

"I've got the shot," Blake hissed.

"*Look.*" Something in Singh's voice gave him pause.

"What?"

The Sikh said nothing, pointing to a stream of dinosaur blood floating gently upward from the torn flesh of the dead brontosaurus. The droplets defied gravity to form delicate, lacy red traceries in the air. Bits of broken Panzer and limestone pebbles slowly tumbled up to join in the silent waltz. A curious hissing began, growing louder.

The hair rose on the back of Blake's neck.

"Run!" he shouted. "Everyone, *run for it!*"

"We're doing it!" Amber shouted, watching the surviving Panzers blast each other as the stampede closed in on them. DeMetta grinned.

Flushed with victory, Amber didn't immediately recognize the sensation thrumming through her body, vibrating through her bones. Then she heard a keening wail, accompanied by a weird, almost electrical crackling and sizzling. So loud… and getting louder.

Oh god.

In front of them, a ragged line of earth disintegrated into a vertical scattering of debris, ash, and dirt, all careening skyward as if hoovered up by a cosmic vacuum, replaced a fraction of a millisecond later by a blinding torrent of sheer, unstoppable power, a pillar of the earth bursting forth to be transformed into the fiery lance of Heaven.

The roar of its overwhelming power drowned out her scream. This close to the raw energy flow, Amber could feel it pulsating through her, all the way down to her fingertips and toes, and up and down her spine.

For an instant she was back on the rowboat with Gavin.

Gavin was dead.

"Stop the bike!" she shouted, sending DeMetta a visceral image of the threat they faced. He slammed on the brakes and swerved, but the motorbike continued on—somehow trapped in a dreamlike slow motion, bouncing along the ground and threatening at any moment to lurch straight into the surging flow of energy flaring up alongside them.

Amber's mind fractured—shifting back and forth between the punt outside Romford while the Event raged... staring in horror out the window of the *Vanuatu* as it plunged into a dive to avoid a wall of fire... between the arms of the Sphinx as a trio of aftershocks split the horizon...

... and then, just like that, time returned.

DeMetta pulled the bike to a skidding halt.

The curtain of energy vanished, along with the thundering percussion of battle. An eerie silence reigned, broken only by the soft crackling and hissing of super-heated sand fused into lines of glass.

The aftershock had fragmented a leaf-shaped patch roughly a mile or two long, taking out most of the necropolis and extending out into the desert. Within the boundaries of the glassy lines, still faintly smoking, the terrain had splintered and multiplied, like pieces of a fractured mirror. The Panzer tanks and the herd of brontosauruses had been diced into pieces, large and small, all of them replicated so many times they formed a grisly collage of metal, flesh, and bone.

"It's over... just like that?" Amber asked, dazed by the extent of the carnage. "Is everyone dead?"

DeMetta shook his head. "I don't know."

A terrible thought occurred. *Where is Blake?*

"Wait." DeMetta pointed south to the desert. "I see somebody. Over there." Out of the dust and heat haze, a lone shape approached on foot, only just shimmering into clarity. With a sharp burst of relief, Amber stood up and waved her arms.

"Blake! *Blake!* We're here! Over here!" she shouted, signaling to the distant figure. Then she stopped, realizing her mistake.

The approaching shape was a German soldier.

He wasn't alone.

Line after line of tanks—another two dozen mixed Panzers and mobile guns, along with supply trucks, all escorted by a full platoon of more *Panzergrenadiers*. Behind them, like ant drones attending to their queen, a crowd of armored cars and half-tracks surrounded an imposing armored command car.

Rommel's mobile HQ.

Or rather, Mehta's. The general and his master stood atop the vehicle, surveying the battlefield through binoculars.

Mehta was pleased at the outcome. The first two waves had been advance probes to draw out any resistance. Now the main body of the Afrika Korps would take Alexandria, and there was no defending army left to offer the slightest resistance.

Amber's heart sank as she and DeMetta watched the encroaching army's inexorable advance. For a few moments it had seemed as if, despite all the odds, they could win this mismatched fight...

"What do we do now?"

"Get out," he answered, his voice flat.

Amber stared at him. "What do you mean?"

"I mean, *get out of the sidecar.*" His expression was deadly serious. "*Now.*"

"But—"

"Go on, do it!" His voice cracked like a whip, leaving no room for argument.

Stunned, Amber pulled herself out. "What are you... are you leaving me here?"

"Yes." His tone was uncompromising. Then it softened, slightly. "Don't worry. I have a plan. You're just not going to like it."

"What do you m—"

She lost consciousness.

* * *

Amber collapsed like a sack of potatoes, and DeMetta dismounted to make sure she was uninjured. He brushed a stray lock of hair from her face and, after a moment, came to a decision. Touching her forehead, he placed a message in her mind for later.

Then he remounted the bike and drove toward the Germans.

"Herr Generalfeldmarschall!" One of the radiomen called up to Rommel from inside the command car. "We've spotted a rider on one of our motorbikes. He is... waving a flag of truce?"

Rommel took up his binoculars again.

"Yes, I see him. Tell the front infantry to allow him safe approach to within parleying distance, and hear what he has to say."

Standing beside the field marshal, Mehta said nothing, but kept his binoculars trained on the approaching motorcycle. He was willing to bet Blake was the rider—the ringleader of the commandos that had harried them all the way here.

An invaluable asset. Mehta smiled at the thought of Blake back under his control. He turned to Rommel. "Tell the troops to bring him directly to me."

The German commander gave a curt nod.

DeMetta kept his speed slow and steady across the flattened necropolis, his makeshift white flag clearly visible. He'd made it from the strips of white silk cloth that he'd found crumpled up on the floor of the sidecar. No way to know where they came from, but they worked well enough.

It seemed as though the entire Deutsche Afrika Korps infantry had their guns trained on him, but no one shot him. One German trooper stepped forward, holding up a hand to halt him, and he slowed to a stop at a discreet distance from their line. Raising his hands to show he was unarmed, he left the bike's motor running. The lead soldier walked up, shouting something at him. DeMetta shrugged and shook his head.

"*Runter vom Motorrad!*" the soldier yelled. "*Das* motorbike— off! Now!"

DeMetta smiled and shook his head. *"That won't be necessary,"* he sent with a gentle psychic push.

"*Sie können auf dem Motorrad bleiben,*" the soldier replied with considerably less antagonism, waving DeMetta forward. "*Lass uns gehen!*" A guard of six soldiers lined up to escort him toward the mobile command.

"Yes, take me to your leader," he sent to each of them in turn. *"He wants to see me. We're old friends."*

Mehta frowned to see the prisoner still on his motorbike, approaching like a foreign dignitary with a full honor guard. *How the hell did Blake manage to sweet-talk those idiots into this?*

"What's going on with your troopers?" he growled at Rommel.

Raising his binoculars again, he zoomed in on the rider for a closer look. What he saw froze him to the core.

It wasn't Blake's face.

It was his own.

He grabbed Rommel by the lapel.

"Shoot him!" he shouted. "*Shoot him now!*"

16

Still keeping his bike to a crawl, DeMetta kept pace with his armed guard, observing his surroundings. He and his entourage made their way past the infantry and the foremost lines of tanks. Beyond that, still more tanks and guns, and then—

Ah. That has to be it.

A motorcade of smaller combat vehicles, all clustered protectively around a single oversized armored van. Clearly it was the mobile headquarters. Two figures stood atop it.

One of the pair was his target, he'd stake his life on it. No time to worry about which one—he just needed to concentrate on staying cool long enough to slip past all the troops and armored units until he was close enough to take both men out with a psionic assault.

Then he realized it was never going to happen.

"Erschieß ihn! Erschieß ihn!" someone yelled.

The time for subtlety had run out. DeMetta's guards stood still, confused by his mental tinkering, giving him just enough time to gun the engine and race forward. Bullets zipped by him, dangerously close to his head, and he wished he had an aptitude for telekinesis—a bullet-proof shield would be just the thing right now.

Being a telepath, he had to pick and choose his targets one at a time—his psychic tricks didn't work *en masse*. He reached out for the mind of the gunner in the closest tank, planting the idea that all the shooters behind him were British infiltrators. The man opened up on the imagined attackers, mowing them down.

As DeMetta sped between the rows of Panzers, another tank's heavy machine guns turned toward him. He quickly struck the gunner psychosomatically blind, and when another tank opened fire on him, he prompted the main gunner of the Panzer behind it to blast it to smithereens.

He ducked as flaming shrapnel flew overhead.

His route was a gauntlet of tanks and infantrymen, all trying to kill him. A rifleman popped out from behind a tank, and DeMetta made himself unremarkable and unnoticeable. As others came into his line of sight, he employed a variety of rapid-fire tactics—terrifying one trooper, inspiring overwhelming anger in another, and turning still others against their own comrades in bursts of paranoia.

Bullets flew everywhere—it was impossible to keep track of all the shooters. He ducked down as shots whizzed past his head, striving through the haze of gun smoke to keep his eye on the bulky command vehicle dead ahead—and on the two commanders atop it. He just needed to get close enough to make eye contact.

Approaching the ring of armored cars, he could see the two officers up top. Both drew pistols on him, and in rapid succession he paralyzed both before they could fire. He could almost make out their faces—

Watching his doppelganger racing through a gauntlet of bullets, Mehta felt an unpleasant new sensation—fear. His supreme self-confidence cracked as the motorcycle charged toward them through the blazing chaos, seemingly invulnerable to gunfire.

When the bike roared up to their defensive line of armored cars, he drew his Luger. Rommel instantly followed suit to protect his master. Mehta spent a moment to take careful aim, unwilling to miss the shot, and squeezed the trigger.

Nothing. His finger—every muscle in his body—would not obey. He could only stand there frozen with his Luger raised. No shot rang out, so Rommel had to be in the same condition.

Fear turned to terror.

DeMetta came within optimal psionic range, when a rifleman popped up from one of the cars, firing at him from close range. The bullet narrowly missed his head. Instinctively plucking the man's worst childhood fear from his subconscious, DeMetta unleashed it on him.

The soldier suddenly experienced the sensation of a wolf-sized tarantula tearing into his face like a rabid wildcat. Screaming, he clawed at it in self-defense, inadvertently discharging his rifle again.

The second shot caught DeMetta square in his ribs. Its impact hurled him off the motorbike onto the rocky earth.

Locked in place, unable to look away, Mehta silently screamed as his double drew closer. An instant later the rider caught a bullet and was flung off his motorcycle. The bike smashed straight into the closest armored car, flipping up and over the hood into the screaming rifleman, killing him instantly.

Mehta was free again.

The two commanders snapped back to life with a sharp dual exhalation. Mehta wiped his mouth with the back of his hand and shook his head.

"Follow me," he barked to Rommel, then swiftly descended mobile HQ's ladder, pistol drawn. The two approached their fallen enemy, sprawled face-up on the ground, the hot parched soil hungrily sopping up the dark pool of blood spreading beneath him. The man's unblinking gaze stared up somewhere far past them.

"He's you," Rommel said. "He even has your *verdammt* witch-eyes."

Mehta looked down in morbid fascination. It was true. The man was his twin, like the one he'd killed just a few days earlier. How many more like him *were* there?

A medical corpsman ran up and knelt over the body, checking for vital signs.

"Is he dead?" Mehta asked the medic. Before the man could answer, Mehta's twin groaned and closed his eyes.

The medic looked up. "We can stabilize him, sir."

"No, not yet," Mehta said. Reaching into his satchel, he pulled out the hypodermic pistol, and knelt down to swiftly inject the fallen man in the flesh of his neck.

17

Outside the tank, the wide Alexandrian boulevard continued to unroll—a glorious sight, magnificent, beautiful and peaceful. Inside, the claustrophobic walls echoed with the insane radio chatter that was coming over the wireless—unintelligible shouts and screams that sounded like the ravings of lunatics. Dietrich frowned.

What the hell is hitting them out there? The temptation to go up top was strong, but he resisted it. They were almost to the palace. *Must stay sharp.* He gave the order to turn left, up a side street lined with fine houses, temple buildings, and a theater reminiscent of the Colosseum in Rome. The palace lay straight ahead, just a few blocks away.

As the seventh and last Panzer turned the corner off the main roadway, the rumble from the column drowned out the sounds of the truck engines and the squeal of brakes. Even so, there was no missing the two trucks coming in from the cross street to cut them off. Quick as a slamming door, the trucks pulled alongside each other to form a double-thick wall, completely blocking the street. No one in the tanks heard or saw the third truck do the same behind the column.

The truck drivers bailed out.

"Ambush!" Dietrich shouted. "Smash those trucks!"

A shrill whistle split the air, and high above them, from the rooftops and the upper decks of the theater, a battalion of street urchins popped up to rain down roof tiles and mud and filth by the bucketful. Machine-gun fire broke out from all the tanks, firing blind, and Dietrich's gunner fired as well, blasting the trucks.

Even in the tank they could feel the heat of the explosion as the vehicles burst into flame. Their windows covered in filth, they could still see nothing, the crews struggling to clear the viewports.

"Driver, forward! Smash through now!" the commander barked. As the driver revved forward, another whistle sounded above, and the pelting stopped.

Then all hell broke loose.

At Hypatia's signal, the women all along the rooftops chopped their ropes, releasing bundles of stone pillars, each one as thick as a ship's mast. They rumbled down the tiles and came crashing down upon the Panzers with the force of an avalanche. Some crushed main guns or stripped the machine guns away, easy as pine needles. Others crumpled turrets or the engines.

* * *

In the lead tank, Dietrich clawed for support as the vehicle rocked crazily, its treads caught on the rubble as it tried to move forward. He heard more impacts up top—gentler ones, like those of shattering pottery—and with them, the smell of oil. Then smoke began to come through the ventilation ducts.

Cursing, he threw open the top hatch, his Luger drawn. A young Arab woman in a headscarf threw a burning blanket on their air intake. He shot at her, but she disappeared down the tank's side. He reached over and snatched away the flaming cloth. Behind him, all down the column, attackers with torches or mallets piled on the tanks. Others simply poured amphorae of oil into the street. None of them were more than teenagers, some even younger.

Firing quickly, he shot down three of them before a shooter opened fire on him. The Arab girl, her headscarf gone now, blazed away at him with a Sten gun. Bullets ricocheted off the turret with a sharp metallic twang, narrowly missing him as he ducked back inside.

Almost immediately a little round jar shattered on the open hatch above him, spilling shards of pottery and a handful of pale scorpions into the interior.

The wireless operator slapped at his neck and began to scream.

Back at the rear of the column, Cam and Kha-Hotep slipped behind the hindmost tank as it went into reverse, trying to ram the truck behind it. Armed with a small boat anchor,

Cam swung it like a hammer into the moving tread. Gear teeth eagerly ground down upon it, and then the whole tread belt buckled, snapped, and clattered off the wheels. The tank lurched to the side and halted.

The top hatch snapped open, and the tank's commander drew his pistol on Cam. Kha-Hotep slammed the hatch down on his head, pulping his face against the mouth of the opening. His features a bloody wreck, the man dropped back inside, and Kha quickly poured in a basket of asps after him.

Nellie blew the whistle again. Her rooftop crew, including Ibn Fadlan and Harcourt, lit their sheaves of straw and sent them cascading down like reverse paper lanterns. A moment later, the whole street burned.

"Get us out of here! Now!" Dietrich yelled, stomping on the tiny monsters. With a last lurch, the tank cleared the stony rubble and roared ahead, smashing with ease through the wreckage of the two trucks.

Thirty meters out, Dietrich gave the order to halt and raised the hatch for a look back at the site of their ambush. Two other tanks had followed them out. The rest of the wedge were crippled and burning.

"Any of ours still alive, sir?"

The only survivors in sight were the enemy, their fleeing shapes silhouetted against the roaring flames like capering pagans at a bonfire. The commander shook his head.

"How many shells left?"

"We're down to four, sir," the loader replied. Dietrich wiped a bead of sweat from his chin and rotated the turret.

"We'll spare one for here. Fire on that balcony!"

He pointed to the terraced upper floor of the highest villa on the block, the palatial home of some great noble house. A moment later, the blast tore it apart, first with a thunderous explosion of tiles, stonework, and marble that rained down upon the pavement stones. Then, with a shudder, the building's entire facade came crashing down, crushing anyone below and shrouding the ruined city block below with a smoking cascade of fiery debris.

Dietrich swung his gun back around to the fore and the three German tanks rumbled on ahead.

Behind the wreckage of the fallen noble house, a blinding cloud of ash, plaster dust, and burning cinders settled upon the atrium gardens and its fruit trees—as well as on Nellie and Hypatia's band of guerrilla fighters. They slowly came to their feet, coughing and waving away the fumes as they dusted themselves off, then quickly slipped away to continue the fight.

18

At the stab of the needle, DeMetta's eyes opened. An agonizing pounding wracked his entire body with every beat of his pulse, and his head spun as he struggled to see through the haze of pain and delirium. A surreal sight came into focus—his own face, staring back at him with a reptilian look of malice.

Even as he fought to stay conscious, part of him recognized that he was face-to-face with his target. Pushing past the pain, he concentrated on bringing a telepathic attack to bear—but nothing happened. Instead, he could feel his will draining away...

Chemical attack, he thought. *I've been drugged.*

His training kicked in. *Counter it. Increase neuroresistance...* He sent orders to the appropriate parts of his brain, mounting a defense.

"Hand me that," he heard the man say. A bright beam shone into DeMetta's eyes, constricting his pupils. The flood of brightness overwhelmed the optic nerve pathway—

Mehta's device was designed to trigger photic reactions in the temporal, parietal, and occipital lobes to augment the drug's psychotropic takeover.

DeMetta tried to fight it off. He couldn't.

"Can you hear me?" Mehta's voice came from far away, like an echo from the bottom of a well.

"Yes," he heard himself answer. "I hear you."

"Very good," the man replied. "Now, here is what I want you to do…"

Sinking deeper beneath the surface, DeMetta knew he was outgunned. Time to try a different defense tactic. He compartmentalized, mentally castling his core psyche even as he felt Mehta's hooks sinking into his mind's higher functions. He would be a free man trapped in the body of a puppet, but all was not lost. Not yet, though life was slipping away from him.

Only one option left, he realized. The part of him that remained free called up the memory of the abandoned mosque in the ruins of Cairo… the secret he had seen there in the girl's mind.

*Sensemay*á.

He would never be able to duplicate her world-shattering abilities, but there was one thing he *had* learned from her.

"Your mental abilities," Mehta said. "You can teach them to others?"

"Yes," his double responded mechanically.

"How long does it take to learn?"

"If you wish, I can… place the knowledge… directly into your mind…"

Mehta smiled, eyes gleaming.

"Excellent! Do it now!"

"Yes…"

While Mehta spoke, the medics huddled over the prone man, trying to save his life. One of them looked up.

"We're losing him, sir."

Mehta shoved them out of the way and crouched down, a new urgency in his voice.

"Listen to me," he demanded. "Before you die, you must show me your power. He peered down. "Do you understand?"

There was no response, and the silence stretched on for so long that he feared it was too late. Then with one final effort, the prone man looked up, locked eyes with Mehta, and smiled. He could not speak, but Mehta still heard the dying man's voice quite clearly in his head.

"Oh, I'll show you my power, you son of a bitch."

19

All is lost.

On Pharos island, overlooking the battlefield from high above, the sentry stood haunted by the apocalyptic visions he'd just witnessed. He gripped the marble balustrade with white-knuckled hands, trying to decide whether or not to throw himself over the railing.

Leaning forward, he peered over the edge, all the way down to the waves crashing against the rocks. Surely it would be a quick death, he thought. Then a flash of movement to the southwest caught his eye. Something was riling up the Germanians at the periphery of the flattened necropolis. He heard the chatter of their weapons, angry shouts in their harsh language. What was causing the commotion?

Then he saw it. A single man, riding one of their small vehicles, speeding into the center of their nest. Furious chaos erupted in his wake until his wild ride ended with a crash, enemy warriors swarming the stricken man. Surely he was doomed.

It would be fitting to join him, the sentry decided, peering outward one last time to see if he could glimpse the man's fate. As he squinted, a blinding brightness flared up, like a newborn sun, swallowing up land, sky, and sea in an eerily silent burst of white-blue light so intense he had to shield his eyes.

An instant later, just as colors started to return to his sight, a thunderclap knocked him backward with the force of a gale, threatening to blow him off of the tower like a speck of grit on the wind. When he dared to open his eyes once more, releasing his death grip on the railing, he stood there, shocked at what he saw.

What just happened?

Amber found herself lying on the ground, staring up at an empty sky. DeMetta was gone. So was the motorcycle. So was the battle.

No sounds of cannon.

No gunfire.

No dinosaurs.

Only a deathly stillness remained. She stood, brushing herself off. Gruesome chunks of brontosauruses and shattered pieces of Panzer tanks were strewn all around. When she turned her gaze to the south, she gasped.

A smoldering crater, more than one hundred yards across, lay where the German army had been a few moments earlier. Looking at it, Amber realized that the core of the German forces had simply been... *erased*. Numb, she stumbled toward it in a daze.

When she finally reached the lip, a crisp ozone smell of burning electrical wires still hung in the air. The heat of whatever caused this had fused the sand into a smooth glassy surface that shimmered with a darkly beautiful iridescence. She stared, trying to make sense of it all, until she realized with a start that she wasn't alone.

A lone figure sat nearby, his back turned to her. It was one of the German soldiers. The man's arms were wrapped around his legs, and he rocked gently back and forth. Kneeling beside him, she gently touched his arm. He looked up at her, eyes wet and uncomprehending.

"*Zu hell...*" he whispered, his voice hoarse and broken, "*zu hell...*"

Too bright... too bright...

A crunching sound behind them caught Amber's ear, she turned toward the noise. In the gloom, ghostly figures were approaching. She stood in alarm, her eyes widening as the three emerged from the last of the dwindling smoke and dust. A turbaned Sikh, a man carrying... bagpipes? And...

"Blake...?"

"You're alive," he said simply.

She nearly knocked him over with her enthusiastic embrace. He returned the hug, arms wrapping around Amber so tightly it took her breath way.

"I thought you were done for after I spotted Mehta, taking you away on the motorcycle," Blake said, voice rough with uncharacteristic emotion. She was confused for a moment, then realized what he was talking about.

"That wasn't Mehta. That was, he—" she hesitated, unsure of how best to explain. "Well, he's kind of like Merlin—he looks like Mehta, but he's on our side." She looked around anxiously. "Have you seen him?"

"Gone." Blake shook his head. "Obliterated, with most everybody else on the field," he said, staring at the devastation. "What the hell did he detonate? He lit the place up like bloody Hiroshima and Nagasaki." The other two soldiers looked at him blankly.

"Oh." That was all Amber could get out before dropping to her knees, head spinning. She felt sick. Blake knelt down next to her, resting a steadying hand on her shoulder.

"Amber…?"

"The… the man on the motorcycle. He was… he…" She couldn't finish. It was like losing Merlin all over again.

"I'm sorry." Blake's voice was uncharacteristically gentle. "Your friend… he saved us. He saved Alexandria."

The soldier in the turban spoke. "What do we do now?"

Amber looked up as the man's question triggered something in her mind.

///Amber, you need to know…

I don't have a lot of answers for you, I wish I did. I only know what I have to do, and that's keep you alive so you can do what you have to.

I don't know what that is, either, but years ago, the PreCogs told me I would meet you, and when I did, you'd be our best hope for saving the world.

I hope they're right. Good luck///

"Right, good question," Blake said, all business again. "I've got a plan for us to get mobile, but it's not going to be easy, and we'll all need to work round the clock. First, we need to take stock of all the engine parts we can salvage here, and then—"

"No."

Amber's voice was soft and distant as she stared off into the horizon, but that one word stopped him mid-sentence.

"What do you mean, 'no'?"

"I know how we're getting to the South Pole."

20

The Mediterranean Sea
off the Coast of Egypt
Two days before the Battle of Alexandria

The ship was gone, destroyed by a surface-to-air missile, but even in its death, it protected its passengers.

Harcourt's emergency cocoon brought him safely to a splash landing on the Mediterranean, where he remained afloat through that day and night. The following morning, a trio of Carthaginian fishermen rescued him. Its job done, the cocoon-turned-coracle dissolved into a tadpole-shaped glob and moved away.

The white glob immediately attracted the eye of a large Jurassic ammonite, its coiled shell the size of a bulldozer tire. The cephalopod lashed out with its tentacles, expertly snagging the pale fishlike prey. Acting on pre-programmed instinct, the white glob promptly dispersed into a cloud of tiny wriggling tadpoles, leaving behind the frustrated octopod.

Each of the synthetic tadpoles contained a staggering amount of information—every cubic micrometer easily encoded more information than one hundred Libraries of Congress. Despite that, each one was focused on just two concerns—where it was headed, and what it would do when it got there.

Attracted by the shimmering movement, hungry fish quickly descended upon the school of ship-stuff. A garfish swallowed one, spitting it out again immediately. Unfortunately, the robot tadpole was snapped up by another less-fussy fish—a bony-beaked prehistoric monster that looked like a demon-eyed tuna in a suit of armor.

Unfortunately for the fish, tunneling out of a Devonian-era carnivore posed no problem for the robot, either technically or ethically. It was bright white, eel-shaped, and ten times its original size by the time it cut through the surf on the Mediterranean shore and began slithering over the wet sand. It wound its way over the rocky breakwater and crossed long, hard-packed stretches of sunbaked grayish-yellow earth—a milky stream flowing with quicksilver grace over the dunes and rolling across rocky flats like a pearl.

At one point it slipped over the knife-edged lip of a *wadi*, a parched streambed etched long ago through the plain. The smooth banks thwarted the droplet's efforts to flow up the side, so it grew tiny crab legs and spidered up the wall before reverting to its mercurial form.

Now and again the motile little globule would meet up with other stray blobs like itself. When that happened, they would glom on to one another, increasing in size and sometimes breaking up again as needed later. But always, keeping on the move, hurrying to rejoin their siblings at the rendezvous point.

Miles inland, the tenacious droplets finally reached their destination, a blackened smudge of scorched earth covering approximately half a hectare of the desert. A network of slender arterial rivulets reached across the blackened ground, bearing steady streams of sand down into an opening roughly a meter across.

Deep inside, the mix of raw matter and ship-stuff underwent a complex series of alchemical transmutations as the body forming underground absorbed nutrients from the surrounding matter. If a single pearl had been buried in solid rock, it could rebuild itself—and if that same pearl had instead been suspended in midair, it could still grow like an aerophytic plant, using sunlight, air, inhuman patience, and its own take on photosynthesis.

Bones of superstructure formed first, then walls and connective tissues, finally giving rise to other sophisticated and specialized configurations. The coding inherent to each pearl engaged, activating higher functions. In the final stages, its internal power systems reached a critical mass. Engines formed and began to recharge. As energy surged through the construct, its mind awakened from its deep coma.

Engines activated, and the pliant body twisted and nosed upward, burrowing up through the layers of soil until the massive shape breached the surface and shook off the dirt.

Gleaming, it powered up the energized fields of its wings, reborn like a true phoenix.

The *Vanuatu* went off in search of Amber.

21

**Alexandria, Boulevard *Aspendia* in the Royal Quarter
just south of the Prefectural Palace
Ten days after the Event**

"The palace is ours. Target is dead ahead."

Oberleutnant Dietrich put down the wireless, feeling much less triumphant than his words had sounded. The time had finally come for them to take the king and checkmate the city. Rommel would be pleased with that, at least.

He wiped his brow, trying not to look at the staring eyes of his dead radioman. How many of them were left? he wondered. What the hell had happened today? How had medieval desert folk mounted such a ferocious defense— *against Panzers*, for god's sake? It boggled the mind.

As they approached the palace grounds, he shook off his dark thoughts.

"Why are we stopped?"

"We're not, sir!" The driver revved the engine. They could hear the treads rolling, yet they were not moving forward.

Dietrich swore and raised the hatch for a closer look. Yes, the treads were moving—just not the tank.

To his left and right, the treads of Wedge Two and Three were in motion, too, but both tanks were suspended a few feet off the ground—and slowly rising. Just like his tank was.

"*Was zum Teufel?*" he murmured.

A shadow fell across him. Startled, he looked up to find a brilliant, prismatic avian shape hanging serenely in the sky directly above them. A voice came down, speaking perfect German.

"*We are outside of your arc of fire. I recommend you surrender now, before we raise you another five hundred meters off the ground.*"

Dietrich stared speechless for a few moments, certain he was suffering from some combination of shell shock and heat madness. His men opened their hatches as well, blinking up at the impossible. Then he pulled out his Luger.

"*Scheiß drauf…*"

He chucked it over the side.

"We surrender!"

The three tanks slowly sank back to the ground once more.

"*Surrender accepted. Welcome to Alexandria.*"

The prefectural palace gardens served as the *Vanuatu*'s temporary berth. There was no time to celebrate or to mourn, or to rest—they had a world to save. Not everyone was planning on going. No one wanted to talk about what would happen if the mission failed—or, for that matter, if it succeeded. Either way, it was time for goodbyes.

Singh and MacIntyre offered to stay behind to help Hypatia and the prefect Orestes restore life to normal—or whatever would pass for it—in Alexandria. They took Blake's advice to board the ship just long enough to get linguistic implants, though both were noticeably uncomfortable aboard the futuristic vessel.

"Sure I can't talk you two into going with us?" Blake asked once the procedure was done. "We're likely to need all the help we can get."

"Aye, right." MacIntyre looked dubious. "Like we'd want tae gang tae th' sooth pole when this place is sae well tidy wi' bonnie lassies." He peered around the *Vanuatu* in apprehension, rubbing his temples as if feeling for the implants. Blake was reasonably certain it wasn't his social life that kept him behind.

He turned to Singh.

"Keep this one out of trouble, will you?"

The Sikh shrugged. "I'll do what I can."

Blake clasped hands with both of them, and they headed out.

Amber and Cam walked up to Kha-Hotep as he stood in front of the *Vanuatu*, gazing up at it in wonder. Cam laid a hand on his shoulder.

"Can you believe it was built by the sons of men?"

Kha-Hotep shook his head. "Who could even dream such a thing? Truly, it is like a lotus-vision become real."

"We have to leave—but will you come with us, Kha?" Amber asked.

"Of course," he said. "How could I leave my brother Cam?"

Cam grinned. "It will be a little colder than Egypt, I think."

"Isn't everywhere?"

Amber hugged him. "I'm glad. Do you think Leila will come, too? Where is she?"

Kha-Hotep pointed to a lane of the garden, where Leila was walking with Ibn Fadlan.

"I am truly sorry you lost your *hijab* during the fighting," he said sympathetically.

You mean when I tore it off and threw it away? she thought. All her life, growing up in 1980s Cairo, Leila had never been out in public without a headscarf, but ever since the firefight she'd wanted to let her hair remain free. It made her feel like an Amazon, somehow, and she liked that. Perhaps it made her a bad person but, secretly, it energized her.

The fact that it made the self-assured tenth-century imam so ill at ease was a bonus.

"Thank you, *Mullah*," she said.

"Trust that God will provide you with another."

She nodded. *We'll see about that.*

"It's time to go. Will you not come with us?" she asked him, uncertain if she really wanted him to say yes.

"It is kind of you to ask," he replied. "But I have no heart to travel so far from Mecca. On the contrary, I would ask you to come with me back to Baghdad."

"To be your wife?" she asked, her voice harder than she meant.

"If God wills it," he answered, "but regardless, if you were to but see its many-splendored beauties, I think you would count your eyes blessed."

She started to explain yet again what was riding on their mission, and that neither of them would be able to go to Baghdad, if it even still existed. But she knew it was no use.

"Perhaps I'll come visit you after all this." She smiled.

"God grant it be so."

"A peaceful journey to you, *Mullah*. Wish ours well, too, will you?"

"Success or failure is in his hands. *Maktub*, Child. It is written."

An electronic chime rang out across the palace grounds, followed by Blake's amplified voice.

"Time to get a move on, you lot. Say your goodbyes already and then all aboard!"

"I guess that's it, then," Nellie said to Hypatia and Orestes. "Prefect, my lady…" She struggled for words, and settled for, "All the best."

"Our city cannot thank you enough for what you and your companions have done, Nellie," Orestes said, taking her hand.

"We will never forget you," Hypatia added. "Farewell."

If we accomplish what we need to accomplish, you will forget, Nellie thought bitterly. *When we succeed, none of this will ever have even happened, and if we fail—well...* She couldn't finish the thought. Somehow it made her heart hurt all the more.

"Thank you both," she said instead. "Best of luck to all of you." There was so much more she wanted to say, and couldn't. What she needed was to get straight up that gangplank and get out of there. Feet and heart leaden, she made herself walk away.

She made it halfway up the gangplank before stopping, and took one last look back at Hypatia. The thought of her terrible fate haunted Nellie. Had she saved Hypatia, only to allow her enemies to murder her, once they regained their courage?

"Let's move it, Nell," Blake called down.

"Hold your horses, I'll be right back."

Hypatia looked up in surprise as Nellie ran back.

"Nellie? Aren't you going?"

"No," she said, catching her breath. "I mean, not yet. What I mean is..."

"What?"

"Please—come with us."

Hypatia opened her mouth in surprise. "I..." She hesitated. "I cannot. I'm needed here. I have a duty to the city."

"*We* need you. Please."

Orestes cleared his throat. "The Lady Hypatia is quite right. Her duty binds her here."

"But—"

179

"There is nothing more to be said," Hypatia said, her eyes downcast.

"There is one thing more to be considered," Orestes said softly to the mathematician and philosopher. "It seems, should their mission fail, Alexandria will be doomed. So if there is a part you can play in saving it, duty compels you to do so."

Hypatia looked up, shaking her head.

"You have learned something of logic, it seems," she said, with the smallest of smiles.

"My teacher was the finest," he said, matching hers. "Thus I release you from your duty for such a quest as this. If it be your will, my lady."

Nellie turned to her, eyes pleading. "Then—you will come?"

"To the end of the world?"

Hypatia took Nellie's hand.

"Of course I will go to the end of world with you."

22

En route to Antarctica
Late evening
Ten days after the Event

Blake had hit the sack almost as soon as the ship had taken off—his reward for saving Alexandria was going to be a night of sound sleep. Nellie had no such luck. She lay in her unquestionably comfortable bunk, staring into the darkness and wondering why, after what had been one of the most taxing days of her life, she couldn't fall asleep.

When she'd parted ways from her companions after dinner, her yawns had nearly cracked her face in half. Instead of falling into peaceful slumber, however, she'd tossed and turned for hours.

Sleep, Nellie told herself.

Her mutinous brain refused to submit, so she finally gave up and rose from her bunk. Wrapping herself in one of the ship's wonderfully soft bathrobes, she decided a brief constitutional was in order, and left her cabin to head down to the commons. Perhaps the ship could mix up a nightcap for her. A disturbing thought immediately followed.

Dear Lord, I hope I'm not turning into Harcourt.

When she reached the door of the commons, Nellie halted in surprise. She wasn't the only one having trouble sleeping.

Curled up against the window, Hypatia sat on a divan, gazing out at the stars. A slant of moonlight framed her perfectly, making it seem as though the most exquisite Alma-Tadema painting had come to life. Nellie held her breath, afraid to spoil the moment.

Acting on some unbidden awareness, Hypatia turned.

"Nellie." She smiled. "Come look at the stars with me."

Nellie stood frozen in place, at an unaccustomed loss for words.

"Did I say it correctly?" Hypatia asked.

Nellie nodded.

"*Téleia.*" Perfectly.

"No, no! Let us speak—" Hypatia paused, her new implant cueing her with the unfamiliar word. "English." She patted the divan, and her eyes went wide when the seat lengthened to make room. Nellie broke into a grin and joined her.

"I couldn't sleep," Nellie said. "I suppose you couldn't, either." Hypatia's eyes were bright.

"Who could sleep while we sail so high above the Earth? Though in your era, I suppose such marvels must be commonplace."

"I'm not quite so jaded." Nellie laughed. "All this effortless air travel came a bit after my time, I'm afraid. What are you looking at?"

"The stars of the south. I've only ever seen the charts of these constellations in the ancient star catalogs of Eudoxus and Hipparchus, but I never dreamt I would ever behold them with my own eyes." Hypatia pointed out a pair of bright yellow stars. "That is *Rigil Kentaurus*, the hoof of the Centaur Chiron." Nellie watched as she pointed out the rest of the constellation. "And see," Hypatia continued, "that one is Eridanus, it marks the path of reckless Phaethon."

"Phaethon?"

"The son of Helios Hyperion, the Radiant. Rashly he took up the reins of his father's sun-chariot, a task outstripping the young demigod's mettle. First the steeds bolted, climbing too high, and the Earth below froze in their absence. Young Phaethon pulled back tight upon the reins, and the chariot plunged down too closely this time, and so scorched the Earth to ashen waste. From Olympus, the immortal gods looked upon this in great distress, thus Father Zeus cast forth a thunderbolt to strike the chariot. And so Phaethon fell, tumbling to his death."

Nellie listened with rapt attention. She liked the way English sounded on her tongue, tinged with the woman's refined Greek accent. Hypatia's eyes lit up with unconcealed delight as she stared at the night sky.

"And here we are, soaring just like Phaethon—and praying we don't get struck down by a bolt from the heavens."

Nellie flashed on all the extraordinary experiences she had lived through over the past ten days. To think that, if they succeeded in their mission, all those memories—even this one—would vanish like a soap bubble.

The thought of that made her heart hurt.

Hypatia entranced her. The woman was so… alive, her eyes bright with the sheer joy of learning. She could see why the legends of her beauty had endured down through the centuries, only to be eclipsed by the dreadful fate Hypatia had suffered… would *still* suffer if they succeeded in saving the world.

Yet if they failed… *everyone* would die.

"Over the long millennia, the precession of the equinoxes—" Hypatia stopped and looked embarrassed. "Listen to me prattle on, as if I was still in my classroom."

"No, not at all!" Nellie snapped back to attention. "I could listen to you all night."

"You are most kind." Hypatia smiled. "Truly, Nellie, you are not a barbarian."

"A barbarian?" Nellie gave a surprised laugh. "Me?"

Hypatia laughed as well, her smile now tinged with embarrassment.

"Forgive me. It is a coarse word, but your tongue doesn't sound like the angry barking of the Ostrogoths and the Vandals. Eng-lish…" She played out the word. "It seems to be a beautiful and expressive language. Where do they speak it—Englicia? No, that's not right…"

"England," Nellie said. "It's an island far to the northwest of Alexandria. But my country is even further away than that—it's in the New World."

"The '*new*' world?" Hypatia sounded intrigued. "What do you mean? What is the 'old' world?"

"I'll show you," Nellie replied, secretly delighted for the chance to teach such a formidably intelligent woman something new. "Ship, could you conjure up a globe for us?"

A hovering pinpoint of light flared into existence, and then expanded into a meter-wide sphere, glittering with brilliant colors and covered in a haze that Nellie assumed represented clouds. Hypatia gasped in amazement.

"Here is a satellite view of Earth taken on February 2, 2219. Would you like to see a political globe instead?" Nellie considered for a moment.

"Yes, please," she responded. "From the year 1888, perhaps?" The gauzy cloud cover disappeared, replaced with distinct lines laying out latitude and longitude, and national borders.

"That's lovely," Nellie said. "Thank you, Ship."

Hypatia leaned closer, focusing on the Mediterranean, laid in perfect detail, then the huge masses of Africa and Asia, and the tantalizing islands of *terra incognita* lurking on the fringes of her familiar world. Nellie continued with her impromptu lecture.

"Now, before the explorer Columbus set sail, everyone thought the world was flat—"

"Flat? Surely not!" Hypatia exclaimed. "Three hundred years before *my* time, Eratosthenes of Cyrene proved the world was round." She put a hand to her mouth. "Forgive my interruption. Please, continue."

"Well then," Nellie said, "in Columbus's time it seems there were many benighted unfortunates who believed the world was flat, but once he sailed to the New World, the truth became undeniable." Tracing a path across the Atlantic Ocean, she pointed at the Western Hemisphere. "Here is that new land he discovered."

Hypatia eyes lit up again. She stared at the strange new continents, sounding out their exotic names as her implant translated them.

"Greenland... Dominion of Canada... United States... Mexico... South America... how marvelous!" Nellie beamed— Hypatia's delight was infectious. She pointed to a spot on the northern continent.

"Now, here is my home. New York, one of the great cities of the modern world."

"Someday you must take me there."

Nellie paused, uncertain how to respond. Before she could decide what to say, Hypatia quickly spoke up again.

"Tell me—does the ship's sight also extend up into the aether itself? Can we see into the celestial spheres? The starry firmament?" She grabbed Nellie's arm. "I want to see everything in the cosmos!"

"Whatever you like," Nellie replied, wanting nothing more than to give her the universe. "Ship, can you do the honors?"

That particular theory of celestial mechanics has not been borne out by astrophysics, nor has the existence of aether. Would you like to see a historical representation of the model instead? That would be theoretical.

"No," Hypatia answered. "Show me things as they truly are."

The globe shrank until the moon joined it, the two spheres rotating as they danced together. Hypatia pointed to the craters, visible in stark detail.

"Its surface is so rough and spattered, like raindrops fallen upon dust. Such raw chaos," she murmured. "Please, can we see the other six wanderers surrounding the Earth? Mars, Saturn, the sun, and the rest?"

"Your request is problematic, but allow me to show you a rough model of the rest of the solar system." As the display grew to fill far more of the common area, the Earth and moon dwindled away, making room for the entire company of planets, moons, and gas giants, all unmistakably circumnavigating the fiery incandescent ball of the sun.

"Such a wondrous display," Hypatia said. "An orrery of pure light."

Earth and the inner planets were tiny bright beads, dwarfed by the outer giants. By comparison Uranus and Neptune were the size of marbles, and Jupiter and Saturn sling stones, with a sun as wide across as a man's outstretched arms.

"This simulation is not to scale," the ship said. *"That would require a display nearly seven kilometers in diameter."*

Hypatia's brow furrowed in intense concentration.

"There are no epicycles, no deferents," she finally murmured. "None of the stratagems Apollonius devised to account for their movements. Their orbits, are they...?"

Her voice drifted off, and the ship responded by illuminating the orbital paths of each heavenly body. Hypatia's eyes widened at a sudden realization.

"Ellipses! All this time, they were elliptical—Aristotle was wrong, the wanderers do not move in perfect circles—and mad old Aristarchus of Samos was right all along. Every one of them revolves around the sun, even the Earth itself." Her thoughts raced ahead, trying to come to terms with this unexpected answer to the ancient riddle. So much that she held as established fact had just been overturned. "Then the center of the cosmos lies not with the Earth… but the sun."

"In actuality, our sun is not the center of the universe, nor can any such point exist, according to current understanding in cosmological physics."

"What of the stars, and the band of the Milky Way? How far off is their sphere?"

"Stars are not confined within a single spherical shell. Here are those closest to our solar system."

The entire display shrank down until the sun was reduced to a single yellow light, surrounded by three dozen others, mostly tiny red ones, many in pairs, a few in trios. The celestial map shrunk further, reducing the lights to pinpoints while more continued to pour into view until the entire commons was filled with tens of thousands of them, like a swarm of fireflies. The collapsing lights began to form into shapes, long chains, then a thick band.

The women sat entranced. One region flared slightly.

"This is the Orion-Cygnus Arm. Earth's solar system lies close to its inner rim."

"Arm? The arm of what?" Nellie asked. In response, the image continued to contract until the arm—along with several others—formed a glittering pinwheel. It filled the entire common room, spinning silently with a serene, unhurried grace.

"This is the Milky Way Galaxy, a collection of gas, dust, and hundreds of billions of stars, all revolving every two hundred and fifty million years around what we call a supermassive black hole. What we refer to as 'the Milky Way' is simply the visible region of our own galactic plane as seen from Earth."

"How majestic it is, just breathtaking…" Hypatia murmured in awe, and Nellie nodded. "The whole of the universe."

"It is not." Hypatia frowned again. The galaxy grew smaller, until dozens of tiny satellite galaxies surrounded it.

"These galaxies, each containing several billion stars, form a tiny portion of the Virgo Supercluster." Still shrinking, they all dropped away. Then the Virgo cluster shrank down to a pinpoint of light, a particle on the outer fringe of a feathery offshoot tendril of what looked like nothing so much as a windblown piece of thistledown.

Nellie could feel Hypatia's body trembling next to her. A tear was running down the philosopher's cheek. Nellie touched her hand, and Hypatia grabbed hold tightly.

"These megaparsec-long filaments form the gravitationally unbound streams of galactic superclusters called Laniakea, meaning 'Immeasurable Heaven' in the Hawaiian language. It is composed of roughly one hundred thousand galaxies, and stretches across five hundred and twenty million light years."

Nellie's mind raced to maintain a grasp on the incomprehensible scale. The image continued to implode as a whole family of similar superclusters appeared. The lights swirled together like plumes of dust in the wind, until the multitudes of clusters representing trillions of galaxies shrank down into fine grains of light. These, too, slipped away into bands of cosmic streams.

Finally the magnification ceased. The holographic display surrounded them, making Nellie feel as though they were no longer aboard a ship, but floating in the heart of a massive sacred space, two microscopic diatoms adrift in a handful of sea foam. Speechless, the two women held tightly to each other's hands.

Finally Hypatia spoke up again.

"So... this is where we come to the uttermost reaches of all things?"

"It is not. This is simply the limit of the observable universe."

"The *observable* universe? How much further must we go before the cosmos reaches its end?"

"There is no end."

"No end..." Hypatia echoed.

Concerned, Nellie unclasped a hand and reached up to touch her companion's shoulder. In turn, Hypatia looked at Nellie, eyes shining. Another tear ran down her cheek.

"Thank you for this."

Unable to speak, Nellie gently brushed away the tear. For a heartbeat the two women looked at each other, their hands still clasped. The moment stretched into an almost unbearably intimate silence, then Nellie broke eye contact and turned away, unable to put her thoughts into words, or even grasp what she was feeling.

"Look," she said softly, pointing to the window. Although it should have been hours before the dawn, the night was already fleeing and taking the stars away with it, undergoing a sea change from hard onyx to a velvety cerulean. "We must be approaching the Antarctic now," she said. "As I understand it, the sun will not set the entire time we are down there."

The two women sat quietly once more, still holding hands. Nellie turned back to her. "Are you alright?"

Sitting very still, Hypatia nodded, taking a deep breath.

"I'm not given to superstition, but it's just… I have the most terrible premonition that I'll never see another star again."

23

Approaching the Princess Ragnhild coastline, East Antarctica
Early morning
Eleven days after the Event

High waves and whitecaps cut across the Indian Ocean's desolate southernmost reaches, never-ending windstorms lashing the seas into a sailor's permanent nightmare. From time to time, the sky was rent by a distant flash.

"Do you think it's lightning?" Nellie asked hesitantly.

Hypatia shook her head. "No."

If she knew nothing of the Event's aftershocks, Nellie might've supposed it was only a trick of lightning, or perhaps some particularly spectacular form of St. Elmo's Fire—except that it ominously remained in place for far longer than any bolt of lightning could.

This was different, and she shuddered.

Eventually the raging seas gave way to the deep blue and increasingly iceberg-studded Southern Ocean. By the time the *Vanuatu* reached the coast of Antarctica, the sky had brightened into the full blaze of day.

All along the ice-sheet-girded coastline, towering slabs of white stood like frozen skyscrapers. Beyond those guardians that stood between land and sea, the continent lay blanketed in white. Further inland, long years of tenacious windblown snow had scoured the tops of glaciers, exposing hints of the ghostly blue ice below—the largest mass of ice on Earth.

The *Vanuatu* crossed the *Thorshavnfjella* mountains, skimming over the peaks, and continued deeper into Queen Maud Land, toward the bottom of the world.

Katabatic winds blowing out from the vast elevated ice sheets—sometimes at near hurricane strength—impaired their progress, and the dynamic energy wings of the *Vanuatu* continually flexed and reconfigured themselves like those of an eagle in a storm. Even at the ship's considerable cruising speed, it took hours to cross the massive continent.

Blake and Amber stood together at one of the windows in the commons, watching the landscape below. Amber had never seen Blake so relaxed—she suspected it was because he'd gotten a solid block of sleep, probably the first he'd had in days. Blake frowned at the irregular stretches of gigantic canyon lands.

"Looks bloody disjointed," he said.

Amber nodded. It was a subtle thing, but looking across the terrain, she could make out the icy mesas and plains forming gigantic puzzle pieces all the way to the horizon.

"This is all new, I think," she said. "Isn't that right, Ship?"

"That is correct. The multi-tiered topography is a result of the Event. There have been considerable geographic changes in the height and distribution of Antarctic ice sheets."

Cam came up to the window to join them. Amber immediately made room for him to stand between her and Blake.

"Isn't it beautiful?" she said.

Cam peered off in the distance. "Look there—can you see that dark patch?" he asked, pointing to it.

Blake shook his head. "You've got better eyes than me."

Amber stared, but couldn't see it, either. "Ship, can you give us a better look at what Cam's spotted?"

The window shimmered and then zoomed in to provide a close-up view. The three were surprised by the sight of a narrow green valley in the middle of all the ice. Sheltered by sheer frozen walls four kilometers high, there lay a prehistoric garden. Placid groups of duckbilled hadrosaurs milled about, casually eating the local vegetation.

"It's like *Jurassic Park* set in the Grand Canyon," Amber said.

The others in the commons stepped up to see the spectacle, staring in awe at the verdant landscape nestled impossibly in the Earth's most inhospitable landscape.

"Look! The dinosaurs must be coming from below the surface!" Harcourt suggested in wonder. "—from the hollow interior of the Earth itself…"

"I am sorry to disabuse you of this notion, Professor, but that hypothesis is incorrect and has long been refuted."

Harcourt let out a disappointed *harrumph.*

"Still," Blake said, "it's a wonder these monsters are still alive."

"How would they not freeze at night?" Kha-Hotep asked.

"It won't be night here for another six months," Nellie replied. "Do you suppose it's volcanism? Thermal springs of some sort?"

"Some clever Edgar Rice Burroughs setup, I'm sure," Blake agreed. "Whatever is sheltering them from the cold for now, I don't fancy their chances when nightfall returns—if the poor beasts even survive that long."

Their close-up view abruptly winked out. All the common room's starboard windows flared blindingly bright, then just as suddenly, went pitch black. The *Vanuatu* gave a quick but violent shake, provoking a shout of alarm from Harcourt.

"Optical filters engaged," the ship informed them. *"Stand by, viewscreen is automatically polarizing for safe viewing."*

The screen brightened again, but the view of the primeval garden had been replaced by a rippling moiré of light.

Amber frowned.

"Ship, can you zoom out, please?" Leila asked.

The ship reduced magnification at once, pulling back until they could all see a roaring aftershock to the starboard of the vessel, blazing away like a curtain of fire. They all stared at it, momentarily speechless.

"I'll never get used to seeing those things," Nellie said with a shudder.

Amber nodded, rubbing her arms. "Just the thought that, at any moment, one of those things can strike out of the blue…"

"No way to protect yourself, no way to run from it," Cam said.

"It's like war that way," Blake added. "As long as they're out there, you never know when your number will come up."

Kha-Hotep stared thoughtfully at the towering conflagration. "And they'll keep coming until they've ripped the whole world apart."

Just as abruptly as it came, the aftershock vanished again. Their altitude gave them an excellent view of the devastation it left behind. It had struck the green valley, the new shard long and wide enough to completely stamp out any trace of the previous one. And there was something distinctly wrong with the new one.

Hypatia squinted at the new arrival. "What *is* that?"

"It's created a new shard," Amber said, "but that *color*…" Against the surrounding ice, the entire shard resembled a blackened burn wound.

"Three days ago, I saw an aftershock hit the desert," Blake said, frowning. "The new shard was like somebody punched a mirror. It fractured everything caught inside, like chopped up bits reflected over and over. It was bloody strange. But this… I don't know what the hell this is."

"Give us another close-up, Ship," Amber said.

With the increased magnification, the bizarre new landscape

showed more of its colors. The darkest regions were actually a scarlet-purple so deep it was almost black, with the rest of the terrain varying in shades from beet-colored to blood red, with highlights of magenta and fuchsia. Strange pale blue-gray coral-like structures dotted the area, a cross between thornless cacti and anemones. A dinosaur-sized caterpillar-thing was grazing on them, its body a weird cross between a zebra-striped walrus and a rhinoceros beetle.

"It must have dropped a piece from another dimension, the way it did with Dee and János Mehta," Amber suggested. "Only who knows where *this* weird-ass one came from?"

"I wonder how many more there are like these?" Hypatia said quietly.

The *Vanuatu* continued on, leaving the alien oasis behind. Far beyond its passive sensor range, scores of other aftershocks erupted all across Antarctica, waves of them radiating out from the South Pole, in a chain reaction spreading across the planet.

"Attention," the ship announced. "We are approaching the Advanced Transpatial Physics Laboratory complex. Extreme cold-weather gear is available in the central corridor near the main exit. Goggles are recommended for any extra-vehicular transit."

Gazing out the forward window, the passengers could see the laboratory up ahead, a bright spot just starting to appear against the flat white plain that surrounded it, glittering with a swirling unearthly iridescence.

"It's beautiful." Leila stared at the view in awe.

"Indeed," Kha-Hotep said. "How like a diamond it gleams."

The impression increased as the ship drew nearer, but so did a sense of unease on the bridge.

"What's causing that strange glow around the station?" Blake asked.

Nellie stared dubiously. "Perhaps the Southern Lights?"

"Good lord," Harcourt exclaimed, "it's some sort of arctic storm!"

"What kind of storm does *that*?" Amber asked, pointing at the scene below.

As they came closer she could make out the gleaming dome of the station, and see that the building wasn't causing the eerie, swirling play of light. Some weird atmospheric phenomenon surrounded it—hard for her to sort out. At first glance it looked almost like a thick flock of birds, or a festival of kites, all circling the station.

No, the jumble of odd shapes was completely *en*circling the dome, from bottom to top, as if trapping it in a thick, dome-shaped shell. What *were* they? Were they alive, or just being blown around in some kind of extremely localized cyclone?

"Ship," Amber said, "bring the view of the station closer, please."

The ship complied, until the objects appeared to be more like floating crystalline fragments in a confusion of different colors. Some sort of giant Antarctic snowflakes? Whatever was causing the phenomenon, though, the shapes weren't being driven by the wind—their movements weren't uniform enough. The outermost ones barely moved at all, some simply hovering in place.

Deeper in, they rose and fell at whim, sometimes slow, sometimes fast, while directly above the station the dance became positively frenetic.

"Ship, what are we looking at?" Blake asked.

"This is the station. We are on final approach for touchdown."

"I can see that," he snapped. "I'm asking you what the bloody hell is that storm surrounding it."

"There are no adverse weather patterns in our immediate vicinity, apart from the expected cold—"

"Damn it, Ship! What is all that muck swirling about?"

"I'm sorry, I am uncertain what you are referring to." Before they could respond it said, *"Please prepare yourselves for landing."*

As the *Vanuatu* banked and began its descent toward the station's landing strip, the unease in the pit of Amber's stomach grew. She peered ahead intently, trying to make sense of what they were seeing.

"Ship, increase magnification, please."

The ship obliged, zooming in further and sweeping across the landing field. Whatever the storm was, their path to the landing strip would cut right through it.

Blake frowned. "Is the ship taking us—"

"Straight into that crap." Amber finished his sentence. *"Ship, pull up now!"*

"Brace for evasive maneuvers," the ship announced. Everyone held on desperately as the *Vanuatu* instantly flexed its hard-light energy wings wide and nosed up into an abrupt power climb, the repulsor lifts whining like banshees.

The sudden aerial maneuver worked. They narrowly skimmed over the top of the dome of bizarre satellites orbiting the station, close enough to see their individual shapes racing by below them. Amber had the *Vanuatu* circle into a new approach and make a gentle landing just meters away from the entrance to the station.

24

"Damn you, Ship!" Blake swore. "Are you telling me you *still* can't see all that bloody shite whirling around right *there in front of us*?"

"I apologize and am commencing a full sensor diagnostic now. I will keep you informed of any new developments."

Still fuming, Blake strode off to his quarters to grab one of the machine guns he had scrounged from the battlefield at Alexandria. Torn, he deliberated for a minute. He preferred the Sten gun, but found his stolen German Schmeisser the more reliable of the two, so he reluctantly chose that one instead. Mentally cursing the ship's programming that forbade it from creating weapons or ammunition, he grabbed the last of his ammo clips and joined the others suiting up in the central corridor.

His irritation faded somewhat when he saw the quality of the arctic gear provided by the ship, grabbing small items passed up by the others—a folding ice axe, a coil of ultra-light rappelling rope, flares. The rest of the group wasted no time bundling up—except Harcourt, who found it beneath his dignity.

"No, thank you," he sniffed. "I believe I will forbear from dressing up like a savage Esquimau." Evidently determined to persevere by dint of his indomitable Victorian will alone, he dusted off his top hat and fixed it smartly on his head while everyone else was busy slipping on big overboots and long parka dusters with shaggy fleece-lined hoods.

"I shall await you all at the station," he pronounced. The ship opened the hatch and a sudden blast of frigid air struck him like a giant slap from the Abominable Snowman.

"C-cl-close it!" he gasped, and the ship shut the door once again.

"Oh, for heaven's sake!" Nellie stamped a foot in exasperation. "We don't have time for all your fuss and bother." Blake couldn't have agreed more.

Harcourt hurriedly donned the arctic gear, but still refused to leave his beloved hat behind. Then the line of parka-clad travelers all plodded out like astronauts, down the ramp to the landing strip. Though it was the Antarctic summer, few of them had ever felt such bitter, pervasive cold.

Encumbered by their thick polar wear, everyone marched along as carefully as they could. The tarmac was solid enough, and by some magic of twenty-third-century engineering it remained clear of snow, but here and there treacherous icy patches threatened. The group cautiously approached the glassy, flying fragments that continuously circled around and over the station.

* * *

Again Amber thought most of the swirling objects looked something like giant snowflakes, albeit chunky three-dimensional ones, or perhaps shattered bits of candied glass. Whatever they were, it was hard to tell if they were solid or not. All of them appeared to be unique variations on a cluster of crystalline shards, but the pieces that made up each one seemed to shift and move around in place—were they drifting *through* one another? It was difficult to tell.

It also was tricky to focus on any one of the floating apparitions. Some undulated along, like heavily pixelated jellyfish. Others orbited like little sputniks, all glassy splinters and daggers in star shapes. The tiniest of all were little more than fireflies, diving and soaring off again. So many visual impressions—it was dizzying. Amber was mesmerized by the sight, in such a variety of sizes and shades of color, glittering in orbit between them and the station's high metal dome.

"Hypnotic, aren't they?" she said.

Leila nodded, and shivered. "But… *what* are they?"

"No idea." Amber shrugged, still staring in fascination. "I can't even tell if they're really there, or just some weird polar mirage."

"Me neither." Leila reached out a hand.

"Don't touch them!" Nellie called out sharply.

Leila jerked her hand back.

"Could they be artificial?" Blake mused out loud. "Some kind of defense mechanism for the station?"

Amber shook her head. "They seem too broken up for something man-made. It's like an asteroid belt, made up of scattered broken bits. Everything between us and the station is one continuous—" Amber paused, struggling to come up with the right word. "—shatterfield."

Cam nodded. "It's a good name, Shatterfield," he said. "These flying ghostlights look like broken shards of frost borne aloft in a dance by winter spirits." He closed his eyes for a moment and went silent. Amber knew him well enough to know he was praying to them in case they *were* spirits. Cam thought gods and spirits lurked in everything—and this time, she could see why.

She leaned forward slightly and stared at the dancing shimmers of color.

"What are you looking for?" Leila asked curiously.

"I thought I saw something…" Her voice trailed off. "Wait! There—can you see it?" She pointed, and Leila nodded.

The closest one drifting by seemed to have tantalizing images playing on the surfaces of its many facets—hints of hazy, ephemeral landscapes, like television screens tuned in to impressionist art.

Hypatia frowned at the flittering images. "Let us take care. Could there be something sinister lurking in them? Might they mean to draw us in to our doom, like siren songs for the eyes?" Kha-Hotep seemed disturbed by the idea, quickly touching his forehead, eyes, and heart.

"Stay close, everyone," Nellie cautioned. "I don't like these… what did you call them, Cam? Ghostlights. So let's not disturb them, eh?" No one objected to that.

"Well, whatever we are going to do, let's jolly well proceed with it, shall we?" Harcourt groused, his teeth chattering as he tried to conceal his shivering.

"Right." Blake stepped up and unslung his firearm. "I'll take point, then." Giving the strange lights a healthy berth, he entered the Shatterfield.

The others followed, single file. Though they tried to stay together, avoiding the passing ghostlights quickly had them spread out. The floating traffic made it difficult to keep the person ahead in sight. From the air the distance from landing strip to the station doors didn't look very far. Somehow entering the field had changed that, as though it were bigger on the inside than the outside.

At first, the only sounds were their own frosted exhalations, the soft crunch of their boots on the landing pad, and their heartbeats. Then came snatches of haunting, piping music, like the hint of some moaning phantom.

That cannot be real, Nellie thought. *A trick of the mind, or of the Antarctic wind*. It wasn't coming from the lights themselves— they moved in eerie silence, circling like sharks. She pulled back the hood on her parka to improve her peripheral vision. Immediately the cold bit into her ears, and she gasped with pain. Concerned, Hypatia turned to check in on her. They paused as a trio of lights floated by, then quickly slipped forward again.

* * *

Cam stuck close to Amber. They weaved their way past the deceptively placid carousel of flickering shapes, a constantly moving, confusing jumble that made it difficult to keep sight of the others.

A large, irregularly shaped ghostlight passed uncomfortably close, its surface boiling with movement. Amber would have sworn this time there really was something in there, watercolor suggestions of lava flowing over some volcanic tableau. They let it pass by and slipped through the gap.

Her sense of direction felt off.

"Cam? Are we still headed the right—"

Harcourt doffed his hat as a particularly fast-moving spikey star-shape dipped past his head and swooped up and away again. One of the more placid lights slowly drifted up toward Leila. She flinched with a little yelp, startled by the closeness.

"Are you alright?" Kha-Hotep said, coming to her side.

"No, it's okay," she replied, embarrassed. "It's just..." She dropped her voice to a whisper. "Are they *following* us? I almost think—"

She vanished.

"*Leila!*" Kha-Hotep shouted, lunging forward to grab for her, but she was already gone.

Then he was gone, too.

25

Blake wheeled at the sound of Kha's shout.

Nellie and Hypatia turned as well.

"You two keep going!" he said as he passed them. "I'll see what's wrong!" He ducked around the nonstop parade of moving obstacles and ran up to where Cam and Amber stood with Harcourt.

"What happened?" he asked. Amber turned to him, her face pale. Speechless, she pointed in horror to the interior of the ghostlight. In its hazy depths, he could make out the panicked figures of Leila and Kha-Hotep, tumbling away in slow motion as if falling horizontally through a long nightmare tunnel. In a matter of moments, their struggling shapes dwindled away into the dark, and disappeared from sight.

"*What the devil?*" Blake murmured, fighting to rein in his own fear. "Did anybody see what happened?" The others shook their heads.

"How on earth could they have got *in* there?" Harcourt exclaimed in disbelief.

"We have to save them!" Cam said. "Quick, break it open with the axe!" "*No!*" Amber cried out. "How do we know that won't just kill them?"

Blake grabbed the young Celt before he could hurl himself after them.

"Hold up!" Blake barked. "All of you, step back!" Pulling a flare from his belt, he lit it with a quick twist, and tossed it underhand at the crystalline shape. The flare vanished on contact, but then they could see it deep inside, its brilliant red beacon still shining like a star. As it spun away from them, the view made it seem as though he was looking downward, watching it fall into a deep limestone cavern.

Or a monstrous throat.

As if pleased by this offering, the ghostlight abruptly changed its shape and color. It seemed to twist and fold in on itself, unfolding again in a different arrangement of glassy projections. At the same time it underwent a rapid shift through the spectrum of jewel tones, fluttering from a dark, bruised shade of blue-black to a ruby-toned red to verdant tourmaline to citrine.

"Ghastly... simply ghastly." Harcourt shuddered. "To be lost forever in such a way."

"We don't know that!" Amber snapped.

"*What's happening back there?*" Nellie shouted from far ahead of them. "*Is everything alright?*"

"Stay there!" Amber yelled back. "Keep away from the

lights!" She turned to Blake. "We've got to do *something*."

"What do you think we can do?" he shouted.

She glared at him, but then softened her tone.

"We're not going to just leave them in there."

He scowled and swiped his chin, trying to think.

"Give me your rope," Cam said. "I'll go in there after them."

"*No!*" Blake and Amber said simultaneously. Then Blake gave a sharp nod.

"Right. We'll do this, but we're going to do it the right way." He unsnapped the rope from off his belt and quickly knotted one end. "Come here, Cam," he said. "You'll be the anchor. You too, Harcourt." He wrapped the loop around Cam's waist, then commandeered the unenthusiastic professor into service, hitching him up as well. That done, he snapped open his ice axe and tied off the other end to the ring on its handle. *Hope this rope reaches all the way down to the end*, he thought. *If there is an end.*

"Alright then, you two hold tight. Amber, you watch out for any more of these things and give a shout if they come too close. Now give me some room."

Here goes nothing. Gently cradling the remaining coil of the rope in his left hand, he let slip a few feet of the axe end. Then, like a cowboy with a lasso, he swung the axe around a few times to build a little centrifugal force, and then, with careful timing, released the rope at just the right moment to send the axe flying straight through the heart of the ghostlight.

All three men vanished instantly.

Amber screamed as the three plunged away down the tunnel.

* * *

"Amber!" Nellie's voice came from somewhere unseen. "Stay where you are! We're coming to get you!"

Amber looked around, but she no longer knew which way to go—every direction was a dizzying, kaleidoscopic swarm of the ever-shifting lights. Wiping her eyes, she pulled herself up, just in time to sidestep what might be certain death.

"Nellie? Where are you?" she cried out. "Stay where you are!" She didn't want to get them killed. "Nellie?" she called out again. "Hypatia?" No answer. A growing dread clutched her.

"We see you!" Hypatia's voice rang out. "Stay where you are!"

She turned toward where she thought the voice came from, spotting Nellie and Hypatia. They had doubled back to get her. The wave of relief was so intense Amber thought she might faint.

They stood, poised for the next break through a gap. Hypatia grabbed Nellie's arm, pulling her to the side as a pack of hand-sized ghostlights rained down on them from above before swinging back up and away again. Ducking, the two women ran for a few more feet before straightening up again.

"I see you two," Amber called. "It's too dangerous— Stay there, and I'll come to you!"

They waved in agreement. Amber looked both ways, then sprinted to make sure her path was clear before jogging toward them. She stopped short when she saw the big ghostlight slipping behind them at an angle.

"Look out!"

Nellie took a step back.

"No!" Amber screamed. "The other way!"

Neither Nellie nor Hypatia saw the blue-tinged shape come up behind them. Amber watched in horror as they vanished into the rippling surface.

This can't be happening, Amber thought. *I want to wake up*. After all the destruction, all the madness, she'd kept her sanity because she'd had companions she trusted. Now, though... If any chance remained to save the world, she was the only one who could do it.

Without warning, a shape reminiscent of a gently spinning buzz saw glided past, so dangerously close she had to instantly jerk her elbow to avoid its surface. She screamed, flinching away so suddenly she nearly pushed herself into another ghostlight behind her. Tension ratcheted through her until it felt as if her nerves were on fire.

Get it together, she ordered herself. *Hug the ground and inch your body the whole way if you have to. Just get to the other side*. She hunkered down and tried to get her bearings. If she could just spot the station's dome...

There it was, but still so far away.

Facing the right direction, she bided her time, waiting for a break in the closest line to move a little closer. Slowly, inexorably, she continued forward. Just three, maybe four more layers of them and she would be home free. Once she reached the station she could figure out what came next...

I have no idea what comes next.

She pushed the thought away. That was the future, this was the present. Standing again, she moved as quickly as she could in her bulky parka and boots, slipping between two more undulating lava lamp clumps of flowing crystals. Then she sidestepped the next, but missed a different one angling up in her peripheral vision.

At the last possible instant, she turned to see the tiniest of fairy lights come softly spirally down to land on her cheek like a butterfly.

She was swallowed without a sound.

26

Blake lifted his head off the ground and touched his cheek, picking off a crushed piece of fern. Pushing his body up, he found himself on the damp carpet of a forest floor.

"Bugger me," he muttered. *What just happened?* He was on the tarmac in Antarctica, and then… falling? Felt more like being pulled like taffy through… what? He stood and brushed himself off, automatically taking stock of the situation. No sign of the rope or ice axe or—*Goddamnit!*—the Schmeisser he had slung over his shoulder. God only knew where any of them were now.

So much for that.

Cam and Harcourt lay dazed among the undergrowth a few feet away. Both were alive.

"*Kych-an-broc,*" Cam groaned, holding his forehead. Blake raised an eyebrow as his linguistic implant translated the Celtic phrase.

"Do what now?"

"Don't worry. It's just something we say."

Blake and Cam peeled off their parkas and overshoes. The professor stayed sprawled on his back, eyelids gently fluttering. Like a faithful dog, his top hat lay where it fell, close to his head amid the ferns and bracken.

"Did you see where we came through?" Blake asked.

Cam shook his head.

"I only remember tumbling to the ground, through no doorway but the air." Warily he walked a few steps, peering here and there, looking for the invisible portal. Patches of mist hung in the air—nothing but the maples and oaks ringed their little clearing.

"Amber!" he shouted, cupping his hands around his mouth. "Amber, where are you?"

No response. Blake stood and walked over to the professor, nudging the prone figure with his boot. Harcourt groaned, putting a hand over his eyes.

"Leave me alone, you contemptible blackguard," he whined. "I've been transmogrified."

"No time for whining," Blake retorted. "We need to locate the Egyptian and the girl, and then find a way to get back to the others." He peered around the clearing again. *Assuming we can get back.*

"Kha-Hotep!" he called out, his shout echoing off of the trees. "Leila!" The growth was thick, the trees tall and old.

Cam and Harcourt joined in as well, but the only answer was the booming hunting call of some oversized carnivore.

Blake smacked a tree trunk with his palm.

"Damn it, how far could they have gone in just a couple of minutes?" He swore quietly to himself. "Right. Come here, you two. See if my machine gun landed around here somewhere." The trio took a minute to scour the little clearing, without any luck. Then, kneeling down near their abandoned coats, Cam pulled something from the leaves and undergrowth.

"Blake," he said quietly. He lifted the burnt-out flare. The little tube was pitted and degraded, and covered in lichen. Beneath where it had been lying, woodlice scurried in the bare patch. The three men stared at the crumbled relic in silence.

"We can't worry about that now," Blake said firmly. "Let's find those two, and bring them back here on the double."

Cam and Harcourt looked dubious, but neither said anything—there was nothing they *could* say. They left their parkas to mark where they had been, and set off through the only clear break in the tree line. Just a few paces through, they found a much larger clearing, its floor made of cracked pavement stones colonized by opportunistic grass.

"*Nev Kawgh*," Cam said.

"Indeed," Harcourt agreed.

An immense figure stood above them, a beautiful winged woman, nude but for a loose drape around her loins and legs, arms bent in an artful, beckoning pose as she gazed off to one side. Even in stone she exuded grace and movement, guarding a gatehouse flanked by huge columns. Bas-relief friezes decorated its walls, dripping with a riot of sinuous vines and moss. The vegetation was thick, preventing them from seeing anything beyond. Both the gatehouse and columns were crowned with dotted cornices and capped by spherical finials, like chess pieces.

Swanlike figures swirled around their bases.

At about ten times the height of a man, the woman stood in the center of the grand entrance, splitting it in two. Her spread wings formed a perfect arc, framing the entryway. Stylized carved beams radiated out from behind her. A heavenly cloud bore a single word.

CREATION

"What goddess is that?" Cam asked in hushed tones. "We should not trespass without offering our respects."

"It's only an angel," Blake replied. "They just work for God."

"Where and when do you suppose this curious citadel came from?" Harcourt stared up. "A sign in English, but inscribed on the walls of an ancient castle? High Medieval, or is it early Renaissance—"

"Harcourt," Blake cut in, "did you hear that?"

"Hear what?"

"Exactly." Blake mimed a lock sign over his mouth. Harcourt started to issue an indignant retort, but was interrupted by the distant roar of something reptilian, large, and hungry. The professor kept his tongue and the three men entered the ruins.

Beyond the gatehouse there was no fortress citadel—only

a cavernous tunnel largely hidden by the jungle. An enticing light shone from somewhere in its depths.

"Kha-Hotep?" Blake called. "Leila?"

No response.

They entered the tunnel and it curved down, plunging them in semi-darkness. As they proceeded, Blake ran a hand over the cave wall. It wasn't rock, but plaster cleverly painted to resemble a cave. After a few twists and turns the tunnel ended abruptly in rubble—real rubble, not *faux*—followed by more trees that let in dappled sunlight.

Ahead was more cracked and crumbling pavement for them to follow—what appeared to have once been a wide thoroughfare. Buildings had once lined both sides, but the forest had reclaimed them so thoroughly that only traces survived. Wherever the shard had originated, there was no sign of its boundary.

What few buildings remained were bizarrely mismatched. Poking through the oaks and maples to the left, there was an ornate multi-tiered Chinese gate in red and gold—replete with dragons and auspicious good-luck symbols. Not far from it stood the bastioned ramparts and towers of a Norman castle. A huge oak effectively blocked its entrance.

Continuing onward, they reached the tree line and stepped into an open area. They had emerged into the heart of a lost city.

At first glance, it appeared as though they had stumbled upon a scenic avenue that ran along a grand lagoon, hundreds of feet across. Canals branched out and streamed under graceful stone bridges, still standing despite the best efforts of the flowering ivy to conquer them.

On either bank of the water lay tree-lined walkways—once idyllic parks now overgrown and wild. Across the lagoon lay ruins, in a mishmash of classical styles—huge Roman columns, golden Byzantine domes, slender Gothic spires, and more. The foliage had turned every building into a hanging garden.

"Every structure rivals Westminster Palace," Harcourt exclaimed. "Perhaps we've discovered a lost city of antiquity. It's remarkable!"

"Truly remarkable, given that they've developed radio," Blake said, pointing to an old-style wireless telegraph tower. "Come on, we need to go back. No time for treasure-hunting— we've got to find Kha-Hotep and Leila, then find a way back to Antarctica, double time."

"Could that be them?" Cam nodded toward a thin curl of smoke coming from one of the buildings.

Blake shrugged. "Let's find out."

From the cover of the trees, keen eyes spied on the newcomers. The scout—coyote-thin and grim-faced—turned to the others concealed deeper in the forest. He gave two sharp bird whistles, and held up three fingers.

They grabbed their weapons.

27

The Street of *Thaumaturgi*, Alexandria
1130 *Ab urbe condita* (AD 367)

In a less-reputable corner of the Rhakotis district, mystics, fortune-tellers, and dabblers in petty necromancy plied their trade. Theon, father to a young girl named Hypatia, despised such superstition, and forbade her to ever set foot there.

So of course she did.

Slipping away from the slaves assigned to watch over her, she approached a forgotten shrine that lay at the crossroads of two alleys, and found a wizened old woman haunting the doorway. One cataract-beset eye glared a baleful white like the full moon, the other gleamed black and eager as a crow's eye. The ancient witch frightened her, but something in the crone's beckoning finger made the girl screw up her courage and enter.

The shrine was very small, and they sat together on a thick black camelhide. In the sputtering light of a few seashells turned into oil lamps, cabalistic symbols trembled on the walls. The old woman meticulously cast pinches of salt to the four corners *of the tiny room, and spat three times.*

"What would your young Ladyship have?" she asked, holding out her palm to be crossed with silver. "The name of your true love? A cure to whatever malady might vex you? To speak with a shade of the dead?"

Hypatia drew herself up. This was base superstition indeed. She knew the soul was immortal, and upon death of the body, the purest ones would ascend to the higher planes, ultimately returning to the One—the source of goodness and beauty from which all things derived. Lesser souls would be purified and descend again, to be reborn in a new body.

"What do you know of the dead?" She meant it as a challenge, but the crone answered.

"Much indeed do I know, ever since Hecate sent a spider to crawl into my ear and whisper her ineffable wisdom. Sit, and I shall tell you of the di inferi, *those who dwell below—of the chthonic ghost-gods, and the* Erinyes, *the Furies that take vengeance on the spirits of men."*

Curious in spite of herself, Hypatia kept her silence and listened to the white-haired woman's rhythmic, almost musical, speech.

"Five are the rivers encircling Hades. You know the Styx, where all must pay Charon his obal ere they cross. Phlegethon, the blood-river of fire that boils souls, and Lethe, the waters of forgetfulness that drown all thought and memory. Cocytus, the black river of lamentation, flows into the river Acheron, the river of woe.

"Now, the souls of men, if they are good, become Lares *in Elysium, or linger in Hades as* Manes *if even the Fates cannot decree whether they deserve well or ill. But woe betide them that die without proper*

burial, for having neglected the sacred rites, they doom themselves to become Lemures, dark and formless shades vagrant and vengeful, wandering ever-lost and insatiate upon the black earth."

The old woman leaned in, and her whispered words made the girl's skin crawl.

"Yet worse still are those wicked souls consigned to the depths of Tartarus, sunken as far beneath Hades as Heaven lies above the earth. There the damned take on the form of Larvae, their bodies becoming that of great, wriggling maggots, still wearing their own wretched human faces. The stinking pit writhes, rotten as a corpse, crawling with these foul abominations—the worms of the earth, twisting in unceasing torment, naught but food and playthings for the Erinyes and other dark unspeakable horrors.

Ever and ever does their gibbering spite and anguish echo through eternity…"

Bright white became blue-black in an instant, as open arctic brilliance changed to blind night, subterranean and close. In the dark, it took a moment for Hypatia to realize her eyes were open.

Though she could see nothing, her other senses were under assault. The roar of a thousand groaning, keening inhuman voices buffeted her ears, and a mix of sulfur and some horrid animal stench filled her nose and mouth. Her eyes watered and she wanted to retch.

Where was Nellie?

Where am I?

Pain along her forearms and knees told her she must fallen forward onto a rough stone surface, though she had no memory of the harsh landing. Picking herself up, she came to her hands and knees and reached out for her companion. Her mittened hand fell upon something, but it scuttled away beneath her touch.

"Nellie? Where are you?"

The sound of her own voice was lost, drowned out by the cacophony. How many were here with her? Hundreds?

"Nellie!" She called out again and again, terrified that she might be alone in here with—who? What? Turning around in the dark, she had no sense direction, but slowly realized that the gloom was not complete. Her eyes began to adjust to the darkness. Teasing, uncertain hints of shape and movement began to take forms she recognized—and she almost wished for blindness.

Everywhere, the ground seethed with squirming, man-sized shapes, howling their agony and outrage. Cold, unreasonable terror penetrated her at the sight. This had to be the Underworld, the black abyss, and the undead, quasi-human *Larvae*.

Tartarus.

The hell of her nightmares, come to life.

Hypatia screamed.

As far as she could see in the dismal murk, the wriggling forms surrounded her, glaring and howling. The stinking air made her fight to keep from vomiting. Trapped with the loathsome creatures—Éleos *tou* Énós! Was she about to transform into one of them herself? *Oímoi!* Her head spun. Suddenly unsteady on her feet, she felt herself slipping back into unconsciousness.

Something lunged out of the darkness and grabbed hold of her. She felt the fat coils of a *Larva*'s body, pulsating maggot-skin dripping with grave rot, caught a glimpse of a horrible demi-human face screaming unintelligibly at her. Shrieking, she recoiled and tried to escape its grasp, but couldn't.

And then it spoke.

"Hypatia!" Nellie said, holding her tight. "It's alright, it's me, it's me!"

The hideous image, conjured by Hypatia's terrified imagination, vanished in an instant, to her palpable relief. She gasped, unable to talk, clinging to Nellie like a drowning victim to a bit of flotsam.

"We—we are..." She couldn't finish. The thought was too ridiculous, and too terrible. *We are damned to Tartarus.* The agitated bodies of the *Larvae* squirmed all around them.

"We're alright," Nellie soothed her, stroking her head. "Come with me. I'll get you out."

"There *is* a way out?" Hypatia's voice seemed small, like the child she no longer was.

"Of course there is. Let's go." Slipping an arm around her waist, Nellie helped Hypatia to her feet, walking her toward a dim silver-blue illumination.

"But the abyss... the *Larvae*..." Hypatia's voice trailed off. Things were becoming clearer with each step. The reek of sulfur, fish, and sea rot gave way to fresher air, bitingly cold.

She was glad for the parka and gloves.

"Look, it's only a cave, see?"

Slowly the terror faded. No demonic worms swarmed around them, only a colony of indignant speckled gray seals, barking in alarm as they humped out of their way. Hypatia leaned her head against Nellie's shoulder as they proceeded forward. The two stepped out of the cave's wide mouth into welcome starlight, a sight that made Hypatia smile.

The universe made sense again.

Hypatia and Nellie found a place to sit overlooking the rocky shoreline. Covering the horizon to the south, the ocean lapped at the jumble of boulders, jagged on the seaward side. Behind their rocky perch, the land stretched away up into forested mountain country, snow visible on the trees even in the night. Tendrils of cloud and mist tangled their way down the mountains to the sea, and the cold air tickled their nostrils.

They began to assess their options.

"Do you think we can go back the way we came?" Nellie asked.

"I don't know," Hypatia replied, "but we should wait until first light to try." Until then, however, they had to survive the bitter cold night. Hypatia looked back at the cave, still echoing with the howls of agitated seals, and hoped they could find a better shelter.

"Where do you suppose we are?" Nellie asked her. Grateful for something practical on which to focus, Hypatia leaned back for a better look at the panorama of sky above them, and pointed out one solitary point of white gold.

"That one is the polar star, *Cynosura*, the tentpole of the heavens. Were we at the North Pole, it would be directly above us. If at the equator, it would rest upon the horizon." She pulled off her mittens and stretched out her right hand. "I would that I had my astrolabe with me, but failing that, we can improvise. The span from the tip of my thumb to the tip of my littlest finger is very nearly twenty-five degrees. So then…"

Hypatia measured the distance from horizon to star, starting with thumb-to-pinky, then added a bull's head made with her other index and little fingers. "Adding another fifteen degrees…" She stacked the width of her little finger three more times. "… and one, and one, and not quite one more. So our line of latitude is a little less than forty-three degrees parallel north—or reasonably close to there." She blew on her already-chilling hands and quickly slipped them back into her mittens.

"Bravo!" Nellie clapped, the sound muffled by her own mittens. "So where do *you* suppose we are?"

"Barbarian territory, I fear," Hypatia replied thoughtfully. "Perhaps in the lands of the Franks or the Ostrogoths? The sea is to our south, so perhaps we are upon the north shore of the Tyrrhenian, or the Aegean. Or perhaps in Taurica?"

Nellie raised her eyebrows.

"The land of the Bulgars," Hypatia clarified. "Across the Euxine Sea from Pontus."

Nellie could only shrug. "Well, I've heard of the Aegean Sea, anyway. From all the mountains and forest, I supposed we might be in the New World. Canada, perhaps. Maybe British Columbia, above Puget Sound, or somewhere above the Great Lakes."

It was Hypatia's turn to shrug.

"This much I *can* tell you," she said, pointing to the sky again. "Those stars, there? That is Aries the golden-fleeced ram, rising. So then, the sun is in Libra."

"What does that mean?"

"This morning at the South Pole, it was the thirteen of February. Now we are at some time in November."

Nellie mulled that over. "I wonder how many Novembers in the future we've come," she said. "Or... but surely we couldn't have been dropped into the past, could we?" Nellie thought of Leila and Kha-Hotep, and the rest of them, all snatched up and flung away to lord-only-knew where and when. She flashed on her last sight of Amber, terrified and stranded all alone in the sinister swirl of ghostlights.

"If that's the case," she murmured, "how will any of us ever get back?"

A tremendous roar answered her, startling them both. They jumped as a superhumanly deep, booming voice came echoing down from the mountains, howling out a stream of raucous laughter. Ducking down behind the boulders to hide, they peered into the gloom to look for the source of the sound.

Nothing. Only forest and mist.

Nellie turned to Hypatia.

"Perhaps the cave wouldn't be such an awful place to spend the night, after all."

28

Trekking over the crumbling pavement along the canal bank, Blake, Cam, and Harcourt could feel the ghostly echo of what was once a delightful place for leisurely strolling to and from the stately buildings—now ruins. They passed statues, benches, and lampposts along the canals, all camouflaged by years of rampant plant growth. The walkways seemed more like trails through a riverine canyon.

The smoke Cam had spotted still lay ahead, and they followed the canal until it veered away at a right angle. At the juncture, fixed atop a high pedestal, stood another statue, this one of a warrior-king in chain mail holding a sword aloft, his surcoat decorated with crosses and *fleur-de-lis*. The statue had been vandalized: a crude, blackened skull design masked the white marble of the regal face, matched by a black horse skull painted on his mount.

A series of twisted glyphs, frightening and primitive,

had been painted on his chest and cape, and on his mount's caparison. Vines, lichen, and moss had colonized the pedestal, but the inscription was still partly visible.

VRCHAS
XPOSITIO
T. LOVIS

CENTENNIAL
– 1904 –

"Who is that rider supposed to be?" Harcourt asked, undisguised disapproval in his tone. "Charlemagne? Bloody vandals."

"*Andraste and Camulos*," Cam murmured, staring up with a look of dread. A human skull, with a collar of red and black feathers, was impaled on the upraised sword. The victim's spine was still attached to the skull, and the spines of other victims had been lashed to it with sinew, forming a long serpentine chain that coiled down and around the king's arm and body.

"Barbaric devilry," Harcourt muttered.

"You alright?" Blake put a hand on Cam's shoulder, making him flinch.

The Celt nodded wordlessly.

As they regarded the grisly display, Blake was all too aware that they had no weapons. He calculated the odds of them finding Kha-Hotep and Leila, and for any of them getting out of this place alive. Making up his mind, he nodded and pulled the other two in for a quick huddle.

"Here's the plan," he said, keeping his voice low. "We're going to check out the source of that smoke. We slip in, we slip out. If Kha-Hotep and Leila aren't there, we go back to our starting point and wait. For now, keep an eye out, and let's hope the building isn't the HQ for some bloody tribe that made this welcome sign."

Cam and Harcourt nodded.

"And Harcourt?" Blake added.

"Yes?"

"You'll keep quiet, or you'll wait here for us. Your choice."

The professor swallowed, then gave a quick salute.

"Quiet as a church mouse in cheesecloth."

Reaching a clearing, the three paused and scanned for sentries. A trio of tall, palatial buildings stood before them. The rectangular courtyard they enclosed might have once been a sunken garden, but more forest had sprung up there.

A few hundred meters away, the thin line of smoke they'd followed still trailed fitfully skyward, coming from somewhere in a grand temple-like structure to their right. Ivy-bound pillars and classical statuary covered its sides, and a pair of colossal obelisks stood at the entrance, tall enough to dwarf the rest of the facade.

Blake went first, cutting through the sunken forest and then slipping across between the obelisks to the broad entryway.

Cam came close behind, silent in his soft deerskin boots. They both cringed as Harcourt crashed out of the trees with coattails flapping, one hand securing his top hat. Loudly snapping twigs underfoot with every step, he panted for breath.

Glaring at him, Blake turned and peered around the corner. Dust-blown outer walkways stretched off to the left and right, empty except for leaves and weeds. Straight ahead, the main entrance hall led them up to enormous twin doors. They stood slightly ajar, held in place by vines and other growth.

Approaching the gap, Blake peered into the gloom. Skylights and long windows, all but obscured by dirt and vegetation, let in slanting, fitful spears of light, making visibility unreliable at best. The chamber was huge, like an aircraft hangar, easily big enough to fit three or four football pitches. Tall shapes with sinister contours loomed in the shadows.

He listened carefully for sounds of human activity, but heard only vague, ambient noise. Waving the other two forward, he stepped inside. The dim light revealed a network of steel girders crisscrossing the ceiling and, closer at hand, a large wooden plaque stretched overhead, boasting flaking gold letters:

PALACE OF MINES AND METALLURGY

The place was a labyrinth of displays and exhibits from around the world, devoted to aspects of geology and mining. In the hazy light from outside, he caught glimpses everywhere of statues, flags, decorative banners, gem and mineral showcases, models, equipment, maps, and a thousand informative displays.

"We should make torches," Cam said, eyeing the cloth banners and wooden poles.

"No need for that," Blake replied, approaching a display of mining equipment. He gave some of the lanterns an experimental shake. "These will do us just fine."

Armed with working lights, the men moved further into the maze. Many of the exhibits were in shambles, although some barely seemed disturbed at all, and none appeared to have been looted. The debris on the floor seemed to have been heavily trampled, though, as if some sort of steamroller had wound a twisted path through the interior.

Climbing to a raised section designed to evoke the deck of a battleship, they passed under heavy steel gun turrets, going past smaller field cannon and stacked pyramids of cannonballs.

Nearer to the center of the vast exhibition hall, rising well over fifty feet high, an iron statue of Vulcan stood at his forge, hammer in one hand, the other holding a spearhead raised to the heavens. They passed him, walking by elegant sculptures of onyx and copper, and elaborate life-sized dioramas of the mining techniques from the California Gold Rush, complete with antique tools. They stopped when they reached an unusual pair of statues.

The first was a giant slab of what looked to be salt crystal, roughly carved into the shape of a fleeing woman wrapped in a shawl, face turned to look back the way she came. There was a placard at her feet.

LOT'S WIFE

In an inspired arrangement, she faced a demonic figure standing with crossed arms, four times her size, a bright yellow column sculpted into the leering visage of a devil. The sign for this one declared it to be "a monument to Mephistopheles," made of twenty-four hundred pounds of sulfur. Its acrid brimstone reek left a dry, noxious taste in the mouth.

Harcourt pulled out his handkerchief and tried to stifle a wheezing, choking fit.

"*Nev Kawgh...*" Cam exclaimed softly.

"You've got that right," Blake agreed.

A drawn-out rustling sound echoed through the building, adding to the uneasy feeling that they were in some dingy carnival's haunted house. The trio quickly moved on, past the battered remains of exhibits from Hungary, Peru, Japan, and Australia, before they caught a glimpse of the orange glow of an open flame, flickering from the cracks in a concealing makeshift shelter.

"Kha?" Cam pitched his voice low. "Leila?" Blake stopped him with a light touch to his shoulder, stepping carefully around the debris.

"It's clear."

Someone had assembled a modest fire, recent enough that its untended embers were still lit. The traveler or travelers had tried to jerry-rig a concealing shelter using tabletops and other scavenged bric-a-brac.

"Do you think it was their doing?" Cam asked Blake, who shrugged.

"No way to know, but if it was, where are they now?"

From the shadows behind them, they heard the crunch of breaking wood, and turned their lantern beams in time to catch furtive movement underneath a lean-to formed by a collapsed tabletop, as though a large man in black was crouching to sneak up on them.

"Who's there?" Blake called harshly.

The figure didn't respond, silently slipping out from under the table to reveal a head the size of a steam shovel.

It wasn't a man in black—it was a giant snake.

29

The sea cave proved its worth as a shelter from the frosty weather outside. Though it stank and was crowded with barking seals and scuttling trilobites, the women were able to stake out a little spot along a side wall to lie down together, bundled up in their parkas.

Whether from all the combined mammalian body heat, or whatever twenty-third-century magic the *Vanuatu* had used to create their polar gear, Nellie was thankful for the warmth. After a time, the seals settled down and it became quiet enough for them to try to sleep.

Between watching for any sign of the mysterious laughing phantom, and anxiously hoping the portal would open again, Nellie found sleep impossible.

Even after the star-studded blackness of the cave mouth washed away into a crisp sky blue, she still lay there, watching

Hypatia sleep, her features framed by the fur-lined hood of the parka. Nellie passed the time noting the ways the diffuse dawn light slowly played across the soft contours of her companion's serene face.

How beautiful she was, Nellie thought. She felt a little strange, allowing herself to entertain such a fascination for an older woman. There was no harm in it, of course. After all, anyone with eyes could see how objectively lovely Hypatia was. Nellie marveled at how strongly her keen intelligence and her kindness shone through her innocent features. She—

Hypatia opened her eyes.

Nellie froze, embarrassed—though she couldn't say why, exactly. But Hypatia only smiled, putting her at ease again.

"Good morning."

"Is it?" Nellie responded with a cheeky little smile. Hypatia sat up, taking in the recumbent crowd of seals.

"May I assume that no malevolent spirits came by in the night?"

"None dared try get past me, or our army of gallant defenders."

Hypatia laughed. "And we did not freeze to death in our sleep."

"All true."

"Then I declare it a very good morning indeed."

Together they decided the first order of business was to locate the portal that had dropped them there. Stepping carefully around the sometimes-indignant seals, they studied their surroundings, and found only damp and slimy cavern walls.

Nellie didn't express out loud what they both were surely thinking—that they were losing precious time. That they might be stranded forever. That they would die here. She stopped and pressed a hand against the cold limestone. Closing her eyes, she tried to reach out with her mind, the way Amber had.

Amber, can you hear me?

There was no response.

"Nellie? Are you praying?"

Nellie opened her eyes again and explained, so Hypatia joined her efforts. However, after a few minutes without a response, they agreed to go out in search of breakfast.

In daylight the features of the landscape became clear. One small strand of sandy beach opened to the sea. The rest of the coast was taken up by tumbled mounds of boulders and sandstone cliffs slanting down from the forested heights above. Cliques of seals had already staked out prime sunbathing spots on the sand. Overhead a sea eagle circled, screeching at an unhurried line of passing pterodactyls.

They scrambled over the rocky tidal pools. Nellie pointed down to the small shapes moving among the shadows, trilobites, crustaceans, and tiny fish.

"Do you like crab?" she asked. "I'd wager we can catch some of these little ones."

Hypatia shook her head. "Let us not eat animals. The writings of our fathers Plato and Porphyry offer many proofs of the impropriety of killing living beings for food."

"Oh," Nellie said. She hadn't expected that particular response. "What about mussels and clams? Surely they're low enough not to warrant any fuss and bother."

"They know enough to cling tight to the rocks."

"True enough, I suppose. But…" She was out of logic. "How are we to survive out here otherwise?"

Hypatia smiled. "If we must become beasts ourselves to live, so be it, but first let us see if there is kelp or seaweed to sustain us."

Nellie nodded glumly, still eyeing the fat little trilobites while Hypatia began to climb down across the tumble of rocks and boulders. She drew closer to the water's edge, where the white surf splashed over the green mossy stones.

There was a long shape in the water.

"Hypatia…?"

The other woman halted and looked back inquiringly. Nellie pointed to the serpentine form gliding through the surf just as it broke the surface, arching up on a neck as tall as a New York streetlight, the jaws of its giant head—both snakelike and sharklike—wide open and lined with a thick fringe of sharp white teeth.

It plunged downward with blinding speed.

"*Hypatia!*" Nellie screamed.

The beast's teeth clamped down, plucking its prey off the ground and lifting back up to rend the body apart with a few crunches of its massive jaws, then swallowing the bloody remains down. Hypatia was gone. The surf churned bright crimson, staining the foam.

Nellie stood frozen in place, staring at the carnage. Hungry for more, the beast pulled itself up closer to the beach, hauling its gargantuan body with powerful rectangular flippers. It arched up again, stretching open its jaws for a new attack.

"Nellie! Get down!"

But she could only stand there, numb with disbelief.

All the seals on the beach were in a full panic, barking in terror and squirming away in all directions like caterpillars. The beast snapped its head down again, striking out to snatch up a nearby seal trying to escape. Nellie watched in a daze as it craned its neck to snatch a third victim, looking around for fresh prey even as it swallowed the previous one.

It turned toward Nellie.

"Nellie!"

Hypatia? Like waking from a bad dream, Nellie saw Hypatia, still alive, huddled among the rocks. *It didn't kill her, it was just a seal. Still alive. Still alive.* Slowly coming out of her daze, Nellie looked up to see the dinosaur turning its attention on her. *It's the Loch Ness Monster*, she thought as the creature rose up, again opening its wide maw.

"Nellie!" Hypatia screamed a third time.

There was no time to think as the monster struck her. Nothing but sheer instinct and adrenaline stirred her muscles to twist and dive just as the monster came crashing down, jaws snapping on air instead of flesh. Throwing her body to the side, she dove headfirst into the stand of boulders. She landed hard on her arm and shoulder in the gap between the rocks, with only dumb luck and the padding of her arctic wear to protect her.

The monster was on her again.

A row of blood-stained Bowie-knife teeth snapped away at her, slaughterhouse breath blasting at her like a bellows as the enraged dinosaur tried again and again to force its way into the rocky crevice. It struggled to haul up its body closer on the rocks, looking for a better angle. Hypatia screamed again, and the monster reared its head back for another strike.

Nellie's world narrowed to a view of the mottled throat and grisly rows of teeth coming for her. The beast screamed out a deafening prehistoric roar that shook her bones and turned her stomach to jelly. Then its serpentine neck jerked back at an unnatural angle—

She wasn't dead.

The monster was moving *backward*.

She scrambled to her feet and looked down toward the shore. What looked like a locomotive-sized killer whale had clamped its own toothy jaws on the dinosaur's tail. The first monster flailed madly, trying in vain to bite back at its attacker, but this only allowed the newcomer to get a grip on its long sinuous neck. Huge flippers beat the air uselessly as the bigger predator hauled it back down into the dark blood-drenched sea.

For long moments, the only sound was that of the surf. Then Hypatia appeared at the crevice and helped Nellie out of it, hurrying the shell-shocked woman away from the shore as quickly as possible.

"That's it, keep going," Hypatia said. "We'll look for food and fresh water up in the forest."

30

Inside the Palace of Mines and Metallurgy, the snake's jaws yawned open, more than wide enough to engulf a full-grown man. The flesh inside glistened white and pink and pale blue, billowing out at them.

"Move!" Blake kicked the fire as he yelled, sending a spray of red-hot coals into the oncoming mouth. Hissing like a locomotive, the reptile arched back, shaking its head violently as the men scrambled to get out of its path. Before Blake could get around the makeshift shelter, the enraged snake struck again, smashing through with the strength of a giant's fist, sending it and the man flying.

Blake hit the floor in a roll, his lantern dashed out of his hand to tumble and shatter across the tiles, igniting in a splattered pool of oil. He turned to see Cam hurdle over the railing into the Peruvian booth, the light from his lantern arcing back and forth. Harcourt squealed with panic as he struggled to run, tripping over himself in his haste to escape.

Rapidly coiling its formidable bulk around a standing pillar, it anchored itself and tried again to snap up Blake, just missing as he dove under a table. The strike shattered a display case above in a noisy burst of splinters, glass, and Australian opals. Its momentum carried it forward and, in a smooth liquid motion, it twisted back around.

Struggling to see in the gloom, Blake scanned for cover. He didn't dare make a straight run for the door—he'd never be able to outrun the thing—but if he could use the terrain to his advantage—

His thought was cut off as the prehistoric nightmare came at him again. Reacting on pure instinct he rose, angling the tabletop and shoving it straight toward the monster.

For such a massive creature—wide as a rhino and as long as a Mack truck—it could move with uncanny speed. They collided and the impact knocked Blake backward across the floor. With only the table in its jaws, the snake reared back, head thrashing back and forth like a dog with a rat.

Ordering his battered body into action, Blake scrambled to his feet again and ran, hoping the snake would choke on the wooden pieces. Those hopes vanished as the table buckled and broke apart with a crunching snap. Needing cover, he dove behind a pillar in the nearest patch of shadows.

Heart pounding, he leaned against the pillar and let his body slump to the ground, fighting to control his unsteady breath. Then came the sound of Harcourt's terrified wailing. A tiny, uncharitable part of him wished the snake would be distracted enough to chase the noisier target instead.

Enough of that.

Blake peered around the corner. In the glow from the flames on the floor, he could just make out a portion of the blackness that shimmered in a sinuous movement, gliding silently and inexorably toward him. The dark that hindered his vision didn't bother the snake at all. So Blake bolted forward, cutting at an angle toward the pool of flames. The snake changed course, circling around the fire to cut him off. With both hands, Blake ripped down a drape of festive swag and dragged it through the flaming oil, gratified to see it ignite at once.

Waving his makeshift firebrand, he stoked the flames, and the serpent shifted again to give the fiery pool of oil a wide berth. With slow, cautious steps, Blake backed away, scanning desperately for a strategic exit, but unwilling to turn his back on the hungry reptile.

He backed into a booth, nearly tripping over debris on the floor. It was the gold rush exhibit. Had it included a pickaxe? He risked a glance over his shoulder.

Bad idea.

A streak of movement flashed in his peripheral vision and he whirled back around, ducking just as the snake lunged past him—missing him by sheer luck, tearing away the remains of the flaming cloth and extinguishing it in the process. Once again the room was plunged into semi-darkness.

Where's that goddamned axe?

Desperate, he dove blindly, without thought, crashing painfully into a wooden sluice. He scrambled to get to his feet—but the snake already had him.

Unable to see, Blake heard and felt the snake's body encircling the sluice, followed by the awful cracking sound as the coils began to constrict the slats. Once the coffin-like trench collapsed, he would be crushed to a pulp.

The darkness was pierced by a flash of light, followed by a loud roar. Cam ran up, swinging his lantern in one hand and holding a long tamping iron in the other, wielding it like a javelin. Howling some Celtic battle cry, he drove the heavy iron's sharpened point into the snake's thick neck, punching through the scales just below the hinge of its jaw.

It was a solid hit, but not a killing blow.

Infuriated, the snake shook off both Cam and his weapon, releasing its death grip on the sluice as it rose up, hissing and spitting. Crouching, the Celt set down the lantern and took a two-handed grip on the iron, bracing himself.

Locating its new adversary, the snake struck out, the lantern light reflecting eerily in its soulless eyes. Snapping at Cam, it got a bite of the iron spear instead, and the impact nearly bowled him over. The creature was all solid muscle—it was obvious who would tire first in a duel.

"Cam, pull back!"

Blake charged up from the side. With an overhead swing, he brought the pickaxe down on the snake's midsection, the spike plunging into its fleshy bulk and releasing a satisfying gout of blood. The muscles tightened around the weapon, trapping it there, and the snake's long tail lashed about, smashing everything around it to pieces.

Diving away to avoid the deadly thrashing frenzy, Blake went for Cam's abandoned lantern.

"This way!" he shouted. "Move now, while it's distracted!"

Cam could barely hear Blake over the crashing din, and didn't dare turn his back on the monster to run. When the lantern light disappeared, however, only one choice remained.

The two men sprinted for the cover of the neighboring exhibit, leaping over the railing. Something solid went whirling crazily through the air between them—the remains of the bloodied pickaxe, snapped off and flung away. It narrowly missed their heads, striking Lot's Wife in her chest, sticking into the pillar of salt like a murderer's dagger.

Blake and Cam dropped into the cramped wall space behind the statue, just as the snake's body smashed against the wrought-iron barrier and plunged its neck in after them. Its head glanced off the salt column and it hissed in frustration while Cam scrambled in the confined space to work his iron spear into a defensive position.

This time the monster didn't risk another strike, rising up instead like a cobra, swaying side to side. From his all-too-exposed position, Cam locked eyes with their hunter, watching as it seemed to study its prey, perhaps noting that there wasn't enough space to safely shelter two men.

"Right," Blake said. He stood up suddenly and hurled the lantern with all his might—not at the looming serpent, but at the towering figure of Mephistopheles.

The lantern's glass chimney shattered, spraying the carving with flaming oil. Fire suited him. It brought the Devil to life, dancing flames happy to spread and engulf him like royal robes. As the column began to melt, his body seemed to stir and, paradoxically, to grow. Fire distorted and stretched his features. Lit from below, the gleeful, menacing gaze and satanic sneer were magnified.

A moment later came more sorcery. A slow-moving pool of eerie blue-white flames began to spill out from the base of the statue, forming a river of flowing heat. Sparks and bright orange-tufted fireballs skittered across its current like elementals. A fog of noxious vapors rose up as well, clouds building in the high ceiling.

Above them, the ghostly blue radiance illuminated the snake's bloodied skin, its entire length glowing like a primal serpent-god. It raised up, hissing its defiance at the flaming apparition come to life.

"Don't breathe the smoke!" Blake yelled. "It'll kill you! We have to get out of here!" The sea of blue fire and its deadly fumes were spreading, igniting everything it touched. Blake had warded off the snake, only to pin them into a corner.

"Against the wall," he said. "It's our only chance."

Hands across their mouths and noses, the two men crouched and then leapt across the spreading blue flames just as a ton of burning, melting brimstone collapsed on the spot they'd just escaped. It crashed into Lot's Wife and with a piercing sound like the shriek of a damned soul, the salt statue burst into brilliant yellow shooting flames.

The pair followed the walls, bas-reliefs honoring the spirits of gold and iron, surreally flickering in the hellish crimson light. Smoke and sweat stung their eyes. Somewhere deep in the inferno they could hear the thrashing snake.

"Where's the door?" Cam yelled. Blake could only shake his head. A terrified, drawn-out scream pierced the roar of flames and crashing debris. They looked at each other, knowing all too well what that sound meant.

Harcourt.

31

If they were passing through different shards—and surely they must be, Nellie thought—there was no sign of it. As with the shards they had seen in North Africa, the same type of landscape had dominated over so many epochs, so there was almost no telling where their boundaries lay. There was no trace of human activity, but a variety of both prehistoric and modern animals all shared the environment. They continued their hike up into the autumnal trees, the undergrowth crunching beneath their thick overshoes with every step. Nellie cradled her stiff shoulder, but kept pace with Hypatia. Though more familiar with terrain like this, she would never fancy herself a woodsman, and by the time they came close to the snowline, she had seen no sign of anything they could eat.

"Something's just occurred to me."

"What's that?" Hypatia kept walking.

"I haven't noticed any aftershocks—have you?"

Hypatia stopped.

"You're right!" she exclaimed. "But surely they haven't stopped on their own. Could it mean they aren't evenly distributed, and this region is one of the doldrums? No, we've seen far too many of them all the way from Alexandria to Antarctica to suppose we're safe..."

They continued to discuss possibilities as they walked, and a few minutes later they approached a fallen oak. The trunk had broken in half, leaving a neat little gap between the two pieces. A small deadfall of branches and antlers had accumulated on both sides of it, as if forming a rough-hewn little gateway.

Something in the arrangement struck Nellie as odd.

"Wait!" she cried out, just as Hypatia stepped into the gap. With a single crisp cracking sound, her body suddenly snapped forward as though some claw had snatched her by the ankle, sending her face first to the ground.

"Hypatia!" Nellie ran forward, then stopped, catching herself just short of the gap. Hypatia lay unmoving, a rough leather cord cinched tightly around her foot.

An arrow protruded from her side.

"Oh god, no..."

Moving carefully, Nellie swept away part of the branches concealing the trap her companion had triggered. She paused long enough to make sure there were no other snares, then quickly knelt by Hypatia's side. The woman lay as still as stone.

"Hypatia?" Her fingers trembled as she pulled the hair away from her face. Was she still breathing? Hypatia's eyelids fluttered.

"Oh, thank heavens."

Hypatia tried to sit up, then groaned.

"Stay still," Nellie cautioned. "Your side—"

Hypatia looked up at her. "Am I—"

"Try not to move," Nellie told her. "You're hurt. Here, let me look." Gingerly, she pulled Hypatia's coat away so she could examine the wound. The arrow shifted along with the coat.

"What's this?"

She opened the flap of cloth, and exhaled. The arrow had missed Hypatia altogether. Instead, it had embedded itself in the thick folds of her parka. Nellie threaded the arrow all the way through and pulled it out. The metal arrowhead was coated with some greasy, resinous substance. Poison, no doubt. Carefully, she wiped it clean on her own parka, and then used the sharp edge to cut the snare off Hypatia's ankle.

"Are you alright?"

Hypatia sat up, rubbing a red spot on her forehead. "Yes, I think so. Just a little stunned. What was that?"

"A hunter's trap. It must have been rigged to catch deer—if not, it would have caught you square in the torso, I think."

"I wonder how long ago the hunter placed it there."

"Perhaps we'll be able to find him."

Nellie helped her to her feet, but Hypatia winced as she put weight on her foot, and Nellie quickly caught her again.

"Are you sure you're not injured?"

"The snare—it twisted my ankle. I can walk, I think. Just give me a moment." She took a few tentative steps, assessed herself silently, and declared herself fit to continue. They looked further up the slope to where the snowline began and icicles dwindled down from the tree branches.

"I truly dislike having to admit it," Hypatia said with a sigh, "but I don't think we'll find anything to eat up here."

"Maybe we should go back down to the beach?" Nellie rubbed her sore arm, feeling tired and cold.

"Yes, but I can barely move from the chill. How I wish we had a fire to warm ourselves!"

"Never fear—I know just the thing!" Nellie said. "Here, make a pile from these older branches and dried leaves. I'll show you an old mountain man's trick I learned in Pennsylvania." She broke off one of the larger icicles hanging from the nearest tree, snapped off the end and tossed it aside, holding the remaining chunk up to the sun to check it for flaws. It passed her approval. Taking the arrowhead she set work, shaving away at the ice until she had a rough disk shape about the size of a hen's egg.

"What is that supposed to do?" Hypatia asked.

"Just you wait, I still need to polish it." She took off her mittens and held the flattened ball of ice in her bare hands. "This part is a bit chillier than I bargained for." Soldiering on, she shaped the ice, painstakingly melting it with the warmth of her palms in order to create a smooth surface.

Hypatia finished piling twigs and kindling, then peered at Nellie's handiwork.

"You're making a lens!"

With a proud nod, Nellie smiled and focused the morning's sunlight through the ice into a single tiny point on the nest of dried leaves. At first, there was nothing. Then, a slight blackened spot appeared, a little curl of smoke emerged, and a tiny flame came to life. Overjoyed, Hypatia leaned in to gently blow life into the red-orange embers. They cheered as the flame took, feeding it the dry twigs until they had a fine little fire.

"Oh, well done, Nellie!" Hypatia exclaimed happily. Taking their mittens off, the two stretched out their fingers to soak up the delicious warmth. Hypatia reached over to grasp Nellie's hand.

"*Toú Irakli!* By Hercules! Your poor hands are frozen. Here." Clasping them in her own for a moment, she tucked them into her parka and slipped them past the coarse fabric of her cloak, holding Nellie's hands against the bare skin between her own breasts. The contact made her suddenly gasp. "Oh! They are so cold!" she laughed.

Mortified, Nellie tried to pull her hands back, but Hypatia held them fast.

"No, no," she assured, "it's alright. I don't want you to lose your fingers to the frost."

The two women huddled up together in one shivering bundle. Nellie let herself sink against Hypatia's warmth as their parkas formed a tent around them, holding in their combined body heat. Leaning her head gently against Hypatia's, she closed her eyes—dizzy with feelings for which she had no name.

32

The sound of Harcourt's agonized death scream rattled Blake. He'd seen his share of the dying, friend and foe alike, and yet it was far too easy to picture the horrified Victorian, arms flailing helplessly while his body struggled in the jaws of the monster.

He forced the thought away.

"Come on. We have to find that entrance."

"Wait!" Cam said. "Listen!"

Harcourt was still screaming. Which meant he was still alive.

When the snake first appeared, Harcourt's gangly legs had failed him, buckling like a newborn colt's while he stumbled over obstacles and ducked flying debris. He tried to find his way back to the entrance, threading his way through one turn after another, until no longer sure in what direction he was running.

Crashes and shouts echoed behind him as he tried to retrace his route. The sounds pricked at what little conscience he had. He listened to Blake's and Cam's struggles, warring with his terror and sense of self-preservation...

Until he turned and went back to help them.

He had rounded the statue of Vulcan just in time to catch sight of the snake rearing up as the sulfurous Mephistopheles burst into flame. His newfound courage evaporated, and he once again ran for his life. He could have sworn they had left open the doors to the main entrance. So where the devil was it?

Wait—something there...

A faint gleam up ahead drew him closer, but when he reached it he realized it was only the grate of some kind of grillwork in the floor. Still, a cool breeze of fresh air flowed from it, so it had to be a way out.

Placing his lantern on the floor, he grabbed hold of the cover with both hands, took a deep breath, and lifted with all his might. The heavy iron grill... did nothing. It didn't budge. He knelt for better leverage and tried again. The cover might as well have been welded shut.

"Right then. Third time's the charm," he muttered. With a sharp exhalation he tried once more, putting his back into it. His spine made a curious popping noise, and he gave out a long, tortured wail. The manhole cover remained steadfast. Meanwhile, the temperature was rising steadily, and smoke was billowing overhead.

Desperation, anger, and pain warred within him, and an alliance of the first two triumphed. He rose in an uncontrolled fit of rage and kicked the nearest chunk of debris, a large gold nugget. Bending down to the grill again, he tried yet again to wrench it free. The only result was another howl of frustration.

"Jesus Christ!"

Harcourt yelped in surprise at the sudden exclamation.

"We thought that bloody snake had done for you." Blake slapped Harcourt on the shoulder. The Victorian sputtered, surprised and delighted to see his two companions alive.

"I think I've found a way out," he said, "but it's stuck fast."

Cam and Blake knelt down, the two of them prying the grill up and off with seemingly no effort. Harcourt swore inwardly. Blake peered down, then reached for the lantern and slipped it inside the hole. He dropped down into the blackness.

"It's safe!" Blake's voice echoed from below.

"You go next," Cam offered. Harcourt didn't stand on ceremony, quickly scrambling down into the shaft. When he was safely down, Cam started to follow. A sibilant noise came from behind him, making him turn his head.

"*Kych-an—*" he hissed as the snake slipped out of the dark and lunged for him.

He dropped at once, half-falling, half-sliding hard onto a brick ramp, looking up to see the giant serpent's head just an arm's length above him. It snapped and hissed, trying repeatedly to cram its oversized skull into the manhole.

Cam rested his head against the cool brick and sighed in relief. He would pray his apologies to the serpent later.

"No, no, you just keep napping," Blake called from below. "You can catch up to us later."

Cam grinned and slid the rest of the way down to join them. They were in a cistern of some kind, surrounded by tall stone walls three times their height. Welcome daylight slanted in from the windows above, along with fresh air.

"What is this place?" Cam asked.

"A pumphouse," Blake replied. "It used to keep the canal water circulating, I expect."

"More importantly," Harcourt grumbled, "how on earth are we to get out of here?"

"Well, now," a stranger's voice drawled from above them. "I reckon that depends on how cooperative you three are prepared to be."

33

"We should leave if we're going to make it back to the beach before dark," Hypatia said. Nellie reluctantly agreed. Their unsuccessful attempts at foraging had turned late morning to afternoon without them quite realizing it. Rising, they hadn't taken more than a few steps when Hypatia began to limp. Nellie slipped an arm around her.

"Hold up, now," she said. "We have quite a distance to go. At this pace, I don't think we're going to make it before dark." The last thing she wanted was to be stumbling downhill in the dark.

"But, we can't stay up here—"

"Of course we can," Nellie said. "I'll make us a lean-to against the tree. We'll sleep by the fire. It can't be any worse than that stench-ridden seal rookery." She hoped that would prove to be true.

Hypatia protested, but Nellie remained firm, leading her

back to their makeshift campsite. While she sat and rested her ankle, Nellie set about breaking off branches for their cover. On an empty stomach, the work was more exhausting than she let on, and late autumn made twilight a brief affair. No sooner had sunset ended than the night dropped pitch black, and Nellie had stop. Taking a seat next to Hypatia by the fire, she looked dubiously at the makeshift shelter.

"It will have to do, I'm afraid. I'm worn to a frazzle."

Hypatia smiled at her. "A superb labor. We'll sleep well tonight," she said, positioning herself in the lean-to. "Thank you, Nellie. Come rest now." She patted her thigh, and Nellie gratefully leaned down to rest her head in her friend's lap. Hypatia ran a finger through the younger woman's hair. Gradually their eyes became accustomed to the light cast by the stars and the nearly full moon.

"Rest now…"

Nellie closed her eyes. She had just started to drift off when a terrible roar split the night—the same thundering unholy laughter from the night before, only much closer. Nellie bolted upright and the two women stumbled out of the lean-to, ducking behind the cover of the fallen oak.

"Look!" Hypatia whispered.

A powerfully built figure, with a fur wrap around his waist and carrying a spiked club over his shoulder, strode into sight on a moonlit precipice high above them. Unless it was a trick of the moonlight, his skin was as blue as the Antarctic ice, and a pair of long intimidating horns protruded from his shaggy black mane. The hulking shape roared his mocking challenge upward toward the moon.

Just like that, spun and disappeared back into the trees.

They waited a long while. When he didn't return, they went back to the lean-to. It was a long time before either woman managed to fall asleep.

Nellie awoke with a start, nearly upsetting the embers of the fire.

"Shhhh… it's alright," Hypatia said soothingly, putting an arm over her and spooning.

"I dreamt we saw it—that laughing, howling… monster." Nellie's voice shook.

Hypatia rubbed her shoulder. "Rest assured, it was no dream. I saw it, as well."

"Where *are* we?" Nellie burst out. "Is this some dark fairy tale? I'm beginning to suppose this has all been a dream, and I'm going to wake up back in New York city with a great big bump on my head."

"Perhaps we're just learning about something new we didn't suspect before. It is a big world, after all."

Nellie nestled back against Hypatia's parka-clad body, taking comfort in the closeness. Her stomach growled. "My whole body aches, but I don't know if it's nerves or hunger."

"Both, I would expect. We need to go back down and try again to find some food, and check for the portal, but first we should find fresh water."

* * *

Though reluctant to leave the limited security and warmth of the lean-to, thirst and hunger won out. Hypatia took a few experimental steps, declaring herself steady enough to continue. Burying the embers, they left the lean-to.

As they left, Nellie retrieved the arrow. "We might need it," she said.

They headed west, parallel to the snowline, hoping for a water source that hadn't frozen over. Less than an hour later, they came across a mossy creek bed with a slender trickle of mountain runoff. Though it chilled their fingers and teeth, they gulped down handful after handful, the cold water delicious as fine wine.

Hypatia stopped in mid-scoop, and then pointed to something above the treetops, higher up the mountain. Instantly frightened, Nellie followed her gaze. A column of soft gray smoke lazily rose into the sky.

"A chimney," Nellie exclaimed. "A house!"

Caution trumped their excitement, and the women carefully, quietly crept through the trees as they moved toward the source of the smoke. To their surprise, when they came to the break in the trees, there was no house at all—only a flat rocky spot housing a wide pool of water. What they took for smoke was steam rising off a natural hot spring, gathering in the clearing like a wispy fog.

Nellie gazed at it longingly.

"It looks warm as anything, doesn't it?"

"Do you want to—?"

"Let's!" Nellie was already stripping out of her parka and traveling clothes, the cold pinching her skin. Hypatia gave a wary look around, then quickly joined in. Kicking the last of her underthings onto the pile of her clothing, Nellie stepped in with a joyful whoop, plunging below the water. Hypatia watched anxiously, still clutching her *tribon* cloak like a security blanket. After a moment, Nellie's head broke through the surface.

"Oh! It's so lovely!"

Relieved, Hypatia discarded her clothes, as well, and carefully lowered herself into the water. The mix of frigid air and warm water made her gasp. Nellie pulled her wet hair from her face and tried not to stare as Hypatia descended into the pool.

"Yes, this *is* wonderful!" the older woman sighed. "My bones and muscles are singing." Nellie stretched out her hands and the two locked fingers. Hypatia shut her eyes and let herself be pulled luxuriously through the warm water. The feeling was heavenly, and for a few happy, quiet moments, they lost themselves and shook off the crushing weight of their dilemma.

As she relaxed for the first time in what seemed like forever, Nellie began to feel strangely out of sorts, unable to make sense of a bubbling jumble of conflicting emotions within her.

"I keep meaning to tell you how sorry I was for what happened to your friend Calix," she said out of the blue, focusing on words instead of feelings. Opening her eyes, Hypatia looked away for a moment.

"Without your warning, it could have been far worse. I'm grateful to you."

"Were you two—?"

"He was my dear friend and partner of many years. I will miss him."

"Partner?"

"Not that. I should have said my colleague. I am not wed."

"I'm sorry, I'm being rude."

"No, it's alright. I've never taken a husband. I never wanted to."

Nellie nodded, avoiding eye contact. "I think I could be persuaded to marry an elderly millionaire with health issues," she joked to hide her nervousness, "but I've never given marriage much thought, either. Too busy, I suppose."

Hypatia laughed. "I certainly have had no time for marriage—but I made my choice most deliberately."

"Oh. Oh! So you've never... or, did you—was there anyone you... In your day, did ladies—I mean, was it acceptable e... or did you—I mean, could you... if you wanted to... know what I mean to say?"

tia looked at her blankly.

bbling like a madwoman, she scolded herself. *Shut up,*

d no man, if that's what you mean," Hypatia said

lidn't mean—I don't know what I meant."

herself to cease the tortured mental gymnastics, erself face Hypatia. The older woman's eyes gs—kindness, intelligence, wisdom, concern, d... perhaps beyond that?

"Nellie? Are you... trying to ask me something?"

"Yes," Nellie said quietly, releasing Hypatia's hands. Then she leaned in, took ahold of Hypatia's face and kissed her. For one beautiful instant no one and nothing else existed in the whole wide world but the two of them in a kiss.

Hypatia suddenly broke away from Nellie, covering her mouth with one hand and her breasts with the other. Nellie screamed inside, caught up in a torrential burst of shame, fear, and self-loathing.

"Hypatia, I'm sorry!" she cried. "Oh please, I'm so sorry! I don't know what came over me!"

Speechless, Hypatia clambered out of the pool. Nellie followed, desperately miserable. The air tore at their bare skin, and only then did she realize they had no towels or fire.

"Please, Hypatia." Her voice quavered like her shivering body. "Please forgive me—I'll die if you don't. I'll just die! You know I'd never do anything to hurt you." Hypatia stood like a pale ghostly revenant, frozen and silent, staring, but nothing escaped her lips except the cold gray wisps of her ragged breath

"Please say something," Nellie begged.

A loud crack suddenly broke through the frosty air.

34

Three figures appeared, looking down over the lip of the cistern. All three carried firearms casually pointed their way. The one doing the talking came right out of an Old West wanted poster, Harcourt thought—a mountain man, bearded, big as an ox, with a face like a mastiff. A shaggy mane, black with iron streaks, hung down past his shoulders, and steel blue eyes that stood out, a pit bull's eyes. They twinkled, as if he was making a private joke.

A horse-faced, pockmarked man stood to his left, dirty blonde hair tied in a lank ponytail beneath a battered black tricorn hat. He wore a British redcoat uniform that had seen better days. The third man looked to be an Indian warrior in buckskins, an iron tomahawk tucked in his belt. Beneath his unbuttoned U.S. Cavalry jacket and bearclaw necklace he wore only tattoos—black handprints and red and white striped patterns across his chest. His head was shaved, with a flare of crimson scalp lock.

Harcourt looked anxiously at his companions, but neither moved. Any chance of a fortuitous rescue seemed to be gone. If Blake was intimidated, however, it didn't show.

"Seems like an introduction is in order before we all get too chummy, don't you think?" he said. Both of the white men smiled back at that—though their faces were not made for smiling. The Indian didn't bother, his weathered, seamed face as unreadable as a stone. The leader spoke up again.

"Oh, by all means, a man should know who he's dealing with." He jerked his chin to the Redcoat. "This here's Private Samuel Shanks."

Shanks doffed his hat. "Late of the King's army, 45th foot," he said in a thick Cockney accent. In Harcourt's estimation, the scruffy fellow appeared to be a veteran—or a deserter—of King George's forces from the Seven Years' War, over a century before his time. The mountain man turned a thumb to the other.

"And I can't pronounce this Lamanite's heathen name, but according to him, it means 'Feeds-the-Crows,' or some such. He was a scout for the army, back in the day. Killed himself a goodly number of redskins in the Comanche campaign, didn't you, Crows?" The Indian nodded. "But that was after my time."

"And who might you be?" Blake asked, keeping his voice nonchalant.

"Me?" The man lowered his voice, gaze fixed on Blake. "Don't you know? I'm a saint. I'm the Sampson of the last days. I'm the Destroying Angel." His icy eyes gleamed. "But you can call me Porter Rockwell." He paused, as if looking for a reaction to his name. None was forthcoming, but if he was disappointed, Rockwell hid it admirably. "So now you know who we are. And you?"

"I'm Blake. Sergeant Blake, Special Air Service. This is Cam"—the Celt said nothing, giving a curt nod—"and this is Professor Harcourt."

The professor tipped his hat nervously. "Pleased, I'm sure."

Rockwell and his cohorts kept their guns where they were.

"That's right neighborly," Rockwell said. "Now that we're all such fast friends, why don't we see the color of your weapons?"

"Nothing to see. We're unarmed," Blake replied easily. Shanks chuckled. Rockwell only raised an eyebrow and whistled.

"Mind yourselves now, boys! These three must be just about the toughest iron-jawed passel of wildcats you ever seen, a-saunterin' across savage territory with no more than harsh language and their bare knuckles!"

Shanks laughed louder, an unpleasant braying sound.

"I have a knife on my belt," Blake admitted. Rockwell wagged a finger at him.

"Yep, so you do. How 'bout you unclip that sheath and toss it up here for safekeeping—and see that it flies up gentle as a dove, now."

Blake obliged, and the man caught it.

"That's a fine blade," Rockwell said before slipping it into his belt. "You lose everything else?"

"Nothing else to lose."

"That right?" Rockwell shook his head. "Unarmed. I

declare, most impressive showing for yourselves. See now, from the sound of the hullabaloo in there, we were afraid for you boys ever coming out again. Mind tellin' us what transpired? Grizzly? T-Rex?"

"Oh, back there?" Blake raised an eyebrow in exaggerated innocence, and Harcourt was impressed. He jerked his thumb back up the shaft. "Snake."

"A ruddy *snake* made all that fuss?" Shanks snorted.

"Big snake."

"I reckon it'd have to be powerful big," Rockwell drawled.

"Right," Blake said. "So we can stay here all day going on about our snakes, but is there any chance we can continue the conversation *after* you get us out of this bloody cistern?"

"Hold up now, gents. There's just one thing I need to know first." Rockwell cradled his rifle and crouched down closer. "See, nobody comes so far out this side of the river unless they're on the run from someone."

"Or if they're chasing someone else," Shanks chipped in with an unsettling smile.

"Point granted," Rockwell said. "So what brings *you* splendid British-type gentlemen all the way here?"

"We're looking for our friends," Cam said.

Rockwell leaned in. "Friends, you say?"

"Two Egyptians," Harcourt supplied. "A Nubian and a girl from Cairo."

"From Cairo, Illinois? All the way down in Little Egypt? That's a fair ways south."

Cam frowned. "I don't know what an Illinois is, but they

are from Egypt, on the Nile. Cairo and Thebes."

"Cam, shut it," Blake urged under his breath. "This isn't helping."

"Hey now, let the young gentleman speak," Rockwell chided. "There a bounty on their heads? The black feller kidnap somebody's daughter?"

"It's nothing like that," Blake cut in before Cam could reply. "They're simply traveling through here with us. We—" He paused for the briefest of instants, trying not to say too much. "We became separated about an hour ago."

"From your wagon train, I reckon," Rockwell said. Blake hesitated, trying to head off any wrong answer that might get them killed.

"Something like that."

The big man's unsavory sidekicks were growing quietly restless, as though eager to get going. Not Rockwell, however. His steely eyes never stopped cross-examining them. Like some frontier trial lawyer, he seemed to be weighing every word out of their mouths.

"Something like that, huh?" Nodding thoughtfully, he idly picked at the barrel of his rifle as though busy cleaning it of some piece of grit. "So if I comprehend you rightly, you're sayin' your traveling companions are a nigger and some little gal from Egypt proper, a-wanderin' around these here parts. No more than an hour ago, you say?"

He brought his rifle up again, bringing it slowly to bear on some target in the pumphouse, somewhere out of their line of vision. Nonchalantly inspecting the sights, he continued.

"Well sirs, you'll pardon me for sayin' so, but I reckon you can forget about those two. More than likely they're already taken up residence in some beast's belly—and if not, I wager they've already been found and gotten themselves a one-way ticket to somewhere's else every bit just as nice and cozy. I might even hazard a guess where."

Pleased with himself, he glanced back at his cronies. Something had caught the Indian scout's attention, and the Redcoat had noticed the distraction, sucking his teeth anxiously and changing up the grip on his firearm. Rockwell stood up again, seeming ready to wrap things up at last.

Blake stood very still, working out a new course of action. *We dive back into the shaft, scramble back up, and take our chances with the snake.* Far from a foolproof plan, but at the moment, he could think of none better. Rockwell turned his attention back to them.

"Don't reckon three Englishmen'd care to tell us where you lit out from, or where your—wagon train, was it?—where your little caravan is bound for?"

"The details are a bit dodgy to explain," Blake admitted.

"I imagine so. Well, don't trouble yourself none to explain to us—but here's how it's going to be. We came here looking for a bounty, and from what you say, I reckon he's likely in your snake's gullet. So you three are coming with us back to the Landing, and then we'll see if there's a bounty on you fellows. If there is, you're our consolation prize. If not, well then, I promise, honor bright, supper's on us for your troubles and you gentlemen can be on your way. Sound fair?"

When they didn't answer, he raised a bushy eyebrow.

"Well, don't worry yourselves too much if it is or ain't, since that's how it's going to be. Now then, let's not tarry any longer. There are worse things in this place than giant cottonmouths. Even Feeds-the-Crows is getting antsy—and he's Pawnee." At the snap of Rockwell's fingers, Shanks produced twin pairs of manacles, dropping the iron chains at their feet with a loud clank.

"You two big fellows put these hobbles on, and then we'll throw down the rope."

Harcourt brightened, relieved there were no chains for him. "I must say, I appreciate you recognizing that as a gentleman of quality, my word of honor will suffice in place of iron fetters. Very decent of you." Shanks nodded absently.

"Mmm, indeed yes, as you say, sir. Oh, that and this," he said, fishing out some modest lengths of boot lacing. "I should think this is more than sufficient to secure your twiggy little wrists, don't you, Your Highness?"

Blake saw the cold fire burning in Cam's eyes and could guess what plan the Celt had brewing. He was running the cold math himself.

He'll let them bring him up, at the top pull the big one face first into the pit, slam the second into the third before they can fire their guns, kill the Redcoat quick and fight the Indian.

He didn't like the odds, not for him, not for Cam.

"Not yet," he said under his breath to Cam. "Let's see if they know more than they're telling us about Kha-Hotep and Leila." After a moment's consideration, Cam nodded.

He and Blake shackled themselves in the irons, and the flimsy bits of lacing proved more than capable of securing Harcourt's hands together. Their captors lowered ropes and hauled them up like fish. Each prisoner's wrists were lashed to a long leather strap, and they were marched from the pumphouse. Rockwell pulled them along on their tether, walking with a noticeable limp as they left the ruins.

Behind them, smoke rose from the roof of the palace, but the massive building seemed in little danger of burning down. Blake was more concerned with the bloody snake emerging and chasing after them. Their captors would sacrifice them in a heartbeat while they made their escape.

The snake did not reappear, however. A few minutes of walking brought them to the abrupt edge of the shard, and a stand of trees where Rockwell and his men had secured their mounts—a trio of ostrich-like dinosaurs, two-legged lizards with pathetic little clawed arms and stiff straight tails. Sleek coats of downy feathers, as smooth as the head of a mallard duck, covered their skin, each beast a different color—green-gold, russet, and dark olive.

The bounty hunters mounted up. Shanks tied their leash to his saddle horn. Blake noticed all three riding-lizards had saddles and panniers—not refurbished horse gear, but ones that appeared to be specially made and fitted. He thought about the time it would take to domesticate, and then outfit, such animals.

This place raised so very many questions...

With a gentle kick to its sides, Rockwell urged his mount forward and the party headed off. Beyond the thicket the land opened into a wide swath of prairielands that extended to the horizon. It was going to be a long walk.

"Rockwell, tell me something."

"What might that be, Mr. Blake?"

"Where are we, and how far have we got to walk?"

The big man and Shanks broke into laughter.

"Look at that, now, you really don't know, do you? You fellows *are* lost! What happened, the stork just up and drop you here?" Blake said nothing. Rockwell's sharp eyes looked for an answer, but when none came, he replied, again with that mischievous kidding-or-serious glint in his gaze.

"Well, sir, I'll tell you. As the crow flies, we are some two hundred sixty miles due east of the Garden of Eden itself."

"Is that a fact?"

"It surely is, and if you head west by northwest just a little further than that, you'd come to Adam-ondi-Ahman, the very altar whereupon Adam and Eve made sacrifice unto the Lord, after their expulsion from paradise."

It was Blake's turn to raise an eyebrow. "I don't suppose this place goes by any other names?"

"Hell's bells! Ain't you just bound and determined to make me utter that god-cursed name out loud, aren't you?" Rockwell spat. "Well, sir, afore the Lord let loose his righteous vengeance upon it, this here was Missouri."

Blake nodded. Finally, he had at least a vague idea of where they were.

"And where are we going?"

"That-a-way." Rockwell pointed east to the horizon. Cam and Harcourt's eyes widened. They were just as baffled as Blake.

What the hell is that? he thought, staring at the silver arch off in the distance.

Something growled to their left, a low and guttural sound.

35

At first, mist from the volcanic pool obscured the half dozen shapes striding out from the pines. Great, shaggy, half-human figures, some armed with hooked spears. Black eye sockets in ursine faces. Monsters of nightmare walking in broad daylight.

Good lord! Nellie thought. *Werewolves?* Her mind reeled in disbelief. *No, were-bears.*

The women stared, transfixed with fear as the silent bear-warriors slowly fanned out around them. As they moved closer, however, she could see that they were just men—sturdy, thick-set and squarely-built, with prominent cheekbones and high foreheads. Four bowmen in bearskin hoods and capes, sporting bushy beards and dark, unruly long hair, with long knives in carved wooden scabbards tucked into their belts. Two younger ones, wearing dark blue headscarves in place of the hoods, carrying hooked spears.

Beneath the cowls, the bowmen's tanned skin and unruly brown hair matched the bearskins they wore.

"*Shamo yan!*" their leader growled.

Nellie stiffened, swiping the tears away from her eyes, trading anguish for fierceness. Snatching up the arrow at her feet, she held it straight out in a challenge. Behind her, Hypatia grasped her arm.

"Stay away," she growled, putting all the steel she could into each word. "I'll not hesitate to put this straight through the eye of the first man-jack who dares lay so much as a little finger on either one of us."

The bear-men neither changed their savage expressions nor replied. The points of their arrowheads gleamed bright and sharp. If any of the archers loosed an arrow from this distance, he would not miss. Wet, freezing, and naked, Nellie stared them down.

"*Shamo isam,*" one of the others said, sounding dubious. The leader cocked his head. Lowering his bow, he set it on the rocky ground, plucking the arrow free. Then he straightened up and held it out, mimicking Nellie's stance.

Nellie didn't take her eyes off him. His beard and hair were shot with silver, his eyes deeply set, under long and shaggy eyebrows. She realized with some surprise, that his eyes and hers were nearly the same shade of gray-green.

Abruptly he knelt and placed his arrow to the ground, point out.

"*Irankarapte,*" he said quietly. Nellie waited for her language implant to translate, but nothing was happening. Either it was malfunctioning, or this tongue wasn't one of the one hundred and fifty in its repertoire. She could only stare, uncertain if this was an offer to parley or a new threat.

"*Nep kusu e'pas wa e'ek ya?*" he said gruffly.

"I can't understand you," she said, trying to keep her voice firm. He frowned.

"*Ku'ye itak e'eraman?*"

"*Yaytupare,*" one of the others cautioned. Without taking his eyes off of Nellie, the leader reached out behind him.

"*Inaw,*" he said. His fellow quickly lowered his own bow and pulled something out of a small woven knapsack, slapping it into the leader's open hand. It was a small white wooden rod, no bigger than a ruler, one end carved with a luxuriant tuft of shaved curlicues, reminding Nellie of the silk on a head of corn.

The leader held the shaggy baton out in front of him. Fearing it was a scabbard for some hidden blade, Nellie kept her grip on the arrow as he cautiously stepped toward her.

"Stay back!" she snarled, but the man did not. Instead, he gently tapped at her arrow, almost as if blessing it.

"*Ay ama yan,*" he murmured softly. "*Wen nupur, kaske a'kus eaykap.*"

"*Inaw wa Kamuy Renkayne,*" the other men said as one. The leader continued to circle the two women slowly, almost leisurely, wielding the baton. He made no move to attack or touch them, and appeared unmoved by their nudity—though he seemed to be examining them closely, all the same. He seemed especially interested in their hair, eyes, the backs of their hands and forearms.

Finally, he brought his baton up slowly toward the back of Nellie's neck.

"See here!" she bristled, ready to stab him, but he held up a hand, and then gently pushed back the slick strands of wet hair with his baton. The long spirals of wood shavings tickled as he inspected the back of her neck, as though expecting she might be hiding some sinister mark of witchcraft.

Gently, he did the same to Hypatia, who clung to Nellie's free arm but allowed the indignity. His inspection concluded, he backed away and turned to their piles of clothes. After shaking the baton over them for a moment, he lifted one of the parkas, admiring it.

"Those belong to us," Hypatia said with aristocratic command.

The bear-man held it up and turned to her.

"*Tanpe niste wa pirka na*," he said. He dropped the parka and then slipped the baton into his belt, next to his long knife. Taking both hands, he pulled off his bearskin cloak, and hissed something to his second, who quickly doffed his own cloak as well. The two came over and held out the bearskins to the women.

"Are they trying to trade their coats for ours?" Hypatia wondered aloud.

"Ghost of a chance," Nellie scoffed. "Keep your smelly old capotes to yourselves!" She shook her head angrily.

The men looked taken aback.

"*Eani teyne*," the leader said. It sounded as if he was scolding them. "*Somo méekot yan.*" He pointed to them, and waved a hand all around. The second man pantomimed shivering from cold, and toweling off, and tried to hand over his cloak again. Somewhat abashed, the two women nodded their understanding. They reached out and snatched the bearskins. Nellie took her arrow and clenched it in her teeth as she dried herself with the thick pelt.

The two warriors stepped back while they toweled off and then hurriedly dressed again. Nellie was disconcerted that none of the men took their eyes off them as they did. It wasn't that they were ogling them in a lustful manner, but more like she and Hypatia were prey animals that they did not wish to escape.

Once dressed, she clutched the arrow tightly again.

As they handed back the bearskin cloaks, she noticed beautiful embroidery on the men's headbands, coats, armguards, and boots. Graceful slender white lines in curves, swirls, and points, hems ringed with linked parentheses of thread forming little hedge-rows.

Who are these people? She had guessed they had landed in Yukon or Alaska now, but surely these weren't Esquimaux or some northern Indian tribe—their faces weren't dark enough, their hair too brown. Could they be some ancient tribal Europeans?

After this small kindness, would these rugged men let them go?

She wondered what Hypatia was thinking. If they did let them go, would she run away and leave Nellie to her own devices? Furtively, she glanced over to read any clues in her companion's eyes, but Hypatia's face was a mask. How could she have been so thoughtless and reckless? She was no… what was the word? She could barely stand to even think it.

A sapphist. A *lesbian*.

The leader interrupted her frantic, galloping thoughts.

"*Paye'an*," he said firmly, waving his hand for them to come along. Nellie turned to Hypatia, who reached over and took her hand without a word.

36

"Saber-cat," Feeds-the-Crows said, the only words he had uttered so far. He showed no more concern than pointing out an interesting rock. Harcourt turned and gasped at the sight of the hunched sabertooth stalking out from the grass, barely a stone's throw away, its yellow eyes fixed on him.

"Oh, bloody hell." Shanks, absently chewing on his thumbnail, snapped out of his woolgathering long enough to vent a curse.

"I see 'em," Rockwell answered without alarm, nonchalantly pulling out a pistol. "Go on, git!" He fired a warning shot just over the beast's head. It let out a loud, defiant snarl that showed off its foot-long canines, then turned and bounded away.

Other than that brief encounter, their party suffered no further difficulties as they trudged across open country. Every so often they came across a man-made artifact deposited by the Event—a truncated stretch of modern sidewalk, or a lone streetlight standing in an ocean of grass. Sometimes a sudden rise or drop in elevation hinted that they were crossing the subtle boundary to a new shard. Still, apart from the ruins and the occasional dried-up prehistoric swamp, virtually all the shards they crossed were prairielands, so there was little telling them apart, no matter how many years—or millennia—actually separated them.

Blake's attention kept being drawn to the mysterious silver arch ahead. It was just over a low rise, perhaps a klick or two away and twenty, maybe twenty-five meters high. After walking that kilometer, however, it seemed no closer, and appeared to be considerably bigger, maybe even twice as tall as he'd first supposed.

With the afternoon sun falling, the prisoners and their captors laid eyes on the leaden waters of the Mississippi River, and took in their first full view of the arch. He was wrong, Blake realized, stunned at seeing it soaring so high above them, bigger than Big Ben—at least twice as tall, he guessed. Sunset made the steel gleam, like firelight on twin scimitars.

"*Kammneves gwrug a'horn*," Cam murmured in reverent wonder. *Sign-of-rain, of iron forged*. "An iron rainbow." He turned to Rockwell. "Did your gods raise it up? Did they entrap the rainbow inside it?"

The big man frowned at the young heathen's ignorant blasphemy.

"No one knows who built it," he declared. "Though surely some lost race of mighty men or angels constructed it out of steel, or better. There's them that say there was once a way to get inside it, though that secret's lost now." He shrugged away the thought. "Well, we paid our respects." He cocked his head to the north, toward a great stone fortress on the banks of the river.

"That's where we're headed."

The aftermath of a battle greeted them at the gates to the fortress. From the looks of things, a hungry predator, some species of carnivorous dinosaur, had tried to tear into the gates to snack on the juicy little mammals inside, and had been repelled.

It lay on the ground, an ugly iron harpoon protruding from its skull as teams of butchers in blood-splattered aprons worked on the carcass, swiftly carving up tons of fresh meat while fending off opportunistic crows. To Blake's eye, they appeared to be of varied ethnicities, dressed in a mix of styles ranging from early pioneer times to perhaps Harcourt's era. The party's arrival provoked no reaction from the butchers, completely occupied with the task at hand.

He was impressed by the ingenuity of the fortifications. The Event had taken away nearly all of the city, leaving behind roughly five or six city blocks square. From where they were standing it was clear that the boundary cut straight through the nearest block. What had once been multi-story tenement buildings now formed the outer wall, with the excess bricks and timbers cannibalized to fill in the gaps left by streets and alleys. Sentries armed with Tommy guns and rifles patrolled the wall alongside Civil War-era cannons, some converted to fearsome-looking harpoon guns.

Half of a stone bridge extended across the river before abruptly terminating. The half that remained had been turned into docks for a dozen small rivercraft and one large steamboat. Men were unloading cargo and tending to boats and fish traps.

Rockwell led his captives straight up to the gates and to a barred porthole set in the middle of one of the big iron doors. A metal plate slid open on the other side, and a guard peered out at them, eyes narrowed in suspicion. With a cursory glance at the new arrivals, he slammed it closed again. The heavy doors opened with a groan. Weathered and chipped lettering painted on nearby brick walls welcomed them to Laclede's Landing.

The gatekeeper motioned them in with a jerk of his thumb. The man fit the very image of a Prohibition-era mobster. Built like a linebacker, unmistakably Italian, his slick black hair gleamed beneath a sharp fedora. He was dressed to kill in suit and tie, even brandishing a Tommy gun. Something, however, didn't look quite right. It hit Blake a moment later.

The man's suit and tie were made of buckskin, dyed black.

The newcomers passed through a short tunnel just long enough to box in any attacking troops. Murder holes dotted the surface above them and on both sides. No flaming oil or crossbow bolts assailed them, so they passed through the open inner gates without ceremony, and entered the fortress-city.

* * *

Inside the high walls, the lively sounds and smells of a crowded city filled the air. What had once been blocks of brick-and-cast-iron factories, warehouses, and rows of tenements now formed the infrastructure of a gangster's paradise. The reptilian mounts padded down cobblestone streets lined with grogshops, gunsmiths, gambling dens, bars and brothels, and literal dens of thieves.

The stink of the place boasted a unique bouquet. Coal-fire smoke and the tang of industrial sweatshops blended with the fishy stink of the muddy riverfront, and open tavern doorways reeking of alcohol and spittoons. On the streets hung the smell of unwashed crowds and the droppings of horses and riding-lizards, of gunpowder and spilled blood.

Gutters ran with an unusually pungent stench. More pleasing aromas came from skillets of frying salt pork in the cook-house kitchens, warm bathwater and soap, the lures of perfumed women.

The cramped city bustled with commerce of every kind—mostly disreputable. Traders, fur trappers, and pimps made deals and hawked their wares. Amateur gamblers rolled the bones on corners while adventurers and con men prepared to hunt prey, and feral dogs and tiny dinosaurs the size of chickens ran wild in the alleys.

The intersection of two main streets had been turned into an improvised arena, wooden posts wrapped in barbed wire. Inside the crude ring, two bare-chested men were fighting with claw hammers, presumably to the death. The onlookers waved their bets, roaring with every blow. Further down the block, a smaller but well-heeled crowd gathered before a wooden stage, while a line of manacled men and women each waited for their turn to be auctioned off.

Cam stared at them, silently swearing to Andraste and Camulos that he would kill his captor or himself before he set foot on that stage.

Ignoring the entertainments, Rockwell and his partners kept going until they reached the steps of a solid, imposing building and hitched up their mounts. A pair of intimidating bruisers dressed in snappy 1920s fashion stood guard out front, armed with Thompson submachine guns. The somber edifice boasted a line of tall brick archways and above those, two levels of high stone pillars supporting the topmost bay and a peaked roof. Engraved letters were carved into stone.

U.S. POST OFFICE AND CUSTOM HOUSE

The inside was resplendent with marble flooring, crystal chandeliers, and Corinthian columns, along with high windows, and wide oak desks and tables. An impressive candle-lit lounge bar dominated one side of the lobby, staffed by a bevy of cocktail girls. Additional well-dressed, heavily armed gangster-types kept watch from every corner of the room. Four of them flanked a bespectacled clerk dressed in a smart waistcoat and sleeve garters sitting at the main desk.

"Not so fast." A pair of guards stepped forward as they entered, one raising a hand to stop them. "Check yer mohaskas." Rockwell and his men handed over their firearms.

Feeds-the-Crows started to pull out his tomahawk, but the guard waved it off.

"The hatchet's fine, Tonto. Just keep it stowed."

Rockwell waited until the clerk waved him forward, and then approached the main desk. Shanks removed his hat respectfully as he and Feeds-the-Crows led the three prisoners up behind. The clerk eyeballed them.

"So what do you have for us today, Rockwell?"

"Three bounties for Boss Giannola, Mr. Alphonse. Caught them not two hours ago."

"That right?" The clerk peered over his bifocals at the cargo. "These three got names?"

"Call themselves Blake, Cam, and Harcourt. The big one says he's a sergeant. I figured 'em for some holdovers of Egan's Rats."

"What, these here? This bunch is Irish?"

"Maybe so." Rockwell shrugged. "They talk awfully British-like, anyway."

Alphonse snorted. "Apples and oranges, friend, apples and oranges. Never seen a Harp decked out like your boys here. Besides, all those Mick palookas of Egan's are ancient history. We rubbed them out years ago."

"Hold on." Rockwell's voice was strained. "You're telling me there's nothing on these fellows' heads? Mind looking over the latest wanted posters to make sure?"

"Look here, cornpone," Alphonse growled, "quit wasting my time. I know the score on every bounty Boss Vito Giannola puts out, and these guys ain't worth bupkis. So *beat it.*"

"Capital," Harcourt murmured audibly. Cam looked to Blake, who remained poker-faced. The clerk pushed his glasses up and waved a finger at Rockwell.

"Besides, I thought you three were out hunting that two-bit weasel Quigley? What, did he give you the slip already?" Rockwell said nothing, turning with a sour frown and grabbing the leather lead out of Shanks's hands.

"Come on!" he snapped, dragging his prisoners across the lobby.

"See here now!" Harcourt said. "Where do you think you're taking us? It's just as we said, there's no bounty on us. Free us this instant as you assured us you would!"

Rockwell stopped in his tracks, and turned slowly to face them, his gaze cold and hard as flint. "Free? Well now, I don't recall ever sayin' the word *free*. Shanks, you recollect what I promised the gents?"

"I do indeed," Shanks replied with a grin. "'Dinner on us, and then they can be on their way,' which in my estimation is very fair."

"By George, that was just right!" Rockwell said. "So now let's make haste to the slave auction and sell these boys in time to get them a ration of cold corndodger and scrap meat before they head off on their way—downriver to the plantations, that is. Hurry now, I'd sure hate to be made a liar."

Harcourt stared in horror.

"But-but—" he sputtered.

"But *what*?" Rockwell snarled. "You got any money?"

"No, but—"

"Anybody here who vouches for you?"

"Well, now, you see—"

"Is anybody coming to rescue you?"

That shut Harcourt up before he could even work up a convincing lie. Blake smiled grimly.

"So, in these parts, that means you're slaves, you git me?" Rockwell spoke gently, as if explaining to a school child. "Another thing." Rockwell plucked the professor's top hat right off his head. "Slaves don't need hats. Timepieces neither," he added, fishing Harcourt's gold watch out by its chain. He turned to Cam and pointed to the silver torc around his neck. "Slaves don't need jewelry neither."

Even in chains and lashed to a tether, Cam bristled.

"Touch it and see who dies a slave."

Rockwell chuckled—but lowered his hand. He turned to his sidekicks.

"Boys, as much as I hate to damage the merchandise, we may need to haul these boys outside and tenderize them a bit afore the sale." Shanks leered, and Feeds-the-Crows fingered his tomahawk.

"I wouldn't," Blake said quietly. Rockwell turned on him slowly.

"Well, you sure fixed on a piss-poor time to start makin' threats."

"No threat," Blake said. "I just mean it doesn't make sense to sell us as slaves when you could do better." Rockwell raised an eyebrow.

"Oh, I want to hear this nugget of good counsel," he said with a mocking grin.

"I mean it," Blake responded. "You *could* sell us as slaves—but you'd make out better if you ran us as gladiators in the arena."

Neither Cam nor Harcourt objected, mostly because his proposition left the Victorian dumbstruck. Rockwell rubbed his chin, thinking it over. He looked over to his men, then back at Blake.

"Boys, I think he means it," he said. "And I don't mind tellin' you, it ain't the worst notion I've heard today."

Cam continued to glower his defiance, but Harcourt paled, looking as though he was about to keel over. Rockwell noticed.

"May as well just sell the scarecrow for meat."

"He's pretty useless, I'll grant you that," Blake agreed. Harcourt looked on in mute terror, shaking like a leaf. "At least, in a fight," Blake continued. "Still, he has some useful skills that would make him valuable to the right people. Don't you, Professor?"

"What?" It took a moment for Harcourt to recognize the lifeline Blake was throwing him. "Oh, yes—*yes*. Indubitably!"

Their captors looked unconvinced.

"If this poncy blighter has any uses 'cept as target practice or fish-bait, I'll eat me hat," Shanks muttered.

"N-no… it's true!" the professor said. "I'm a most… a most learned professor, with degrees in a multitude of scientific fields." His stammer eased up as he slid into his familiar spiel. "My skills are invaluable for a wide variety of projects and consultations, as I often provided for the crown heads of Europe. To give merely one example, I know the formula to create a Special Galvanic Nerve Elixir—"

"Galvanic?" Rockwell asked. "What's galvanic?"

"Why, it refers to power of electricity in liquid form. Lightning in a bottle!"

"You know a thing or two about electrickery, do you?" Rockwell's tone changed.

"Certainly. I harness it to remedy all manner of physical and cerebral ailments, complaints, and maladies, both common and exotic. There is no end to the number of practical applications…"

"Alright, alright, keep your voice down," Rockwell hushed him. "Get over here." Now they had the big man's attention. He pulled them aside, to a quiet corner of the cocktail lounge.

"Don't suppose you can show any proof, can you?" he asked in a low voice.

"But of course!" Harcourt beamed, fully in his stride. "As all we electrophysickers—that is, practitioners of the galvanic arts—well know, voltaic energy is found in two primary varieties, vitreous electricity and resinous electricity, which together compose the electric fluid. Now, by simply constructing a small tower of copper, silver, and tutanego calamine disks, separated by ordinary brine-soaked cloth, connected at both top and bottom terminals by silver wire, an accomplished electriconeer such as myself can easily create a single current, and thereby produce the electromotive force, to be employed however one desires. *Quod erat demonstrandum.*

"Nevertheless," he continued, "if you would prefer a more practical proof of concept, I can easily provide a rheoscopic demonstration by constructing a working galvanoscope using only a small length of metal wire or foil, a scalpel, and three pairs of frog's legs."

Rockwell was silent for a moment, then dusted off Harcourt's hat and politely returned it to his captive's head, as if bestowing a crown. He kept the gold watch.

"Never you mind about the frog legs. You've sold me, sir. I believe this is the beginning of a profitable partnership." Then he gave a dark look. "... as long as you deliver the goods." The threat delivered, he brightened again. "Alright then, let's put this pair in the arena to see if we can rustle up a little folding money—"

"Oh, but I'll need my assistants," Harcourt said. "They may not be the smartest, but they are nevertheless completely indispensable."

Blake shot him a look, but kept a straight face. "The professor's right. He needs Cam and me to... radiowave the atomic... jazz gizmos."

Cam nodded solemnly. "Yes."

Rockwell stared at them, and appeared to be torn. Then he nodded decisively, and slapped Shanks on the shoulder.

"Come on," he said in a low voice. "Let's get these three out of here before someone figures out what we got."

Puzzled, Shanks peered over his shoulder to see if the guards were eavesdropping. "What about taking them to Vito Giannola?" he whispered.

Rockwell only shook his head. Shrugging, Shanks and Feeds-the-Crows retrieved their firearms from the doormen, and they all went outside and down the steps. When they were mounted up and out of earshot, Shanks spoke up again.

"God blind me, Old Port! What's your game? After all that fuss and bother, we're *not* selling them to Vito?"

"Nope."

"Well, why the bloody hell not?"

"We're taking them somewhere very special. Goin' cross the river."

"Across the river to *where*?"

"Way I reckon, Sun-Raven will pay even better for a crew that knows electrickery and such."

"*Sun-Raven?*" Shanks stared at him in disbelief. "The bloody Indian god-king? Are you barking mad? Crows, tell the man this is a spectacularly bad idea."

"Bad idea," Feeds-the-Crows agreed flatly. The Englishman arched his eyebrows and held up his palm to show his point was made.

"Listen to you old hens cackle." Rockwell laughed. "You don't see our guests wettin' themselves at the prospect. Now come on, we have a ferry ride to book."

"Sun-Raven." Shanks shot the prisoners a sour look. "Our guts for garters, that's what we'll get from that moony bastard."

37

As they trudged through the snow with the strange shaggy men, Hypatia wrestled with troubled thoughts. In her rational mind, she knew concentrating on survival was paramount. So, with a supreme effort of will, she banished her tangled emotions and fears to be dealt with later.

Her ankle still troubled her, but with Nellie's arm around her waist she was able to keep a steady pace. The six men surrounded them but kept their distance, remaining silent and avoiding eye contact. They carried game in woven knapsacks. Birds, small mammals, and trilobites. Hunters, then.

She wondered how the rough men saw them—as captives? Guests?

Prey?

They came to an intimidating display—a wall of skulls with a towering arch. The gateway was formed by a pair of curving elephant tusks, but of a titanic size. Hypatia had never seen the like. Stretching away from the gate, the wall was a rough palisade of sharpened tree trunks mounted with a menagerie of huge, toothsome skulls—what appeared to be bears, wolves, carnivore lizards, the crested skulls of winged reptiles, and other imposing monsters completely unknown to her.

Rows of their pale willow-wood staves ringed the wall, each one spear-sized and sporting tuffs of the curling ringlets. The various skulls were decorated with the curls of willow shavings as well.

Hypatia feared the hunters were taking them to a slaughterhouse.

"*Akon kotan*," the leader announced to the women. The group paused before the gateway, murmuring what seemed to be quiet prayers. They reverently touched the great tusks as they entered.

Inside stood a small cluster of thatched-roofed wooden houses, along with a pair of smaller structures raised on poles—one a thatched storehouse, the other a raised wooden cage containing a young brown bear cub. She was surprised to see the hunters greet the little captive warmly, feeding it morsels of dried jerky by hand.

Women and children came out of the houses, collecting the men's game and staring at the new arrivals. The women saluted the hunters in what seemed to Hypatia a most slavish fashion, covering their mouths with one hand and fixing their eyes upon the ground. Some made a whining, crying noise, as if keening for them. She found it most troubling.

The boys wore the same embroidered robes and trousers

as the men, while the women and girls wore long dresses. She noticed the women bore tattoos, no two alike, black geometric shapes and lines wrapping their fingers, hands, and forearms. Except for the young girls, the women all had wide blue smiles tattooed on their mouths—a curious adornment.

Their arm tattoos reminded her of designs she had seen at the library in Alexandria, in drawings made of Scythian women who lived beyond the Black Sea. Perhaps that was where they were now, in Scythian territory or some mountainous region of the Sarmatians.

The gods help us.

The hunting party took them to the largest house in the village, where their leader stepped up and gave a low cough. After a few moments an elderly woman emerged, her eyes downcast. Covering her mouth, she spoke quietly to the man, then retreated out of the way as he and the rest of the party solemnly entered. Hypatia and Nellie followed, still clasping hands.

Woven tapestries in geometric diamond shapes hung on the walls inside, along with rows of the ubiquitous shaved willow sticks. A large rectangular firepit lit and warmed the room. On the wooden shelf above it, sheaves of millet lay alongside racks of drying salmon, filling the room with their pungent aroma. The old woman joined three young ones sitting quietly against the wall, trying to remain invisible.

A stout old man, face wizened and impressively bearded, sat cross-legged at the head of the hearth. Pulling back his cowl, the lead hunter respectfully approached with quiet, careful steps to sit down at his right. He cleared his throat once again and extended his hands, palms together, fingers splayed. The old man, who seemed to be the chief, did the same. They moved their hands in synchronicity, back and forth, each movement made with great formality.

The other hunters stood waiting, unmoving and silent. Hypatia and Nellie kept silence with them. While Hypatia carefully observed all the subtle nuances, Nellie tapped an anxious foot, still clutching her arrow tightly.

The ritual continued for some time, after which the two men sat in silence, each stroking his own beard while making a soft rumbling sound in the throat. Then they began to speak, and the lead hunter turned to indicate the two women. The chief turned to them, as if only now noticing their presence, and waved the rest of the group over to join them by the fire.

Nellie and Hypatia sat, pulling back the fur-lined hoods of their parkas and removing their mittens. The chief peered at them silently. Hypatia cleared her throat politely, averting her gaze while covering her mouth. Then she put her palms together as the men had done. Nellie hastened to follow Hypatia's lead.

"We are Hypatia of Alexandria and Nellie Bly of New York," Hypatia said. "We greet you, and thank you for your gallant rescue."

"Yes, thank you very much," Nellie chimed in.

The headman blinked in surprise at this development. Then he spoke.

"*Irankarapte.*" Returning their salute, he began the hand-rubbing gestures all over again. The women followed suit, until he stopped and patted his chest.

"*Isonash tapne, an pe ku'ne wa.*" He paused, then repeated the gesture. "*Isonash. Káni Isonash.*"

"Chief Isonash," Hypatia acknowledged. "*Káni...* Hypatia."

"Hi-pay—"

"Hypatia."

"Hi'e-Pay-Shah."

Hypatia smiled with a gracious bow of her head. Nellie spoke up.

"*Káni...* Nellie."

"Ne'ee?" the chieftain struggled with the odd sounds.

"Nell-ee."

"Ne-hee."

Nellie smiled and nodded. "That's me." Acting on a sudden inspiration, she ceremoniously lay down her arrow before the chief as a gesture of good faith.

The mood of the room warmed at once, and the other men introduced themselves, as well. Their lead hunter was Harukor, his cautious second Turushno. With introductions out of the way, Isonash had another question for them.

"*Eani Shamo kur yan?*"

Hypatia and Nellie looked at one another blankly.

"That word *Shamo* again," Hypatia said softly, frowning in concern. "I think they want to know if we are *Shamo*— whatever that is."

"Well, whatever it is, they don't seem to like it much," Nellie replied. She turned back to Isonash.

"No! No *Shamo*!" she said, waving her arm for emphasis. She spit on the floor. "*Shamo*, ptooey!"

Everyone in the hut glared at her in shocked silence. Hypatia's expression was horrified.

"*Yaysama...*" the old man exclaimed quietly. Alarmed, Hypatia cleared her throat to try and offer an apology, but before she could, Harukor grinned and shouted, "*Sonno! Shamo ptooey!*" He spit, and all the other hunters laughed and joined in as well, shouting, "*Sonno!*" and spitting against the cursed *Shamo*.

"*Sonno!*" Nellie yelled happily. The room erupted with wild cheers, and Hypatia exhaled in relief. Pleased, the headman clapped his hands and whistled what sounded like a merry little birdcall. The women of the house stood up and began to prepare for dinner.

Hypatia is a far better diplomat than I am, Nellie thought, stewing in self-recrimination. They had been lucky. That *Shamo* business could just as easily gone the wrong way, and then where would they be? She resolved to restrain herself and follow the older woman's lead, and tried to wait patiently for the meal to begin. Their dinner simmered in thick trough-like hammocks of folded tree bark, suspended above the low fire with sticks and knotted fibers. Hungry as she was, its aroma was both exotic and intoxicating.

While Hypatia sat as serene as porcelain, it took all Nellie's willpower to hide the jumbling pain in her heart. She desperately wondered what her companion was thinking—the older woman felt so closed off to her. To make matters worse, her empty stomach was rumbling so loudly she was sure everyone in the room could hear.

Perhaps they did. Isonash called for the other men to gather around the fire pit alongside them, and the young women came forward and sat in a row behind the men. The woman they took to be his wife went and fetched a little wooden slat and an ammonite shell the size of a wheelbarrow wheel. Taking them, he seemed first to speak to both implements, then dipped the slat into the shell, and methodically sprinkled a few drops onto the fire, offering more words in a reverent tone.

Then he used the slat to pull his beard aside as he drank heartily from the shell, and passed them to Harukor, who did the same, before passing them on to Nellie.

Nellie hefted the stick and shell awkwardly, braced herself, and risked an experimental swig as the men cheered. It was a thick white beer that smelled of millet, and wasn't half bad. She took a second, bigger quaff and wiped her mouth, flashing a cheeky grin which made the men hoot and cheer all over again.

Hypatia, of course, was the soul of poise and dignity, giving a slight bow of her head to the host and to the hearth before taking a long graceful drink, and sighing her contentment before passing them on to Turushno.

The beer made its way around the group. Once the last of the girls took a drink, the chief and then the rest of the men began to clap in rhythm—except one of the youths who pulled out a tiny wooden frame with a thread attached. He held it in his mouth, harmonica-style, while plucking the thread to create a twanging music like a Jew's harp.

As Isonash's wife croaked out a chant, the three younger

girls broke into a shuffling dance, bowing and flapping the hems of their robes like bird wings. The dance showed off the detailed embroidery of their dresses and headdresses to good effect. The designs made Nellie think of the Coastal Indian art motifs she had seen in exhibits back at the natural history museum in New York. Is that where they were now, among some whiter-skinned tribe of the Tlingit or Haida?

Her musings, the dance, and the music were suddenly cut short by a sound that drowned out all the merriment—the now familiar mocking roar and terrifying laughter, echoing across the mountains. The girls quickly dropped to the floor, prostrating themselves toward the house's main window. The others did the same, leaving only Nellie and Hypatia still upright.

They looked at each other in alarm.

Chief Isonash rubbed his hands together as he had before with Harukor, speaking rapidly while the laughter continued to echo through the evening air. When the unholy sounds outside finally faded away, the room relaxed again. Everyone regained their seats and placed their backs to the window, returning their attention to the fire pit and their chief.

The headman finished his incantation or prayer, whatever it was, and turned to Nellie and Hypatia. Seeing their alarm, he pointed to the window, and first placed his hands up from his forehead like horns.

"*Kirawe.*"

"Yes, horns," Nellie said, repeating the gesture. "Horns."

He held his pinky fingers up in front of his lips, like tusks. "*Esaw poro.*"

299

"Yes, he had big teeth, too," Nellie said, mirroring his pantomime. "And his skin was blue. His skin—"She rubbed her cheeks and forearms. "Blue. Like, like…" She touched his sleeve. "Like this. We saw him last night." She mimed looking up and seeing.

"*Atuy-Siwnin Wenkamuy*," Harukor said grimly.

"*Wenkamuy*," Turushno agreed.

"*Daimon*," Hypatia said.

"Yes, a demon," Nellie murmured.

Isonash waved for his wife and daughters to start the dinner. Impatient to eat, Nellie wrapped her arms around her aching stomach and tried her best to hide how ravenous she was. She felt painfully alone. Other than the brief moment when the thing outside had roared, Hypatia had avoided eye contact with her, and sat gazing into the flames, stoic as a Buddha.

The old chieftain continued to talk—he seemed to be either praying or giving thanks to everything in sight, from the hearth to the birch-bark serving bowls, to the walls of the house, the row of little sacred willow-wands—there was that word again, *inaw*—the ceiling, out the open window, and then finally, to the food itself, still simmering over the fire.

Poor souls, Nellie thought. *Do they have to pray to every last thing they see before they can eat? They're worse than Cam.*

At last she received her own steaming bowl of gruel—a mix of grains, leeks, other wild plants, seaweed, cubes of red meat, little chunks of trilobite and salmon. It looked and smelled absolutely mouthwatering. She started to raise the bowl to her lips, but Hypatia cleared her throat and shot her a quick look of reproach.

Chagrined, Nellie quickly set it down again and waited until everyone was served. Once the last girl received her food, Isonash raised his bowl to his lips, and the rest followed suit.

Finally, Nellie thought, lifting her bowl once more. She breathed in the salmon's rich aroma—nothing had ever smelled so fine in her life.

Hypatia will hate this, she thought. *Hypatia hates* me.

Suddenly the smell of the gruel became overwhelming, and her stomach took a frightful turn. Clapping a hand over her mouth, Nellie dropped her bowl, then stumbled to her feet toward the door. The doorway seemed to reel crazily, and she tumbled outside to the frosty ground and vomited. Even after she had spewed what little she had in her belly, the horrible retching continued.

The villagers froze in shock, stunned at Nellie's sudden departure and the awful noises she was making. Hypatia sat still for a moment, then took a long, unhurried drink from her bowl before nodding and carefully setting it back down again.

"Delicious," she said, with a gentle bow of her head. "I thank you." Then she placed her hand on her chest. "I am sorry, but please excuse me—I must go check on my friend."

No one moved as she rose and slipped out the door.

Nellie lay sprawled out on her elbows, her head barely raised, sobbing and shaking. Hypatia knelt down beside her and slipped a hand past the parka's hood to gently stroke the back of her head. Nellie flinched at the touch, then looked up at Hypatia with eyes drenched in sorrow and pain, exhaling heavily, her breath turning to puffs of fog in the cold. She wiped her mouth.

"I-I'm, I'm so sorry, Hypatia..." Still trembling, she struggled to unload each word.

"You needn't apologize," Hypatia soothed. "You've suffered, and now your stomach troubles you. It's perfectly natural."

"No! Not that. I mean before—back... at the pool." She hid her face against Hypatia's lap. For once, Hypatia did not know what to say, so she remained silent, continuing to stroke Nellie's neck and run fingers through her hair.

"Please don't hate me," Nellie whispered.

"Hate you? Of course I don't."

"But... earlier. You seemed so furious at me." Nellie reached a hand to grasp the hem of Hypatia's parka.

"Furious?" Hypatia shook her head. "No, never. I... It's merely that you surprised me."

"Believe me, I'm not... I mean, I've never... It's just, I don't know what came over me."

"Love, I should think—don't you?"

Nellie froze at Hypatia's words. Then she sat up, looking at her with wide, questioning eyes.

"Yes," she finally replied. "I do love you, oh so truly."

Hypatia placed a hand on Nellie's cheek, then moved it further, gently cradling her ear.

"And I you, Beloved." She kissed Nellie's cheek, and pressed their faces together for a long moment, feeling the tickle of a tear run down Nellie's cheek onto her own. "We'll talk more tonight," she said, with another quick kiss to Nellie's cheek. "But now let's return to our hosts and see if you can eat a little, shall we?"

* * *

The dinner continued long after their awkward return to the fireside. Nellie tried to make her apologies, but with the formidable language gap, it was hard to say if the chieftain forgave her or not.

One of his daughters brought out another round of the millet beer, and the feast continued without further incident. Nellie ate the rest of her bowl and a second helping, and when she and Hypatia could no longer keep their eyes open, the hunters quietly took their leave. The old chief and his wife went off to one of the side rooms, and the daughters cleaned up and brought out piles of furs and blankets, placing them next to the hearth for their guests.

As the girls retreated to their own room, Nellie and Hypatia smiled their thanks. It felt decadent to be able to finally doff their arctic parkas and regular clothes and strip down to just their underthings—or in Hypatia's case, nothing—before slipping under the soft pile of covers.

They lay looking up at the wooden rafters, their faces lit only by the embers of the fire. Acutely aware of the warmth of Hypatia's body beside her, Nellie lay perfectly still, afraid if she moved or spoke she might break the fragile peace between them. Finally, though, she thought she would explode if she didn't speak.

"Hypatia?" Her voice came out so quiet it was barely there, but Hypatia heard it.

"Yes?"

"You said something earlier. Perhaps I misheard, but I think… you said…" She paused, then finished in a rush. "You said that you love me, too?"

"I believe I remember that," Hypatia said. "And it seems to me I owe you an apology."

Nellie turned to her. "*You?* Apologize to *me*? Whatever for?"

"For making you believe I was repelled by your kiss."

"You—you weren't?"

Hypatia rolled onto her side, her eyes serious. "It thrilled me like nothing before in my life," she said quietly.

Nellie's heart began to race again.

"We Greeks know many kinds of love, and many words for it," Hypatia continued, "but I always sided with those who divide it into two sorts. First the higher love, that delights only in the intelligent nature of others, true and faithful to the end, without wantonness or lust. The second is only its copy and its shadow, a coarser kind of love, a love of the body rather than of the soul. All my life I have prided myself that I was immune to such temptation.

"Until you." She reached out her hand, and the two gently locked fingers.

"That is what terrified me so. That is what I ran from."

Nellie said nothing, but kissed the back of Hypatia's hand.

"Now all too often I find myself thinking of lines from the poet Sappho," Hypatia continued.

Nellie raised an eyebrow at the name.

"Tell me one."

Hypatia thought for a moment, and then quietly sang out a few lines in Greek. Nellie blushed as her implant translated it for her.

"You came and I was mad for you,

and you cooled my mind that burned with longing…

In the crooks of your body, I find my religion. Someone will remember us, I say, even in another time."

"I like that," Nellie said, "but… is Sappho's poetry conducive to a purely platonic friendship?"

"Of course. I am a Platonist, after all."

"Then tell me more."

Hypatia smiled. "I will, but kiss me again first."

"Nellie?

"Nellie?"

Nellie opened her eyes and sat up, startled by the familiar voice.

"Amber! Are you there?"

"Nellie, where are you? I need your help! I'm trapped!"

"Amber! I hear you! We're here!"

"Nellie, why did you leave? Now it's too late…"

"No! Don't say that! We'll come back right now!"

Hypatia rolled over and peered at her. "Who are you talking to?"

"It's Amber! She's found us!"

Hypatia stared back at her, expressionless. "No, Amber's dead. Look."

Outside the window, Amber fought to get to her feet, orbited by a patchwork carousel of ghostlights that closed in

305

on her. She screamed Nellie's name as they converged on her, bisecting her, swallowing her up.

Nellie screamed, too, but her voice made no sound. Completely nude and untroubled by the cold, Hypatia yawned, her outstretched arms making the movement a seduction.

"Forget her," she said. "Come back to me."

Nellie bent down to embrace her. The sound of Amber's screams no longer seemed so important.

Nellie sat up with a start.

Hypatia lay deep asleep, her back to her.

The tuffs of the *inaw* stirred faintly in the open window. Outside, only the moon and stars, and the cold air. How could they stand to not cover up that eastern window?

She rubbed her face, deeply disturbed by the nightmare, and let out a deep exhalation. Shivering, she ducked back down under the covers and clung to Hypatia's warm curves. But even as she did, something half-noticed drew her back out. She looked over to their pile of clothing.

Their parkas and snow boots were gone.

38

Blake, Harcourt, and Cam had spent the night in unforgiving chains, locked in the basement of Rockwell's favorite groghouse and bordello. Their promised dinner had been no more than an old piece of fried cornbread each, so hard it hurt their teeth.

Unable to sleep, Blake wondered if they had missed their chance to escape, worrying whether Kha-Hotep and Leila were even still alive, second-guessing the decision to go looking for them in the first place. Next to him, Cam and Harcourt seemed to have no trouble sleeping.

Breakfast the next morning was a barely drinkable cup of what the house called coffee—though when pressed, the serving boy who delivered it admitted the watery concoction consisted mostly of brown bread, barley, acorn mash, and dandelion roots, flavored with a dash of snuff.

* * *

Rockwell rushed his crew and captives out to the riverfront early enough to hitch a cheap ride along with the freight and produce on that morning's northbound steam packet. The steamship was a weathered old sidewheeler, a bulky, deep-draft workhorse of a riverboat christened the *Zebulon M. Pike*.

They quickly staked out a pocket of deck space on the bow amid crates, baskets, and bundles of cargo, bid goodbye to the fishing skiffs and flatboats, and the enigmatic silver arch towering above them, and set off upriver.

Once we're out of this mess, Blake thought, *we head back to the Landing and make inquiries at the slave market. With any luck, Kha-Hotep and Leila were sold there, and we'll find out who bought them. Then we'll get a boat and a guide to take us downriver to wherever these plantations are.*

He avoided the bigger question.

How they would get back to Antarctica.

"I thought you said we would be crossing the river." Blake addressed Rockwell as they sat crowded together. "Where are you taking us?"

Rockwell jerked a thumb toward the far shore. "That look like a landing to you?"

On closer look, Blake saw that what at first appeared to be a natural bluff was in fact a walled defense. A stranded freight train had been turned into the base of a fortified barrier, the gaps between cars filled in with brick and earthen ramparts.

The train looked modern enough to be from the mid-twentieth century or later, maybe part of the same shard as the giant arch across the water.

The walls of the fort had been built atop the train. Banners hung from tall lances all along their length, and just like the walls of Laclede's Landing, they boasted field cannon and soldiers armed with Tommy guns and other firearms. These troops, however, were clearly native American.

"That fort's just their border," Rockwell informed him. "We're going all the way to the big city itself."

"What city would that be?"

Rockwell had either grown used to their stupid questions or was simply tired of slagging them off for it. "Biggest metropolis around nowadays. They call it—what is it they call it, Crows?"

"Sacred Place Where the Star Woman Came and Touched the Earth, Near the Joining of the Five Great Rivers, in the Year when Three Moons Danced and Sang," the scout rattled off.

Rockwell nodded. "Well, the whites just call it Cahokia."

The *Zebulon M. Pike* proved to be a sluggish vessel with a primitive steam engine. Even so, it made steady progress, chugging along slowly northward. Except for their circumstances, Blake thought, it would have been an idyllic scenic cruise, right out of a Mark Twain novel, albeit one where Huck Finn shared the wide river with placid brontosauruses foraging in the water. Unimpressed, Harcourt managed to somehow look simultaneously bored and indignant.

Animal life abounded. Fearless little otters played on the banks, fascinating Cam. They chased the ducks and cormorants, annoyed the turtles, and launched flocks of small white plovers into the air. Overhead, somber lines of pterodactyls sailed across the sky.

Before long, the steamship took a lazy starboard turn to follow a tributary, and they spotted a mounted Cahokian cavalryman watching them go by. Bare-chested and long-haired, the native American rider bore a lance twenty feet long and carried a Winchester rifle in his saddle scabbard. He rode high on his mount's back, saddled well behind the reach of its horns.

Cam's eyes widened. He had seen similar creatures before. Larger than a bull rhino, an impressive frill of horns crowned the stocky beast's massive crested skull, with two more on each cheek, and one long central horn emerging from its bird-beaked face. Its thigh had been painted with a compass or crosshair design, a white circle crossed by double lines, and its crest and horns were accented with fearsome blood-red lines.

"They say their fort and the mounties are there to keep watch for T-Rexes crossing the river," Rockwell drawled, "but everybody knows the big fellas don't much care to swim. They just want to keep us reprobates on the badlands side."

The further they traveled, the more they could see where the Event had played havoc, reconnecting old waterways and cutting new ones. Their path wound in drunken twists through oxbows and horseshoes, past miles of outer suburban townships and small fishing villages. Children ran along the riverbank, laughing and waving at the boat. There were also settlements of pioneer cabins, and rancheros of cattle, horses, tapirs, or various sorts of smaller prehistoric livestock, both reptiles and mammals.

The sun wasn't yet directly overhead when they finished threading through the maze of waterways to arrive at another landing, and another fort. Smaller watercraft clustered around the docks—flatboats and keelboats, fishing boats and canoes.

Snatches of English, French, Spanish, and more filled the air as teams of stevedores began to unload cargo from the *Zebulon*. The mixed crews appeared to be native Cahokians, most wearing little more than high leather sandals, loincloths, and tattoos. Judging from the differences in clothes and languages, Blake guessed there were also other native American tribes working there, as well as whites, blacks, and Creoles in various modes of mostly nineteenth-century dress, several in a mix of native and European styles.

He tried to listen to their chatter, but his linguistic implant was no help for any of the native languages.

Like the dockworkers, the Cahokian custom officials wore little, though they boasted bright red woven capes and necklaces of authority. While most inspected the arriving cargo, one stood by the gate with a circle of guards, each armed with a rifle and a brace of pistols.

The custom official looked dubiously at Rockwell and his entourage. Clearly their job was to keep the riffraff out. Neither he nor his guards seemed to regard Feeds-the-Crows with much warmth, either, but he stepped up and did the talking for the group anyway.

It didn't seem to be going well.

"Told you this was a bad idea," Shanks muttered.

"You just stand there humble-like and keep your trap shut," Rockwell growled under his breath.

Sensing a fight might break out at any moment, Blake looked sidelong to see if this could be the right time to escape. The only flight options were back into the river or up to the heavily guarded city gates. He had no idea what language they were speaking, or what was being said, until Feeds-the-Crows pointed to Harcourt, and apparently said the magic word.

"Anagalisgi."

That broke the ice, and then it was just a matter of them being checked for more weapons and contraband before the official handed them a thin bar of copper. It had been engraved with intricate designs of a bird-man figure, along with lines of text written in some strange variant of Roman lettering.

"Your pass into the Sacred District and the palace," the officer said, pointing toward a towering green ziggurat perfectly framed by the gateway. The colossal terraced mound looked to be about ten stories tall, and lay about two kilometers to the north.

The border patrol guards stepped aside as their superior waved the group on. As they passed through the landing's fortress gates, the officer signaled to a teenaged boy, who quickly ran up. The man whispered a message into his ear and the rangy youth nodded before running off again.

"That went well," Blake said.

"Yes, thank you, Crows," Shanks grumbled. "Right out of the frying pan into this great lovely fire."

"Shut your braying donkey face before I box your ears in, dough-head," Rockwell growled. "What are you bellyaching for, anyhow? Did you see how quick that jumped-up redskin let us in once Crows told him 'bout the electrickery? We're headed for the big time now, boys. Off to the palace!"

A mercantile district spread out before them, its main streets thronged with people and animals. Faces of every hue passed them, dressed in a variety of mixed-and-matched styles, speaking a dozen languages or more—their implants could only make out a fraction of them.

Clusters of earth mounds rose above the crowds and buildings, some topped with still more structures, others blazing with ceremonial fires. Teams of builders swarmed around new construction. They were in a true cosmopolitan metropolis, a growing, vibrant city. Even Blake was impressed.

What year is all this from? he wondered. *And just how big is this shard?*

Alongside the multitude of human pedestrians and porters, horses, riding-lizards, and oxen passed still more curious beasts of burden—mastodons, turtle-shelled armadillos the size of igloos, and full-bellied dinosaurs that looked something like giant horned toads, bristling with sharp points along their flanks. All of them were decorated with painted designs, with elaborate saddles for riders or rope nets heavy with cargo.

Shops, workshops, and patios lined the wide boulevard. The sounds of blacksmiths, potters, carpenters, and other artisans competed with the ruckus of construction teams, the cries of vendors, and haggling of merchants. The storefronts ran the gamut from simple open-air markets and outdoor drinking tents to fancy shops and restaurants of brick and timber. Multilingual signs abounded, advertising in both text and pictographs.

They moved out of the mercantile quarter and past blocks of tight-packed neighborhoods. Most were native Cahokian, timber houses constructed and decorated in a hybrid architecture of native American and European. Heavenly smells of frying corncakes, fish, and venison came from the kitchens, along with aromatic stews of squash and peppers simmering in pots. Here and there they passed the outskirts of more communities, from different native tribes as well as European settlers—French Creoles, Spanish, Yankees, and English, clustered in their own barrios.

The road ahead split to loop around a perfectly circular court, more than a hundred meters across, ringed by dozens of tall standing totem poles. The space within was covered by a layer of fine white sand that gleamed like bleached bone. As crowded as the thoroughfares were, no one dared step near it. They continued around with the flow of traffic, and soon came to a high palisade wall surrounding the inner city.

The defensive wall, studded with fortified bastions at regular intervals, stood as tall as the totem poles, ten meters high, made from tens of thousands of logs, each nearly a meter in diameter. Rockwell flashed their pass, and the soldiers waved them on.

They went through a narrow gap between twin objects guarding the southern entrance—one a giant conical mound, the other an enormous stepped pyramid—and then found themselves entering the city's grand plaza. The wall enclosing the inner city radiated out from either side of the south gates they had entered and then became fairly square on the other three sides.

Blake tried to estimate the size of the central precinct. It covered scores of acres—*no, bigger than that*—at least two hundred acres if it was an inch. He had been to Rome after the war. This was easily five times as large as St. Peter's Square.

Aristocratic neighborhoods of fancy houses and other important-looking buildings clustered along the flanks, along with more earthen mounds and cones surrounding some kind of sports field or parade ground in the center. But the most impressive structure by far lay straight ahead of them—the multi-leveled Royal Palace of Cahokia, dominating the whole northern end of the inner city.

"I never thought I'd look on any work as mighty as those I saw in Egypt," Cam mused aloud, "but this palace is even broader than the Great Pyramid itself."

Blake nodded, also impressed. "Bigger than my kingdom's Buckingham Palace, too."

"Egads, you're right," exclaimed Harcourt. He looked personally offended at the thought.

They continued across the plaza, past nobles and their retinues, message runners and servants on errands, haughty city officials, and merchant caravans. A sporting event was commencing. Parades of athletes carried spears and thick plate-sized stone disks to the playing field and its crowds of eager spectators.

Finally they arrived at the palace.

After showing their pass at the lowest foot of the stepped pyramid, the Palace Guard collected their weapons, searching them for hidden ones. They climbed up the long broad steps to the middle tier's plaza, where more soldiers stood on guard and a great number of Cahokian and foreign nobles milled around the edges of the terrace, admiring the view.

In the cool shade of a luxuriously decorated woven canopy, another official wearing eyeglasses sat at a table. An older man, he was dressed much like the border officials, though his fine-beaded cloak and jewelry were more splendid. He sent away a pair of disappointed merchants and waved Rockwell and his group forward, calling out something in Cahokian.

"The Sun Raven is not seeing petitioners today," he tersely repeated in English and French. Rockwell stepped up and spent a few fruitless minutes pleading their case.

Cam nudged Blake. "That woman is watching us," he said, nodding toward a noblewoman currently standing amid the other ladies of the court. Blake peered in her direction as inconspicuously as possible. She was a young Creole, he guessed, her sleek, pomaded hair in a stylish Roaring Twenties cut, dressed in a white wrap of cotton that flowed around her body like silk, accentuated by a scarlet headscarf.

She looked like something out of *The Arabian Nights*.

Laughing with a trio of other women, they appeared to be in their own little world, enjoying the view and chatting about nothing—but she clearly had her eye on the three of them.

Do I know her? Blake wondered. She looked familiar, but he'd be damned if he could figure out who.

If she spotted them spying on her, she gave no sign of it, but she nonchalantly left her friends and strode over to the court scheduler, lightly touching his shoulder as she bent down to whisper in his ear. Then, gracing them with just a flash of dazzling smile, she went back to her friends. Clearly, she was used to being looked at—she made an exquisite art of it.

"You're in luck after all," the official said without explanation. "The Sun Raven has deigned to see you."

A squad of the palace guards escorted them up the long high steps to the final terrace. As they ascended, Blake surreptitiously leaned toward Harcourt.

"I've been meaning to ask you," he said under his breath. "Was any of that electricity song-and-dance you gave Rockwell true?"

The professor paused thoughtfully, as though he had never stopped to consider such a question.

"I only ask," Blake added, "because our lives probably depend on it."

Harcourt opened his mouth to reply, then shut it again.

Blake was not reassured.

39

Early the next morning, before the first light burst out over the mountains, the chieftain Isonash hurried across the village, making his way as fast as his old legs and walking stick allowed. Though he had called for this gathering, he was unhappy about it. Bad enough that the meeting could not come to him, but he had to get up early to make amends to the *kamuys*, the gods, for the poor manners of his guest the night before.

His people had many gods. Their spirits dwelt everywhere, and in everything. He had made his apologies to the mother-goddess of his hearth fire and the other gods of his house, the spirit of its door, the sacred eastern window, and its divine hedge of *inaw*. He berated the god of the porridge for making the woman ill, explaining to the god of the earth that the fault for the desecrating gruel so unceremoniously spewed upon the ground of the village lay with that god, not humble Isonash, set-upon host to a crazed foreign woman with no manners.

318

Lastly, he thanked the *Atuy-Siwnin Wenkamuy*, the sea-blue demon of the mountain, for his daily forbearance in not raining down wrath and pestilence upon their little *kotan*, their village.

When he came to the house of Harukor, the hunter's young wife was waiting for him at the doorway. She greeted him modestly and bade him come inside. The rest of the men and elders were waiting, as well, crowded around the hearth. Harukor's wife sat in the corner and made herself very quiet. Isonash took his place of honor at the head of the fire pit next to Harukor, and made the briefest of necessary ritual greetings, eager to proceed to the business at hand.

"The youngest of you will not remember this," he began, directing his attention to Harukor's two sons, "for it was before you were born, before the Day of the Lightning-Dance, the Time of the Coming-and-Going, when many old things disappeared and many new things appeared. We were here for a hundred thousand years before the *Shamo* came up from the south in their ships. They were strong and cruel, with many strange ways and most ignorant of the land and the gods. In those years before the Lightning-Dance, the People became slaves of the *Shamo* in all but name, and the People and the land—who are one—suffered much under them. The gods were greatly displeased.

"But the People did not neglect to honor the gods, and remembered their manners. So one day, when your father, mighty Harukor, was but a crying stripling, and I a young hunter, the gods struck down the prideful *Shamo*. The power of their mighty lords in the south, across the great water, disappeared in a single day, and only the tribe of the lone *Shamo* lord Matomai remained here in our lands, far to the south of us.

"Matomai did not escape his punishment, for the gods sent enemies to attack him from across the seas, from the cold lands where no trees grow. The gods rewarded the People, sending much wondrous new game to hunt, and great sea monsters to protect us from any more ships of the south. And so all the *kotans* of all the People have thrived these five and twenty years, thanks be to the gods."

"*Kamuy Renkayne,*" the men echoed reverently. *Thanks be to the gods.* Isonash nodded, then heaved a sigh.

"Know that all things change in time. Now there is trouble again. Some of you have heard this, what the neighboring *kotans* across the valley have said—that the *Shamo* have beaten their enemies and grown again in strength. That now they have returned to our shores. Already they have recaptured the Lake People of the western hills, and the People of the smoking mountain. I think what they say is true. This is a serious matter, and we must think on it."

He allowed that to set in, then continued.

"We must also speak of the two found yesterday by Harukor's band, for they bring many questions. Who are these strange women? Where did they come from? Do they mean us good, or harm? What shall we do with them?" He stretched out a hand. "Harukor, speak."

The hunter cleared his throat, stroking his beard thoughtfully.

"They are sisters, I think. When we first saw them, we took them for *Shamo* spies, but they were only strange women, bathing in the hot spring by the split creek. We surprised them. They were crying, upset about some women's argument, but when they saw us they were very brave. Yet silly. You all saw their strange clothes are very fine, but they wander the land like lost babies. They bathed without a fire, or furs to dry them, and they carried no food or tools. Only a single arrow and no bow."

The others chuckled.

"Here is a mystery," Harukor continued. "They look neither like *Shamo* nor the People. Their tongue is strange, not the *Shamo* tongue, not any language of the North or the West. I inspected the backs of their necks for a third eye, or a second mouth, but found neither. So they are not witches."

"Perhaps they came from the water," Turushno interjected. "River *kamuy*, come here from the land of the gods."

"Or evil ones of the forest," another said.

"In my grandmother's *kotan*, an owl took human shape and lived among them," the hunter Makanakkuru mused. "The younger sister, I think she could be a fox, and the older sister a swan or a crane." The others clicked their tongues in agreement.

"It makes sense," Isonash said. "The one is wild and reckless, the other strives to be very polite, but neither knows how to be human. Then again, perhaps they are simply travelers from a distant land, unfamiliar with our ways."

"So I thought, too," Harukor said, "but hear this. When we returned yesterday, I sent young Chikap out to follow their trail. It was easy. He tracked them to their camp, a lean-to at one of our deer-traps—they made no effort to hide it—and from there, all the way down to the cave of the spotted seals."

"No sign of a boat or a sea vessel?"

"None. What's more, he says their tracks went back into the cave itself."

Isonash considered this new information. Caves were gateways to the land of the gods. If these women emerged from there, it was clear they were no mere travelers.

"Ah! Do you think they are just seal-*kamuy*?" Makanakkuru asked. "I wonder if seal-women make good wives?" He appeared to be putting much thought into the question.

"Perhaps we could keep them?" another added. "They would look pretty if they tattooed their lips."

"Perhaps they are wives already, who have escaped from their husband," Turushno said, always the one to see the danger in any situation. "If so, he may come from the land of the gods looking for them. He would be very angry."

Isonash clicked his tongue.

"Turushno speaks rightly. Whatever they may be, we should be very careful with these women, and treat them well. If no one comes to claim them in a few days, we should return them to the land of the gods."

The others sat up at this. They and their neighboring *kotans* returned bear-*kamuy* to the land of the gods every year—but never a spirit in human form. The killing of a bear to release its spirit was no easy thing, involving restraints, shooting many arrows and sometimes the pressing of its neck between heavy logs so they could slit the throat and drink the blood. Sending a bear spirit home meant a great feast of bear meat and blood, stewed and roasted on skewers, since its earthly flesh was left behind, a gift for them.

But *kamuy* in the shape of human women?

"How… would we do such a thing?" Turushno asked. Isonash understood his apprehension.

"We will invite everyone, all the neighboring *kotans*, to a great feast in their honor, and after celebrating them with food and drink, we should send them off gently. Poison first, I think. Then strangling them to be certain."

The others sat thoughtfully, but then clicked their tongues.

It was a good plan.

40

The throne room was designed to impress, and it succeeded. As dark and spacious as a theater, with light from dozens of stained-glass oil lanterns that only reinforced the atmosphere.

They illuminated rich mosaic murals on the walls, scenes of divine figures, lush depictions of the land—the great river, forests, hills, mountains, and city—and faces of the various peoples and races of Cahokia. Each mural glittered with gold and silver, and thousands of tiny pieces of shell, stone, metal, glass, and gems. The music of flutes and lutes accompanied their arrival.

Banks of courtiers stood in attendance on either side of the great throne, with servants along the walls. As with the city below, the court included a variety of ethnic groups and fashions from both European and native American strands. Somehow they all formed a cohesive, cosmopolitan whole, Blake thought. The royal guards looked a lot like Greek

Hoplites with their red cloaks of office, helmets, swords, and armored chestplates, though with one significant difference. Each stood at attention holding the same Tommy guns as the gangsters across the river.

As the music came to an end, one of the women came forward and sat on the steps to the throne. With her head bowed modestly and the hood of her wrap veiling her face, it was impossible to tell if it was the same beguiling creole woman they had seen on the terrace, though the skin of her hands was the same shade. Moving together on some unseen signal, the honor guard brought them before the throne.

A single skylight shone down upon the god-king, bathing him in a pillar of radiance even as it backlit him—simultaneously highlighting and hiding him—so that he was no longer merely a man, but a larger-than-life figure composed of shadow and light. Sunlight gleamed on the glossy blue-black feathers rising from his ornate headdress and sparkled off his silver armlets and copper breastplate.

"*Tsileyusga utanu* üguhwiyuhi *Kalanu Nuhdaegehi. Detsuyadaniluga*," he said. The clever acoustics gave his already powerful voice an even deeper, superhuman resonance. The woman at his feet began translating, but Blake was pleasantly surprised that his linguistic implant recognized the language as Cherokee.

"The Sun Raven bids you welcome," she said.

"Thank you, Your Majesty." Rockwell stepped up, his limp lending him an odd sort of gravitas, and gave an awkward bow. He cleared his throat nervously. "Great King, my name is Orrin Porter Rockwell. Well, sir, my associates and I have come to your fair city to offer you our services, and those of our prisoners. Now, it's no secret that your Royal Majesty has a great desire to obtain skilled men such as can work scientific—"

The king cut him off with a rapid-fire torrent of Cherokee. The implant's translation was intriguing.

"Enough from him. Now let us roast them. You know what to say, my love."

"His father the Sun tells the Sun Raven all that he sees during the day," the woman said in a strong, melodic voice. "His mother the Moon and his sisters the stars tell him what they see at night. So Mr. Rockwell, understand the Sun Raven knows well who you are, and of your reputation as a gunfighter and hunter of men. He knows, too, the Pawnee and the Englishman with you, and the deeds they have done. He suffers very few such men to live. Be thankful he has allowed you into his presence."

Feeds-the-Crows said nothing, but the muscles in his neck tensed. Shanks's grip on the leather leash tightened as his fist trembled.

"Well, sir, our reputation is exaggerated, surely," Rockwell stammered. "Let's put all that behind us. We're not here today as outlaws, or enemies of Cahokia, just as humble merchants, only interested in fair trade."

"The Sun Raven knows why you have come to the great city, as he knows the claims made by the prisoners you have brought," the woman replied. "The manacles on these men offends the Sun Raven. There are no more slaves here. Remove them."

"Yes, yes, of course, Your Majesty." Rockwell snapped his fingers at Shanks, and the Redcoat made haste to unlock them.

"Now, Rockwell, you and your men are dismissed. You will find abundant refreshment and lodgings in the Mericat Quarter, where you will wait for your reward while your three associates are put to the test. If they are worthy, your payment will be generous. If they prove to be false or weak, they shall suffer for it—and your payment will be of a different kind."

Rockwell stood for a moment, dumbfounded that his sales pitch had come to such an abrupt and unsatisfying end. As a quartet of palace guards stepped up to escort them out, he composed himself, quickly bowed and hustled his men out, pausing only long enough to shoot a last fiery stare at Harcourt, who now held their lives in his hands.

Sun-Raven sat in silence during these exchanges, letting his translator do all the talking. He waited until the three bounty hunters had been led out, and then spoke again, his stern voice gentle.

"Now that they are gone, know that I understand your tongue, and you are very welcome here."

Harcourt quickly stepped forward and bowed deeply, hat in hand. After a moment's stunned surprise, Cam and Blake followed suit.

"Your most gracious Majesty! We thank you and I promise I shall do my utmost to provide—"

Sun-Raven made quick hissing sounds behind his teeth, as though chasing away a buzzing fly. Harcourt stopped in mid-sentence, petrified.

"Spare me your pretty lies, you red-haired fox," the king said tersely.

"Your Highness," Blake said, stepping up. "You are right—this man is a scoundrel and a fraud." Harcourt stared at him in undisguised outrage. "None of us know anything about electricity, but his lies were only meant for the men who captured us, never to deceive anyone else."

Cam stepped forward. "High King, we are only here to search for our beloved friends who are lost, yet we will do anything in your service if we can only—"

"Enough!" Sun-Raven slammed his hand upon his throne. "You fearless rascals! What am I to do with you?" He stood up, body quaking with apparent anger. Suddenly he gave a long laugh that echoed through the whole throne room.

"Ha! A fine pharaoh I make!"

His translator had kept her veiled head downturned and poker-faced. Now she sprang up with a huge smile and ran up to a stunned Cam, seizing him in a tight bear hug.

"Cam! Oh, Cam!"

It wasn't the mysterious woman from before.

It was Leila.

The Sun Raven stepped down out of the blinding spotlight, his arms spread wide.

"Kha-Hotep!" Cam cried out in disbelief as the man joined the embrace. Blake and Harcourt snapped out of their stunned silence and joined in, as well, the whole huddle whooping like drunken madmen as the bemused court watched on.

Cam grabbed their heads in joy. "We were afraid we'd never see you two again!"

"*We* thought all of you were dead!" Leila said through happy tears.

"But this—all of this," Blake said, shaking his head. "How in bloody blazes did you ever pull this off, you magnificent bastard?"

"Come! We'll share each other's story over some food and drink!" Kha-Hotep grinned. "Look at you, *all* of you—you haven't changed a bit!"

Cam laughed. "What do you mean? It has been a rough two days and a night, I know, but it hasn't..." His smile faded in confusion.

Kha and Leila *did* look different, he realized.

Kha-Hotep looked at him solemnly.

"It's been eight years, my brother."

41

"Are we prisoners, then?" Hypatia asked.

"Come on," Nellie said, her Irish up. "Put on your clothes and we'll demand our things back at once." As soon they were dressed, Nellie strode over to the doorway of the chieftain's room.

"Nellie, wait!" Hypatia whispered. There was no door to knock, only a beech-bark framework with thick furs, so Nellie pounded on the wooden wall instead.

"Come out, you! We have a serious problem to discuss!"

Neither the headman nor his wife made a sound.

"You've stolen from us! This will not stand!" Incensed, she pulled open the curtain of skins.

"Nellie, no!" Hypatia gasped at the breach of protocol.

The chief's room was empty, but across the room on the other side of the fire pit, the chief's daughters emerged from their own room, eyes downcast, with the stolen parkas and boots in hand.

"Nellie…" Hypatia murmured.

Nellie turned, eyes still flashing with ire. "You three! What are you doing with—" Her reprimand fell away as the girls held up the snow coats and overshoes, now richly embroidered with their own curving lines and patterns, forming waves and birdlike shapes.

"They must have worked on them all night long," Hypatia said.

"They're so beautiful…" Nellie sighed, shaking her head as she felt tears coming on. "Oh, thank you, girls!" She gave the closest daughter a fierce hug, and then grabbed up the other two.

Hypatia looked on, dismayed at the lack of etiquette, but seeing the girl's obvious pleasure at Nellie's delight, her sense of formality melted away and she joined in as well.

They all sat down for breakfast, while the girls tried to explain the symbols they had stitched into the parkas. The oldest traced out the line of parentheses on the sleeves, touching the point on the embroidered line with her finger, and miming as if it were a sharp thorn. Her sister held up her hands to her head to make devil horns and growled, and the oldest crossed her fists against her monster-sister.

"I think the designs are magic, meant to protect us from the *daimon* of the mountain," Hypatia said.

"Well, I think they will bring us splendid luck!" Nellie enthused.

It seemed they did bring them luck. For the next week, their days were tranquil. Even across the steep language barrier, Chief Isonash and his family were kind and unfailing hosts. During the shortening days, the men would go hunt, and Nellie and Hypatia would join the younger wives and daughters as they foraged for the last of the autumn's harvest.

They worked in sewing circles and prepared the food stores for winter. The work made them feel as if they were contributing, helped them bond with the other women, and gave them the chance to pick up snippets of the language.

In the evening, like clockwork, the blue demon would call up the moon. Before long they thought of him more as a nocturnal rooster than a threat.

The men treated Nellie and Hypatia as their equals, drinking with them at dinner. They swapped songs, the hunters singing in their barbarian language while Hypatia would recite epic poems in Greek, and Nellie would sing "Oh My Darling, Clementine" and her favorite vaudeville numbers.

Nellie made a point of spending the beginning and end of each day in silent meditation, mentally calling out for Amber. Once she explained what she was doing, Hypatia quickly took up the practice, too—but no response came. They comforted each other with the hope that she had been successful. Hypatia suggested that perhaps a passing merchant caravan might show up in the springtime, and they could make their way to the Mediterranean and back to Alexandria.

Neither woman voiced the thought that they might be forced to stay where they were for the rest of their lives.

* * *

On the tenth day, the chief announced that he had important news. By signs and gestures, and with the help of his daughters, he informed them that there would be a great and important feast the next day.

42

"It's beautiful, is it not?"

The palace's uppermost grassy terrace stood nearly as high as a ten-story building, offering a breathtaking view over the metropolis. It proved to be a perfect place for the friends to sit and catch up over a royal picnic. Kha-Hotep gestured proudly at the roads, waterways, border forts, farms, and rural suburbs that stretched for leagues in all directions.

"The city is a mirror of the cosmos, its four sacred circles all meticulously aligned to serve as astronomical timepieces. The northern circle represents the Sky World above, the one to the south—the one you walked past in the outer city—signifies the Earth World below, and the east and west circles, sunrise and sunset. The palace and the inner city stand at the conjunction of the four, symbolizing the human world."

"How is it that such a huge shard survived the Event?" Cam asked.

"It started as a cluster of three moderate-sized ones, spanning a few centuries," Leila explained. "One contained the inner city and part of the outlying suburbs to the east, another pair mostly fields and villages—one from a few generations earlier, the other a few generations later. The rest we've rebuilt or expanded upon since."

"The big question," Blake said, "is how we came out eight years after you did, even though we followed you into that bloody thing not five minutes after."

"And yet it seems as if we all emerged at the same spot, in the woods of the haunted ruins," Kha-Hotep said. "Though when Leila and I arrived, it appeared to have been about five or six months after the Event."

"When we got here, the city ruins crawled with Stone Age savages," Leila said. "They spotted us almost immediately, but we were lucky. As they chased us through the forest, they disturbed a pack of these big shaggy lizards, bigger than grizzly bears." She shuddered. "It was ugly. Kha and I spent hours hiding, and then cut across the prairie until we reached the Mississippi. We arrived to find open war being waged between Cahokia and what remained of Saint Louis."

"And dinosaurs who preyed on both," Kha-Hotep added.

"Our timing was perfect," Leila continued. "The Cahokians had Laclede's Landing under siege, but even though they were outnumbered, the gangsters still had the firepower—so, *boom*, it's a stalemate. When we arrived, both sides were desperate. The crime boss Vito Giannola had run out of food, and was getting short on ammunition."

Kha-Hotep nodded. "By then, his guns had already killed the Cahokian king, and nearly all of their high priests, and every war leader they had sent against them, along with hundreds of their bravest warriors, so the Cahokians were utterly demoralized, with no idea what to do next."

"We came out of the west at sunset," Leila said, "right when the Great Arch looks its most gorgeous, and the Cahokian soldiers were amazed. For one thing, they'd never seen an African before, and though we didn't speak their language, we did have Cherokee and Lakota Sioux in our implants. They knew enough of both to communicate with us.

"We didn't know it then, but we had arrived at the end of a sacred day for them," she continued. "A minor lunar eclipse had occurred the night before, what they call a 'blood moon.' For them, it meant the sun and moon had been fighting, and this was a sacred time to resolve feuds. They were astounded when we introduced ourselves. To them, Kha's name sounded like *Ka'a* and *Ho*, their words for 'Raven' and 'Sun.' All the tribes here love ravens. They tell stories of his cunning, how he stole fire from Heaven, brought messages from the gods, that kind of thing.

"So to have a black-skinned man, with braided hair that sort of looks like feathers, I guess, come out of the setting sun six months after the Event, on a sacred day and introduce himself as 'Raven of the Sun,' well… you can guess what they made of it."

Kha-Hotep grinned. "Rumors spread like a Nile flood," he said. "Some started saying Leila was the moon-spirit, and others said we were both god-children sent by the sun and moon."

"So many weird coincidences—*Alhamdulillah*." Leila shook her head. "That night the Cahokians celebrated as though they'd already won the war. We had to get stern with the remaining priests to keep them from sacrificing a dozen virgins in our honor. The next morning, we sent a nicely worded message in English to the mobsters, telling them if they happened to be running low on food and ammo, that we were willing to act as negotiators to cut a deal."

Kha-Hotep laughed. "Poor Vito had no idea what to make of us."

"He still doesn't." Leila grinned. "Anyway, we met with him. That was the first time we did our god-king act, using the translator, and it worked like a charm. We brokered a peace that's lasted eight years, although it gets pretty shaky sometimes. After all—well, you saw the place—the Landing has attracted every kind of thug and lowlife from every shard up and down the river. Still, the end to the war sealed the deal with the Cahokians."

"And so I became their king," Kha-Hotep said, "and in time…" He took Leila's hand and kissed it, locking eyes with her. "This woman became my queen, my sister, and my love."

She smiled at their friends. "I had to—who could keep him out of trouble if I let him try to run a whole kingdom by himself?"

"You see how I have to suffer?" Kha-Hotep appealed to Cam, who grinned and shrugged. "Now, if I were Pharaoh, your head would have been lopped off your rebellious neck a hundred times over, woman!"

"Oh, like you'd last a day without me," Leila scoffed. "Besides, who would save you from *these* monsters?"

Happy shrieks announced the arrival of a pair of giggling twin girls and a solemn boy in buckskins and an Egyptian scalp lock, accompanied by the mysterious cinnamon-skinned woman from before. She held the girls' hands as the pair tugged her toward their parents.

"Light of my eyes!" Leila spread her arms wide to embrace them. "Did you two drag your poor auntie Josephine all the way here?"

Nodding, the girls laughed in triumph.

"It was my pleasure," the woman said with a smile, bending down to kiss Leila on the cheek.

"Nuh-uh!" one girl exclaimed. "She said she would eat us!"

"My goodness! Did she now?"

"Yes, she said she would gobble us up for being rotten!" the other reported happily. Josephine made tiger claws of her hands and growled at the twins, who again burst into squealing giggles.

"I'll be damned!" Blake stared at her. "You're... you're Josephine Baker!" Cam and Harcourt stared at him. They had never seen the commando flustered before.

The young woman smiled. "Sorry, you've got the wrong girl," she replied. "I'm Josephine McDonald, but it's nice to meet you all the same, soldier. I do love a man in uniform."

Blake tried to speak, but nothing came out. Cherished memories of wartime shows in Morocco came flooding back to him—staring at her as she dominated the stage in

a dazzling evening gown, captivating entire regiments of soldiers, singing to every man in the audience as though her song was only for him.

"These silly monkey-birds are our girls," Leila said, coming to his rescue. She lay a hand on each girl's head. "This is Heba, and this is Amber." By contrast, their older brother regarded the newcomers with a most serious expression. He had Leila's eyes. Kha-Hotep lifted up his young son and sat him on his knee.

"And this is Enkati, named after his uncle." He turned to the boy. "Show them how well you speak. How old are you now, my prince? Five?"

"My sisters are five! I am almost seven."

"Indeed you are. Come, do you remember the story I told you, about the crocodile back in Egypt?" Enkati nodded. "This is my brother Cam, the man who saved us."

The boy's eyes grew large. "You killed a monster crocodile with a magic sword! Do you still have it?"

"Yes," Cam replied solemnly, "but I left it behind, sadly."

"Enkati, help me show our friends the map," his father said. A servant approached, bearing a leather case, and removed a large scroll, spreading it out before them.

"Fine grade birch-bark paper," Leila said proudly. "We make it ourselves."

The exquisitely hand-drawn chart covered some fifteen hundred miles or better, laying out the main body of the Mississippi and its tributaries, spotted with a handful of settlements, from the Great Lakes to the Gulf of Mexico.

At the center lay Cahokia, its subdivisions and outskirts, the heart of the New World. To the east lay a mosaic of shards all the way to the Appalachians—mostly alternating fingers of forested waterways and prairie, with some jungles and tall, isolated glaciers still slowly melting, eight years after the Event.

Virtually everything west of the Mississippi was largely *terra incognita*. Kha-Hotep explained that the city traded with the German and Irish miners in the mountain ranges of the Ozarks to the southwest, but otherwise—past Laclede's Landing and the ruins—the great plains were marked as Nomad Territory. There, tribes still followed the buffalo or brontosaurus herds and occasionally clashed with one another.

Through diplomacy, Kha-Hotep and Leila had unified several feuding tribes, and some had put down roots in Cahokia, along with Spanish, French, and American settlers.

"And our canny Nile merchant prince has cultivated trade routes up and down the river," Leila said, "as far north as the Chippewa and Ojibwa nations and the Yooper Republic, all the way down to the Duchy of New Orleans." She pointed out each area in turn. Whatever lay beyond the Rockies or the Appalachians was a mystery, but Kha-Hotep stretched a finger to the south.

"The peace between us and the Landing is shaky at best. Boss Giannola trades with the slaver plantations, and they don't like us anymore than we like them. Below them is New Orleans, our most important trading partner in the south. Then there is the great desert, and below that"—he indicated a pair of shaded blotches filling the region below the vast desert—"two rival empires, the Empire of the Tenochca—"

"We'd call them Aztecs," Leila cut in.

"—and their enemy, the Conquistador States, who call themselves the Viceroyalty of Nueva España. Long may they stay at each other's throats."

The three newcomers had continued eating with gusto while Kha-Hotep and Leila talked, but as soon as he finished his meal, Blake grew restless.

Eight years... How much time is passing right now back in Antarctica? If we make it back, will we show up at the same time we left—or eight years too late? Christ, we need a bloody Einstein to get this mess sorted.

"Listen," he said. "Don't get me wrong. Thank you. We needed food and rest, and it's good to see you—but there's no time for this. We have to go. I'm not saying that you need to come, too. With all respect, you two have gone native and made a home here. That's fine, but we have to get back now."

An awkward silence dropped.

"How would you do that?" Kha-Hotep asked, his tone strangely cool.

Blake shrugged. "I assume back through the portal."

"Didn't you already try?"

"Yes, but—"

"Don't you see?" Kha-Hotep said. "There *is* no going back. That was all eight years ago." He paused to let that sink in. "Listen to me. Those aftershocks that were tearing up the world, they had already stopped here before Leila and I arrived. So Amber and the other women somehow succeeded

341

in halting the destruction. They probably died in the effort," he added.

Harcourt stopped eating and looked up, shock on his face.

Leila gasped. "Kha!"

"I'm sorry, my love," he said. "We don't know what their fate may have been. We'll never know, but whatever became of them, it is a thing completed. They succeeded, they saved the world from shattering, and restored *Ma'at*. They brought life and order to our new world, strange and troubled as it is. *We are the proof*."

"You two have done great things here, my brother," Cam said, "but… Merlin had said that once we set things aright, it would be as though the Event had never happened at all."

"He's right," Blake affirmed. "None of this should be here."

"Then your Merlin was wrong," Kha-Hotep replied.

"Or this is all just some temporary fluke," Blake countered. "Some random eddy in the timestream."

"This is our world!" Leila exclaimed, glaring at Blake. "This is our life now! We have children. We're rebuilding civilization!" She clutched her daughters tight, and the girls stared back at the adults, suddenly as solemn as their brother.

Kha-Hotep raised a hand. "You are right, Beloved, but come, let there be no strife between us, for there is no need to fight. Our lost friends are returned, and now they join us. This is a gift—how splendid a gift!" He turned back to the three men.

"Know this now, my friends. There is no return. The portals of time that brought us here, they flow like a cataract.

342

We have been dropped here, and none can return up those streams again.

"Yet take comfort," he added, his voice conciliatory. "Mighty battles you have fought. Truly, you have saved the world. You have earned your reward—a hero's welcome in this great city of peace and abundance. Your new home welcomes you with a full heart." He raised his glass. "Welcome home."

Blake started to reply, but changed his mind and joined the toast with the others.

Later that night, side by side on their royal bed, they lay in silence, listening to the cicadas. Their children and their old friends had all been seen to their rooms, but Kha-Hotep and Leila could not sleep. After a long period of stillness, he reached over to give an enquiring caress of Leila's forearm.

"So remarkable a day, our brother returned, our friends with us again," he said. "Don't you think?"

Leila didn't reply.

Kha rolled over to face her. "Are you happy?"

She turned her face to his, eyes gleaming in the moonlight. "Yes. Very." Her beautiful smile almost worked.

"But… what is it? Are you frightened?"

"Yes. Very."

"Tell me your heart."

"Kha." She faced him completely, taking his hand in hers. "What if they *did* find a way to go back?"

"How could they?"

"I don't know, but think about it. If they went back and did what they said, it would destroy everything we've built—our lives here, our family. *Habibi*, we would have to stop them. By any means. No matter what it takes. You know that, right?"

A shadow passed over Kha-Hotep's face. He quickly banished it with a reassuring smile.

"Hush now, my love. You worry for nothing. We are safe."

"But what if they could," Leila insisted. "Promise me you would stop them."

"And with what sorcery would they accomplish this miracle?"

"Promise me!"

Sitting up straight, Kha touched his lips, heart, and forehead. "As truly as lives the divine Ra, Ptah, Isis, and Osiris, so I bind myself to this oath. The great gods bear witness to the words I speak. I keep the oath and abandon it not, for all my days." He raised his eyebrows. "Satisfied?"

"No." She stared back, unmoved by his theatrics. "No, swear by *me*. Swear by your love for me and your children."

He took her hand and kissed it. "I swear it truly, with all my heart."

"No matter what it takes?"

"No matter what it takes."

Leila took a deep, ragged breath, and as she exhaled, the tears she was holding back slipped down her cheeks, catching the moonlight. With gentle strokes of his thumb, Kha wiped them away. Taking him by the hip, she pulled Kha-Hotep atop her like a blanket.

"Love me?"

"You know that I do."

"No," she whispered. "I mean *love* me. Now."

He bent his head down to kiss her as she spread her legs, wrapping herself around him.

On another terrace of the palace, in the guest wing, Cam lay waiting for sleep that would not come. Instead, a silent voice called to him in his head.

"Cam? Are you there? It's me, Amber..."

43

It had started with a jolt, enough to wake Rose from a sound sleep. She wasn't due to be at the Todd's abode until ten, so she had planned on sleeping till the luxurious hour of seven.

The jolt was deep and sudden, but not immediately frightening. Before making the journey to San Francisco, she'd been warned about the possibility of earthquakes. Still, the siren call of Paris of the West was far stronger than any fears of what nature might do. After all, she'd experienced tornadoes in Missouri, and surely nothing could be as terrifying as being in the path of one of those monsters.

She was wrong.

Rose burrowed back down under the single quilt, determined to go back to sleep. Not a minute later, the earth screamed in pain and the walls, her bed, the very foundation of the house itself shook.

Before she could get out of bed, Rose had been thrown to the floor, landing with a jarring thud that rattled her brains. There was no chance to gain exit to the streets—the floors collapsed one on top of the other, the weight driving the building and its occupants into the ground. The screams and moans of the injured began, and the swampy ground on which the structure had been built began swallowing pieces of wood, bricks, furniture... and people.

"God, help me! Please, help..."

The cry trailed off into a thick burbling as watery mud clogged the poor soul's throat. Rose tried to pretend otherwise, but she couldn't fool herself.

It would have been easy enough to give up if not for a crossbeam that had fallen, one end onto the rapidly disappearing floor, the other still attached to a chunk of ceiling near the exterior wall. She managed to scramble onto the steeply slanted beam, but didn't dare move for fear of upsetting the delicate balance of her perch. Yet she was alive. Which was more than she could say for those drowning in the muck below her.

The smells were horrific.

"Rose..." A rattling cough followed her name.

She jerked, nearly upsetting her precarious perch. The beam listed to one side with an ominous creak from above. She froze, barely breathing until it stopped moving.

"Vera?"

"Oh god, Rose, help me!"

"I… I can't move," Rose replied weakly. "If I do, I'll fall." She hated herself for her cowardice. Vera was only thirteen, living with her aunt in the room next door.

More coughing, a wet sound.

"Please, I can't… I can't get out," Vera pleaded. "There's something on my leg and there's water and mud, and it's getting higher." Vera's voice broke. Rose heard splashing. "Rose, I can't—" Vera's voice cut off in a choked, waterlogged cough.

Rose shut her eyes, not daring to speak. If she tried, she would scream her throat raw, and she wouldn't be able to stop.

Vera didn't call her name again.

Within the first hour after the quake, all sounds ceased from those trapped in the lower levels of the crumpled rooming house. Drowned or crushed, Rose knew. The part of her crossbeam that rested on the buckled second-story floor was under muddy water. Only the fact the beam still clung to its original mooring kept Rose from the same fate.

She focused on the sounds coming from above. More cries and moans, to be sure, but also the muffled sounds of rescuers. Voices and noises that indicated digging, wreckage being cast aside.

The sounds of hope.

"Hello…? Hel—" Dust filled her nostrils and she coughed, choking on crumbled plaster and god knew what else.

"Hello, miss? You alive?"

"Yes! Please, help me!"

"What's your name?"

"Rose. Rose Pearson."

"I'm John. Don't you worry, Rose," the calm male voice assured. "We're here and we'll get you out."

She believed him. He meant what he said. She still believed him, even when the acrid tang of smoke stung her eyes and nostrils.

"John," she said, raising her voice to be heard of wreckage being shifted and cleared, "I smell smoke."

"Don't you worry, Rose," he repeated. "We'll get you out."

The sounds of activity increased in tempo and volume. Shouts and crashing as pieces of wood were flung aside. The thankful cries of lucky people being extracted from the ruins of the building.

The distant crackle of flames, growing louder with each passing moment.

Still, Rose believed John's repeated assurances that they would get her out, even when she heard worry replace the confidence in his tone. She believed him right up to the moment she heard his voice crack.

"Rose. The fire. It's nearly here. I... we have to leave."

"Oh god. No. Please, John, can't you—"

"I'm so sorry, Rose." A pause. Then, "I have a wife. Two children. I'm so sorry."

And then he was gone.

The smell of smoke grew stronger. A muffled roaring sound, crackling, roaring... and heat. So much heat. Sweat beaded on Rose's brow and between her breasts. The hair on her arms, face, head started to singe…

Flames roared over the ruined structure, down to where Rose straddled the beam. Searing heat streamed into her nostrils and lungs.

Oh god. She tried to hold her breath, even though she knew it was pointless because her next breath would be her last. She held the breath, held it… held it… and then the earth shook with another sharp jolt, nearly unseating Rose from the crossbeam as a high-pitched keening filled her ears. Rose couldn't help it—

She closed her eyes and screamed.

Instead of flames, however, cold air rushed into her lungs. The smell of smoke dissipated, whipped away by a bone-chilling, whistling wind. Rose opened her eyes.

There was no fire bearing down on her. Instead of the hopeless tangle of fallen beams and walls, instead of fleeing rescuers, she found herself staring at a grassy plain. A family of large elk stopped its grazing to stare at her in surprise.

Crawling carefully to the end of the beam, she shimmied up onto the earth, shivering as her sodden nightgown pulled up and ice-encrusted grass scraped against her bare flesh.

44

Nauvoo, Illinois
August 8, 1844
Three hours before the Event

"They have killed him! Goddamn them! They have killed him!"

At dawn, he thundered out of the wilderness at full gallop through the streets of Nauvoo, a howling, wild-haired Sampson. The faithful leapt up from their troubled sleep as Porter Rockwell wailed the terrible news coming from Carthage jail.

"Joseph is killed!"

Porter Rockwell snapped out of his painful memory, startling those seated on the pew beside him. He sat there, inconsolable, heavy as stone. The loss of his prophet, leader, and childhood friend had hollowed him out.

His fellow parishioners were just as lost. He stared up, mouthing the gilded words written across the arch of the ceiling.

The Lord Has Seen Our Sacrifice

He watched as the Church's designated heir apparent squirmed in the front pew next to his stricken mother Emma—the Prophet's oldest son, Joseph Smith III, all of eleven years old. The next choice would have been the Prophet's older brother Hyrum, but he'd been martyred alongside Joseph in Carthage. Barely a month later, their younger brother Samuel suddenly dropped dead at age thirty-six.

The official cause of death? A mysterious "bilious fever"—but others whispered about the unidentified white powder his personal caregiver fed him until his death, saying Samuel died trying to spit out his daily "medicine," crying out that he had been poisoned.

So much for the obvious choices.

Rockwell knew all too well that behind the scenes, the Church was fragmenting, and factions were already squaring off for power. In the six weeks following the Prophet's death, plenty of rivals had claimed that Joseph had personally ordained them as his successor when no one else was looking.

One of them, a new convert named James Strang, claimed that both a signed letter from Joseph Smith and a vision from an angel appointed him as president of the Church. As further proof, Strang had unearthed and translated a book of ancient brass plates, the final testament of an ancient American king, Rajah Manchou of Vorito, a place known to them as Voree, Wisconsin.

Rockwell fully expected to be called upon to deal with the man at some point, just like he'd dealt with the ex-governor of Missouri when he'd fired four lead balls into him. Instead, Strang was excommunicated.

So now it was down to two, and at the conference assembled in the Nauvoo temple, it was the frontrunner's turn to speak. First Counselor Sidney Rigdon had hurried to town, announcing to everyone he had just received a revelation from Joseph at the right hand of God, appointing him the Guardian of the Church. Sickly, peevish, and overly emotional, he gave an overwrought performance for an hour and a half, while Rockwell fought to stay awake.

Most of the faithful had long grown inured to his hysterics. As Rigdon sensed his drama souring, his performance suddenly shifted from pious, aspiring shepherd to a diva scorned. Rockwell sat up for that, as the counselor's failing bid for leadership ended with him slinking away from the pulpit, fuming and swearing he would expose the Church.

The second round went to the president of the Quorum of the Twelve Apostles. Rockwell felt another sharp pang of regret watching the beefy man take the pulpit. Coarse and foul-mouthed, unpleasant, spiteful, a brass-tacks meticulous workhorse without warmth or charisma—in nearly every way Rockwell could imagine, Brigham Young was the very opposite of Joseph Smith. But watching the man roar into action and tear into his rival, even Rockwell had to admit Young had a formidable presence. There were moments he turned into a second Joseph, and then his silver tongue turned sharp.

Joseph had given the Church's apostles all the secret knowledge of church rituals, Brigham declared. They alone had the keys to the kingdom, all the signs and the tokens to give to the gatekeepers of Heaven to allow them in. He warned them nothing less than their salvation and celestial glory hung in the balance.

Rockwell nodded his head. It was perfectly obvious to him, if not everyone in the room, how the vote would go. The Saints would vote in the Quorum of the Twelve Apostles to act as the new First Presidency—which meant that the de facto leader of the Church was now the president of the Quorum, Brigham Young.

Suddenly Rockwell needed to get some air. He slipped out of the Great Hall, hoping Young didn't notice him go—the man never forgave any sign of disrespect. In an uncharacteristically contemplative mood, Rockwell exited the temple and headed out toward the bluffs overlooking the lowlands and the local bend of the muddy river.

Rockwell would gladly have taken—or given—a bullet for Joseph's sake. Now Brigham Young was to be his new prophet and leader. Rockwell deliberated what he was prepared to do for his new prophet.

So be it. The man was a contemptible bastard, but if anyone could save the Church, it was him. Rockwell turned and gazed back at the still-unfinished temple. If they were forced to move yet again, it might never be completed.

Abruptly the church spire wavered, undulating like a desert mirage. He frowned. No, not just the spire. The whole building seemed to be twisting, then even the ground itself. The very air suddenly danced with will-o'-the-wisps and shooting stars. Rockwell backed away in horror, fearing he had lost his senses.

Then some raw, divine miracle manifested. With a sizzling rush, a geyser of angel-fire burst up from the earth before him, reaching up to Heaven itself like Jacob's Ladder. He threw himself to the ground, as Moses had before the burning bush. The upward torrent was too bright to gaze upon, its fury unbearable. Clapping his hands over *his ears, he felt the hair on his head and arms rising. Even his beard stretched out, electrified.*

And then, just as it seemed the whirlwind would consume him, together with the world, it disappeared, snuffed out like a candle. He remained on his hands and knees, shaking uncontrollably. When he finally stumbled up to his shaky feet, he shaded his eyes and stared out across the rocky bluff.

The temple was gone.

The city of Nauvoo was gone.

Nothing remained of either but barren wilderness. The meaning was clear. All the Saints had been lifted up to Heaven—but not him. He was forsaken.

He fell to his knees again, wailing.

"Old Port! Wake up, man!"

Rockwell jerked awake, rousing himself from the messy oaken tabletop, and Shanks yanked his hand back from his boss's sleeve. Rockwell glared at Shanks and Feeds-the-Crows, then saw that the fear in their eyes was not on his account.

The music had stopped, a hush fallen over the raucous crowd. He turned and looked across the tavern at the squad of Cahokian guards taking up the doorway. The spectacled royal secretary stood front and center, regarding them.

"You have a serious problem. Come with us."

Leaving behind their half-finished dinners and celebratory tankards of potent local corn whiskey on the table, Rockwell and his men stepped out into the night. To their surprise, the

Cahokian soldiers did not escort them back to the palace, taking them instead south through town to the gate of the outer city and the docks beyond. This late, the dark and deserted waterfront felt sinister.

Looks to be a fine place to get bushwhacked and dumped in the river, Rockwell thought. "What kind of hogshit jiggery-pokery are you playing at?" he demanded, refusing to show any fear. "Is that it—we're being deported? Where's our goddamned money?"

The royal secretary peered at him like an unimpressed schoolmaster. "Payment comes after delivery," the man said, sounding bored. "Your experts failed to provide their services. No merchandise, no payment."

"The hell you say!"

"Not only that, but they have escaped the palace. They slipped out through a window in the night and climbed down to the ground. Presumably they have fled the city. The Sun Raven is most displeased."

Well, hell, Rockwell thought. Out loud he said carefully, "I can surely see his predicament, but how's that on us? We did our part."

"No merchandise, no payment."

"You pack of goddamned Lamanite Injun-givers!"

The secretary remained unfazed. "It is strange that you three do not see the pot of trouble you stew in."

Shanks bristled visibly. Outgunned as they were, he and Feeds-the-Crows had their hands on the hilts of their knives, eyes peeled for any false move from the soldiers.

"Still," the secretary continued, "the Sun Raven offers you one more chance to redeem yourselves."

"And what would that be?" Rockwell raised a suspicious eyebrow.

"Here it comes now."

A peculiar mechanical sound came across the water as a long, low barge pulled up to the docks. The old wooden vessel had no sails, smokestacks, or paddlewheel, but some sort of engine chugged along, propelling it at a surprising speed. The only cargo was covered by a canopy of tawny-brown tarpaulin.

He was surprised to see a negro captain at the bow, dressed in as smart a navy uniform as he'd ever seen, a double-breasted blue frock coat with gold piping and buttons. The officer stepped off nimbly and touched his cap in greeting, though he didn't bother doffing it or shaking hands.

"I am Captain Kha-Hotep," he said. "I'll be in charge of this mission, on the direct orders of the Sun Raven himself."

Rockwell scowled. "See here, Captain Coon! Since when does a white feller take orders from some jumped-up darkie in a fancy suit?"

"Am I mistaken?" The captain flashed his teeth in a panther's smile. "So sorry, I was under the impression you wanted to get back into his good graces and be paid handsomely, instead of being creatively executed over the next few days and nights."

The big man blinked. "Well, now," he said after a moment of silent reflection. "Orrin Porter Rockwell, at your service,

Captain. My associates, Mr. Shanks and Mr. Feeds-the-Crows, and I are a-chompin' at the bit to hear more about our exciting excursion. *Sir*."

The captain's smile warmed by a degree, and he waved his hand with a flourish.

"Welcome aboard, Gentlemen. Let's be off."

As the barge chugged away downriver, the captain explained their mission.

"Most likely, we won't encounter anyone else on the far shore, but should we, I am just another wasteland bounty hunter, like you. We are tracking our quarry, and Cahokia knows nothing of this. We do *not* want to provoke a war with the Landing. Understood?"

The three bounty hunters nodded.

"Good. There's a particular spot in the woods near the haunted ruins. As I understand, it's south of where you first picked them up, and I think I can locate it without trouble. We need to stop them before they get there. If we succeed, we'll be back in the city by morning, and you three will be rich men."

Shanks nodded, pleased at the prospect, but Rockwell frowned.

"What makes you so sure that's where they're headed?"

"That's where they're headed," the captain replied calmly.

"If you say so. How much of a head start they got on us?"

"We suspect they left the palace shortly after nightfall."

Feeds-the-Crows shook his head. "No good," the Pawnee said. "They'll beat us there."

"He's right." Shanks scowled. "There's no chance we'll catch up to them in time by now."

"No, we will be waiting for them," Kha-Hotep stated.

"How do you figure?" Rockwell looked at him skeptically.

"We'll go ashore just as soon as we've gone a mile or so past the Great Arch, far enough from the Landing that no one should spot us, much less think we've declared war. From there, we should reach the ruins in about twenty minutes. We will catch them, and we will take the fugitives *alive*. The Sun Raven made that very clear, and I am here to make certain his instructions are followed to the letter."

"Twenty minutes!" Shanks snorted. "In a pig's eye! There'd have to be some bloody fast horses waiting for us!"

Kha-Hotep walked over to the tent and pulled open the canvas flap. "We have one hundred and fifty of them." Inside the tent sat the strangest coach Rockwell had ever seen—four-wheeled and open-topped, its long blocky metal body housing strange machinery as complicated as one of the whiskey stills in Laclede's Landing.

It had two rows of fine cushioned leather seats for a pilot and crew, some sort of pint-sized ship's wheel, and a pane of window glass mounted across the front—though what *that* would protect them from, Rockwell thought, God only knew. A busy team tended to the vehicle, poking its metal innards with long rods, adjusting valves, pouring tin canisters of coal oil, and funneling water from nearby water barrels.

There were, however, no horses.

"What the hell's *that* contraption supposed to be?" Rockwell asked.

"It's Lacledean," Kha-Hotep said with pride. "They call it a Scott-Newcomb steam car. It's a *horseless* carriage."

45

It was dark and the stars were still out when Hypatia roused Nellie from deep sleep.

"It's too early…" she grumbled, but Hypatia quickly shushed her and pointed silently to the entrance of Isonash's house.

Someone was there.

Both women froze. No villager would dare enter another's home without waiting to be invited, let alone try to sneak inside. An unthinkable violation, yet a wedge of moonlight appeared as the figure in the doorway pulled back the fur screen, then slipped inside. A shape approached them, a darker shadow in the gloom, keeping its footsteps careful and quiet.

Nellie tensed, readying herself to attack or flee—she wasn't sure which. The figure crouched down, reaching for her. Sitting up, Nellie snatched the intruder's wrist, drawing her other hand back to strike—but then recognized the intruder's tattooed face.

It was Imekanu, Harukor's young wife. She didn't cry out, holding a finger to her lips to urge their silence.

"Imekanu?" Hypatia whispered. "What's wrong?"

"*Shhhhh... Yaytupare,*" she cautioned them. "*Paye'an.*" They had picked up enough of the language to know that she wanted them to come with her, and immediately.

As Imekanu led the two women out of the *kotan*, her heart beat so hard it hurt her chest. She had never done anything rebellious, and it terrified her to think of what would happen to her if anyone saw her, let alone suspected what she was about to do.

Fear sent a shudder through her.

She had packed a small knapsack and tied it around her forehead. Passing through the village gate, she paused to pull a small whisk broom from it and quickly brushed away their footprints before leading them back around the village fence.

Imekanu pointed out patches of snow on the ground, cautioning the two women from stepping on them. They seemed to understand, and the three continued to circle around the back of the village until they came to the rocky patch in the river, crossing it where the stones made a bridge in the ice, and where no tracks would show on the opposite side.

It was slow going through the forest, but she hadn't dared bring a torch. They crept along carefully until she found enough of a break in the timber to let them see by moonlight. She thanked the gods the two puzzled women trusted her enough to keep their silence, and continued to follow her lead.

As they drew closer to her goal, Imekanu's doubts increased. She had been second-guessing herself ever since the men had decided what to do with Ne-hee and Hi'e-Pay-Shah. They were convinced the two women were *kamuy* to be returned to the land of the gods.

Imekanu didn't pretend to know what they were—animals in human guise, water spirits, forest spirits, shamanesses, sorcerers, so many possibilities. Perhaps they *were* from the land of the gods, but her *ihuminu*, her psychic sense, told her that no matter how strange they seemed, or where they came from, they were women like herself, with good hearts.

She took a deep breath, steeling herself. There was no certainty that her plan would work. Still, she had to try. If she did nothing, the two were doomed. There was only one place she could go for even a chance of help, and they were nearly there.

The pre-dawn twilight felt somehow clearer than the full light of day, Hypatia thought, and the cerulean tone of the star-frosted sky gave everything a hint of magic as the women hiked higher up the slope. When they reached a small mountain tabletop jutting out from the trees, Imekanu finally stopped.

"It's a completely different shard," Nellie exclaimed. "Everything's so wild here, I'd quite forgotten that there must be several of them around." Imekanu raised a finger to her lips, and Nellie held her tongue.

The flat ground they stood upon was smooth stone. Years ago it must have been part of a much wider terrace, but the

Event had left only a small scrap behind. It formed a courtyard of sorts for the entrance to a large cave. Imekanu was clearly afraid of the cavern, grabbing Nellie and Hypatia each by an arm to hold them back. She spoke quietly but firmly in her own tongue, apparently urging them to not go any closer.

Something in the cave's high doorway seemed deliberately constructed, albeit with great cyclopean stonework. How old was it? Perhaps it was a shrine to Imekanu's people.

Setting down her knapsack, Imekanu removed stacks of millet cakes neatly bound up with long grasses, a leather flask, and bundles of dried salmon. She laid them all out in a line, and last of all, pulled out two of the short knives favored by the women of the village.

"*Taan uk*," she said, offering each of them one of the iron blades. Nellie and Hypatia stared at them in their meticulously hand-carved wooden sheaths. They knew how valuable they were.

"*Taan uk*," Imekanu said again, more emphatically.

Accepting the blades, the two watched quietly as Imekanu knelt down and began to perform a short ritual. First, she removed her headdress and hung it neatly over her left arm. She brushed back her long hair, then placed her hand over her mouth, and ran a finger along her left arm from hand to shoulder, then across her upper lip, ending by smoothing her hair behind her ears again. Then she folded her hands in her lap and facing the cavernous entrance, began a prayer or invocation in a firm voice.

"*Irankarapte na, Atuy-Siwnin Wenkamuy kirorkor…*"

"I greet you, O mighty Sea-Blue Demon,

"Please forgive our trespass and accept my gifts.

"I bring you good food and drink. Please accept them.

"I also bring you these two women to be your wives.

"Please be good to them and protect them from all harm, and in return they will bear you many children and bring joy to your life. For this we thank you."

Imekanu ended her plea, wanting to say more, hoping against hope her words were enough to save her friends—and afraid she had already stayed too long. She needed to return quickly, before she was missed. She would tell her husband she rose early to forage for the feast.

She looked up at the two women, standing there watching her with uncertain and anxious eyes. If only she could tell Nehee and Hi'e-Pay-Shah exactly what was happening…

But there was nothing to be done about that, and no more time to spare.

Rising, she quickly hugged each woman tightly and then backed away from them. As they started to follow, she held up a hand and told them no. She pointed back down to the *kotan*, and to them again, speaking to them in words she hoped they understood.

"No. Never." Her own eyes were stinging with tears now. She had to go. She pointed to the cave, speaking to them like toddlers. "Go. Go on inside."

She turned before they could see her crying, and ran off down the valley.

Nellie and Hypatia stared in shock as Imekanu bolted away into the trees.

"Whatever was *that* all about?" Nellie wondered. "She seems so very distraught. Is she cross with us? Do you think she's alright?"

Hypatia shook her head. "Something is very wrong, but I cannot say what or why."

"So… are we just to wait here until she comes back?"

"I would think so. She seemed most emphatic about that."

"But today's the big festival—surely we have to be there for that!"

Hypatia cradled her chin in her hand, thinking it over. "You're right," she finally said. "Then again, she was so secretive about everything. Perhaps this is part of the festival. Otherwise, why would she bring us all the way up here?"

As if in answer to their question, something stirred in the cavern. The pavement shook repeatedly like a beaten drum, and a huge shape emerged.

"Oh my lord," Nellie said faintly.

The demon was bigger than they'd realized, standing over twice their height, nearly as tall as the fir trees. The club he carried over his shoulder was iron-bound and spiked, bigger than a grown man and thick as a pine. His fur wrap, a rough tiger-skin toga. His skin was the deep blue of a midwinter sky, and his shaggy black mane and long horns would have put a buffalo to shame.

His bright eagle's eyes, each as big as a shot put, gleamed at them with cold-burning anger and ravenous hunger. When he spoke, the rumbling stone-timbre of his voice resonated deep in their bones.

"Nante oishī o yatsu," he said, eagerly staring not at the food or drink, but at them. Their translation implants recognized his words.

Such delicious morsels.

46

Except for the stars, dancing fireflies, and a sliver of moon, the three fugitives had no light to navigate by. Still, Blake and Cam jogged at a good clip across the open prairie, with Harcourt struggling to keep pace. They were within sight of the dark shape that marked the woods of the ruined city.

"Half a moment!" Harcourt wheezed. "Hold up, you louts!" Cam and Blake halted to allow the Victorian to catch up to them. Panting, Harcourt leaned over for breath, propping himself on his thighs. "It's all well and good for you soldier-boys to gallop away like a pair of Percherons, but these calisthenics are most unbecoming of an English gentleman!"

Blake raised an eyebrow. "Is that what you'll tell the posse when they catch us?"

"Be reasonable, man," Harcourt scoffed. "What is the chance they'll even take notice until breakfast-time?"

Blake opened his mouth to respond, but was distracted by

a pair of bright spots appearing in the distance behind them. They didn't move like lanterns carried by men on foot or horseback.

What the hell? he thought.

They moved like *headlights*. That could only mean...

"They're coming!" he said. "*Run!*"

Terror lent the three a second wind as they sprinted for the woods. Eerily, their pursuers made no sound—neither the familiar clomp of horse hooves nor the roar of a German war engine. Still, the lights of the vehicle drew closer at a frightening rate.

Lungs on fire, Cam and Blake bolted as fast as they could toward the relative safety of the trees ahead. Even as they drove themselves forward, though, both men knew with growing despair they had lost any chance of entering the woods unnoticed.

Harcourt worked his skinny legs madly, like a broken-winged bird struggling to lift off the ground. It was no use. He could scarcely match half the other men's speed.

"Wait for me!" he called, then wailed with an incoherent cry of alarm when he saw them disappear into the dark of the forest. He was still a hundred yards out, utterly abandoned and completely exposed. And then he was caught in the lights from the approaching hunters.

* * *

Breaking past the edge of the woods, Cam and Blake each took cover behind a tree, fighting to catch their breaths. Harcourt was still wailing from the prairie, and Cam risked a look back. The lights of their pursuers were blindingly bright now, clearly outlining Harcourt in his flapping coattails and top hat, their unmistakable beacon.

"They've spotted him!"

"Of course they have," Blake said impatiently. "We need to keep going."

With a pathetic yelp, Harcourt tripped and fell flat on his face.

Blake shook his head. "There's nothing we can do. Come on."

"We have to help him," Cam insisted.

"He'll lead them straight to us."

"So there's no use hiding now," Cam said—and dashed back toward the light.

Blake swore, gritting his teeth. Fighting the urge to punch the tree trunk in anger, he could only watch helplessly as the reckless Celt sprinted to Harcourt's rescue.

The few seconds it took Cam to reach Harcourt felt like forever. Rushing up, he held out a hand to help the man to his feet. Harcourt took it.

"I-I thought you'd left me." His voice was pitifully grateful.

"Never," Cam replied. "Now let's—"

A blaze of fire came out of the night, as a burst of automatic fire cut him off.

47

Nellie and Hypatia froze in terror. The blue-skinned ogre towered above them, his outstretched arms allowing no room to slip past him for the safety of the forest. That left only the lip of the precipice behind them, a sheer drop to the death.

He leaned in closer.

"Yūshoku no jikandesu." His low voice rumbled, deep as a dragon's. *Time for dinner.*

"Wait now!" Nellie cried out. The ogre raised an eyebrow the size of a stretching black cat.

"Oh ho! You speak English! Fee Fi Fo Fum!" He laughed, a terrifying sound like battleship chains scraping anchor on the bottom of the sea.

"Please…" Nellie fought to keep her voice from shaking. "Please don't eat us."

He seemed to consider her request.

"I am most hungry, and you two will make a delicious

meal—but first, I will let you take your picture with me before I throw you into my cooking pot."

Nellie gaped at him in confusion. "Take... a picture? But we have no camera... or photographer." Even as she spoke the words, she recognized how ludicrous they sounded.

"Hmm, very well. Then I shall let you go this time—but you must promise to attend my performance at the Sapporo Pavilion. Four o'clock this afternoon."

The women stared at each other.

Madness upon madness, Nellie thought.

"Then we shall," Hypatia said with all sincerity. "You have our word."

"Excellent!" the ogre exclaimed. "I shall not eat you today. My *Oni* brothers and I shall perform our wondrous Ainu Demon-Dance, brought to you by Sapporo. You shall be amazed at my agility and thrill to my feats of strength!"

Nellie raised a hand. "Pardon us, Mr. Ogre—"

"I am Kon'iro Kyojin, King of the *Oni!*" he thundered. "Disrespect me at your peril!"

"I... I beg your forgiveness," Nellie stammered, "but can you just tell us—where is this pavilion?"

The Oni king held out one big blue palm, the nails of his fingers resembling blackened shark teeth. A shimmering ball of pearlescent light sprang to life in his hand, reflecting back from his huge eyes, and resolved itself into the glowing figure of an elegant fairy princess, one foot tall. She appeared to be Asian. Japanese, Nellie thought.

"Welcome to Ezo-Land, the enchanted Ainu realm of

Hokkaido!" the pixie-voiced princess exclaimed with a courtly bow. Like a magician's assistant, she held up her hands broadly, showcasing a glowing translucent map that appeared between them.

"You are at the Demon's Cave, here. You must be very brave, and beware the fierce demons! To reach the Sapporo Pavilion, kindly take the stairway to your left to Mononoke Hime Station. The magic monorail arrives every fifteen minutes, and will take you to RoboMech Paladins Station, where the Sapporo Super Ninja Adventure Pavilion is only a short walk away. Thank you and enjoy your special day!" She bowed again and disappeared along with her map.

Nellie and Hypatia looked around, seeing no trace of the promised stairs or station, or anything of this Ezo-Land that had filled the whole valley on the princess's magical map. There was nothing but snow-streaked forest.

Gazing out over the rugged yet beautiful vista, becoming clearer as the day became brighter, Hypatia scarcely knew what to make of the demon and the fairy princess, or the vanished land of which they spoke. She turned to Nellie to ask what she thought.

Something was wrong.

"Nellie? Are you—?"

Nellie seemed caught in a trance, staring out into the empty vastness of air spread before them. She opened her mouth as if to speak. Then her eyes closed, she raised her fingertips to her temple, wavering unsteadily.

"Nellie!" Hypatia gasped as Nellie suddenly toppled forward. She tried to catch her, but the momentum was too great, carrying them both off the ledge.

Air whooshed past them, then twin blue streaks caught them up and brought them back. Kon'iro Kyojin had grasped them in midair with surprising speed and deftness, lifting them back up and gently setting them back on their feet at a safe distance from the precipice.

"Are you in distress?" the giant asked. **"Would you like me to summon a nurse from the first aid center?"**

"I... I'm not certain," Hypatia said, still dazed from the drop and the rescue.

"I apologize, there is a delayed response from Guest Services, but I will stay here with your party until a medical professional arrives. In the meantime, may I offer you a drink of water?"

She found the fierce ogre's reassurance as touching as it was unexpected.

"Thank you," Hypatia said, distracted by concern for her friend. "Nellie? Are you alright?"

Standing somewhat upright, but still supported by the Oni's great blue fingers, Nellie nodded absently.

"I'm fine," she replied to no one there. "You just caught me by surprise, and I had a dizzy spell at a bad place, but we're alright!" She nodded, and seemed to be fighting back tears. "Yes. Me too."

Hypatia stared at her. Though Nellie's eyes were open, she was miles away.

"Nellie? What are you saying?"

Then, a moment later, she turned to Hypatia, eyes gleaming.

"Hypatia! It's *Amber*! She's found us!"

"NELLIE!"

"We're still here," Nellie replied. "We hear you! Please don't shout. It's overwhelming when you do."

"Sorry! I keep cutting in and out. But listen! I'm losing rovers—they break apart if we try to keep the portal open for very long. I need you two to jump through now before I lose you altogether."

"Oh, but we're miles away. We'll hurry, but we need more time to get to you."

"Damn it!" Silence. *"Okay, I'm sending a rover to find you."*

"Wonderful! The portal is in a cave, but we're in the mountains a few miles due north of it. We'll leave at once to rendezvous with your robot."

"Hurry Nellie, I can't—"

"Amber? Amber?"

She was gone again. Nellie turned to Hypatia.

"We have to leave for the seal cave at once. Amber is going to send one of the ship's little flying satellites to search for us and help lead…" Her voice trailed off. "Oh."

"What is it?"

Nellie pointed down over the lip of the precipice. A gleaming dot was floating up the mountainside toward the top. The rover had already found them.

* * *

The softball-sized obsidian sphere stopped and hovered in the air before them.

"This is the Ship," it said. *"Ms. Bly and Lady Hypatia, it is urgent you follow me immediately down to the portal."*

"Marvelous!" Nellie exclaimed. "How did you find us so quickly?"

"I have been in search mode for three hours and nineteen minutes."

"But… I was just talking to Amber a moment ago. How could you possibly…?" She shook her head. "Why do I even bother asking questions anymore? Never mind. Let's just be off."

The rover set off toward the trees, back in the direction Imekanu had brought them up. Kon'iro Kyojin seemed to take no notice of the drone whatsoever, but when they started to leave, he raised a hand to stop them.

"So sorry, but it is very important you remain here until medical personnel have arrived to confirm that you are alright. They will be here soon." For a giant horned and fanged blue monster, he sounded quite protective.

"Why don't you come with us?" Nellie said. "We could use your company."

"No, please, I must insist that you both remain here until a nurse arrives." He shifted slightly, making a wall of himself. The flying drone turned around and sailed back to them.

"I'm afraid we don't have time to discuss this with such antique and obsolete neurohardware," the rover said. It emitted a beam of greenish-amber light which struck the giant's face.

Kon'iro Kyojin froze in place, and then his forehead—horns and all—slid back like a rolltop desk, exposing an interior filled with intricate translucent grillwork and tiny blinking lights. The drone moved closer, emitting needle-thin beams of light in rapid bursts. A few moments later, the rover retreated and the giant's skull slid seamlessly back into place.

"**Come!**" he said, rumbling back to life again. "**I shall take you on a fabulous tour of Ezo-Land before I cook you up for dinner!**"

With the rover as guide and Kon'iro Kyojin as escort, Nellie and Hypatia made good time retracing their route down from the precipice as their breaths puffed out in the cold midmorning air.

Though she knew it was foolish in light of their situation, part of Nellie hoped this route would take them back by the village so they could thank their hosts and say goodbye. It was a shame they'd had to ruin the festival by disappearing the way they did. Then again, they couldn't very well expect a warm welcome with the giant blue ogre in tow.

The going was rougher for him, ducking under the tree canopy or bulldozing his way through, keeping his palm held open so that his holographic princess could act as a rather odd tour guide, pointing out features of a park that no longer existed.

They reached a small clearing in the forest, the glade formed by the crossroads of two trails, and the rover abruptly paused. The others halted as well, and the ogre closed his hand, snuffing out the princess in mid-sentence.

"What is it?" Nellie whispered.

The rover was silent for a moment. *"I detect—"*

Sudden commotion broke through the trees to their right, sending a flock of birds bursting into flight. A herd of terrified deer came bounding toward them, charging through the undergrowth in great waves, kicking up snow as they ran. The women ducked behind Kon'iro Kyojin for shelter as the herd thundered past them—disappearing again just as quickly as they had appeared.

"That bunch was certainly in a hurry." Nellie laughed as the two emerged from behind their oversized protector.

"But what set them to flight?" Hypatia asked.

As if in answer to her question, lines of armored men began to fill the glade from the north.

Squads of medieval Japanese foot soldiers swarmed toward them, lacquered leather cuirasses and conical black helmets gleaming like beetle carapaces. The front rows bristled with long polearms tipped with spearheads, sword blades, and hooks. Behind the lines of spearmen marched archers and sharpshooters, long muskets on their shoulders.

Alongside them, two surly, rhinoceros-like beasts pulled a platform. Each was nearly the size of a stagecoach, their massive, hunchbacked bodies covered in shaggy white fur and boasting two sharp horns, the foremost as big as a scimitar. Atop the platform rode a grim-faced Japanese officer with a shaven head. He wore a dark blue military uniform and cap much like the European armies of Nellie's time.

Beside him stood a sturdy metal tripod. Nellie recognized the instrument it supported—a Gatling gun.

Nellie gasped. "Japanese *samurai*! They're terrifying warriors." Suddenly she made the connection.

Shamo—Samurai…

The dreaded *Shamo* had arrived.

48

The shot went wide, sending the targets diving to the ground for cover.

"I have them!" Shanks hollered, raising the Tommy gun to fire off another burst.

"*No!*" Kha-Hotep yelled, shoving the firearm away as he slammed on the brakes, spoiling a second barrage. "*Seshuw heset net Selkis!*" Kha hissed at the startled Redcoat. "The scorpion goddess shrivel your worthless throat! I said we take them alive!"

"Get you hence!" Shanks snapped. "Besides, I was only shooting at the savage!"

"Jackal! I said we kill them only as the last resort—the very last! Mind my words or suffer the consequences—and mind your ammunition, the bullets come dear." At the prices Cahokia paid Laclede's Landing for their hand-tooled bullets, they may as well have been firing diamonds.

Behind them, Crows elbowed Rockwell and pointed to their quarry. The two had already slipped out of the headlights' glare into the dark.

"They're getting away," Rockwell said. "Do you want us to shoot them, or not?"

Kha-Hotep said nothing, flicking the switch to vent the boiler with a sharp hiss, and then took up his own Tommy gun.

"Not yet. Come. We pursue them on foot."

Even while diving for cover under fire, Harcourt's precious hat had somehow managed to stay on his head. They kept up their desperate belly-crawl, moving sidelong out of the beams of light, until they heard the doors of the horseless carriage crack open.

"We have to run!" Cam urged. "Come on, get up!"

"No!" The professor shook his head. "They'll gun us down!"

"They're only getting closer." Taking him by the arm, Cam hauled the Victorian to his feet and the two sprinted into the woods. The shouts of their pursuers followed as they ran almost blind, their only illumination the dappled bands of the carriage's lights shafting through the trees.

"Which way do we go now?" Harcourt asked breathlessly. Cam shook his head, his sense of direction uncertain. With the sound of their hunters closing in, he chose the darkest path available and pulled Harcourt with him.

"Not that way." Blake emerged from a different pool of shadow. "Follow me."

The three crashed through the near dark, more concerned with speed than stealth, while the hunting party seemed to be fanning out—their echoing shouts seemed to come from every direction. In front of Cam, Blake came to an unexpected halt and then angled back sharply to the right, into a small break in a stand of oaks. Enough moonlight knifed down to illuminate a welcome sight—a trio of arctic parkas laid out like directional beacons.

There was no sign of any portal.

Blake paced back and forth like a leopard in a cage.

"Damn it, Amber," he muttered, "come *on*."

Cam closed his eyes. *"Amber, we're here at the doorway."*

Her voice came rushing back.

"Cam! I can see you! Come through!"

"Amber!" he said aloud. "She's here! Amber, we can't see you. Where are you? Where is it?"

"Turn around, and go slightly to your left."

He followed her lead.

"Wait! You just passed it! Back up and try again."

"Are you sure? There is nothing."

"Trust me!"

He tried again, walking slowly with hands outstretched.

"There's nothing here!"

"We're running out of time," Blake muttered. "They're close…"

"Amber, I can't—"

"Hold on, I'll send the rover."

A diffused white glow suddenly brightened the clearing.

"There! I see it." Blake pointed. Above Cam's head, just out of arm's reach, a shining haze of distortion rippled in the air like the surface of a pool after a pebble drop.

"What now?" Harcourt asked.

Blake looked up at the aerial display.

"Come here, Cam. Help me with him."

"What's that now?" Harcourt asked. Following Blake's lead, Cam grabbed a leg and lifted him up. "Wait, wait, I'm not r—" he cried out as they fed him headfirst into the light. It drank him in as if it were a swirling drain—one moment he was all flailing gangly limbs, the next instant sucked through and gone.

Blake and Cam looked at each other.

"Think you can jump up there?" Blake asked.

Cam nodded. "You?"

"Give me a hand." Blake laid a hand on Cam's shoulder as the Celt bent and made a stirrup of his hands to boost him up. The vortex took him away as swiftly as it had the wailing professor.

"Cam, you did it!" Amber's voice was urgent. *"Come through quick, we don't know how much longer we can keep the portal open!"*

"Here I come."

A cracking sound suddenly came from further in the woods. They were close. Cam put them out of his mind, focusing on the jump. The rippling in the air seemed higher now. He flexed his hands nervously, crouched down, then took a deep breath and leapt up. His hand swept through empty air and with a grunt of frustration he fell back down again.

He quickly picked himself up for a second try.

"Cam," a quiet voice said. He turned around slowly to see Kha-Hotep step out from between the tree trunks, firearm raised. "Step away from the portal, my brother. You're coming back with us."

"I'm sorry, Kha."

"Don't make me do it." The Egyptian's gaze was deadly serious. Cam had no words to convince him.

"I'm sorry."

"I'll shoot."

Cam lowered his head as if in defeat, and then bent to flex his legs and jumped as high as he could.

"*Cam!*" Kha-Hotep yelled.

The Celt stretched out his arm as if to touch the sky—and this time the vortex accepted his offering. He felt himself moving ever upward, slowly, and then twisting in the air—no, it was everything else that was twisting, the world and the sky swirling around him until he plunged through a tunnel of air turned into water, into dreams…

49

They kill bears here, Commander Tokushirō Noda had thought
to himself a few minutes earlier. His unit, the 7th Hokkaido
Infantry of the Imperial Army, had been the *Kuma-Heidan,* the
Bear Division, the strongest unit in the army of Japan. *Now let
them see what this old bear knows of revenge.*

He flashed on memories from a quarter century ago, as a
young lieutenant in the winters of 1904 and 1905, when the
Russian and Japanese empires clashed on the plains of frozen,
desolate Manchuria.

*Grueling marches through blinding snowstorms, days and nights
of endless artillery bombardment, chattering of machine guns and
screams. Flat battlefields turned into hills of twisted, fallen dead.
Bone-white landscape, dyed red and blasted black.*

Every day, every attack, for a year and a month, his troops took up the banner of the rising sun and swore by the spirit of Yamato, promising ten thousand years for His Majesty the Emperor. They reflected on the cherry blossom, the warrior's flower, its beauty, short life, and glorious death. Those ready to die could accomplish anything.

At night, he affixed his bayonet with frozen fingers and they charged in waves of suicidal assaults through minefields and entanglements of barbed wire, silver blades flashing in the dark like reeds in a storm. Blinding Russian searchlights swept across the field, and the star-rockets burned over their heads, making them easy targets. His unit was thrown into the worst meat grinders of the war—203 Meter Hill, Port Arthur, the final battle of Mukden. There, on a front extending more than ninety miles, the Russians dug in at the old Manchu capital, and for ten days the outnumbered Japanese threw themselves at them.

By the end, when the Tsar's generals knew all was lost and they were closing in to finish them, the Russian troops abandoned their wounded and fled under cover of a massive dust storm. Once again, the Russians were saved by their oldest and most implacable field-general, the weather.

In the moment of victory, tighten your helmet-strings, *Iyeyasu the first* Shōgun *had warned. Even as Noda and his men, too exhausted to give chase, stood watching their defeated foes slink away into the howling oblivion, a still greater battle commenced before their eyes.*

Divine beams of light from a hidden sun broke through the crumbling earth to touch the sky, forming sheer mountain ranges of pure lightning and blinding radiance, resplendent and terrifying. This was more than the might of Raijin-sama *the thunder god, it was the karmic energy of the entire universe on full display.*

And then, as all things do, it vanished.

The old world passed away on that afternoon—the Day of the Battle Between Earth and Heaven—replaced by a wild, strange new land he barely recognized. Like Odysseus, Lt. Noda suffered much, lost many comrades, and saw many strange things during his yearslong voyage home through the monster-ridden anarchy of Asia.

From crisis, opportunity. A survivor, he knew the man who controlled bullets controlled guns controlled the future. Harvesting the spent cartridges at Mukden, millions scattered across the battlefield for the taking, he worked with Chinese alchemists to produce bullets again for his unit's firearms. He took Castle Matsumae, what the Ezo *called Matomai, and gathered new vassals—*samurai, *stray* ronin, *and* ashigaru *footsoldiers.*

His army.

His Kamchatkan and Koryak scouts, bundled up in their reindeer hides and thick fur capes, came running back past the ranks of spearmen and arquebusiers to get to Noda. Had they spotted the village already? Rarely were the taciturn, weathered men so agitated.

"A giant, my lord! A giant!"

"A giant? Indeed?" Noda permitted himself a smile, absently leaning a hand on the Maxim gun. His force was more than a match for any prehistoric beast still roaming the Hokkaido wilderness. "Let us bring it down!"

With a chop of his hand, he waved his troops forward toward their prize.

* * *

Nellie and Hypatia froze as spearmen, archers, and gunners spilled into the glade, fanning out in a wide formation to better encircle them. Kon'iro Kyojin smiled at the newcomers.

"Such delicious morsels…"

Reaching over to the closest fir, he casually broke it in half and stripped off its branches with a single sweep of his hand. Then he raised the trunk high, hefting it like a batter at the plate.

"No!" Nellie cried out. "There's too many of them!"

"We will take care of these," the rover said. *"You two go."*

"But—"

"He is right," Hypatia said, grabbing her hand. "Come!"

Nellie looked back at the blue giant, but his attention was on the warriors now. He let loose his roar of demonic laughter—thunderous this close. She turned and ran.

Arrows were already whizzing past them.

"Uchikata hajime!" Commander Noda shouted. At his signal, bowmen and arquebusiers opened fire, the muskets belching smoke and fire. While the gunners hurried to reload, a second and third flight of arrows struck the ogre until his blue hide bristled with them like a porcupine. Noda nodded in approval… then he realized the *oni* was still advancing. Bright blue sparks flew off his shoulders and chest, but if the bullets and bow-shots had wounded him, he otherwise showed no sign of it.

"*Totsugeki!*" Noda shouted to the front line.

The soldiers charged, rushing toward their foe *en masse* with spears and *naginatas* to finish the monster. Laughing maniacally, the giant swung his makeshift club in great sweeping arcs, shattering polearms and sending warriors flying with each swipe. The archers fired at will, while the panicking arquebusiers gave up on the reload, dropping their guns to draw *katanas* instead.

Noda swore and crouched at the heavy machine gun, quickly and efficiently locking the cartridge belt in place and racking the charging handle with an experienced hand. He raised the barrel and fired on the demon's horned head.

A flash of blinding light filled the clearing for an instant. He shielded his eyes—and suddenly there were *four* of the giant blue ogres. Sinister flying shapes swarmed overhead, and dark things came crawling out of the woods.

No more arrows flew past, but the women still ran as fast as they could in the bulky overboots, their parka hoods falling back from their faces. Terrible sounds, thundering mixed with men's screams, echoed from the battle above, but worse, strange yipping, whistling hunting calls still dogged them. They wove through the trees, crashing through pockets of snow and scrub, recklessly bounding down the mountain like the fleeing deer.

Without warning, something fast and deadly came slinging through the air, catching Nellie from behind—in a sudden flurry of movement, it whipped around her neck, choking her and striking her in the head. She pitched forward, arms splayed wide, momentum sending her tumbling, first onto the frost-slicked ground, and then over the side of the nearest cliff. Hypatia screamed her name.

Heart pounding, Hypatia rushed to the edge and carefully crouched down to peer over. It made her reel with vertigo, and then the pit of her stomach dropped as she looked down upon Nellie's body. The young woman had plummeted down a snowy embankment and slid to a precarious halt, halfway to a sheer drop-off of hundreds of feet. She lay unmoving, eyes closed, her body threatening to slide headfirst even further toward that final edge.

It took all her concentration not to slip and fall herself, but Hypatia hurried down the slope, half-sliding, half-walking until she reached Nellie's side. There, she saw that nothing more than a simple trio of leather-bound stones connected by lengths of sinew had brought Nellie down. She knelt and threw off her mittens, working her fingers quickly to unwind the strands wrapped tight around Nellie's throat, praying she still lived.

Engaged as she was, Hypatia still heard the sudden whipping of the air and ducked, just as another leathery snare went whirling just over her head. She looked up to see a trio of men dressed in ragged suits of patchwork leather hide and bushy fur capes. Beneath their thick black fur caps, they looked wizened, with beardless wind-carved faces the color of camelskin, their eyes like knots in a tree.

They were coming for her, knives out.

* * *

Will-o'-the-wisps and malevolent spirits filled the air—pale gaunt specters floated overhead in trailing burial robes, repulsive night hags cackled and swooped like predatory birds, a tall black shade with no face but an austere *kabuki* mask moaned and stretched out grasping arms as it drew closer. Gray-skinned, hollow-eyed dead girls, their limbs impossibly contorted, crab-crawled down tree trunks, alongside staggering fire-blackened corpses with melting eyes and red flames in the sockets.

A menagerie of hungry demonkind descended upon them. Cyclops *oni* whose heads were little more than a massive evil eye, and gelatinous *oni* with a hundred eyes. Headless *oni* whose torsos bore a malicious face, and humanlike *oni* with necks that stretched like serpents. Crow-*tengu*, and river-*kappa*. Seductive spider demonesses beckoned to the soldiers from their web-shrouded bowers in the trees.

The identical quartet of giants still roared and brandished their clubs with perfect synchronicity, but the terrified foot soldiers—those still alive—scrambled back. The bravest among the surviving *samurai* still wielded their *katanas* against the howling demons, but the insubstantial evil spirits were immune to steel or arrow. The rest of his men dropped their spears or swords and fled for their lives.

Howling like wolves, the three *Shamo* scouts came tearing down the embankment toward Hypatia, heedless of its steepness or the nearness of the cliff's edge. She still struggled to loosen the snare from Nellie's neck. But the fastest two were on her before she could even rise to defend herself.

"Melagetashlen!" one barked as he bounded down to grab for her. She drew her arm back and swung with all her strength, flailing him with his own corded weapon. Its three stone weights hit him full in the face with a crack, breaking teeth. He careened to the side, unable to stop himself from toppling off the cliff. A long, agonized cry trailed after him. The other scout grimaced and leapt to tackle her, sending them both sliding further down dangerously close to the edge.

They struggled in the snow, but the rugged tribesman was stronger. Seizing Hypatia by the throat with one hand, he slammed her body down, once, twice, and then raised his blade with the other, aimed at her heart. But she had already drawn her own knife, and now slipped it under his thick hide shirt into his unprotected belly. He gasped, and she plunged it in deeper. His blade tumbled out of his trembling fingers over the cliff, and then, with a push from her, he followed it.

Her head spinning, breath heaving, and blood pounding through her chest and arms, Hypatia forced herself to get to her feet again, raising her knife to face the third attacker. But he was up the slope. His beefy hand held Nellie by the back of her hair, her limp body dangling from his grasp. Pointing his knife toward Hypatia, he gestured with it angrily for her to drop hers. She refused and took a step closer, shaking drops of blood off her blade.

"If you've killed her…" she said, her voice deep and guttural. Locking eyes with him, she took another deliberate step. Rattled, the man swiftly brought his knife to Nellie's throat. Hypatia froze. They continued their stare-down for a few tense heartbeats, before she slowly lowered her knife, and then lightly let it fall to the snow.

The tribesman smiled, not a pretty sight. With a nod of his head, he beckoned her closer, then pointed to the ground with his knife. It seemed he wanted her to kneel down, so she did, never taking her gaze off his. Pleased, he grunted in reply, dropping his catch. He stepped toward her, reversing the grip on his knife.

He grunted again, louder this time. Then, with a fixed look of surprise, he stiffened and dropped like a fallen tree. Nellie stood behind him, her knife buried deep in the small of his back.

Hypatia gave a choked laugh that was swallowed by tears. Rushing to her side, Nellie dropped to her knees and the two held each other.

"I thought they'd killed you," Hypatia said, her voice muffled against Nellie's shoulder.

"No, just made me see stars for a minute," Nellie said, soothing her. "So sorry to scare you just now—I was only playing possum for his sake. Are you alright to keep moving?"

"Oh, yes."

The commander was not a superstitious man.

"It's a trick!" he bellowed at the top of his lungs. "Stand your ground and fight the giant!"

None followed his orders, if any could even hear them over the din. He swore again. Ignoring the phantasms, he took aim at the closest of the giants and opened fire with the Maxim gun.

Nothing. The blaze of bullets passed through the horned blue colossus as if he were a ghost. Another trick. *Damn all the smoke and mirrors!* Noda roared his own war cry as he swiveled the barrel, sweeping the entire clearing to catch all four in his arc of fire.

All of them went down in concert.

Even so, the rest of the creatures continued to terrorize his forces. He wanted to fire another burst to be certain he had finished off the giant, but there was so much panic he couldn't get a clear shot without gunning down his own men. He considered the option, his finger flexing on the trigger... then he spotted the mysterious floating sphere. It hovered at the very center of the commotion. What technological marvel allowed it to defy gravity, he had no idea—but he understood the concept of a cinematograph projector well enough.

Time to exorcize these ghosts.

He raised the angle of the gun and trained it on the hovering little orb. Before he could pull the trigger again, the blue giant—just one this time—was back on his feet again, his chest smoking. Men's screams and flying bodies marked another swing of the blue giant's club, and then the horned brute turned his eyes on Commander Noda himself.

"Be amazed at my agility!" the *oni* roared as he leapt into the air with club raised, bounding over the fleeing *samurai*.

The rhinos bucked in fear, and Noda struggled to hang on to the platform.

"Thrill to my feats of strength!" the giant bellowed as he came crashing down upon Noda and the gun.

Even after they could no longer hear the terrible echoes of battle rolling down the forested slopes, Nellie and Hypatia continued to run, not daring to stop even as their lungs and limbs burned. As the mountains swallowed up the wan winter sun, they finally staggered their way down to the little beach and its sea cave.

The seals were agitated. Light shone from somewhere in the depths of the cavern, suffusing its inky depths with a welcome glow. The mammals barked and wiggled away as the two women entered and approached its source, a shimmering spot of gauzy brightness on the cave wall, thrumming with unearthly life. Nellie put a hand to her forehead and concentrated, trying to reopen the psychic link.

"Amber? Are you there? Amber?"

The connection returned.

"—can't tell how much longer I can hold the portal open. Keep an eye out for the rover, it should reach you soon!"

"Amber, you already sent it. That was this morning. We're here!"

"What? Okay then, come through!"

Hypatia took Nellie's hand, and the two stepped into the vortex.

50

Earlier...

Her head hurt. Even so, the first thing she noticed when she woke up was how warm she was. Not just warm, but impossibly cozy, as if she were wrapped in luxurious fur blankets. Blankets that rose and fell as if...

As if they were breathing.

Amber opened her eyes. It took all of her self-preservation instincts not to scream and run. She was nestled against something large and furry.

A mammal of some sorts, a *big* honking mammal. It had an arm flung over her, large enough on its own to be a bolster pillow.

The thing suddenly growled, a deep, rumbling stretched-out sound. Amber stopped breathing. It shifted slightly, then settled back down with a snuffle. Without moving, she looked at the arm, following it to the end where the sight of four velociraptor-sized claws nearly stopped her heart.

Oh my god. Oh my god.

I'm so dead, I'm so dead…

Lying very still, she focused on her breathing, and slowing her heart rate so it didn't reverberate in her chest and head like bongo drums. Then, slowly… very slowly, she started trying to wriggle out from under the arm, hoping against hope that those intimidating talons wouldn't suddenly dig into her flesh.

They twitched… then settled back down, then the huge animal slowly curled up, bringing its head down to Amber's face, opening its jaws wide. They were more than big enough to take off her whole face.

It yawned.

She dared to breathe again, exhaling in relief.

The creature wasn't a grizzly, though it did have a bearlike, stretched-out face. Its long conical head ended in a mouth that seemed more made for a camel or a giraffe. Then she recognized it from pictures in library books, the scary-big claws, the face… an *adorable* face. She'd been spooned by a giant ground sloth.

Okay, they're herbivores, she thought. *I should be alright*. If it hadn't messed her up so far, it probably wasn't going to. Still, she moved very slowly and carefully, sliding out from under its massive arm. Scuttling low to the ground, as quietly as she could, she waited until she was a good twenty feet away to stand up again.

Amber looked back at her furry friend. The giant sloth was curled up against the base of a cypress tree, making little snoring noises almost impossibly cute for something that big.

Relieved beyond belief, she took a look around. There didn't seem to be any other super-sized Ice Age beasts in the immediate vicinity, for which she was grateful. She'd had enough of prehistoric carnivores trying to turn her into a meal.

She was also grateful for the parka and overboots the *Vanuatu* had provided. It was cold here—wherever here was—though not as cold as Antarctic summer. Still, chilly enough. Tentatively she wiggled toes and fingers, relieved to find everything apparently in working order other than a slight crick in her neck.

Taking stock of her surroundings, Amber saw that she was in a clearing at the top of a hill, surrounded by stony outcroppings and trees. Two green picnic tables stood in the middle, and the smell of smoke drifted on the breeze. Down below a little lake encircled the hill. Past that lay a long patch of carefully manicured park, now a refugee camp.

Makeshift tents and campfires dotted the meadow. In between them, hundreds of shell-shocked people milled about, or huddled together for warmth and comfort. Most wore turn-of-the-twentieth-century clothing—ladies in big hats who looked as if they should be strolling with parasols, and mustachioed men dressed up for barbershop quartets. A handful sported more contemporary outfits.

On the outskirts of the camp sat a circle of what she supposed was a native American tribe, roasting fish on the fire. The men, their long black hair tied back in ponytails, were naked except for shell necklaces and nose rings, while topless women wore deerskin aprons and ornate necklaces of feathers and shell, their chins tattooed with a trio of lines. Some had capes and blankets made from animal skins, and all had plastered themselves in mud for warmth.

Where the hell am I?

The hilltop afforded Amber a clear view. Beyond the roughly half-mile-wide shard of parkland, alternating patches of frosty tundra and sand dunes stretched to the south and west. Far off on the western horizon, she could make out a glazed sliver of ocean.

Past the tents to the east and to the north lay devastation—a blasted hellscape of still-smoking rubble and whole city blocks still being devoured by flames, clouds of smoke billowing up from the burning buildings. Yet even in the destruction, there were isolated patches of other shards—glacier and dune, city and jungle, each one an island of color in a sea of blackened ash.

To the north, a flash of red-orange caught her eye—the partial span of what had once been the Golden Gate Bridge.

Time stopped.

San Diego—and her family—was only a nine-hour drive down the coast. No, that was pre-Event.

I have to get there.

Could she find a working vehicle?

Would there be passable roads?

She closed her hands into fists, and took a deep breath. This was the closest she had been to her hometown since the Event had hit. If she couldn't drive, she *could* walk there. Sure, it would be dangerous, and take days or even weeks, she knew that. But for the first time since the world had gone haywire, she allowed herself a slender thread of hope that maybe... just maybe... she could see her family again.

After all, how could she save the world now? She was even further off track, running out of time, and her friends were gone away to—god, who even knew?

And would it really be so bad to be with her family when the end came?

Cam's face suddenly flashed into her mind. Cam, who would do anything for her. Who would die for her. And Blake, who had crossed miles to find her again in England after they were separated. Nellie, Kha-Hotep, Leila, and even Harcourt. They were family now, the relationship forged through survival and sacrifice. She owed it to them, and to the world, to figure out how to stay on course. DeMetta had said it when he'd emerged from his sarcophagus.

"I think we're supposed to save the world."

He'd sacrificed himself to give them a chance to restore the world to the way it was before the Event. All the people who'd died since this nightmare began... if she succeeded, she could give them their lives back.

She wasn't going to let them down.

New plan. First, find the others. Keeping Cam's face in her mind's eye, Amber closed her eyes and sent out a mental call, focusing on the strength of her feelings for him. If he was anywhere nearby, she could find him. *Would* find him.

Down in the desperate tent camp below her, the minds of grief-stricken people lit up in her psyche like fireflies. He wasn't there. She scanned through them for anyone familiar.

Nothing. Not a hint.

Amber tried to expand her range, but without Dee's help it was too overwhelming. There were too many minds to grasp, let alone to sort through. Her head began to pound harder. Feeling suddenly weak and dizzy, Amber stumbled over to the nearest picnic table and sat down. Maybe when she'd landed, she'd hit her head and now she was losing her psychic ability.

Despair swept over her like a flood, so raw and deep that for a moment she thought she'd drown in it.

"No," she muttered. "I don't have time for this."

Forcing herself to concentrate, she recalled the first time she'd been on her own, immediately after the timeline had shattered. She'd found it impossible to think, and then Blake had found her, saving her from a pack of wolves. After that, she'd rarely had *time* for despair—and she hadn't been alone—but now her new family was gone, and she didn't know how she was going to survive. There had to be a reason she'd uncovered her newfound abilities, but right now she couldn't figure out what it was.

Amber rested her head on the table and tried to think.

Across the clearing, the giant sloth snored.

"Excuse me… Excuse me, miss? You okay?"

Amber jerked awake. Her eyes snapped open and she sat up so quickly it hurt her neck.

Standing in front of her were a man in his twenties and a girl who couldn't be much older than eighteen. She was dressed in a too-big brown duster which fell open to reveal a filth-stained and tattered linen nightgown that had once been white, and a pair of brown Ugg boots. Smears of dirt and soot streaked her delicate features, and she had her mass of long dark hair tied back with a scrap of checkered cloth. Her china-blue eyes were sunk deep into their sockets, and she looked like she'd been through hell.

The man wore a black duster over nice jeans and a hunter green long-sleeved shirt, with a backpack slung over his shoulders. It made Amber immediately miss her own beloved backpack, still back aboard the *Vanuatu*. He looked the very epitome of Casual Friday, good-looking in a non-threatening way. Her mom would have liked him, Amber thought, apropos of nothing.

"You okay?" he repeated. The two stayed back a few feet.

"Yeah," she replied. "I fell asleep. I think I'm dehydrated."

The man immediately shrugged out of his backpack, which looked stuffed to the gills, and pulled out a bottled water.

"Here," he said. When she hesitated, he added, "Don't worry, we've got more."

"Thanks." Amber gratefully took the bottle, unscrewed the lid, and took a long swallow. Almost immediately she felt more alert, and saw how tired both of them looked. "Do you want to sit down?" The man nodded, and the two stepped over and sat down on the other side of the table, the girl looking as though her bones were ready to melt with exhaustion.

"I'm Andrew," the man said, "and this is Rose." He put a protective arm around the young woman, who leaned against him and closed her eyes.

"I'm Amber."

Andrew reached into his backpack again, pulling out more bottles of water, two bags of chips, and a chocolate bar.

"We've been walking for hours," he said. "Might as well have a picnic, since we're here." He indicated the tents down below. "Didn't want to take this out down there—people are going crazy at the sight of food. Saw one guy get the shit kicked out of him for an apple."

Rose nodded, but didn't say anything.

"I was working late when this crazy shit went down," Andrew continued. "It was like an earthquake, but like the northern lights were going on all around, and suddenly half of the Transatlantic Pyramid is gone." He shook his head. "I mean, literally gone, like someone took a giant axe to the building and just chopped it away. And suddenly it's not night anymore, and I'm stuck on what's left of the eighth floor along with the janitor. Luckily it was the part that still had stairs, so we could get out of the building. But when I got outside…"

He swallowed, his shock still evident. Rose squeezed his hand in mute support. Amber liked her for that.

"There were buildings I didn't even recognize on fire, with a bunch more already collapsed into rubble, and… and people were dressed all old-timey. Like… well, like Rose here. It's like the 1906 earthquake happened all over again."

"But it *is* 1906…" Rose said softly.

"See what I mean?" Andrew said. "If I didn't know better, I'd think they were filming a movie, but it's *so* much crazier than that—some real Marshall, Will, and Holly *Land of the Lost*-type shit, you know? Frickin' *dinosaurs*, man! My whole neighborhood is just *gone*, I mean gone like-it-never-existed gone." He stopped and took a deep breath. "What the hell has happened?"

Amber nodded. "Yeah, I pretty much went through the same thing." She didn't elaborate, since Andrew didn't look as if he could handle much more of the weirdness.

"Anyway, I followed a bunch of people toward Golden Gate Park," Andrew continued, "and ran into Rose. Bare feet, no coat…" He paused, shook his head again. "Weirdest thing—there was this little Aussie import store just sitting there in the middle of all these ruined buildings. Fire hadn't reached it yet. Got her these boots and our coats."

"There was an earthquake," Rose said suddenly. "I was trapped in my boarding house. Sinking into the muck. The fire was coming, and then… something happened." She smiled, but it wavered into confusion. "I could just walk out the building… but half of San Francisco was gone." She picked up a bottle of water, stared at it for a moment. "And I'm still alive."

The three of them sat in silence for a moment, sipping water and eating junk food as the sun began to set.

"Do you mind if we stay up here?" Andrew asked. "I think it's safer for Rose if we don't go back down."

"Sure," Amber said. "Just don't bother my friend over there." She nodded toward the sloth. "I think he's safe, but I wouldn't want to risk it."

Andrew's and Rose's eyes widened.

"Yeah, we'll just stay over here," Andrew said.

He and Rose set up a little camp on the opposite side of the clearing from the sloth. Amber gave them their space, but she wasn't ready to start settling in. Not just yet. Judging from their story, she'd somehow ended up in San Francisco just a few hours after the initial Event. That meant she was in her own immediate past, two weeks and some change before the *Vanuatu* had landed at the station in Antarctica.

God, wrapping your head around time travel is a bitch. Apparently the aftershocks hadn't started kicking in yet, which meant there was a little bit of time before the world started breaking down further. *What should I do now?* She thought about the ship, waiting for them back in Antarctica. She'd failed to reach Cam, but she'd been able to communicate with the *Vanuatu* more than once. Plus, Antarctica wouldn't have other minds to get in her way.

Might as well give it a try, she thought. *But if it doesn't work, what do I do then?*

"*I think we're supposed to save the world.*" Dee's voice echoed in her mind.

Fine, Amber told herself. *Sure. That's a* great *Plan B.* Before she could talk herself out of it, she sent a thought winging out into the aether. "*Ship? Ship, can you hear me?*"

Nothing.

She waited a moment, then tried again.

"*Ship?*"

Still nothing.

Damn it. She grabbed handfuls of her hair, squeezing her skull in frustration. A cold wind suddenly began to knife through the clearing. *Alright, come on*, she told herself. *Let's do this.* Doing her best to ignore the wind, she reached out, focusing on the unique signature of the ship's artificial intelligence. *Ah. Much better.* There were millions of human minds, but only one of the *Vanuatu*.

Except... there were *two* of them.

How was that even possible?

She zoomed in on the pair of signals. Sensing the *Vanuatu*'s thoughts didn't feel the same as reading a human mind. That felt like listening in on a conversation, or watching a movie. This was more like reading a textbook, or looking at a phone directory or a map. She mentally skimmed the first of the contacts, and identified its location as somewhere over the South Atlantic Ocean, speeding north. There was a human mind aboard the ship, as well. It was Dr. Meta—her Merlin— dazed from the Event and uncertain as to what to do.

Merlin before she'd met him.

Of course. *Think fourth-dimensionally, McFly.* She was two weeks back in time.

She toyed with reaching out to Merlin or his ship, and flashed on the butterfly effect. The thought of being caught in some kind of time-loop horrified her.

Nope. Uh-uh. Not gonna screw with the timeline.

The thought almost made her stop altogether, but she decided to check in on the second *Vanuatu*. The result was instantaneous. The ship was close by—just a few yards away.

Her eyes flew open. There was nothing to be seen, and yet the contact was so close—no further than... than where that giant prehistoric ground sloth lay curled up asleep.

The spot where I arrived. That meant the hole in space and time was still active. Screwing her eyes tightly shut again, she focused on reaching through it, feeling on the other side.

"Ship?"

"Amber?"

"Ship! It's me!"

"Amber, where are you? I cannot determine your location. How are you able to effect this mode of communication?"

"It's a long story, and we don't have time for it. Are you still where we left you?"

"Yes. All of you disappeared from my sensors shortly after you left for the station. I have been waiting for you and the rest of the passengers to return."

"I'm in San Francisco, back in time, right after the Event happened. I guess it's two weeks ago."

"Is everything alright? You have all been gone for a considerable amount of time."

"Yeah, I've been stuck here for about three or four hours now—"

"No, you vanished more than nineteen hours ago. Global Event aftershock activity has increased substantially since then. I'm afraid there is not much time before the planet reaches critical mass."

Amber paused for a moment. She couldn't begin to unwrap that bit of news.

"Listen," she replied. "I must've slipped through some sort of, I *don't know... some sort of wormhole or something."*

"Give me a moment to set up new sensor arrays. I need to augment my baseline parameters." After a few beats the ship's voice returned. "Thank you for your patience. Since this morning I have been making a topological model of the local chronotopography, and am tracking its perturbations by monitoring particle interaction."

"Um... okay."

"Earlier, I was unable to detect the visual interplay between various nuclear force particles manifesting as bijective isometries in this curious n-dimensional hypervolume region of schizochronal disruption. That has since been remedied."

Amber just let it go.

"This has enabled me to study the anomalous chronospatial phenomena you labeled 'the Shatterfield.'"

"Wait! So you can see the Shatterfield now?"

"That is correct. Now that we are in contact, please stand by..." The ship paused for a moment. "Yes. I believe I have identified the particular portal from which you are contacting me."

"Good. Keep an eye on it." She thought for a moment, then continued, *"Okay, now see if there's a way to isolate it on your end. I need you to capture it somehow, pull it away from the rest of the field so I don't just fall out of it and into another one."*

"I'm sorry, Amber, but my data strongly suggests that would be impossible. All the portals on this end appear to be anchored in a very particular orbital zone surrounding the center point of maximum chronospatial disruption."

Amber frowned. *"That's less good."*

"However, I think I may have found an alternative. I have employed the gravitoelectromagnetic systems to stabilize the Shatterfield's rotary movement, enabling you to better navigate it without risk of further chronolinear quantum enmeshment."

"If that means you've stopped the crazy merry-go-round, that's excellent! Now we need to see if we can open the portal on my end. So if you send a drone through, do you think you can keep it from getting spit out at the other end?"

"I concur with your plan. Dispatching a rover now."

Amber opened her eyes. The giant sloth still slept, curled up at the base of the big cypress tree. Suddenly the air began to distort, and like a magical window, a circle of light materialized. She looked at it unhappily. She would have to climb over the sleeping giant to reach it.

"Nice sloth," she cooed, as she climbed atop its bulk, as slowly and gently as she dared. The creature twitched, its fur rippling as if she was tickling it. She froze, and it raised its head, blinking at her, then it settled back down and began to snore again.

Amber glanced over at Rose and Andrew. They looked to be as out of it as the sloth. Silently she wished them well, then made a grim realization. If she did restore the timeline, it would undo Rose's miraculous escape. The girl would die a horrible death in the San Francisco fire.

I'm so sorry, she thought.

She stretched up to the swirling light. The sloth made a grunt of protest, and then she was gone.

51

The baseball-sized rover appeared in front of her as a slick black bead, holding firm to a position deep inside a tunnel of warped space-time.

Then she was back, falling to the ground, tucking a shoulder, and rolling in a somersault. All around her, the Shatterfield's floating carousel of brilliantly colored extra-dimensional scraps were frozen in place. They still creeped her out, even with the *Vanuatu's* assurance that its electromagnetic hold on them was secure.

Amber got to her feet. "Okay, Ship," she said. "Let's find my friends."

One by one the others appeared. Blake and Harcourt, then Nellie and Hypatia.

"Ship? I think something's wrong," she said aloud. "Is there any sign of Cam?"

"Portal integrity is still holding, awaiting visual contact," the *Vanuatu* responded. Chafing with frustration, Amber tried to contact him, but it was hard to focus with all the distractions, and time seemed to be flowing differently at different ends of the portals.

What was taking so long?

Nellie put a reassuring hand on her shoulder. "He's coming, girl. I'm sure." Amber nodded. "I know you're right. I only wish Kha and Leila—"

"I know," Nellie replied sadly. "Me too."

Kha-Hotep and Leila aren't coming with us, Cam had told her. *We're their prisoners here.* Their friends had vanished down a rabbit hole, and just like that, everything had changed.

The ghostlight seemed to flutter. Was the connection closing? If the portal's link collapsed now, would he be stuck in another place and time? Every minute they waited might mean they'd never get him back.

She would never get him back.

An even worse thought occurred to her. What if the portal collapsed in mid-trip *before* he was through?

The shimmering steadied, and abruptly a figure lunged through the portal, stumbling onto the tarmac.

"Cam!" Amber threw her arms around him, almost afraid to believe he was there. She listened to the sound of his heartbeat. "I was so afraid we'd lost you…"

"I'm here." He rested his cheek against the top of her head.

"Are you okay?" she asked.

He nodded.

"Good, because we're running out of time." She looked at the door that would allow them to enter the laboratory facility.

"I'm ready."

"No, you're not." Blake strode down the gangplank of the *Vanuatu*, cradling a Sten gun in one hand. In the other hand he gripped Cam's sword belt and scabbard, and a new repeater crossbow. He handed them to the Celt.

"*Now* you're ready."

52

"Here we go," Blake said. "Everybody ready?"

The others nodded.

"Right. Rover first. The rest of you hold back, but stay sharp." Gun in one hand he listened at the doors, then pulled one open, moving his body out of the line of fire while the drone flew in.

"All clear," it reported a few seconds later.

First Blake, and then the rest filed into the dome. The lights were on—station power was still operational. The entrance opened onto a wide corridor that led straight ahead for thirty meters to a second set of double doors—this pair transparent, with a sign above.

Advanced Transpatial Physics Lab
Antarctica

With the rover on point and Blake and Cam just behind with weapons out, the group moved toward the doors. The two checked around corners as they passed side corridors arcing away to the left and right.

About halfway down the main hallway, the rover came to a sudden halt.

"Warning—approaching zone of increased chronotopological disruption."

"Ship, what does that mean?" Amber asked.

"Waves of space-time displacement are rippling out from Event ground zero. Expect significant temporal and causal anomalies, and—"

"And… what?" Nellie asked.

"And—

"And—

"And significant causal and temporal anomalies, anomalous causalities of temporal significance expecting and possible disruptions to our cognitive processes and sensory functions. This is the Ship."

The hover sphere jiggered crazily in place.

"Oh, this is not good," Amber said.

"This is the Ship. This is increased chronotopological disruption. Also, I am detecting four—

"This is the Ship."

"It's gone stark raving," Harcourt muttered. He let out a squawk of alarm when the rover vanished. It reappeared a few meters ahead of them.

"—chronotopological disruption. This is—" The rover

415

vanished again, only to reappear a few meters behind them.

"Warning—approaching zone—" It disappeared again. Its artificial voice came echoing from down one of the side corridors.

"This is—" Then from somewhere on the opposite side,

"This is—" from somewhere further off.

"This is the Ship..." its voice echoed, impossible to locate.

"Warning, four—" it said one last time, so faint it could barely be heard. *"... are approaching from..."*

"Did anybody catch any of that last bit?" Blake asked. The others shook their heads. Then Cam cocked his head, listening carefully.

"I don't think we're alone."

Blake frowned. "I don't hear—"

Then they could all hear it—a susurration of voices, like the sound of an anxious audience, or perhaps a crowded restaurant.

"It's coming from behind those, I believe," Hypatia said, pointing to the glass doors. They appeared to open onto a large, empty room.

Hypatia vanished, and Nellie screamed.

Hypatia reappeared almost at once, a few paces ahead of them.

"It's coming from behind those, I believe," she said, pointing ahead. Nellie ran up and grabbed her arm tightly. Then she turned.

"Anyone else feeling... unwell?" Nellie asked.

* * *

Cam stayed close to Amber. She could tell that he was feeling more fear than he showed.

A trio of Harcourts suddenly appeared in front of them, one after the other all in a row down the hallway. A moment later they disappeared again, in reverse order, leaving only the original.

"Good lord!" he gasped, patting his chest.

Amber began to say something, but everything moved in slow motion, and she couldn't hear herself talk. Time sputtered forward a few beats, then sped ahead in rapid motion. Finally it just *stopped*—and then resumed again.

"This is… this isn't right," she said. *Are we going to go crazy in here?*

"Stay close and keep going," Blake said. His voice was cool as ice—as always, but even without telepathy she could sense he was rattled, too. They continued their approach, passing a second set of side corridors and stopping just short of the transparent double doors. The sound of a milling crowd was definitely louder.

Amber held her breath as Blake leaned forward to peer through the panes of glass, and the doors slid open. They continued into a room large enough to comfortably hold a school cafeteria or even a gymnasium, its open space empty. Alternating mirrored panels on the walls made it look even larger than it was.

All was perfectly silent. Blake spoke.

"Nothing to see in—"

The burst of a machine gun sounded behind them.

* * *

"Get down!"

Combat instincts kicked in. Blake whirled in a crouch and returned fire as the others ducked out of the way. Nothing was there. His bullets only shot up the outside door to the station.

"Damn it," he swore. "Wasting ammo on bloody carnival tricks."

"What in blazes is all this?" Harcourt asked. He sounded on the verge of panic.

"Stay calm," Blake said. "First order of business is to find a map or a directory. Then—"

Behind them, the outer station doors slammed open to reveal Kha-Hotep and his posse, all four men armed with Tommy guns.

53

"You want us to go chasin' 'em though *that*?" Rockwell said incredulously, jerking his thumb up to the faintly rippling spot of air.

"Just so," Kha-Hotep replied. He kept his voice calm, even though he wanted to throw the men through the portal.

"'Just so,' he says." Rockwell spat on the ground. "Kindly allow me to propose an alternative plan. We plug you right here, head back to Cahokia, and tell the Sun Raven those hombres shot you and got clean away." He raised his Tommy gun, training it on Kha-Hotep's heart.

"Or, better yet," Shanks said as he and Feeds-the-Crows turned their guns on him, as well, "we might just wash our hands clean of the damned king's promises, and sell the car in Laclede's Landing." The three men grinned unpleasantly— even the Pawnee scout.

Kha-Hotep lowered his gun. "That plan doesn't work, and

let me tell you why," he said calmly, as if explaining to a child. "First, Boss Giannola and his goons would skin you alive before he ever paid you a cent for that car. But that is beside the point." He pointed to the wavering patch in the air. "Second, take a good look at *that*. Does it look natural to you? It is not. It is nothing less than a hole in space and time itself. That is the kind of power we are dealing with. The power of the gods to create and to destroy." He paused to let that sink in.

"And third, we are not here because the Sun Raven wants some prisoners back, or just so you can become rich. You're here, and we're going to stop them, because otherwise they are going to destroy the world, killing you, me, and everyone else."

"Sun-Raven told you all that, did he?" Rockwell said.

"No, he didn't tell me anything—because I am Sun-Raven."

"God's hooks!" Shanks swore.

"Thought your voice sounded familiar," Rockwell muttered.

"The question is, are we going to stand around until it's too late, or are you three coming with me so that you can save the world—as well as your own worthless hides?"

The bounty hunters lowered their guns.

They emerged through the portal into a burst of Antarctic white, dazed and shaken. The men stared in wonder at the expanse of snow, the silver dome of the station and the carousel of glittering crystalline forms suspended in the air all around them.

"Christ Jaysis, I'm ottomised!" Shanks groaned. "Next time I'll padlock my arse so I don't shite meself."

"What icy-cold circle of hell have you brung us to?" Rockwell said with a scowl.

"This is the island below Africa," Kha-Hotep replied. "Come. We have no time for chatter"—he pointed to the hovering lights—"and don't touch those, or you'll regret it."

They followed him through the station doors.

"Run!" Blake fired off another burst.

The intruders scattered before returning fire. Blake and the rest fled down a side corridor, out of their line of sight. A ghostly technician appeared midway, walking casually.

"Good luck, Dr. Meta," he said to no one there.

They hesitated for a moment, then ran past him. Another wave of distortion rippled through, popping them down the hallway like jig-jagged bursts of teleportation.

"There's a stairwell this way," Amber yelled—then suddenly the six of them were at the bottom of three flights. They burst through a new doorway while their pursuers appeared at the top of the stairwell. Blake and Cam covered them, trading shots with the gunmen. Blake looked over at Cam's repeater crossbow, wishing it was another machine gun instead.

"How many bolts do you have left?"

"Two."

Blake scowled. "Take that kiddy-toy of yours and get them out of here!" he barked at Cam. "Go!"

When Cam hesitated, Blake grabbed him, yanking him inside the room as another fusillade of bullets came raining down. "Get out of here while you still can!" he growled.

Amber turned to Cam. "We have to go."

"Now!" Blake yelled. He gave Amber one last look, then turned back to return fire from the cover of the doorway.

"Please, Cam," Amber urged. She held out her hand. After a brief hesitation, he took it and let her pull him away to follow the others.

"Blake!" Kha-Hotep called down. "You are a good man, and you know I don't want this."

Blake said nothing. After making sure Amber and the others were well on their way, he risked a glance up the stairwell. No exposed targets. Were all four of them still up top, or were some attempting a flanking maneuver?

"I can't let you destroy everything we've built," Kha-Hotep continued. "I won't. Throw down your weapon, and you and the others come out. I give you my word you will be safe."

"I believe you," Blake said, stalling for time while he checked his ammo. Not good. The magazine was well over half spent. "Now, how about the word of those three with you?" He carefully clicked the clip back in, as quietly as he could.

"They have no reason to kill you," Kha-Hotep assured him. "They'll do as I say."

"Give us a minute to talk it over," Blake answered. Without waiting for a reply, he pulled back through the door and kicked it closed, locking it behind him.

He found himself in some extensive engineering sublevel, a gloomy industrial dungeon filled with a confusion of machinery, various conduits, and other mechanical monoliths he could never hope to identify. It looked as if the station had installed multiple generations of technology over the course of a century or two. Plenty of prime spots for a sniper to set up shop.

Blake quickly scoped out his choice, an overhead gantry with good vantage points. Looping his arm through the Sten's skeleton stock, he slung it over his shoulder and began to climb. He could clamber up awkward surfaces quicker than most men, but three-quarters of his way up a burst of Tommy-gun fire rang out.

Kha's thugs, shooting out the lock.

With a twist of his arm, he reached behind and swung the Sten around to spray a little suppression fire back at the door. While the attackers ducked away from that, he re-slung the gun, quickly scaled the top of the gantry and took position, lying flat. Quiet fell over the area, and he could hear them arguing outside the door over who would enter first.

He grinned. *Let's make it harder on them.*

First, he switched from full-automatic to semi. Not enough rounds left to keep up the fireworks show, but plenty for a few well-placed shots. In rapid succession, he targeted and took out the three closest banks of lighting fixtures, until the chamber truly looked the part of a dungeon.

On shot number three, the door burst open. Two silhouetted figures laid down heavy suppression fire while two more rushed into the darkened room. Blake fired off four more quick shots at the running figures—and then the Sten jammed.

Damn it! Temperamental bitch.

Rolling back from the edge of the gantry, he rose into a crouch, silently moving further down its narrow length to take cover behind a thick steel support beam.

The diminished lighting turned the sublevel into a haunted house ride. Indicator lights became sinister red eyes and flickering torchlights. Every pipe, generator, or random mechanical outcropping a shadowy, menacing shape— stalactites, gravestones, specters.

At least the near-darkness didn't impede him from working on the Sten—he could field-strip and reassemble it blindfolded. Popping out the magazine, he tapped it against his knee to unjam the cartridges, replaced it, and re-cocked the handle, ready to fire again. Judging from the weight, though, he had no more than a few rounds left.

Blake lay flat again, scanning the room. If the mood lighting made him harder to spot, that cut both ways. He had lost all sign of his opponents.

Harsh whispered commands and furtive movements came from the floor below, but he would have to wait for the perfect moment to shoot. On the plus side, every second he kept their pursuers busy meant better chances for Amber and the others to get to whatever big red button would fix this nightmare.

Hiding with the others behind a bank of strange machines, Feeds-the-Crows was having problems with his own jammed weapon. Finally giving up, he set the bulky thing on the floor. New tactic. He tapped Rockwell on the shoulder, made a few quick gestures, and pointed forward. The big man nodded, and gave a low whistle to Kha-Hotep and Shanks, bringing them back for a quick conference.

"Blake's holed up here as rear guard," he whispered. "How 'bout you two keep going and find the others. Crows and I will take care of him and catch up to you."

They nodded and slipped off, taking advantage of the gloom. The Pawnee scout drew his long knife and took point, slipping from shadow to shadow, completely silent in his moccasins, watching every corner, listening intently for the slightest sound from his quarry.

Abruptly he stopped, listening intently.

The white man was fiddling with his gun, and he was somewhere in the metal framework above. Crows clenched the blade in his teeth and set to climbing up the strut, quick and quiet as a spider.

The tension grew nerve-wracking. Blake continued to scan the room, waiting for his chance. Part of him hoped they might try to parley some more, but it looked like that ship had sailed. He could still hear them rustling about somewhere amid all the futuristic machinery.

Then, abruptly—nothing but silence. The absence of sound ate at him worse than anything else—it tempted his imagination into places he'd rather not go.

He caught the hint of rustling, this time from far to his left—the direction Amber and the rest had gone. Had their pursuers already gotten past him? If they had, he needed to stop them, and fast.

He'd have to leave his position. Setting the gun down as gently as possible, he silently rose off the cold metal. A furtive movement in his peripheral vision set off a reflexive alarm, but it came too late—Crows rushed him, driving a knee into the small of Blake's back and yanking his head back by the hair to expose his neck. With one swift movement, Crows dragged the knife across Blake's throat.

Before the blade could connect with his jugular, Blake caught his attacker's wrist, yanking the knife-arm forward and slamming the back of his head hard into the man's face. Gushing blood from nose and lips, the Pawnee lost his grip on Blake's hair, and the commando twisted to follow up with two savage elbow strikes to his attacker's belly.

Grunting in pain as he wrestled Blake for control of the knife, Crows kicked and twisted and managed to wrench his arm free. Rising up, he stabbed at Blake's face—but this time Blake seized the momentum of the attack, pulling him into a kick-assisted judo flip that hurled the man face first off the gantry and into the dark.

Crows hit the hard concrete with a sickening crunch.

"Blake!" Rockwell roared. "I see you now, you son of a bitch!" He blasted with his Tommy gun. The thundering blaze lit up the dark like a welder's torch, jack-hammering the steel girder that was Blake's only cover. Gritting his teeth,

Blake ducked from the sparks of ricocheting lead. His own gun still lay on the gantry, far out of reach.

The Tommy gun went silent.

Rockwell swore and tossed his gun aside with a clatter, striding out of the dark bold as brass. This was no time to cower in the shadows. After all, he was the new Sampson—hadn't the Prophet himself declared no bullet or blade would ever harm him?

He drew his trusty pistols.

At the telltale clicking sound from Rockwell's gun, Blake bolted from cover and ran to sweep up the Sten.

Rockwell kept walking, talking as he fired on his running target.

"Tell you something, Blake. I don't shoot *at* people."

Totally exposed, Blake crouched, firing off three quick shots from the hip. Rockwell didn't flinch as the bullets narrowly missed his head.

Blake stood and raised the gun up for a better shot, aiming right between the big man's steely blue eyes. The Sten clicked.

Out of ammo.

That's it, then, Blake thought.

Rockwell didn't miss a beat, firing back with both pistols. Blake's body caught the bullets, the impacts smashing him backward and off the gantry.

* * *

Echoes of the gun battle rang out through the circular industrial wing, reaching the other end of the section, where Amber and the rest had already found a door to a second stairwell. Quickly, they took the stairs down as far as they could, coming to another door.

Cam pulled it open and peered in.

54

Soft-lit and calm, this new level hummed with an oddly serene grace after the grim engineering sublevel above. Here towering computer banks—each lit up with a thousand tiny lights—rose high above them in stately rows, as mysterious and majestic as a ring of menhirs. Though it somehow felt sacrilegious to run in a place like this, they hurried on until they came to another door.

A Level – Central Hub
Primary Chamber

"Not too much further now," Amber said quietly, trying not to think of Blake's possible fate. The door slid open onto a new corridor, bending away on a long arc. Another time glitch hit, popping them further along the corridor. It was getting harder to keep their thoughts straight.

"Come on," she urged them. "We're running out of time."

They followed until it came to a T-junction, a main passageway cutting across their ring route like the spoke of a wheel.

To their left came the sound of unexpected conversation. Down at the end of the main passage an argument was unfolding between two translucent figures in lab coats. One was a bookish man with serious determination on his long face. The other was very familiar.

"Merlin!" Amber ran toward them, but neither man paid her any attention.

"You think I'm worried about going to *prison*?" the first man said with intensity. "Or *dying*?"

"You can't stop this, Iskandar," Merlin replied.

"We'll see about that." He pushed past the project director, storming off down the corridor.

"You can't stop this!" Merlin yelled after him, and then they both simply evaporated. Amber stared for a brief moment, then turned back to the others.

"I think we've found it."

There was no mistaking the entrance to the Primary Chamber, even without feuding ghosts to mark the way. A great round door big enough to be a bank vault, with a heavy steel lever beside it. The entire setup smacked of power and secrets.

Amber's thoughts raced. Blake, Nellie, Hypatia, Harcourt... and Cam. In just a moment, she would never see them again.

If they were successful.

"So... this is goodbye," she said quietly. "If we fix this, I'll never have known any of you. None of us will. We won't even remember saving the world." She paused, swallowing hard. "So even if it's only for this one moment, and then it will be gone forever, I want you all to know that I love you."

Nellie hugged Amber tightly. After a moment's hesitation, Hypatia did the same.

"It's been an honor to know you all," Harcourt said.

Cam set down his crossbow, slipped the silver torc from around his neck, and placed it on Amber.

"For good luck," he said.

"Cam, I can't—"

"If we fail, you can give it back to me." Gently he touched the side of her face.

"I..." Amber felt her resolve slipping, so she tore her gaze away from his and took a deep breath.

"Are we ready?"

Unexpectedly, Harcourt put a hand on her shoulder and squeezed.

"We are, m'dear."

Together she and Cam pulled down on the steel lever. With the metallic hiss of plates sliding across one another, the doorway irised open onto the very heart of the station, the primary reaction chamber.

Except there was no chamber.

There was nothing at all, except a howling, spiraling vortex, like a black hole.

"We're too late," Amber said. Particles of violet light streamed into the voracious maw, the vortex drawing them all into sheer oblivion.

"Gods of my father…" Cam murmured.

How could they get to the override switch now? Did it even exist anymore? Her vision spinning, her legs began to buckle. Cam reached for her, but she waved him away and steadied herself.

She looked to her companions as they stared at the horrifying sight, faces pale and eyes wide, trapped in an uncomprehending dread at the swirling blackness that drank in the light. It was as if it were dragging them away, too. Even stoic Hypatia looked horrified, and Harcourt was positively green.

"What is it?" Nellie's voice trembled.

"I don't know." Amber shook her head. "It looks like a black hole—a spot in outer space that sucks in everything that comes near it, even light. But it can't be a black hole, or we'd already be dead. It has to be something else."

"Whatever it is, there's no way to get past that," Harcourt said. "I'm afraid this might well be our curtain call."

"It can't be." Nellie's voice was flat. She looked at Amber, and then to Hypatia. "Surely we can do something."

"Let us think," Hypatia replied. She regarded the vortex. "It doesn't appear strong enough to pull us inside, nor does it seem to be consuming the rest of the station. In fact, it seems confined to this one spot. Could it be a portal?" Her scientific curiosity overrode fear. "Perhaps something akin to the ones in the Shatterfield?"

"Maybe so," Amber said, following the logic. "It must be connected to them somehow, but can we risk getting too close?" The maelstrom roiled perpetually, its movement both hypnotic and unsettling. She held her fear at arm's length.

"Do we have a choice?" Cam hefted his crossbow, looking back down the corridor the way they had come. "We may not have much more time." Amber frowned, but he had a point. As far as they knew, their pursuers were still coming, armed with machine guns. And the Event aftershocks were still tearing the planet to bits.

Damned if we do and damned if we don't.

"Truly, we are caught between the Scylla and Charybdis," Hypatia murmured, echoing her thoughts.

Amber looked at the vortex again. It *did* remind her of the ghostlight portals, and whatever timey-wimey hyperspace mojo was going on with them.

"You're both right," she said. "We *don't* have a choice. Either the switch is through there, or it's not—and if it isn't, this is pretty much game over. So I'll go through. I don't know if I'll be able to get back out again, but maybe I can connect with you telepathically from wherever—"

"If you go, I go with you," Cam said.

Amber looked at him, filled with a sudden rage.

"It's just so *wrong* that we won't be able to remember any of this," she said, angry tears spilling down her face. "I can't imagine living my life not knowing you."

"Fear not," he said with a wry smile. "I won't ever forget you. You'll haunt me, even if I never know why." His gaze carried a deep, unshakable sincerity. Amber opened her mouth to reply, but no words came. So she kissed him with all the passion she'd ever dreamt of feeling.

"Enough of that, you two," Nellie said. "We'll all go, Amber. At the worst, it's choosing our own doom instead of letting it choose us."

"Certainly not!" Harcourt shook his head. "I've had enough of falling through the looking glass!"

"Suit yourself, then." Nellie turned away from him. "Let's go, then. It's the waiting that's murder."

Leaning in, Hypatia whispered, "I love you."

Nellie squeezed her hand.

"Are we ready?" Amber asked.

Nellie looked at Hypatia. She nodded.

"Let's go," Nellie said. Without looking back, she added, "Goodbye, Harcourt."

With that, the four stepped forward. One, two, three steps—the black hole swallowed them up. One instant, they were alive and well, walking and breathing, in a warm, well-lit corridor, and then they simply…

Weren't.

55

Are we dead? The four of them seemed to be walking—or were they sleep-walking?—through one of the station corridors, but something was very wrong. *How long have we been here?*

To call it a corridor felt wrong—it didn't feel like a *real* one, it didn't feel like anything man-made. More like they were walking through a reflection, or maybe a shadow, of the station's hallways, if shadows could be solid things with color and substance.

It almost made sense, in an ephemeral, dreamscape sort of way.

"Are all of you seeing this, too," Nellie's voice was hushed, "or have I completely lost my mind?"

Amber could only nod.

There were no walls or ceiling—just a curving, stationary pathway that seemed to be suspended in an infinite ocean of blackness, punctuated every so often by a crossroads or set of steps going up or down.

Other corridors, identical to theirs, stretched out in gravity-defying inclines, above and below them, coming in or jutting out at weird angles—virtually every possible angle imaginable. A dizzying, kaleidoscopic maze all around them, an Escher print come to life.

We're in Escherspace, Amber thought.

Spaced out randomly along each corridor, most a few meters or so apart, great spheres of hazy light hovered in place at varying distances above the floor, silent and serene. Together, the network of walkways and spheres made Amber think of old tinker-toy models of molecule and atoms.

"Look!" Cam pointed. "It's us."

He was right. There were other sets of *them*, each quartet walking their own corridor, many walking upside-down or at a forty-five-degree angle. The other sets of people, the other *thems*, pointed, as well. When Cam gestured, his twin did the same.

All of the Cams did.

Amber's mind raced with questions. Which ones were the *real* them? Was *she* the real *her*? How did gravity work here? What would happen if *she* took a wrong step and fell off the path?

They approached the first of the globes on their path. The illumination inside seemed to flicker and move, reminding Amber uncomfortably of the Shatterfield again. This one was about two meters across, hovering about a meter off the floor and taking up an uncomfortably large portion of the walkway.

The surface rippled with a weird effervescence, a million tiny stars floating up toward them, perfectly mirroring the pinpoints that cascaded down Merlin's eyes in all of his iterations. Some tableau appeared to be unfolding in slow motion.

She leaned closer.

"Don't touch it!" Nellie cried out. "For god's sake, girl!"

"I think there's something inside this one," Amber replied. Even so, she was careful to keep her distance.

When they looked closer, the image coalesced—a woman floating in outer space, caught up in some explosion of violet light. She wore a spacesuit of some advanced design, so formfitting it looked more like scuba gear, and she cradled an exotic instrument that looked awfully like a weapon. The suit's bubble helmet clearly showed her bronze face and silver Mohawk.

"Merlin…" Amber gasped.

"You're right!" Nellie exclaimed. The resemblance was unmistakable. This was Merlin in female form—complete with those uncanny, star-flecked eyes. A name was stenciled across her right breast.

J. METAA

Her silent vignette went on for about half a minute, then went back to the beginning and repeated.

"Look over there," Hypatia said. She pointed up to another group of their doppelgangers on a nearby corridor, peering into a sphere of their own. Inside it was another Merlin, this one a monk with a shaven head, sitting in a lotus position. Ripples of visible energy surrounded him in thick waves. Their twins peered back at them, too. They were close enough for everyone to make out subtle differences between themselves and the individuals in the other group.

"Over here, too," Nellie said, nodding her head toward a sphere below to their left. It was nearly upside-down, yet they could see clearly that the sphere contained a Victorian-era Merlin with long disheveled hair, struggling in the midst of a quintessential mad scientist's laboratory, all Tesla coils and baroque gadgetry. Like the astronaut and the monk, this Merlin shared the same starry eyes, and like them, his story was set on repeat.

Walking carefully around the astronaut's sphere, they walked past the next one—where a gleaming cyborg Merlin stood in the center of a laser array—and then on to the next, where Merlin seemed to be a god-king from another world, part Aztec, part Chinese. His attire of silks and feathers was as flamboyant as a Rio de Janeiro samba dancer, and whatever power he wielded was coming from arrays of giant, energized crystals.

Everywhere they looked they saw spheres containing some new iteration of Merlin, each unique, stretching back as far as they could see. Scientists in lab coats, astronauts in space, soldiers on futuristic battlefields, wizards, psionic practitioners, shamans, robed hierophants, and an uncountable number of other, less identifiable variations.

And then they came to one that made them all halt.

This sphere's interior was darker than most. It showed an ill-lit cavernous lab space where a colossal assemblage of machinery, instrument panels, and power cables were surrounded by levels of grated metal walkways. A man in a lab coat sat in a chair, his head lolled back. Next to him, caught in a beam of violet light coming off a control panel, stood János Mehta.

"I think I understand."

They turned to look at Hypatia.

"These are all the final moments before the Event," she said, "every one of them from a different world, a single strand forming a great rope. We are looking at the frayed ends."

Amber shook her head, trying to make sense of it all.

"So… it wasn't just our Merlin's experiment which caused the Event—it was *all* these different factors, all colliding together at a single point on the timeline… putting so much stress on, well, on reality itself, I guess, that it didn't just shatter our timeline, but all these others as well," she said. "And Merlin is at the heart of every one of them."

Hypatia nodded. "I believe he is the catalyst in all these dimensions. In an untold number of forms. Shattering not just the past, but the future, spanning across any number of other worlds. How staggering a concept. I struggle to comprehend it fully." She looked almost reverent.

"Does that mean we've got to get out of here to get back to the control room?"

"No," Hypatia replied, "I think the control room we want—the one with your Merlin, *our* Merlin—must be here, contained in one of these spheres."

The four of them looked out at the countless globes.

"It could take forever to find it," Amber said. "We don't have time."

"But *you* can, Amber," Cam said. "You can find him with the second sight Dee gave you." She wished she shared his confidence in her, but she also knew he was right.

"Yes!" Nellie said. "Your mind-reading powers, or astral projection, or whatever it is."

She shook off her doubts. "I'll try," Amber said, "though I wish Dee was here to help." Closing her eyes, she reached out with her mind. Instantly she was hit with sensory overload, and she had to brace herself to keep from falling. It was as if she had plunged into an ocean of Merlins…

"My god," she gasped, "there's so many of them. Way, *way* too many. I don't think I can do this."

"Focus, Amber," Hypatia said. "Train your thoughts on the one you know best."

"But there's millions of them!"

"What other choice have you but to succeed?" Hypatia said softly.

Nodding, Amber took a deep breath and tried again, fighting with the sheer numbers that threatened to drown her in psionic overload. Steadying herself, she let her psyche acclimatize to the overwhelming near-infinite number involved, the crushing intensity of it all. Each Merlin had his own unique signature, she saw. So she began by winnowing her way through them all—sorting through all the permutations, honing in on the ones she *knew*.

* * *

Cam noticed the change first. Already on the lookout for trouble, he feared it might be an aftershock.

"Something's happening," he cried out.

The uncanny landscape around them was subtly shifting, altering its physical layout as easily as a gem split a beam of light in all directions just by turning in the sun.

Amber felt a tangible change as she sifted through whole realms of possibilities, massaging the impossible into the conceivable, the conceivable into the workable. Tangentially, she was aware of a million other Ambers, some like her, others distinctly *not*, doing the same thing.

She was in a pocket universe with its own laws of physics, and she was learning to surf them. All of the trippiest Alice-in-Wonderland physics concepts came to mind—phrases like "quantum entanglements," "dark matter," "strange attractors," and Heisenberger, Heisenberg…

Was that his name?

She was uncertain, but the thing he had said about Schrödinger's cat… suddenly it seemed to make sense. His principle was at play here. Somehow, the act of searching for Merlin was bringing him closer to her—she couldn't explain how she knew, but she could sense it happening. On this side of the looking glass, observation really could change the nature of reality. It already was.

Then she was back.

"I think we can do it now," she said. "We just need to keep walking."

Nellie looked confused. "How far, exactly?"

Amber shrugged. *Exactly* was such a woefully inappropriate word here in Escherspace. Everything was relative, everything was paradoxical.

"We just need to turn around here, it's only a couple of spheres away." She set off back the way they had come.

"What?" Nellie said, trailing behind her. "Wait, Amber, we've already seen all those spheres—" She looked over her shoulder, to Cam. "Tell her. It doesn't make sense."

He shrugged. "It's magic's nature to be strange."

"Oh! Here he is!" Amber said, stopping at a sphere. Inside was her Merlin—*their* Merlin—standing like a symphony conductor, a holographic orchestra of lines, shapes, and text coloring the air around him.

Nellie caught up. "You'd think I'd have gotten used to being flabbergasted."

"I'm getting a feel for it," Amber replied. "It has something to do with quantum mechanics, I think." Nellie looked blank. "In this little universe, where we're standing, we're all connected somehow. It constantly reflects us, or maybe it reacts to our thoughts by re-shaping itself. I don't know, but the sense I get is that to find each other, we have to focus, and let the universe do the rest."

"A labyrinth from which you can neither escape, nor become lost in," Hypatia said, intrigued. She stepped up to peer into the sphere. "What you are looking for, you find."

"I think you are right," Cam said, pointing to a figure coming down a side branch. "Harcourt has found us."

"Quickly! You have to get out of here!"

The professor looked utterly terrified as he ran toward them, holding on to his beloved hat for dear life.

"There's no need to panic, Harcourt," Nellie chided. "It's really no more dangerous here than in a hall of mirrors."

"No!" He shook his head violently. "They're coming!"

56

Kha-Hotep, Rockwell, and Shanks stared at the vortex into which the professor had disappeared. Harcourt had panicked at the sight of them and, in despair, thrown himself down the rabbit hole.

It was terrifying to witness. The Egyptian was awestruck, and his two companions looked on uncertainly.

"Well, shitfire," Rockwell growled at last. "If that twiggy little lily-livered English pansy-picker can do it, so can we." The other two nodded, bolstered enough to step through together.

As they found themselves walking in an inky black limbo, looking out on all the sphere-studded walkways, doubts arose.

"Cast into the outer darkness with the sons of perdition," Rockwell said with uncharacteristic apprehension. Shanks didn't like seeing his leader so shaken. Kha-Hotep nodded, but kept his jaw firm.

"Come," he said. "We'll find them and return."

* * *

Even as Harcourt ran over to join his friends, three unwelcome figures came into sight. He had led their enemies straight to them. Their doppelgangers appeared on each and every infinite pathway, but Kha-Hotep's posse didn't seem to notice.

Cam moved in front to face them, and lifted his crossbow. He had only two bolts left, Amber remembered. Then he would have to rely on his sword against their guns.

Kha-Hotep and Shanks approached with their submachine guns raised, Rockwell with a pistol in his hand and another in his holster. Amber backed away instinctively. The bounty hunter's gleaming eyes and wild long hair terrified her.

Jesus! He looks like Chewbacca with rabies.

"Easy, my brother," Kha-Hotep said as if calming a panicked horse. "It's over, Cam. There are three of us, and our weapons are greater."

"Nothing is over," Cam said, his crossbow trained on the man he considered his brother.

"Where's Blake?" Amber demanded.

"Dead," Rockwell answered with grim finality. "So is your friend, if he doesn't drop that pepperbox."

Cam said nothing, but merely swung the repeater over to the big man.

"You can't kill me with that, you know," Rockwell said, taking a step closer.

"Nor you, me," Cam answered.

"I mean it." Rockwell advanced another step. "I'm the new Sampson. Made a Nazirite vow. No bullet or blade can ever harm me."

Cam shrugged. "These are bolts."

Harcourt's eyes twitched back and forth between Cam and Rockwell as the tension between the two rose like a head of steam, finally becoming unbearable. Without warning, he grabbed his top hat and snapped it through the air at Rockwell's face, dashing forward to tackle the man.

Rockwell snatched the hat in midair. Harcourt bounced off the burly man as if he had collided with the side of a barn, and fell to his knees on the walkway, stunned.

"A goddamned *hat*?" Rockwell exclaimed. "*Now* I'm insulted." Throwing aside the offending object, he reached down to grab Harcourt by his scrawny neck and snap it—but Nellie darted forward and shoved Rockwell off the walkway. He fell with a long shout, and all his doubles did as well, each plummeting away at a different angle into the endless void.

"Porter!" Shanks's cry, multiplied a million-fold, reverberated throughout the space. He wheeled on Nellie, his ugly teeth bared. "You filthy scapegrace bawd. I will put you in hell for that."

Nellie backed away from the Redcoat, frightened, but Kha-Hotep intervened before Shanks could carry out his threat.

"Hands in the air, all of you," he commanded. Shanks paused. Everyone but Cam complied.

Kha-Hotep brought his gun to bear. "Please, Cam. Do not make me do this."

Relaxing his grip on the crossbow, Cam raised both hands above his head.

"Good, my friend. Now drop the crossbow."

Cam hesitated, but before Kha-Hotep could enforce the request, Shanks shoved in front of him, his focus on Nellie.

"As for you, murdersome bitch," Shanks growled at her. "Step off that ledge. Do it yourself, or I'll just shoot you off where you stand."

Cam stayed perfectly still and kept his hands in the air, but turned his gaze up and away—at their doubles walking upside-down on another walkway. He pulled the trigger.

The quarrel struck the other Redcoat. Instantaneously, a quarrel came down on their Shanks, sinking deep into his flesh between neck and shoulder. All across Escherspace, a million different Shanks dropped dead.

"That was a nice trick," Kha-Hotep said, keeping his gun trained on the Celt. "Will you shoot me next?"

Cam thought about it for a moment.

"Why don't we talk instead?"

"Good. First, drop your crossbow, kick it off the edge, and step away from the sphere. It's going to be alright. We're all going back home now."

Cam obeyed. In every direction, a million other crossbows sailed away, too.

"Kha," Amber said, keeping her voice calm. "It's not going to be alright. If we don't find Merlin's override and stop the

Event, the aftershocks are going keep tearing the planet apart until nothing's left."

"*No!*" The vehemence in Kha-Hotep's voice made her flinch in surprise. "No," he repeated, softer this time. "Leila and I made a life together. We raised a family, for eight years. The aftershocks stopped on their own. Don't you see?" He stared at them with a fanatical intensity. "I am living proof that nothing needs to be done."

"Listen," Amber said. "Outside, it's already happening and if we don't act now, we're all doomed. The *world* is doomed. Kha, I know you don't want to hear this, but those eight years you've spent with Leila…" She hesitated, then forged ahead. "You have to face it, that all that time may have just been a glitch."

"A *glitch*?" he spat out the ugly word. "What is that?"

"I don't know what else to call it," Amber replied. "It's just a… a wrinkle in the timeline that will get smoothed out, sooner or later. Like everything that's happened to us—*all* of us—ever since the Event hit. It will be gone, painlessly, naturally." She let that sink in, then continued, "But if we don't act, *everything*—everything that had ever existed, will be destroyed—down to the subatomic level."

"Enough!" Kha-Hotep shouted. Amber stiffened, but he did not pull the trigger. Instead, he collected himself, lowering his voice. "Come back with me, and you'll see. You'll understand when we get back. We will all have a long and happy life together." He paused, then pleaded, "Please… please do not make me kill you."

Cam stepped closer.

"Kha… you know you can't kill me with that, don't you?"

Amber stared, horrified. *Oh Cam, you have no idea what a machine gun can do to you.*

Kha-Hotep remained calm, keeping the Tommy gun trained on Cam's chest, even as he took another step closer.

"I think I can, if I cut your head off," Kha-Hotep replied.

"Cam, don't," Amber said softly. "Let's just—"

Cam snapped forward to tackle Kha-Hotep, but the Egyptian pulled the trigger and fired off a burst. Harcourt screamed as the bullets went flying wide, and then the two crashed together.

A split-second later, Cam and Kha-Hotep's bodies hit the sphere, disappearing instantaneously.

57

The Primary Chamber
Forty-five seconds before the Event

Cam could neither move nor see. Was this *Dubnos*—the dark world, the realm of the lost dead, deep beneath the earth? Or some hidden fortress-palace of the *Sídhe*? Somewhere nearby, a man was talking, his voice echoing strangely.

"Targets acquired in the operating theater," the familiar voice said. "Advancing to stage two. Stand by to initiate on my mark."

Cam tried to wiggle his fingers and toes but couldn't be sure he still had any.

"Approaching optimal..." the voice continued.

Cam snapped awake. He had fallen onto a hard metal floor. The air before his eyes swarmed with the tiny blue lights of mischievous fairies, reveling in his misfortune. Shaking his head, he raised himself to his elbows and looked at his surroundings.

He lay at the precipice of a vast subterranean chamber, its perfectly spherical walls gilded in a tartan of stars. Before him stretched out a narrow bridge that ended mid-span in a round platform. A man in white clothing stood there, his arms outstretched like a druid sorcerer, as a host of lights, glyphs, and sigils danced in the air.

Entranced, Cam stared in wonder at the sight, until he heard a moan from behind him. His Egyptian sword-brother Kha-Hotep lay nearby, rubbing his eyes, his firearm close at hand. The two locked eyes, and with a jolt Cam's memory came rushing back. He was here to stop Merlin.

Kha-Hotep was here to stop *Cam*.

He lunged for the weapon just as Kha-Hotep's hand darted out.

"Steady… steady…" Merlin's voice again, calm and even, focused on the task at hand. Although he was all the way at the end of the walkway, his voice resonated throughout the chamber.

Cam grabbed Kha-Hotep's arm, twisting to ground himself as each man strived for control of the gun pinned between them. Kha-Hotep had one hand on the trigger and the other on the barrel—Cam fought to keep it away from his face. They rolled, both teetering on the edge of the drop. Then Cam shifted his weight, kicked his way free, and sent them tumbling backward to relative safety.

He couldn't keep this fight up for long. Kha-Hotep was bigger and stronger than he was. He struggled to get to his feet and gain the advantage, but the Egyptian rose with him, and the pair locked together as Kha-Hotep tried to shake him loose. But the Celt held on for his life, trying to pry Kha-Hotep's hand from the trigger, the barrel of the gun wavering dangerously near his face.

"Commence warp," Merlin said.

The machine gun went off. A blaze of fire burst forth in a deafening roar, and sent a spray of bullets past Cam's face toward the center of the chamber.

Where Merlin stood.

Meta stiffened as the hail of bullets struck, and then dropped to the floor of the platform.

"Intruder alert in Primary Chamber!" The loudspeaker's mechanical voice came booming off the echoing walls. *"Security alert omega! We have gunfire in Primary Chamber!"*

Meta lay unmoving in a crumpled heap, though his eyes remained open. He had felt nothing as the barrage went shrieking through the holographic displays, narrowly missing him as they impacted the walls beyond.

Was he hit? Miraculously, it seemed not. Overhead, the three drone cameras automatically swooped in for dramatic footage of his would-be assassination.

Intruder alert? he wondered. The only way into the chamber was still sealed tight—how could anyone else be inside with him? Continuing to play dead, he turned his gaze to locate his attackers.

What he saw confused him. The two were fighting *each other*. One a saboteur, then—and the other fighting to save him? But which was which? In a few moments, it wouldn't matter. The security team would take both of them out with a scythe beam or a burst of nanoflechette clusters.

"Primary Chamber, do you copy?" Main Control said over the neural link. *"Dr. Meta, are you—?"*

"I'm alright," he responded, hoping the intruders couldn't hear him. "Don't worry about me. What's happening to the warp containment?"

"It's happening! We've done it! But, Doctor…" Even through the neural link Meta could hear the man's fear. *"We're—we're reading multiple anomalies within the containment area."*

What?

Meta risked a look up at the holographic interface. If the containment field failed, they were all dead. The Calabi–Yau display painted the air with impossible space-time topology. The lines of the eleven-dimensional modeling were tesseracting in a rapid series of mind-bending origami folds.

Playing dead couldn't save him now. Damning the consequences, he leapt to his feet and checked the quantum micro viewscreen. The display teemed with pairs of waltzing particles. Another pair suddenly appeared.

Then another.

And *another*.

"Shut it down!" he shouted. "Abort! Abort *now*!"

Trinity Test Site near Alamogordo, New Mexico
July 16, 1945 – 5:29 a.m.
Twenty seconds before the Event

In the control bunker, Dr. Oppenheimer adjusted his welding goggles one last time and held on to the nearest post to steady himself, tension growing as the final seconds ticked off. He stood like stone, scarcely breathing, listening to the announcer's voice do the countdown, until at last he spoke the final word.

"Now!"

The pre-dawn darkness of the Jornada del Muerto desert suddenly burned bright as a thousand suns. His face relaxed.

Now I am become Death, the destroyer of worlds.

58

Cam's ears rang from the blast, and Kha-Hotep snapped the Tommy gun's barrel up with a jerk of his hand, clubbing Cam in the face. He reeled back from the blow, and Kha kicked him backward, sending the Celt staggering onto the catwalk.

He froze as Kha-Hotep turned his gun on him. The two friends locked eyes. Kha's face was stone.

"I'm sorry."

Kha-Hotep pulled the trigger.

The mechanism clicked.

Nothing.

In a flash Cam drew his twenty-third-century sword and brought it down toward Kha's head. The Egyptian barely stopped the blow with an awkward parry of the gun barrel. The diamond-edged blade bit deep into the weapon, and Kha quickly reversed his grip to make a club of it.

Cam had the advantage now, and Kha knew it. With wild

swings of his makeshift bludgeon, he drove Cam further down the gangplank, while Cam continued to hack away at him, chopping off pieces of the gun with every strike.

As Kha reversed his grip again to better parry Cam's sword, the ultra-keen blade sliced off a tip of the gun barrel, striking at an angle—inadvertently turning it into a bayonet. Kha slashed a long red wound across Cam's chest, and then plunged the sharpened barrel at his throat.

Cam only just dodged the thrust, and Kha followed up with another reverse, smashing the butt against Cam's skull. Stars exploded behind his eyes.

Reeling from the hit, he fell back a step too far—only the slender guardrail kept him from toppling over to his death as Kha pressed the attack. The Egyptian charged, gun held out in both hands, and then suddenly threw the weapon at Cam's face.

Cam ducked, and the battered Tommy gun spiraled away, falling out of sight. Kha used the feint to grab Cam's sword arm and bend the Celt over the railing. Off balance, legs flailing and his body pressed over the edge, Cam threw all his strength into one last desperate try to break free.

He couldn't.

Gritting his teeth, Kha pressed his hand over Cam's, twisting the grip of the sword. Turning Cam's own blade against him.

Cam cried out as the razor-sharp tip pierced his chest. He grabbed at the blade with his free hand, trying to halt its progress, but its preternatural sharpness slashed open his palm, nearly cutting his hand in half.

And then Kha-Hotep slid the sword into Cam's heart.

* * *

Meta stared in horror, paralyzed by what he saw in the viewer. The containment field wasn't losing integrity—it was being joined by other fields and other particles.

Where were they coming from? The screen began to glow with a deep violet intensity—*some form of Cherenkov radiation?* At the same time, a torrent of particles began streaming up toward him, rising like champagne bubbles in an endless cascade.

"Primary Chamber, controls are not responding to abort command. Repeat, there is no response to—"

The neural link cut out.

The light from the viewscreen suddenly roared to life as a beam of pure energy. Meta reached for the manual override, but the pulse struck him face first and the impact sent his body tumbling backward through the air. He landed on the catwalk with a painful skid, nearly losing consciousness.

Kha-Hotep's face was a rictus of rage and anguish as he worked the blade into Cam's chest. The Celt's grip softened, the eyes lost their focus, and he could feel Cam's death rattle shake against him as he gently lowered his friend's body down to the catwalk.

At the far end of the walkway, a violet burst of light sent the scientist flying backward without warning. Kha looked up in surprise.

It begins, he thought.

A second blast of raw energy transformed the vast open space of the spherical chamber into blinding whiteness. Kha-Hotep pressed his head against Cam's shoulder as the walkway quaked.

A scriptorium near the Palace of Cyrus the Great, Babylon
538 BC
Three seconds before the Event

His prayers done and tools laid out, the exiled scribe spread forth the fresh scroll of cured gazelle skin and, with exquisite care, set quill to page, opening his story with a single word in Hebrew.

B'reshith.

In the beginning…

59

Meta clung to the catwalk, fighting to remain conscious. His eyes burned, his vision a dizzy, jumbled mess. Shaking his head to clear it, he managed to scramble to his feet, shielding his eyes with one hand. It took a moment for his eyes to come into focus.

Where are the intruders?

No matter. He had to get to the safety cutoff before all was lost.

There was no platform anymore—the long walkway now ended in a fiery ball of multicolored plasma, burning freely like a new sun.

Another tremor shuddered through the station, nearly jostling him off the catwalk entirely. Even the three rovers seemed to be affected by the ripples. They seemed to be flying blindly in crazy loop-de-loops, systems hopelessly scrambled.

Meta clutched at the rail as the narrow walkway began to

buckle beneath his feet. He pulled himself hand over hand back toward the entryway.

Someone stood in his way.

"Get out!" Meta yelled over the tumult. "It's going to blow!"

Kha-Hotep nodded—and then another tremor shook the catwalk like a branch in a windstorm, its tortured frame giving a horrifying metallic groan. Both men grabbed at the rail and pulled themselves along.

Kha came to a sudden stop just before the walkway's end. He turned, staring at Cam's body.

"We have to go back."

Meta stared at him, his eyes bright with cascading stars.

"He's dead!"

"No—he's not," Kha yelled back.

"You're insane," Meta replied. "Do what you want, but I'm leaving." Kha started to let the man pass, but a sudden impulse—instinct?—struck him.

"No," he said. "You can't leave yet."

"He's gone," Meta insisted, an edge of hysteria in his voice, "and the pulses of time-space distortion are tearing the place apart!"

Kha knew the man was right—still something was eating at him. It wasn't just that he couldn't leave Cam behind. He couldn't let Meta go, either. But why?

"We're going back."

"If we go back, we'll die!"

"Then we die." Another tremor shuddered down the walkway, and he shoved, sending Meta skidding back the way he came, toward the sun burning where the platform used to be. Toward Cam's corpse. A strange calm fell over Kha-Hotep as he followed.

We're not going to die, he thought. *This is the way it has to be.*

They reached Cam's body. The sword still jutted out of his chest, and Kha-Hotep realized the blade was sticking through Cam into the catwalk itself, keeping the corpse pinned in place. He crouched down and, with an effort, pulled the blade free. He slipped it into his belt.

Meta stared at him, terrified and baffled. Kha-Hotep pointed beyond him at the ball of plasma.

"That is the source of the—the pulses?"

"Pulses of time-space distortion, yes!"

Kha held on to Cam's body, and both men grabbed the rail tighter as another tremor rippled the catwalk beneath their feet. It was starting to all make sense. Leila had been right— they and their children... their entire life over the past eight years, were all proof that the aftershocks had stopped.

They had stopped because *he was here, to make them stop.*

But how?

"You have to end it here," he yelled to Meta. "Now!"

"I can't! It's ignoring my commands!"

"But there was supposed to be a way, damn you! You told them yourself!"

"What the hell are you talking about?"

"A—what was it called?—an override!"

"There is no override! The override is buried in *that*!" He pointed to the blazing sun. It pulsed again, bucking the walkway with another screech of metal.

Kha-Hotep felt a stab of doubt. Had he just doomed his children? Had he just killed his best friend—and himself—for nothing?

Was *all* of this for nothing?

"Wait," Meta said suddenly. "I can't abort the sequence, and I can't release the field, but…" He touched a hand to his head. "I can release the coupling that supports the staging area via my neural link." He closed his eyes. The energy sphere suddenly dropped away toward the bottom of the chamber, leaving the platform behind, still pulsating with ripples of errant space-time.

"*Em heset net Ma'at!*" Kha-Hotep exclaimed, touching his eyes and heart. "You've done it. Go! I'll finish it!"

"Are you sure? I can—"

Kha shook his head. "You've done more than enough."

Meta nodded. "The cutoff is the big red switch on the far right. Thank you," Meta said gratefully. "I won't forget you."

"You will, but no matter. All will be well."

Meta frowned, then raised his hand in gratitude before sprinting down the catwalk and exiting through the great round doorway. Kha-Hotep made sure the man and his trio of rovers were gone before he made his way back to the end of the catwalk, and threw the override switch.

60

Kha-Hotep wasn't sure what to expect, but he was surprised when nothing more than a final ripple went through the chamber, and then the catwalk was still again.

Cam suddenly coughed up blood and groaned. Kha-Hotep put a hand on his friend's chest. The medical nanites had already formed a hexagonal mesh closing up the stab wound through his chest and heart. The Celt's eyes fluttered open. Though his hand was still healing as well, he felt around for his sword.

"Easy, my brother," Kha said. "Let your body's sorcery do its work."

"The world—"

"Be at peace. It still holds up the sky."

"You forgot to cut off my head," he replied, his voice faint. Kha laughed in spite of himself, even as he fought to hold back tears.

"No, I remembered." He took Cam's hand. "Forgive me,

my brother. We were both right, and wrong. But now the thing is done. The storms are no more."

Cam smiled in turn, then grimaced in pain as he sat up.

"Easy! Easy!" Kha admonished him. "You were dead only a moment ago."

"I hate being dead," Cam said, wiping the blood from his chest. Kha-Hotep helped him up to his feet, supporting him as they walked back toward the doorway.

"*Cam!*" Amber's voice rang across the vast chamber as she ran to them. Nellie, Hypatia, and Harcourt came up behind. He yelped when she grabbed him in a fierce bear hug but made no complaint when she kissed him.

"You did it!"

"Kha did it," Cam said, clapping a hand on the Egyptian's shoulder.

"We *all* did it," Kha-Hotep corrected him. "The storms are ended, and damn all the gods, we yet remain."

"*What in the bloody hell?*" Harcourt raged, seemingly unrelieved to be back on Earth again. "You ignorant savages! *What* have you done? You haven't fixed the world! You were supposed to return us all to our lives—it was supposed to be as though none of this ever happened, the man said!"

"Shut up," Amber said quietly. Harcourt ignored her.

"Did Blake die for nothing, then?" he continued.

"*I said shut your mouth right now!*" Her voice crackled with grief and rage.

Taken aback, Harcourt swallowed his retort.

"Good lord," Nellie said slowly. I hate to say it, but he's right. After all we've been through, nothing's really changed, has it?"

"Perhaps you *have* stopped the time-quakes for the time being, I couldn't say." Harcourt sniffed. "But what I *do* know is that you two have managed to ruin our only chance to get back home again!"

Kha-Hotep stepped up, fury and the pain of loss in his eyes. "Isfet and Set take your tongue! You think we have done nothing this day? That no sacrifices were made? If any of you are so shrouded in misery, go ahead and throw yourselves into the pit then—it lies here before you!"

"Think, man!" Harcourt said bitterly. "You had a life once, your home, your country, your ship, your family. We all did. Now our world is gone—all our worlds are gone—and we are trapped forever in this patchwork nightmare—madhouse and menagerie in one!"

"Our world *is* gone," Amber said, her voice hollow. Was any of her family still alive? Her friends? What *was* left of San Diego now, if anything? Whatever remained, as much as she ached for something of her home to have survived, her old life was completely gone now. All of them could say the same.

"Not all our worlds are gone," Kha-Hotep muttered, his eyes narrowed.

"Hold a moment," Hypatia said, raising her hand. "We argue two sides of the same coin. It's true, we haven't saved our world. We all have lost much, and still have much to mourn. So we shall." She was quiet for a moment before continuing.

"Now we all dwell upon a new world. New companions—" She reached out and clasped Nellie's hand in hers. "—and new family. With what we have been given, much is asked of us, and great works we can do to make this our home. There are tasks ahead, cities and libraries to rebuild, crops and gardens to plant, and a boundless world to explore. Our ship awaits."

"Amen to that," Nellie replied softly.

"Indeed," Kha-Hotep agreed, and even Harcourt nodded.

"Come on," Amber said, pulling herself together. "Hypatia's right, the whole world is waiting for us now." And with Blake gone, she needed to step up. She wasn't sure how they'd manage without him, but it was time to start practicing. "We'll... we'll need to find Blake. I don't want to leave him here. He deserves a decent burial."

She mentally reached out to the *Vanuatu*.

"Ship, have you regained contact with your drone? Sergeant Blake is dead. We need to get his body out of here and prepared for a burial." She flashed an image of the last place she had seen him.

"I read you, Amber. Please permit me to extend my condolences to you all. I am dispatching the rover to look for him in Engineering Sublevel Alpha."

It seemed like only a few minutes had passed before the *Vanuatu*'s rover drone sailed into the chamber.

"Pardon the interruption, but I have located Sergeant Blake."

Amber wasn't ready to see Blake's body yet, didn't think she ever *would* be. But she owed it to him to bear witness to his sacrifice. "Thank you, Ship. Take us over there."

"Forgive me, but I have taken the liberty to send a med unit. Sergeant Blake is not dead. He has suffered serious injuries and is being taken back to the ship for treatment."

The stretcher floated Blake down the station's hallways. Its robot tentacles were already hard at work administering first aid and field surgery. Amber walked alongside him, one hand laid over his, while the rest followed behind.

"You got shot twice and fell onto concrete?" Amber said. "I'm surprised you're still alive."

"The ship was surprised, too," Blake replied, his voice a pale imitation of its usual brisk certainty. "But not dead. Just broke every bone in my body—feels like it anyway." He gave her an uncharacteristically mellow smile. "Whatever morphine they use now sure does the trick, though."

"There are multiple transverse fractures along the left side of his body, and he has sustained considerable blood loss. However, his primitive gunshot wounds were fortunately not critical. I give excellent odds of his recovery."

"Good," Amber said. "Because there's a whole new world out there, just waiting for us."

"We saved the world, did we?"

They reached the open doors leading out of the station and went out into the cold.

The Shatterfield was gone, the sky an unbroken expanse of blue. The *Vanuatu* stood ready for them, its prismatic wings unfolding in the sun.

Amber smiled. "The next best thing," she replied with certainty. "We saved *this* world."

EPILOGUE

The Palace of Cahokia
Eight years after the Event

Leila rose early and sat at the window, wrapped in her robe, watching the rising sun gleam off the great silver arch across the river. From the moment her husband had put on his riverboat captain disguise and set off in the royal barge, sleep had been impossible.

She rested her chin on her crossed forearms while worries churned in her mind and stomach. It had had to be done, at any cost, she knew—but just how high a price would they pay in the end? How many would return with him?

Would Kha-Hotep return at all?

Josephine, whom she loved more than anyone but her husband and children, came in with a tray of sweetgrass tea and honey.

"You slay me, sister," she said, setting the tray down and hunkering down next to Leila.

"What?" Leila asked.

"You haven't slept a wink." Josephine slipped her arm through Leila's and kissed her friend's cheek. "Me, neither, but don't you worry none, Bearcat. He'll be back soon."

Leila sighed and nodded, fighting back tears. Resting her head against her friend's, she snuggled closer and the two women watched the river for the returning barge. If Josephine had her own fears and doubts, she kept them to herself.

The two looked up and quickly stood at the sound of footsteps out in the hallway, signaling the approach of the guard, who halted at the door and announced themselves. Leila assumed a more regal stance, and bid them enter. A pair of the royal guardsmen entered.

"What news of my husband?"

"This man brings news, my lady." The captain stepped aside to let a tall figure in a gray hooded cloak enter. Leila's heart dropped, and Josephine quickly put a steadying arm around her shoulders.

A priest? Oh no, no, no…

"Tell me, Priest, is my husband alive?"

"No."

The man pulled back his hood.

"Not a priest."

Kha-Hotep stood, resplendent in an immaculate new kilt of bright white Egyptian cotton, gauzy tunic-shirt, and jeweled collar.

"*Kha!*" Leila flew into his arms. Josephine beamed, heaving a heartfelt sigh of gratitude. Laughing with gusto, he swung her around, and when he stopped she clamped her legs around him and kissed him until he finally pulled back. Leila touched a hand to his cheek. "Oh, Kha—are you alright? Did everything—" She was afraid to finish the question. He stared at her intently, tried to speak, and had to swallow before trying again.

"Tell me, my love," he said, his voice suddenly, strangely, quiet. "Do you notice anything different?"

"What do you mean?"

"I don't look... different?"

Staring at him intently, Leila tentatively touched the silver in his hair, the lines of his face. Tears welled up in her eyes.

"You look more handsome than the day I first laid eyes on you, my Egyptian Prince, my Sun-Raven." She kissed him again, and this time he held her as tightly as he could, aiming for forever after. Outside, a roar arose from the city below, as though all of Cahokia could see them.

"What is it?" Leila looked around in apprehension.

"Let us go see," he replied mysteriously. He led her out to the terrace that overlooked the inner city. The crowds below were waving and pointing up to the sky, where the *Vanuatu* hung above the palace, shining like a brilliant bird.

"We have company for breakfast."

To think we are so important,
is an obvious crime
We know that we are specks on a tiny dot
Hurtling through space and time

And yes I understand that my whole life
is just a blink of an eye
in the history of the earth,
as with each moment that goes by

But this moment that I'm with you
It feels like time has stood still
It feels somehow like it matters
And that it always will…
—from "Apocalyptic Love Song" by Shelley Segal

ACKNOWLEDGEMENTS

As always, thanks to our Dark Editorial Overlord, Steve Saffel, for endless tough love throughout the years of writing this trilogy, and to Hannah Scudamore, Natasha Qureshi, David Lancett, Louise Pearce, Kevin Eddy, and the rest of the crew. A shout out to the skilled and exceptionally sharp-eyed Louise Pearce of Pearce Proof for her brilliant copy edits. Boundless appreciation also to Jill Marsal, our amazing agent, and to the magnificent voice artist Aaron Shedlock, who has brought our entire cast of characters to life—in over twenty-two different languages.

Thanks to all of the following (and anyone we've forgotten!) for their invaluable support and generous assistance with research: Dr. M. Tariq Bhatti, Professor of Ophthalmology and Neurology at the Mayo Clinic, Susi and Uwe Bocks, Beth Collins, Sue Erokan, Hector Esparza, Owen Hodgson, Kendra Holliday, Alisha Koch, Junko Maekawa, Irene Minabe,

Minas Papageorgiou, Harold Perry, Jennifer Rattazzi, Crystal Roseman, David Speaker, Brian Thomas, and Mary Walls. Thanks also to Shelley Segal for the use of "Apocalyptic Love Song" from *An Atheist Album*. Words and music by Shelley Segal, copyright ©2011 by True Music. All rights reserved. Used by permission.

ABOUT THE AUTHORS

Dana Fredsti is an ex B-movie actress with a background in theatrical combat (a skill she utilized in *Army of Darkness* as a sword-fighting Deadite and fight captain). Through seven-plus years of volunteering at EFBC/FCC, Dana's been kissed by tigers, and had her thumb sucked by an ocelot with nursing issues. She's addicted to bad movies and any book or film, good or bad, which includes zombies. She's the author of *The Spawn of Lilith*, *Blood Ink*, the *Ashley Parker* series, touted as "Buffy meets the Walking Dead", the zombie noir novella, *A Man's Gotta Eat What a Man's Gotta Eat*, and the cozy noir mystery *Murder for Hire: The Peruvian Pigeon*. With David Fitzgerald she is the co-author of *Time Shards*, *Shatter War*, and *Tempus Fury*, and she has stories in the *V-Wars: Shockwaves* and *Joe Ledger: Unstoppable* anthologies.

David Fitzgerald is a historical researcher, an international public speaker, and an award-winning author of both genre fiction and historical nonfiction, such as *The Complete Heretic's Guide to Western Religion* series and *Nailed*. He is also a founding member of the San Francisco Writer's Coffeehouse. He lives with his wife, actress/writer Dana Fredsti, and their small menagerie of cats and dogs in a 130-plus-year-old Victorian house in Northern California. His latest fiction is the *Time Shards* series.